A DETECTIVE CHIEF INS

HIS DEAD MAN'S HAND

NEW YORK TIMES #1 BESTSELLER **TONY LEE** WRITING AS

JACK GATLAND

Hooded Man MEDIA
INSPIRATION • PRODUCTION • PUBLICATION

Published by Hooded Man Media.

First Edition: December 2025

PRAISE FOR JACK GATLAND

'Fast-paced and action packed, Jack Gatland's thrillers always deliver a punch.'

'This is one of those books that will keep you up past your bedtime, as each chapter lures you into reading just one more.'

'This book was excellent! A great plot which kept you guessing until the end.'

'Couldn't put it down, fast paced with twists and turns.'

'The story was captivating, good plot, twists you never saw and really likeable characters. Can't wait for the next one!'

'Totally addictive. Thoroughly recommend.'

'Moves at a fast pace and carries you along with it.'

'Just couldn't put this book down, from the first page to the last one it kept you wondering what would happen next.'

Also by Jack Gatland

DECLAN WALSH BOOKS

LETTER FROM THE DEAD

MURDER OF ANGELS

HUNTER HUNTED

WHISPER FOR THE REAPER

TO HUNT A MAGPIE

A RITUAL FOR THE DYING

KILLING THE MUSIC

A DINNER TO DIE FOR

BEHIND THE WIRE

HEAVY IS THE CROWN

STALKING THE RIPPER

A QUIVER OF SORROWS

MURDER BY MISTLETOE

BENEATH THE BODIES

KILL YOUR DARLINGS

KISSING A KILLER

PRETEND TO BE DEAD

HARVEST FOR THE REAPER

CROOKED WAS HIS CANE

A POCKET FULL OF POSIES

CHEATING MY DESTINY

STAND AND DELIVER

WE PLAY WITH DEATH

HIS DEAD MAN'S HAND

DIGGING YOUR GRAVE

TOM MARLOWE BOOKS

SLEEPING SOLDIERS

TARGET LOCKED

COVERT ACTION

COUNTER ATTACK

STEALTH STRIKE

BROAD SWORD

ROGUE SIGNAL

SNIPER ALLEY

SHADOW THREAT

SENTRY POINT

BURNING LEDGERS

ELLIE RECKLESS BOOKS

PAINT THE DEAD

STEAL THE GOLD

HUNT THE PREY

FIND THE LADY

BURN THE DEBT

TAKE THE KING

LIAM HARPER BOOKS

FINAL STRIKE

BLOOD RIDGE

TRACK SHIFT

CROSS ROADS

CARLYLE & SILVER BOOKS

SILVER AND THE SUNDAY CYPHER

SILVER AND THE CHRISTMAS CAPER

SILVER AND THE MOONLIT MURDER

DAMIAN LUCAS BOOKS

THE LIONHEART CURSE

THE EXCALIBUR QUEST

STANDALONE BOOKS

THE BOARDROOM

As Tony Lee

STANDALONE

TWELVE TASKS

THE PLAYING CARD WAR

KNAVE OF SPADES

QUEEN OF BLADES

CHARMING

LAST PRINCE STANDING

HAPPILY NEVER AFTER

For Mum, who inspired me to write.

For Tracy, who inspires me to write.

CONTENTS

FOREWORD

I don't often write forwards to books, but I felt this one should have one.

In the book you're about to read, I kill off a character named D.Q. James, a poker player. This isn't a spoiler, I've already mentioned this on the Amazon blurb page when you ordered it. However, I do need to point out a little thing about D.Q. James.

You see, he exists, and in fact, actively *wanted* to be killed off in one of my books.

Back in February 2025, I was a guest at the Gallifrey One *Doctor Who* Convention in Los Angeles, and as part of the charity auction, I gave away "one person to be murdered of your choice" when bidding for a set of my *Doctor Who / Star Trek* crossover comics. I hadn't expected it to go crazy, but suddenly I had three different people all bidding to have someone murdered in my books. It was D.Q. James, who looks exactly like he does in the book with cowboy hat and aviator sunglasses, who suggested instead that the three bidders should all pull together, pay a set fee each, and have *three* people murdered. This brought the collected money for charity from this one item to over $11,000, way more than the couple of hundred bucks I was expecting, and I was more than happy to do this.

Two of the names have already been used in previous books. These were personal, and I was quite happy to not mention them publicly. But as for this one, when I asked D.Q. James who he wanted to murder, he asked for *himself* to be the victim.

And therefore, in this book, D.Q. James is the victim.

I will, however, point out that this is a work of fiction. Everything that *this* D.Q. James does, or *has* done is completely fictional and is in no way connected to the actual D.Q. James, apart from his hat, aviator glasses, and public "poker player" initials and surname.

But I wanted to take this moment to thank Mr. James for his kind donation to charity, and I hope he isn't too unhappy with what I have done, as I've character assassinated him so visibly!

Tony Lee / Jack Gatland,

London, November 2025

PROLOGUE

Terry Callahan hefted the sledgehammer in his calloused hands, over two decades of construction work behind him, as he faced the basement wall that currently stood between Terry and a lunch at the nearest chippy. The Harrison Casino had been stripped bare over the past month; poker tables hauled away, roulette wheels dismantled, chandeliers almost ready to be boxed for auction. Now his crew had three weeks to gut the basement before the developers started building luxury flats and a full-service health spa where high-rollers had once lost fortunes.

The Harrison Casino had operated for nearly eighty years before closing last year. The place had started as a gentlemen's club in the fifties and evolved into a high-stakes casino by the nineties. Exclusive membership, invitation only, the kind of place where politicians and media moguls rubbed shoulders with people whose business dealings preferred darkness.

The basement itself, though, reeked of damp plaster and

decades of neglect. It had been mainly held as a storeroom over the last ten years, but once everything had come out, the builders had realised that water had been seeping through the walls for years, leaving dark stains that no amount of cleaning would shift, and giving the place a musty, off-putting smell. The developers didn't care – everything below ground level was coming out anyway. It was prime Mayfair property, and that meant they'd probably be turning all this into a car park, or a cinema, maybe a pool and sauna combination or something for rich people to occupy their time with while they weren't being rich people elsewhere.

'I'm telling you, mate, she's been seeing someone,' said Dave from across the space, his voice echoing off the plasterboard walls. He was measuring distances with a laser level, preparing to mark the wall for demolition, but his hands were shaking slightly. 'My neighbour saw her car at the Travelodge last Tuesday night. Tuesday bloody night, Terry. Kids were at mine, she said she was working late.'

Terry had watched Dave's marriage deteriorate over the past year like a slow-motion demolition. First, the arguments that Dave would share during tea breaks, then the silences at home that stretched for days, and now this paranoid surveillance of his wife's movements. Dave had been Terry's best worker for eight years, reliable and skilled despite his moods. Lately, though, the moods had been getting worse. Terry didn't respond immediately. He'd heard variations of this conversation for months now, Dave's marriage falling apart in real time, aired out on every job site from Canary Wharf to Camden. The man's obsession with his wife's imagined affairs had become background noise, like the rumble of traffic outside. But that said, Terry knew the desperation behind it. He'd been married once himself, back when he still believed in permanence. Sarah had left him for a bank manager twelve years ago, taking their eight-year-old son with her. Now Ronnie was twenty and barely spoke to his father, and Sarah was Mrs Something-Else, living in Surrey with a swimming pool and a mortgage Terry couldn't pronounce.

Like the wankers who were probably moving in here once the apartments were built.

The construction business was hard on marriages. Long hours, physical exhaustion, the constant uncertainty of when the next job would come. But Terry had learned to live alone in his small, terraced house in Ilford, cooking for one, and watching television shows no one else would discuss with him on Monday mornings. It was a quiet sort of loneliness, but at least it was honest.

'Maybe she was working late,' offered Mickey Webb, the youngest member of their crew. At twenty-two, Mickey still believed in the basic decency of people. *Give him ten more years in this business and he'd be as cynical as the rest of them.* The lad was sharp though – he had a head for figures and could read building plans better than men twice his age. Terry was training him up as a potential foreman, assuming Mickey didn't get bored and run off to one of the bigger, international firms like so many of the bright ones did. Mickey's generation didn't understand the kind of loyalty that kept a man in one trade for decades. They job-hopped like their parents had channel-surfed, always looking for something better, something more exciting. Terry sometimes envied them that freedom, but mostly he pitied them. There was something to be said for mastering a craft, for knowing exactly what your hands could do with steel and wood and brick.

'Working late selling insurance?' Dave's laugh held no humour. 'At a bloody Travelodge? Come off it.'

The Harrison Casino basement had been home to more than just storage over the years, though, with a rich history of off the books gambling. Terry had done enough Central London renovations to know these places usually had multiple purposes. During the casino's heyday, this basement had hosted private poker games for oil sheiks and Russian oligarchs, millions changing hands on the turn of a card. The stories he'd heard from the demolition crew upstairs were the stuff of legend; briefcases full of cash, gangsters like Billy Hill and The Krays being treated like rock stars, beautiful women who spoke six languages, and men who owned football clubs arguing over cards like schoolboys.

Now it would become parking spaces for stockbrokers' Maseratis, and gym space for people who lived or died on their Instagram feeds where punters once lost fortunes, and Terry's crew had three weeks to erase eighty years of history. It was good money – a contract that would keep his small firm afloat through another winter – but something about the place made him uneasy. And it wasn't what he'd been told about it recently, either.

'These casino places,' Mickey said, trying to change the subject. He was a good lad, didn't like conflict. 'Bet they've got stories, right? All those wealthy punters, foreign money, dodgy deals. Probably half the Russian mafia's been through here.'

Terry had worked on enough Central London renovations to know Mickey wasn't far wrong. The city was full of buildings with questionable histories, places where money had been laundered, deals struck, problems solved with a combination of cash and violence. The legitimate businesses provided cover, but underneath London's financial district ran currents of corruption that occasionally surfaced in newspaper headlines or police raids.

Dave, meanwhile, was still muttering about Sandra, his attention split between his measurements and his marriage.

'I've been with that woman twenty-three years. Met her when she was nineteen, married her at twenty-one. Built her a conservatory with my own hands, extended the kitchen twice, put in new windows throughout the house. And this is what I get.'

Dave's voice carried the bitterness of a man who'd kept score of every favour, every sacrifice, every gesture of love, and was now tallying them up like debts owed.

'Look, Dave,' Terry said, studying the wall. 'Why don't you knock off early today? Go home, talk to Sandra properly. Maybe there's an explanation.'

'Oh, there's an explanation all right. She's shagging someone else, isn't she? Probably that ponce from her office. The one with the BMW and the flash suits. Bet he doesn't come home stinking of plaster dust and honest work.'

Terry had met Sandra a handful of times at company dos. She seemed decent enough, but tired, maybe worn down by years of Dave's increasing bitterness. If she was stepping out, Terry couldn't entirely blame her.

Mickey was checking his phone again. The lad did that every ten minutes, waiting for messages from some girl called Kelsey he'd been seeing for six months. Young love; Terry remembered that feeling, though it seemed a lifetime ago. Back when he thought things would turn out different, when he believed hard work and good intentions were enough to build a life that wouldn't crumble.

He looked around, shaking the memory off. Dave had given up on the laser measurer now.

'What's the problem?' he asked.

'I can't get this right,' Dave muttered. 'My head's not in the right space. No matter how many times I do this, the bloody thing's off, not matching the plans.'

Terry pursed his lips as he considered this. He didn't think Dave was wrong at all – the basement was smaller than it should have been. Terry had read the building plans repeatedly before coming down here and mentally compared them to the actual space. The measurements were off by about six feet along the eastern wall.

But Terry already knew why. He knew there was a space behind the wall, and he'd been told about the potential of the space, enough to want Mickey and Dave to piss off for lunch while he took down this wall himself.

'You're off by what, a couple of feet?' he offered.

'Yes!' Dave took the question like an offered lifeline, showing the display. 'Look.'

'Maybe it's a priest hole,' Mickey suggested, pocketing his phone reluctantly. 'Rich people love that stuff, don't they? Secret passages and that. Like in the films.'

'It's not the bloody Middle Ages,' Dave snapped, 'and people in Mayfair didn't need bloody secret passages.'

He was in one of his moods again, anger simmering just below the surface. Terry had seen it building all week; Dave's temper had always been short, but lately it had turned mean. The kind of mean that came from knowing your life was unravelling and there wasn't much you could do to stop it. Construction work attracted men with anger issues. The physical nature of the job provided an outlet, a way to channel frustration into something productive. But when the anger started controlling the man instead of the other way around, it became dangerous.

Terry studied the wall he planned to demolish. The plaster and brickwork looked newer than the rest of the basement, the mortar too clean in the areas where the bricks had been exposed. Hastily done, maybe ten, possibly fifteen years ago. He'd seen enough bodge jobs to recognise one, and whoever built this wall had been in a hurry, more concerned with getting it up quickly than making it pretty.

The sort of rush job you did when you needed to hide something fast.

Casino. Hidden Room.

Money. It had to be. More money than they made in a year, stored away and forgotten.

'This wall,' Mickey said in a moment of clarity, running his hand along the surface. 'It's not load-bearing. Wasn't on the original plans either.'

'So what?' Dave said, looking up from his laser level. 'Probably storage or something. These casino types, always hiding something. Tax dodgers, the lot of them.'

Mickey had pulled his phone out again, and was waving it around the basement, still unable to get any signal.

'Put the phone away, Mickey,' Terry said, not unkindly. 'Take Dave over to the nearest pub and buy him a pint. I'll sort this out and come join you.'

Mickey pocketed his phone with the reluctance of a teenager being asked to do homework. His generation lived on their devices, always connected to networks of friends and information that older men like Terry found exhausting.

Terry hefted the sledgehammer again. They needed to

take this wall down anyway – the plans called for the entire basement to be opened up. *If he found anything that nobody knew about? Well, the new owners didn't need to know, did they?*

Dave, however, wasn't as dim as Mickey. And personal issues or not, he folded his arms.

'You know about this, don't you?' he accused.

Terry made a weak attempt at a smile, shrugging – his way of pretending that he didn't understand really what Dave meant.

'I just thought I'd give you a break,' he replied. 'It's been a busy day.'

'Bullshit.' Dave looked over at Mickey and then returned his attention to his boss. 'You've been eyeing this bloody wall all day. You think we haven't noticed? And then I find that there's a few feet missing? Come on. What do you know?'

Terry sighed, looking around. It was only the three of them, and he had worked with both enough to trust them.

'I heard from a mate at the gym,' he explained softly, 'and he said this place down here? Big games. Dangerous games. And now we've got a fake wall. What do you think?'

'I think you're about to try and make yourself some money,' Dave replied, looking over at the wall and picking up the sledgehammer. 'I think you're trying to get rid of us so whatever you find—'

'Can be split three ways.' Mickey interrupted, seemingly unable to not look up, even when the phone wasn't in his hand. 'That's what you meant to do, wasn't it? Me, you, Dave. Split three ways.'

'Sure,' Terry replied, resignation settling in. The secret was out; there was no way he'd be able to take the wall down without the other two. 'But I've got a few requests.'

'Like what?'

'The guy who told me about the space was a gambler back in the day and thought there might be something hidden that has a personal history for him. He also wanted a ten per cent finder's fee if there is anything back there.'

'Whatever,' Dave replied. 'At the moment it's still ten per cent of sod all. Let's see what's behind here.'

There was a ding of a message – Mickey pulled out his phone, looking down at the screen, but then frowned.

'That wasn't me,' he grumbled. 'Dave, you got *signal* down here?'

But Dave wasn't listening any more. He was staring at his phone, his face pale in the basement's artificial light. Terry saw his hands shaking as he read whatever message had just come through, the haft of the sledgehammer forgotten in his other hand.

'What is it?' Mickey asked.

Dave's voice was barely a whisper.

'It's Sandra. She's... she wants a divorce. Says she's been trying to tell me for months, but I never listen.' He looked up, eyes wild with disbelief. 'Says she's moving in with that BMW-driving prick from her office.'

The silence stretched between them. Terry had seen men break before; the moment when the thing they'd been fighting finally won. Dave looked like a man whose world had just collapsed, taking everything he thought he knew with it. Twenty-three years of marriage ended with a text message while he stood in a damp basement holding a sledgehammer.

'Dave,' Terry started, but the man wasn't listening.

'Twenty-three bloody years,' Dave whispered, then his voice rose to a shout that echoed off the brick walls. *'Twenty-three years!'*

The weight of the sledgehammer, the solid reality of steel and wood, seemed to focus his rage into something pure and destructive. This was something he could control, something he could break when everything else in his life was breaking him.

'Dave, don't—'

But Dave was already swinging, putting twenty-three years of hurt and betrayal behind the blow. The sledgehammer connected with the wall in an explosion of brick dust and mortar. Once, twice, three times he swung, each impact sending chunks of masonry flying across the basement floor.

'Dave!' Terry grabbed for the hammer, but Dave jerked away, swinging again with wild, desperate energy. The fourth blow punched through completely. Instead of hitting solid brick, however, the hammer disappeared into darkness beyond. Dave stumbled forward, off-balance, as the weapon met no resistance. The sudden absence of impact sent him staggering, and he nearly fell through the hole he'd created.

'Jesus,' Mickey breathed, backing away from the wall.

Terry pulled out his phone putting the torch on and shone it through the jagged opening Dave had made. The light revealed a space perhaps four feet deep, and brick-walled on three sides.

'What's in there?' Mickey asked, jostling for position to look through. 'Are we rich?'

'No, I don't think so,' Terry whispered in horror. The air that drifted out was stale and sweet, carrying the smell of old leather and something else that made his stomach turn.

This wasn't treasure, after all.

There, crumpled against the far wall in what had once been an expensive suit, were human remains.

The skeleton sat against the wall, jaw hanging open. Scraps of fabric clung to yellowed bones, and a wristwatch glinted on the left wrist. But it was the skull that made Terry step back, his torch beam wavering.

Under an oversized black cowboy hat, the left temple was caved in, a spiderweb of fractures spreading from a depression the size of a man's fist, a pair of battered aviator glasses half-hiding it as they hung skew-whiff from the remnants of hair and skin.

'Call the police,' Terry said, his voice steady despite the way his hands were shaking. 'Call them now.'

'But what about the hidden money—'

'There is no bloody money!' Terry spun around, snapping. 'This wall wasn't built to hide treasure; it was built to hide a secret!'

Behind him, Dave sat heavily on a pile of rubble, the sledgehammer forgotten at his feet. He was staring at his phone again, at Sandra's message, as if by reading it enough times he could make it say something different.

Mickey was already halfway up the stairs to gain a signal, dialling 999, his young face pale in the artificial light.

'Police,' he said when the operator answered. 'We need police. We've found a body. A skeleton. It's been here for... for a long time.'

Terry stepped back from the hidden room, careful not to disturb anything else. Someone had killed this person and walled them up like something from a horror film. But this wasn't fiction – this was real, and now it was their problem. His friend from the gym wouldn't have known this, and for a moment, Terry almost texted him, asking what ten per cent of the body he'd want.

Outside, London carried on oblivious. Traffic hummed

past on the street above, people hurried to lunch meetings and shopping appointments, tourists queued for attractions. But down here in the basement of what had been the Harrison Casino, the past had just reached out and grabbed them by the throat.

Terry didn't want the chippy any more.

He'd lost his appetite.

1

SPARRING SESSION

The rhythmic thud of leather against heavy bags provided a steady percussion to the conversation, punctuated by the occasional grunt from the handful of boxers training in Johnny Lucas's gym as Declan Walsh sat on a folding chair beside the Globe Town boxing ring, watching Monroe circle Johnny Lucas on the worn canvas, both men wearing head-guards and light gloves. Their sparring was more theatrical than athletic – Monroe throwing lazy jabs that Johnny easily deflected whilst delivering his latest intelligence report.

'Come on, Ali,' Johnny said, slipping a half-hearted right hook. 'Rosanna's right, you know. You've gone soft since the wedding.'

Monroe grunted, throwing a combination that had more enthusiasm than technique.

'Bloody woman's got me on some health kick,' he bemoaned. 'Salads for lunch, early morning runs, and now this.'

'Could be worse,' Johnny replied, tapping Monroe's ribs

with a gentle uppercut. 'Could be yoga. Or worse still, running.'

'Very funny.' Monroe backed away, breathing harder than he wanted to admit. 'Besides, this is supposed to be my intelligence briefing, not your entertainment.'

'There's nothing wrong with running.' Declan, a keen runner, smiled. 'I can always take you to a parkrun.'

'Aye, and I can always take you round the back and beat the shite out of you for considering that,' Monroe grunted back, ducking a swing.

'Watching you here? I'll take my chances,' Declan chuckled.

'The Albanians are getting bolder,' Johnny was saying, changing the subject while ducking under Monroe's guard and landing a playful body shot. 'Word is they're moving into Whitechapel, testing the waters. Nothing major yet, but they're asking questions about protection rates.'

Monroe paused his movement, lowering his gloves.

'How reliable is this?'

'Pete heard it from his cousin who works the docks off Wapping.' Johnny nodded towards the trainer working with a young boxer at the far end of the gym, then resumed his stance. 'The cousin's not exactly Einstein, but he knows who pays his wages. Keep your hands up.'

Monroe raised his guard again, throwing a clumsy jab that Johnny caught on his gloves.

'Christ, I'm knackered already.'

'You're out of shape, is what you are,' Johnny replied with amusement, moving around Monroe with the easy grace of someone who, although being older than Monroe, had been boxing for decades. 'When's the last time you did any proper exercise?'

'I walk to work,' Monroe protested, attempting another combination. 'Ish.'

'Walking to the car doesn't count.' Johnny tapped Monroe's temple with a feather-light jab. 'Your wife's a doctor, she knows what she's talking about.'

Declan made a note in his phone, grinning as he watched Monroe's increasingly laboured movements. These regular chats with Johnny had become routine over the last couple of months, ever since a new player on the London crime scene had made a play for the crown, and Monroe and his one-time protégé Ellie Reckless had gained Johnny's help in fixing it. Monroe had explained little about what happened, but after that he started spending more time here – unofficial intelligence gathering that kept them ahead of emerging criminal trends. The boxing club provided neutral ground, a place where information flowed as naturally as sweat. The sparring sessions however were a newer addition, Rosanna's idea after she'd pointed out that Monroe's idea of exercise was reaching for the remote control, and if he was going to be here anyway, he could be here exercising and not eating doughnuts.

'Anything else moving in the East End?' Monroe asked between breaths, attempting to land a jab on Johnny's shoulder.

'Couple of new faces sniffing around the drug trade. Chinese lads, but not local. They've got that mainland swagger, you know? All flash and no understanding of how things work here.' Johnny moved fluidly around Monroe, making the older detective look clumsy by comparison. 'Kenny Tsang's not happy about it.'

'Kenny's never happy about competition,' Declan observed from ringside.

'True enough. But this feels different. They're not trying

to integrate; they're trying to take over. Making promises they can't keep, threatening people they shouldn't threaten.' Johnny caught Monroe in a clinch, both men breathing heavily. 'Give it a month and they'll either be gone or floating in the Thames.'

Monroe pushed away from the clinch, pulling off his headguard.

'Right, that's enough punishment for one evening. I'm getting too old for this.'

'You're getting too unfit for this,' Johnny corrected, removing his own gear. 'But you're improving. Last week I could have knocked you over with a strong breeze. Soon you'll be past the training wheel stage with me and off to the races with a real boxer, like Pete.'

'Charming.' Monroe climbed through the ropes, accepting a towel from Declan.

'Your dad would have loved this,' he said, wiping sweat from his face. 'Patrick always said the best intelligence came from people who lived in the community, not from files in an office.'

'He wasn't wrong.' Johnny climbed out of the ring, still barely winded despite the workout. 'He understood how to work the criminal networks. Never judgemental, never threatening. Just... curious.'

'Curious how?' Declan asked.

Johnny grabbed a water bottle, taking a long drink before answering.

'He'd ask about motivations, not just actions. Why someone turned to crime, what pressures they were under, how family dynamics played into their choices.' His expression softened slightly. 'Most coppers, they see criminals as problems to solve. Patrick Walsh saw them as people with stories.'

Monroe finished towelling off and sat down heavily on a bench.

'That approach got him results, but it also got him enemies.'

'Yeah, it did.' Johnny's tone grew more serious. 'There were people who didn't appreciate being understood. Made them feel... exposed, I suppose. Patrick had a way of getting under your skin, making you think about choices you'd rather forget.'

Declan leant forward.

'Anyone in particular?'

'Christ, where do I start? You already know about most of them.' Johnny took another sip of water, then his expression shifted to something that might have been admiration. 'Though there was one case Patrick worked that always stuck with me. Showed me how different he was from other coppers.'

'Go on,' Declan said, genuinely curious. Stories about his father's investigative methods were rare – most people who'd known Patrick either couldn't talk about the work or wouldn't.

'This was... mid-nineties, I think.' Johnny sat down on the ring apron, settling into the story. 'There'd been a warehouse fire in Rotherhithe. Massive thing lit up half the South Bank. Body found inside – warehouse night watchman, poor sod. Everyone assumed he'd been caught in the fire, maybe fell asleep on shift, cigarette started it, tragic accident.'

Monroe stopped towelling off, interested now.

'I know this one,' he said. 'Patrick mentioned it.'

'Well, it's my story, so shut up with the punchline, yeah?' Johnny smiled.

'So, Patrick? He wasn't sure this fitted, so he asked when the fire started. Fire brigade said they got the call at half past midnight, flames visible from across the river. Coroner put time of death around midnight to one a.m. based on the body's condition. Everyone was satisfied – the timing matched.'

'So, what was the problem?' Declan asked.

'Your dad pulled the warehouse security log. Last entry from the night watchman was at eleven forty-five p.m. – routine patrol check, everything normal. Now, every other copper looked at that and thought *"fifteen minutes before the fire started, makes sense".*' Johnny smiled. 'But Patrick looked at that log entry and thought *"that's forty-five minutes too early".*'

'How do you mean?'

'The watchman did his patrol every two hours like clockwork. Had done for three years but always started from midnight. Twelve a.m., two a.m., four a.m., six a.m. – never varied. His last entry should have been at around twelve-thirty, not eleven forty-five, which was forty-five minutes earlier than usual. So, Patrick asked himself, why would a creature of habit suddenly break his routine?'

Declan leant forward.

'Because someone made him write it early.'

'Exactly. Someone forced him to make an eleven forty-five entry, then killed him. They started the fire at midnight to cover it up, figuring the coroner would assume he died in the fire. And it worked – everyone was looking at when the fire started, not when the watchman broke his routine.'

'But Patrick spotted it,' Declan said quietly.

'He did. Went back through three months of security logs,

proving the pattern. Then he worked backwards from that eleven forty-five entry – who'd been in the warehouse earlier that evening? Who'd have known about the patrol schedule?' Johnny shook his head. 'Turned out the warehouse owner had been embezzling. Night watchman had noticed inventory discrepancies. Owner came back that night, forced him to make the early entry so it would look like normal routine, then killed him and burned the place for the insurance.'

There was a moment of silence before Monroe spoke.

'I would have told it better.'

'Your dad didn't look at when things happened,' Johnny continued, ignoring Monroe and looking directly at Declan. 'He looked at when they *should* have happened and didn't. While everyone else was checking alibis for midnight when the fire started, Patrick was checking alibis for eleven forty-five when the watchman broke his routine. That's how he caught the bastard.'

'I never heard this story,' Declan said.

'Patrick didn't talk about his methods much. Said it made criminals too careful if they knew how he thought.' Johnny stood up, stretching. 'But I remember it because it taught me something. Everyone focuses on the dramatic moment – the fire, the body, the discovery. Patrick focused on the boring routine that got broken. The thing everyone else overlooked because it wasn't obvious. Either way, going back to your question, your dad worked cases across London for years. He accumulated grudges like some people collect stamps.' Johnny took another sip of water. 'But he also earned respect. Even from people who had every reason to hate him.'

'Like you?' Monroe asked with a slight smile, still catching his breath.

'Like me,' Johnny confirmed without embarrassment.

'Patrick arrested me a few times over the years, but never once did he treat me like scum. Never once did he make it personal. Even when he was putting handcuffs on me.'

The conversation was interrupted by the sound of the gym's front door opening. Declan glanced over, expecting to see another boxer arriving for evening training. Instead, he saw a familiar figure in workout clothes, pulling earbuds from her ears as she scanned the gym.

'Jess?' Declan stood up, confusion evident in his voice.

Jessica Walsh froze when she spotted her father. Her now dyed-black hair was pulled back in a ponytail, and she wore athletic gear that suggested serious training rather than casual exercise. The surprise on her face matched Declan's own.

'Dad? What are you doing here?'

'Working,' Declan replied, still processing the unexpected encounter. 'What are *you* doing here?'

'Training.' Jess walked over to them, her initial surprise giving way to slight defensiveness. 'I've been coming here for a few weeks.'

'Well, this is cosy. The Walsh family gym reunion.' Monroe's eyebrows rose with amusement, though he was still breathing hard from the sparring session.

Johnny chuckled.

'She's got natural talent. Quick hands, good instincts. Reminds me of her grandfather, actually.'

'My grandfather boxed?' Jess looked between Johnny and her father.

'We were just talking about it,' Johnny confirmed. 'Patrick could handle himself in a ring. Not professionally, but he understood the sport. Respected it.'

Declan felt the familiar protective instinct rising.

'And you offered Jess a membership here?'

'I did.' Johnny's tone remained casual, but Declan caught the slight wariness in his eyes. 'Good to have young people in the gym. Keeps the energy up.'

'Out of the goodness of your heart?'

'Laddie...' Monroe's voice carried a warning note, though he was still wiping sweat from his face. But Johnny held up a hand.

'No, he's right to ask. I've got a reputation, and he's got a daughter.' He looked directly at Declan. 'Truth is, I liked Patrick, and I like you. You've saved my arse a few times, and I hope I've returned the favour enough. But when your daughter showed up wanting to learn self-defence, I saw it as a chance to do something positive. No strings, no expectations.'

'I can look after myself, Dad,' Jess said, her tone mixing affection with exasperation. 'And I'm good at this. Really good.'

Monroe wandered over to the heavy bag Jess had placed her bag beside.

'How long have you been training?'

'Three weeks. Johnny and Pete have been teaching me combinations, footwork, basic defence.' Jess glanced at her father. 'I was going to tell you, but...'

'But you knew I'd worry,' Declan finished.

'But I knew you'd make it complicated,' Jess corrected. 'Which you're doing right now. Dad, I need to be able to take care of myself better if I want to be a police officer. Sure, I've been taught stuff here and there, but this? This is something that's mine.'

Johnny cleared his throat diplomatically.

'Perhaps this is a conversation for another time?'

Monroe nodded and walked over to his things. As he did so, Jess pulled Declan aside.

'Dad, about the training...'

'I'm not angry,' Declan said, which was mostly true. 'Concerned, yes. But not angry.'

'Pete, Johnny's trainer? He's been a good teacher. Patient, professional. He doesn't treat me differently because I'm a woman or because of who my father is.' Jess's tone was earnest. 'He just treats me like someone who wants to learn.'

Declan studied his daughter's face. She'd inherited his ability to read people, but she'd also inherited Elizabeth's determination once she'd decided about something. Fighting this would be counterproductive.

'All right. But I want to know your schedule, and I want you to check in with me after each session. And no staring at Leroy over there when he's shirtless.'

'Deal.' Jess smiled.

Before Declan could respond, his phone rang. Temple Inn.

'Walsh.'

'Guv, it's Cooper.' PC Cooper's voice carried that particular tension that meant something significant had happened. 'We've got a body discovery that's been passed to us. DCI Cohen at Paddington called it in.'

Declan straightened, his attention immediately focused, putting the call on speaker so Monroe could hear it.

'I'm on speaker with Monroe. What's Cohen got for us?'

'Construction workers found human remains in a basement renovation this afternoon. Curzon Street, formerly the Harrison Casino. Builders were demolishing a wall and found what looks like a concealed room with skeletal remains inside.'

'Why's Cohen passing it our way?'

'He said, and I quote, "This one's got complications written all over it, and I'm up to my eyeballs with a money laundering operation." Wants a fresh pair of eyes on it.' Cooper paused. 'Also mentioned the casino's got a "colourful history" that might need delicate handling.'

'How long has the body been there?'

'Hard to say without Doctor Marcos, but the construction foreman thinks the wall was built to hide it. Could be years, maybe decades.'

Declan was already reaching for his coat.

'Where are we with the scene?'

'Cohen's people have secured it, but they're waiting for us to take over. DI Kapoor, Sergeant De'Geer and Doctor Marcos are on the way.'

As Declan ended the call, Johnny's expression had shifted to one of interest.

'Harrison Casino, you said?'

'You know it?' Monroe asked, folding his towel and placing it in his makeshift gym bag, currently a Waterstones tote bag.

'I should do. Jackie and I provided security there for private games back in the nineties – back when Jackie was Jackie, and not...' he tapped his head, indicating that it was before "Jackie" became a persona inside of Johnny Lucas. 'High-stakes poker, international players, serious money changing hands. If someone's buried in that basement, there's a story there. That place attracted the sort of people who solved problems permanently.'

'What sort of people?' Declan felt the familiar stirring of a case beginning to take shape.

'Rich people with expensive habits and who liked their

gambling untraceable. Professional players who took the game very seriously indeed.' Johnny paused. 'People who didn't appreciate losing, and who had the resources to do something about it.'

Now all business, Monroe pulled out his notebook – a battered thing held together with an elastic band.

'Tell us more about these games. What kind of security work?'

Johnny glanced around the gym, ensuring they weren't being overheard. The boxers were focused on their training, and Pete was busy adjusting equipment at the far end.

'Making sure players felt safe bringing that kind of cash into central London. The casino had a reputation to maintain – completely secure, completely discreet.' Johnny's expression grew thoughtful. 'We weren't just keeping the riff-raff out. We were managing... tensions.'

'Aye? What tensions?'

'Ones that come with serious money and bigger egos. Players who didn't like losing, business rivals forced to sit at the same table, foreign nationals with complicated histories.' Johnny shook his head. 'Dangerous mix, that. Money makes people do stupid things.'

'But you kept the peace?' Declan asked.

'Mostly. But Jackie was getting unpredictable, and the casino decided they needed more... *diplomatic* security.' Johnny's tone suggested this was something of an understatement. 'We were effective, but we weren't subtle.'

Monroe made a note.

'When did you stop providing security there?'

'After Jackie disappeared, I took my eye off the ball. When he "reappeared", I popped by here and there, but we carried on providing the service until 2009, maybe 2010. The new management switched to smaller games after that, safer clientele. The high-stakes international crowd was too much trouble, even for the money they brought in.' Johnny smiled. 'Tell you what, after you've had a look at whatever they found down there, come back. I might remember more details about the players, the layout, the way the place operated.'

'That would be helpful,' Monroe agreed. 'Professional consultation.'

'Within reason,' Johnny added with a slight smile. 'I'm a legitimate businessman and ex-member of Parliament these days, but I'm not completely reformed.'

Monroe was already moving towards the door, his earlier exhaustion forgotten.

'Come on then, laddie. Let's go see what secrets the Harrison Casino has been keeping.'

Declan paused Jess as she grabbed her bag.

'No,' he said gently, almost mockingly. 'You can't come with us. You have boxing training.'

As he turned, Jess, pouting, caught Declan's arm.

'Dad? Be careful. If Johnny's right about the people who used that casino...' She paused, choosing her words carefully. 'Some secrets are buried for very good reasons.'

THE DRIVE TO CURZON STREET TOOK THEM THROUGH THE heart of London, past the Thames and into the West End, where old money met new ambition in an endless dance of power and influence. As they navigated the evening traffic, Declan found himself thinking about Johnny's words regarding the casino's clientele.

'Do you trust him on this?' he asked Monroe.

'Johnny? As much as I trust anyone with his background. He's never lied to us directly, well, nothing major anyway, and he's never given me information that turned out to be false.' Monroe paused, his breathing finally back to normal after the sparring session. 'But he's also never told me the complete truth about anything. It's not in his nature.'

The traffic slowed as they got nearer Mayfair and, as they approached the one-time Harrison Casino, Declan could see the police tape and the gathering crowd of onlookers. Doctor Marcos's distinctive frizzy hair and custom grey PPE suit were visible near the building's entrance, her forensic kit already in hand as she entered the building. The evening's comfortable routine at the boxing gym felt like a lifetime ago.

'Right then,' Monroe said, checking his watch. 'Let's go see what the past's dug up for us.'

The casino building stood like a monument to faded grandeur, and whatever secrets lay buried in its basement had waited years for discovery. Now, with apparently a construction worker's sledgehammer blow, the Harrison Casino was about to give up its dead.

And Declan Walsh, armed with Johnny Lucas's warnings about high-stakes players and permanent solutions, was about to discover that some casino games never really ended.

2

BASEMENT JACKS

THE HARRISON CASINO'S BASEMENT SMELT LIKE VICTORIAN London had crawled down there to die. Brick dust hung in the air, lit up by the harsh contractor floodlights that made everything look like a film set – which, Declan supposed, it was in a way. Crime scene photography was just another kind of movie-making, except the actors were all dead and the plot never made sense until the end.

Doctor Marcos was crouched beside the hole the builders had smashed through the wall, muttering to herself as she examined the skeletal remains. Her dark frizzy hair had escaped whatever she'd done with it that morning and was now doing its own thing, which seemed appropriate given the circumstances.

'About bloody time,' she said without looking up as Declan and Monroe reached the bottom of the stone steps. 'I've been down here documenting things while you two were having a lovely chat upstairs.'

'We literally watched you enter before us,' Monroe

replied with a smile. 'I thought you were travelling here with Anjli?'

'She's coming with De'Geer.' Doctor Marcos sat back on her heels. 'I wanted to come and see the fancy dress cowboy first.'

The skeleton sat against the far wall of what was once a hidden room, still wearing the remains of what had clearly been an expensive suit jacket. The black cowboy hat sat at an angle on the skull, like he'd tipped it to a lady before settling in for a long wait. The aviator sunglasses hung askew, one lens cracked, giving him a rakish air even in death.

'Interesting fashion sense,' Declan observed.

'Not your typical London look,' Monroe agreed. 'Unless there's a line dancing club in Mayfair I don't know about.'

'American, maybe?' Doctor Marcos suggested. 'The dental work will tell us more but the clothing's definitely expensive. Custom tailoring, silk lining. This was someone who could afford Savile Row but chose to dress like he was heading to a rodeo.'

The gold Rolex on the left wrist caught the light. Still attached, but now frozen, the battery having run out at approximately four-thirty-three, but whether it was morning or afternoon wouldn't be known until they examined it. Even after years in a basement, it was clearly worth several thousand pounds. The gold case had tarnished slightly, but the distinctive Submariner design was unmistakable.

'So, not a robbery,' Declan concluded. 'A watch like this would be the first thing any thief would take.'

'Definitely not. And look at this.' Doctor Marcos held up what looked like a small rectangular tile in her tweezers, recently gained from the jacket pocket, and looking like a domino that'd been drawn over. 'Gaming piece of some kind.'

The object was made of what appeared to be bone or ivory, with Chinese characters carved into one side. The craftsmanship was exceptional – hand-carved with an attention to detail that suggested serious value.

'Mahjong?'

'Possibly, but the quality's unusual. This isn't something you'd buy in a tourist shop. Hand-carved, probably worth a chunk of cash too.'

'Johnny mentioned this place had international players. High-stakes stuff,' Monroe took a look around the room as he replied.

'Was this when you "boxed" together?' Doctor Marcos made air quotes with her fingers as she spoke, smiling. 'Or rather, when you stumbled sweatily around a boxing ring, complaining about exercise?'

'It's almost as if you were there with us,' Declan replied, placing the game piece carefully into an evidence bag.

The sound of footsteps on the stairs announced Anjli's arrival, followed by De'Geer's heavier tread. Both were already pulling on gloves – the routine of crime scene protocol beaten into them by years of this work.

'Sorry we're late,' Anjli said, taking in the scene with the quick assessment of someone who'd done this too many times. 'The Miller interview ran long.'

'How'd he take the charges?' Monroe asked.

'Like you'd expect. Claims the drugs belonged to his mate's dog's previous owner's third cousin.' She paused, looking at the skeletal remains. 'What have we got?'

'Cowboy who never made it home,' Doctor Marcos replied. 'Been here fifteen, twenty years, give or take. Someone hit him very hard in the left temple – you can see the fracture even through the sunglasses.'

De'Geer was examining where the false wall had been, running his hands along the edges.

'The brickwork matches the original construction perfectly. Whoever built this knew what they were doing.'

'How long would this have taken?' Declan asked.

'Quality materials, proper mortar, time to let it cure properly... a day or two. This wasn't panic work.'

'Planned,' Anjli said.

'Very planned. And look at how he's positioned.' Doctor Marcos indicated the body. 'Sitting upright, hands folded. Someone took care with this.'

'Care?' Monroe's eyebrows went up. 'They murdered him and then tucked him in for a nice sleep?'

'Happens more than you'd think with killings where the killer has personal history with the victim. They feel obligated to treat the body with respect even while disposing of the evidence.'

'So, there's a possible personal connection here,' Declan nodded as he noted this down. 'Good to know.'

The basement felt colder as they processed this. Above them, London carried on – taxis honking, tourists taking photos, politicians lying about something or other. Down here, they were standing over a decades old secret that someone had taken considerable trouble to keep buried.

'Right,' Monroe said, closing his notebook. 'We need to talk to the builders. Get proper statements.'

'They're still here?' Declan asked.

'Waiting upstairs. Cohen's people took initial statements, but you know how that goes,' Anjli replied.

As they headed back up the stairs, Declan took one last look at the hidden room. Someone had dressed like a cowboy in the middle of London, played high-stakes games in an exclusive casino, and ended up dead in the basement. The question was whether the costume was part of who he was, or part of what got him killed.

'One thing's certain,' he said to Monroe as they climbed towards daylight. 'He wasn't planning on a quiet night in.'

THE THREE CONSTRUCTION WORKERS WERE SITTING IN THE MAIN gaming room, two of them at one of the half-dismantled poker tables looking like they'd rather be anywhere else. The room still had traces of its former glory – crystal chandeliers wrapped in plastic sheeting before boxing, mahogany panelling, thick carpets rolled up and stacked against the walls like sleeping dragons.

Terry Callahan, the site foreman, looked up as they entered. He was a man who'd spent his life working with his hands, and it showed – calloused fingers, sun-weathered face, and the build that came from decades of lifting things that didn't want to be lifted.

'Mister Callahan? DCI Walsh, Detective Superintendent Monroe, DI Kapoor. We'd like to go over what happened this afternoon.'

'Told the other officers everything already,' Terry replied. 'Dave found the body; we called it in straight away. Didn't touch anything we weren't supposed to.'

'Tell us about the wall. You knew it wasn't original?'

'Could tell the room wasn't to the dimensions we were told. Once we saw through the plaster, we could see it wasn't the same builder. Similar, but slightly different brickwork, newer mortar. Bodge job, really, though a professional one if you know what I mean.'

The youngest of the three was fidgeting with his phone like his life depended on it.

Probably some girl, Declan thought. *There was always some girl when you were that age.*

'Mickey, right? What did you see when the wall came down?' he asked.

'Just... the body. Sitting there like he was waiting for someone.' Mickey's voice was shaky. 'Never seen anything like it. That hat, those glasses... looked like something from a Western.'

'Bit theatrical for London,' Monroe observed.

'That's what I thought. Like he was playing dress-up or something.'

Terry gestured towards the back of the room where Dave sat alone, staring at his phone with the intensity of a man reading his own death sentence.

'Dave's having a rough time. Wife left him, took the kids. He got the divorce message right before we started on the wall. Finding a skeleton didn't exactly improve his mood.'

Declan understood that feeling. He'd felt the same when Lizzie had finally sent him the divorce papers.

Or was she still calling herself Bet now? He'd have to ask Jess.

Monroe approached Dave, who looked up with hollow eyes; a look that came from having your life fall apart in slow motion while everyone watched.

'Dave? We need to ask a few questions about what happened.'

'Just wanted to get the wall down,' Dave said quietly. 'Thought some demolition work might help clear my head. Hit it with the sledgehammer and... there he was. Just sitting there. Formal. Like he was holding court or something.'

Declan made notes. *Not dumped, not hidden in panic, but arranged almost ceremonially.*

'You've been working on this renovation for how long?' he asked Terry.

'Three weeks. The building's been empty for over a year, since the casino closed. If that body had been there the whole time...'

'The smell would have been noticeable,' Monroe finished.

'Exactly. But there's been nothing apart from the damp, but that's common in old buildings like this. Which means that wall was sealed tight as a drum. Probably didn't expect someone like Dave to stick a sledgehammer through it.'

Before Monroe could ask another question though, there was a commotion at the main entrance. A woman's voice, sharp and authoritative, could be heard cutting through the dusty air of the gaming room.

'This is my building. I have every right to know what's happening here.'

They turned to see a well-dressed woman in her forties arguing with one of the uniformed officers. She had the kind of presence that came from serious money and the expectation that doors would open when she knocked on them.

'Ma'am,' Declan said, approaching. 'I'm DCI Walsh, this is Detective Superintendent Monroe. You're the building's current owner?'

The woman turned her attention to the two detectives, and she smiled, relaxing slightly.

'Katarina Kováč,' she replied, extending a manicured hand. Her accent carried traces of Eastern Europe, softened by years of living elsewhere. 'I bought this property six months ago. These are my contractors.'

She gestured towards Terry and his team.

'What exactly have they found?'

'Human remains,' Monroe said simply. 'Been there for some time.'

Katarina's composure cracked slightly.

'Human remains? How long?'

'Fifteen years, possibly more. You're familiar with the building's previous use?'

'Of course. It was the Harrison Casino until last year.' She looked around the dust-sheeted room, her business mask slipping. 'I can't believe someone was… was down there all this time.'

'You bought it for development purposes?' Declan asked.

'Yes, luxury flats and a spa. The location's perfect, with Georgian architecture, planning permission approved. It was going to be worth…' She stopped herself. 'Well, this changes everything, doesn't it?'

'How so?'

'A murder scene! The publicity alone will destroy the property values. Years of work down the drain.'

'So, this is purely business?' Monroe made notes.

'Not entirely.' Katarina hesitated. 'I used to play here myself, actually. Years ago. When I heard it was for sale, there was some… nostalgia involved.'

'You were a regular?'

'For a few years, yes. High-stakes poker, private games. Very exclusive, very expensive. A place where you needed references just to get through the door.'

'When was the last time you played here?' Anjli asked.

Katarina thought for a moment, and Declan wondered if this was a ploy to gain time to position her answer.

'Years ago. When I was younger, just a girl, really. After

the financial crisis, things changed. The clientele became… less international.'

Declan thought back to the financial crisis of 2008. If this was the one Katarina Kováč was talking about, she would possibly have been late twenties, not really "girl" status.

'What kind of clientele?' he pressed.

'Business people, some celebrities, professional players from Europe and America. The buy-ins were serious – ten thousand minimum for the real games.' She gestured around the room. 'It was magnificent then, with proper dealers sometimes flown in from Monte Carlo.'

'You knew the other players?'

'Some of them. It was a small community, in its way. People came from all over the world for these games.' Her expression darkened slightly. 'Though I can't imagine any of them being involved in murder back then. Poker was big. Television shows. Poker players on world tours. No longer the seedy backroom games of old.'

'We'll need you to come in for a formal statement,' Declan said. 'Tomorrow morning?'

'Of course. Should I contact my solicitor?'

'That's your choice. This is routine questioning at this stage.'

'In that case, you can come to me.' Katarina looked around the casino one more time, taking in the dust sheets and renovation equipment. 'To think I've been renovating this place with someone's body in the basement. It is horrifying.'

She turned to leave, but Declan noticed one last look at Terry, who avoided her eyes.

Some kind of workplace issue, perhaps?

After she left, Monroe pulled Declan aside.

'What do you think?'

'Someone who knew the building, knew the players, and has the resources to buy the entire property for millions of pounds.' Declan watched through the window as Katarina climbed into what looked like a very expensive car. 'Nostalgia's an expensive hobby.'

'Or a very good cover story,' Monroe replied. 'Question is, did she buy this building to develop it, or to control what was found before *someone else* did?'

Declan studied the gaming piece through the evidence bag. Hand-carved Chinese characters on genuine ivory, craftsmanship that took years to learn and cost serious money to commission. This wasn't something you picked up at a souvenir shop. The victim had been someone with expensive tastes and dangerous hobbies. Someone who dressed like he was auditioning for a Western but played games where the stakes were measured in tens of thousands. Someone who'd made enemies who didn't forget and didn't forgive.

The cowboy hat and aviator sunglasses suggested a persona – someone playing a role, creating a character for the high-stakes poker world, perhaps. But personas could be dangerous things. They attracted attention, made you memorable, and sometimes made you a target.

His phone buzzed. A text from Jess.

How's the casino? Find any treasure?

Something like that. Stop texting and start boxing.

Tomorrow would bring the formal briefing, team assignments, and the methodical police work that turned mysteries into arrests. But tonight, looking at the evidence, Declan couldn't shake the feeling that they'd stumbled into something much larger than a simple killing.

The Harrison Casino had given up one secret, but buildings like this – with their history of high-stakes games and dangerous players – usually held more than one. Someone had gone to considerable trouble to hide this particular body, and some secrets stayed buried forever.

Others just waited for the right moment to surface and remind everyone that the past never really stayed in the past.

The question was whether they were investigating a cold case murder or walking into something that was still very much alive.

3

THE POKER PLAYER

'Right then, my collection of misfits, degenerates, and general disappointments to their respective mothers,' Monroe began, standing beside the large plasma screen rather than Declan as DCI should have, an arrangement that had evolved naturally over the months and worked for everyone involved, mainly as Monroe hadn't wanted to give up active policing to sit beside the D Supt desk. 'It seems our wee basement mystery is starting to reveal itself, and what a bloody pantomime it's turning out to be.'

Declan sat in his usual spot to Monroe's right, Anjli beside him, both nursing their second cups of coffee of the morning. Billy had claimed his customary position to the left with his laptop already connected to the primary display, whilst Doctor Marcos sat at the back with her forensic files spread out, De'Geer and Cooper occupying their regular seats beside her. Finally, visiting for the day, Detective Chief Superintendent Bullman stood by the door in her customary position, looking like a rather irritated bouncer.

'Now then,' Monroe continued, 'let's see what our wee

cowboy has to tell us. Billy, enlighten us about the dead poker cowboy?'

Billy stood, grabbing the remote and moving to the front of the room. The plasma screen behind him now glowed with a frozen image of a man grinning, arms raised, stacks of poker chips piled in front of him.

'That's Chris Moneymaker,' he said, addressing the room. 'Yes, that's his real name. And in 2003, he changed everything.'

He clicked the remote. The screen shifted to grainy footage from a Las Vegas casino – rows of poker tables, cameras rolling, crowds cheering.

'He was an accountant who paid forty pounds to enter an online poker satellite. Won it. Got a seat at the *World Series of Poker Main Event.* Then won that and walked away with two and a half million dollars. First amateur to do it on that stage. The media went mad. It looked like anyone with a laptop and nerve could do the same.'

He changed slides. The next showed early-2000s poker websites – cluttered interfaces, digital tables, blinking avatars.

'That kicked off the poker boom. Between 2005 and 2010, online poker exploded. *PokerStars, Full Tilt, PartyPoker* – all raking in millions. Tournaments running twenty-four-seven. It was digital gold.'

'Any regulation?' Anjli asked.

'At first? Not much. Wild West stuff. People deposited with credit cards and started playing straight away. By 2006, millions of players and sites pulling in billions of hands a year.'

He clicked again, showing a bar graph of rising player numbers at the *World Series of Poker Main Event.*

'Live tournaments followed suit. *World Series of Poker Main*

Event 2004, with two and a half thousand players. 2005, over five thousand. 2006? Eight thousand, seven hundred players. Winner took home twelve million dollars.'

Declan raised an eyebrow.

'Twelve million?'

'Yup, all for playing cards. Hollywood got involved too.' Billy showed a promotional still from the movie *Molly's Game*. 'Private games in penthouses. Huge buy-ins. Movie stars, tech moguls. When it went bad, it went really bad – players in debt, fixers, threats, bankruptcies.'

He paused, letting that settle.

'For about five years, poker wasn't just a game. It was a career, lifestyle, payday. And, for a lot of people, an addiction with a six-figure price tag. But then things started to change.'

'How?' De'Geer asked from the back.

Billy clicked to another graph – this one flatter.

'After 2006, it slowed. That's when the U.S. passed a law, the *Unlawful Internet Gambling Enforcement Act*. Made it harder to get money onto poker sites. Some companies pulled out of the U.S. entirely. Others kept going, but the easy-money, gold-rush vibe faded.'

He turned back to the room.

'That said, poker was still massive. In 2006, *Casino Royale* used Texas Hold 'Em as the game Bond played, rather than the Baccarat he was better known for in the earlier movies, and the original novel. From 2007 to 2010, it stayed huge – just more regulated, a bit more under the radar. But casinos still drew the big money players, and the online experts? They simply migrated from the kiddie pool to where the sharks swam. The dream was still alive. It just cost more to chase.'

Monroe waited patiently until Billy finished.

'Aye, that was very educational, laddie. Now, what about our actual victim?'

Billy looked slightly embarrassed.

'Right, sorry. I thought it was important to understand the context, as he was operating during the biggest poker boom in history. Makes his behaviour and the money involved much more significant.' Now back at his desk, Billy clicked onto the image taken in the basement of the Rolex. 'Okay then. The victim's watch provided our breakthrough late last night. Rolex keeps obsessively detailed records – serial number, model, purchase date, buyer details, the lot. Swiss efficiency meets luxury paranoia.'

He clicked to the next slide.

'Watch was purchased on March fifteenth, 2008, from Mappin & Webb in Regent Street. Twelve thousand, four hundred pounds. Registered to...'

The screen changed to show a photograph. A man in his late thirties or even early forties with a black cowboy hat tilted back, what looked to be steel-grey eyes behind barely tinted aviator sunglasses. Even in an official photo, he radiated theatricality.

'David Quincey James. Known professionally as D.Q. James.'

Monroe looked up from his files.

'Well, that explains the Wild West fancy dress. Americans and their bloody themes.'

'Actually born in London,' Billy corrected. 'Moved to Las Vegas at twenty-one. According to interviews, made his name on the American tournament poker circuit, then came back to Europe. This photo's from his *World Series of Poker* registration.'

Monroe leant forward.

'You got this from a watch, and not his dental records?'

Doctor Marcos looked up from her notes.

'Now that we have a name, I'll submit a formal request through Interpol for James's dental records from Las Vegas, to confirm the identity. From what I can see, he was never reported missing, so nobody ever asked for them before this.'

'Why Vegas?' Anjli frowned.

'That's where he apparently resided before he dropped off the grid,' Billy replied. 'His last registered dentist should have them on file.'

'How long?'

'Best case? Five to seven working days,' Doctor Marcos admitted. 'US dental practices need proper legal authorisation before releasing patient records, especially for someone who was never officially reported missing. Add in the time difference, international channels, and the fact that records often end up in storage when practices change hands...'

She shrugged.

'Could be ten days if we're unlucky.'

'We're not waiting around,' Monroe said. 'Johnny mentioned the casino attracted serious international players. This D.Q. James fits that description?'

'Professional poker player, known for psychological warfare at the table. The cowboy persona was part of it – made him memorable, gave him an edge. Opponents would underestimate him.'

'Glasses?'

'Players use them to hide their eyes, stop any tells,' Declan said. 'Probably wasn't allowed a full shade, hence the light shading of those.'

'Or he didn't want to look hungover on TV,' Anjli suggested.

'And the casino manager?' Monroe asked.

'Casino's been sold to developers, but the last manager was someone called Richard Statham. Was there since 2000, retired last year when they closed.'

'Any relation to Jason Statham?' Cooper asked half-jokingly.

'We can only hope.' Billy smiled.

'What about the owner?'

Billy consulted his notes.

'That's interesting. The casino was owned by Harrison Gaming Ltd until it closed last year, then sold to a property developer called Katarina Kováč for renovation.'

'She's the one who hired the construction crew who found the body.' Declan checked his notes. 'We spoke to her yesterday. She claims she used to play there in the old days, wanted to restore it to its former glory—'

'I thought it was apartments?'

'Yes, but posh looking ones. But she'd have known the layout, had access to the basement during renovation.'

Monroe made a note.

'We'll want to speak to both of them. What else about our cowboy?'

'Tournament winnings in the millions, but poker's volatile. You can win big one month, lose everything the next. From what I can gather, James lived hand to mouth despite occasional massive paydays. Barely anything in his accounts when he disappeared off the scene.'

'And enemies?'

'Plenty. Poker at that level isn't just about cards – it's about reading people, exploiting weaknesses, getting inside their heads,' Billy continued. 'James was apparently a master at making the game personal. He'd research opponents beforehand, find out personal information, then use it against them at the table. Financial problems, relationship issues, family secrets. Anything that would make someone play emotionally instead of logically.'

Billy pressed a key, and a YouTube video appeared that showed tournament footage. Declan could see D.Q. James at a poker table, leaning back in his chair, cowboy hat tilted, addressing another player.

'You think you can read me, partner? I've been playing this game since before your mama taught you to tie your shoes. How is she now – I heard she had a stroke? That must play on your mind, that you're here with me, and not there with her. Fold now, save yourself some embarrassment, maybe get off early, go see her. Say hi from me.'

'What a tosser,' Monroe muttered. 'No wonder someone wanted to cave his wee head in.'

'Gets worse. According to forum posts, he had a reputation for sleeping with opponents' wives and girlfriends, then bragging about it during games. There's a whole thread about a game where he apparently drove someone to a complete breakdown. The player lost everything – house, marriage, career.'

'Okay. Anything else?'

Doctor Marcos held up an evidence bag containing the mahjong piece.

'This still doesn't fit the poker narrative. This is Chinese, high quality. Not something you'd find in a Vegas gift shop.'

'Could be a lucky charm?' Anjli suggested.

'Maybe. But the craftsmanship suggests it's more than just a souvenir. This is hand-carved ivory or bone, probably worth several hundred pounds on its own.'

Monroe turned to Doctor Marcos.

'What else can you tell us about our Mister James?'

'Male, aged approximately late twenties to thirties when he died, which fits the photo of James if you squint – poker life obviously ages you. Cause of death was blunt force trauma to the left temple, single blow, probably from something like a hammer or heavy poker – not the game, but the pointy metal stick. The impact fractured the skull and would have caused immediate unconsciousness, death within minutes. The Rolex stopped at four-thirty-three, though we can't determine whether that was morning or afternoon without more analysis, and the mechanism likely seized at some point after the murder. What's interesting is that there's no impact damage to suggest it was damaged in the attack, and Rolex don't build batteries into their watches, so this would have been a wind up dial, and once left would have died out around forty-eight hours later. Also, he was killed elsewhere and moved because of a distinct lack of blood in this space, and the positioning suggests someone took considerable time with the disposal.'

'Someone who knew him,' Declan said.

'Very likely. The construction work was good quality too.' Billy brought up new images – detailed shots of the basement wall. 'Whoever did this knew building techniques, had proper materials, took time to make it look authentic.'

'How long would that take?' Declan asked.

'Couple of days if pressed,' De'Geer replied. 'The mortar would need time to cure; brickwork had to match perfectly. Meticulous work. Apparently, according to building records passed to the contractors, there was work done in November 2009, and the Harrison Casino was closed on two weekends during this time – but we don't know yet if this included the basement or not.'

'Any missing person reports?' Bullman spoke from the door.

'That's where it gets interesting,' Billy said. 'Professional poker players at James's level were nomadic – tournament to tournament, city to city. For all anyone knew, he'd simply moved on to another game. Or he'd decided to do something else. Maybe he got his buzz from trading, or cryptocurrency?'

'Perfect victim,' Monroe observed grimly. 'Someone who could disappear without reports being filed. Anyone know what happened to our Mister James after 2008?'

Billy smiled and nodded towards the door.

'Actually, I outsourced that research.'

As if on cue, Jess appeared in the doorway, laptop bag slung over her shoulder, looking slightly nervous.

'Sorry I'm late,' she said. 'Traffic was murder getting here.'

She paused.

'Sorry, probably not the best choice of words.'

'Come in, lassie,' Monroe said. 'Billy says you've been doing some detective work for us.'

Jess moved to the front of the room, clearly trying to look professional despite her nerves. Monroe stepped aside, giving her space at the plasma screen.

'When Billy called me this morning I focused on what happened after 2008 – or, more importantly 2009, when he disappeared from the poker circuit,' she began, connecting her laptop to the display system. The screen now showed poker forum screenshots. 'Look at this thread from January 2010 – people asking, "Whatever happened to D.Q. James?" Most responses assume he'd burned through his money again and was taking a break. Apparently happened regularly with high-stakes players.'

'Anything after that?'

'Actually, it gets a little more toxic,' Jess continued, pulling up more forum posts. 'By mid-2010, some people were speculating about why he really disappeared. Posts like "Maybe someone finally shut D.Q. up for good" and "Karma catches up with table terrorists eventually." Nobody took it seriously at the time, but looking back...'

'They were right,' Monroe said grimly. 'Table terrorists?'

'Hyper-aggressive types. Raising every hand, bluffing like lunatics, making you fold hands you'd normally bet the house on,' Jess replied. 'It wasn't about the cards for them, it was about control. They made everyone else play on edge. This D.Q. James made enemies everywhere he went. Last time he was seen was around November 2009. There was some kind of issue there, but I've not worked it out yet.'

'Which fits in with the timeline. Nice work, lassie,' Monroe told her as she sat down next to Billy, but not before getting a proud pat on the arm from Declan.

'Thought you were at college today?'

'This afternoon.' Jess smiled. 'I can help until noon.'

'And Billy just so happened to outsource?'

'Well, I might have contacted him repeatedly all night once I knew you had a case.' Jess grinned. 'I must have worn him down.'

De'Geer's phone rang, causing him to jump slightly. He glanced at the caller ID and frowned.

'Excuse me,' he said, standing and moving towards the door. 'I need to take this.'

He stepped into the corridor as Monroe turned to the remaining team.

'Right, assignments. Declan and Anjli, former casino staff. Find out who remembers D.Q. James, what games he played, who he might have pissed off enough to want to kill him.

Billy, deep dive into James's background. Complete tournament history, where he stayed in London, criminal associations, financial problems. Get Jess to help while she's here and look into this brouhaha thing.'

He looked to the back.

'Cooper, when our sergeant finishes his mysterious phone call, go with him and canvass the area. Any businesses operating in 2008–2009, any CCTV archives, anyone who remembers unusual activity.'

'The Chinese connection?' Doctor Marcos asked.

'I'll handle that personally,' Monroe said. 'Kenny Tsang might have insights into high-stakes gaming from that period. I'll see what I can discover about that mahjong piece.'

'Ah,' Declan said. 'You're thinking underground Chinese gambling.'

'The very thing. If there were illegal operations running parallel to the legitimate casino business, Kenny would know.'

In the corridor, De'Geer's conversation seemed to get heated. His voice had dropped to urgent whispers, but his posture suggested increasing agitation.

'Anything else we should know?' Monroe asked Bullman, now straightening from the doorframe.

'Standard bureaucratic nonsense. Questions about overtime budgets, progress reports. High-profile case involving expensive real estate – the press will be sniffing around once word gets out.'

De'Geer returned, pocketing his phone with a troubled expression.

'Sorry about that,' he said. 'Old business from training college. Nothing urgent.'

But Monroe's sharp eyes caught how De'Geer avoided eye contact, the slight tremor in his hands as he sat down.

'Doctor Marcos, how soon for complete forensic analysis?'

'Another few days for toxicology. Want to check for drug or alcohol traces that might tell us about his last hours – the body's been alone and decomposing for over a decade so I'm not holding out much hope there.'

As the briefing broke up, Declan noticed De'Geer lingering, checking his phone again with a deepening frown.

'You sure everything's alright, Sergeant?'

'Fine, sir,' De'Geer replied, but his voice lacked conviction. 'Just someone from the past asking for a favour. Nothing I can't handle.'

'Who do you want to start with?' Anjli asked, pulling on her jacket as she rose from the chair.

'We'll start with the manager,' Declan said. 'Richard Statham should remember a flamboyant American poker player in a cowboy hat.'

'Yee-haw,' Anjli mimed a lasso. 'Let's just hope there aren't that many of them.'

4

MUSEUM PIECES

In Bermondsey, Richard Statham seemed to have already been waiting for Anjli and Declan with the sort of patience that came from decades in the hospitality business when they arrived. His small, terraced house overlooked the Thames, and from his sitting room window, Declan could see the spot where the old London Bridge had once stood.

'I remember D.Q. James very well,' Statham said, settling into his armchair with a slight wince. 'You don't forget someone like that. The hat was theatrical, but it worked. People underestimated him.'

The sitting room was neat but lived-in, with faded photographs of what looked like casino events dotting the mantelpiece. A walking stick leant against Statham's chair, and his movements suggested arthritis was making retirement less comfortable than he'd hoped.

'What kind of games did he play at the casino?' Anjli had her notebook ready.

'High-stakes poker, mainly. Texas Hold 'Em when it became fashionable, but he preferred the psychological games – Seven-Card Stud, Omaha. Anything where he could get under people's skin.' Statham's expression grew thoughtful. 'Very methodical about it. He'd arrive early, watch players during the warm-up games, take mental notes.'

'Notes about what?'

'Tells. Nervous habits. But more than that – he'd listen to conversations, pick up personal details. Then during the actual games, he'd use those details like weapons.'

Declan leant forward.

'Can you give us a specific example?'

'Oh, I remember one night particularly well. It was a February, I think. We had a regular tournament, about eight players, buy-in was twenty thousand each. James was playing against this property developer – nice enough fellow but going through some personal difficulties.'

Statham paused, seeming to organise his memories.

'The developer was playing well, actually. Had a good stack, making smart decisions. Then James started making little comments. "Difficult times in the property market," that sort of thing. "Must be hard keeping the business afloat with everything that's going on at home." Nothing too obvious, you understand.'

'What happened?'

'The developer started losing his composure. His betting became erratic, started making calls he shouldn't make. By the end of the night, he'd lost everything – not just his buy-in, but an additional forty thousand he'd borrowed against his business.' Statham shook his head. 'James collected his winnings and actually had the gall to offer his condolences about the man's divorce and hoped his "coming out" wasn't too painful.'

'The divorce wasn't public knowledge?'

'The papers hadn't even been filed yet. And nobody knew the man was gay, either. Somehow James knew about it before anyone else. And once you realise he knew that, then you realise the comments about the property market? They were laser focused on his competition, deliberate.'

Anjli made notes.

'How did he find out personal information like that?'

'That was always the mystery. James would disappear for days, sometimes weeks, then return with detailed knowledge about players' private lives. Financial problems, relationship issues, family secrets. We assumed he had contacts, people who fed him information.' Statham struggled to his feet and moved to a cabinet, pulling out a thick photo album. 'I kept pictures from the casino's better days. Thought they might be worth something someday for a book or documentary.'

He settled back into his chair and opened the album, pages crackling slightly with age. The photographs showed the Harrison Casino in its heyday – crystal chandeliers, Persian rugs, well-dressed people around green baize tables.

'Here we are,' he said, finding a particular page. 'This was taken during our Valentine's tournament, 2009.'

The photograph showed D.Q. James at a poker table, cowboy hat pushed back, aviator sunglasses reflecting the camera flash. Even in a still image, he radiated theatrical confidence. Around the table sat five other players, their faces showing various degrees of concentration and barely concealed frustration.

'James won big that night – nearly five hundred thousand pounds,' Statham continued. 'He was in an excellent mood afterwards, buying drinks for everyone, tipping the staff generously. Said it was one of his better performances.'

'Performances?'

'That's how he saw it – theatre. The cowboy persona, the psychological games, even the way he stacked his chips. Everything was calculated for maximum effect.'

'Who are the other players in this photo?'

Statham put on reading glasses and squinted at the photograph.

'That's Corey Moore, professional from Manchester. Excellent player, but James got to her that night with comments about her father's gambling debts. The man next to her is Tony Norton, property development. The woman with dark hair is Linda Burrell – she used to work for us actually, cocktail waitress, but she'd sit in on games when we needed numbers. Good player too.'

'What about the others?'

'The gentleman in the dark suit was a regular – came up from Brighton most weekends. I can't recall his name now. The woman next to James was visiting from Germany, I think. High-roller, serious money.'

Declan studied the faces in the photograph.

'Did any of these people have particular problems with James?'

'Oh, all of them at some point. Tony Norton especially – James had somehow discovered Norton's company was being investigated for tax evasion. Made several pointed comments during play about the importance of keeping proper records. Norton lost nearly sixty thousand that night and banned himself from the casino afterwards.'

'Banned himself?'

'We had a self-exclusion programme. Players could request to be barred from entering if they felt their gambling was becoming problematic. Norton signed the papers the next morning, said James had made him realise he was in over his head.'

Statham turned the page, revealing more photographs from the same event.

'Linda was cleverer about it. She'd worked for us for three years, knew James's methods. When he started probing about her personal life, she fed him false information. Told him she was getting married when she wasn't, claimed she'd inherited money from a relative. Threw him off his game completely.'

'So, it was possible to counter his tactics?'

'If you knew what he was doing, yes. But most players were so focused on their cards they didn't realise they were being manipulated until it was too late.'

Anjli looked up from her notebook.

'What happened to the casino after James disappeared?'

'Business dried up slowly, over the years. The poker boom was ending – online gambling was taking over, and frankly, some of our clientele were getting involved with people we didn't want in the building.' Statham's expression darkened. 'Too many stories about money laundering, too many questions from authorities. We started losing our legitimate customers.'

'What people were you trying to avoid?'

'Organised crime, mainly. Eastern Europeans, some Chinese groups, couple of Albanian outfits. They'd use poker games to move money, settle debts. The stakes got higher, the atmosphere became... unpleasant.'

'Was James involved with any of these groups?'

Statham considered this carefully.

'Not directly, as far as I knew. It was early days back then. But he was playing in games with their money on the table, winning from their associates. Dangerous territory for someone who made enemies as easily as James did.'

'When did you last see him?'

'November 2009. He'd had a particularly good run – won over three hundred thousand in the space of two weeks. Then he managed to piss off a Triad-connected gangster and just stopped coming. We assumed he'd moved on to other casinos, other cities. That's how it worked with professional players.'

'No one filed a missing person report?'

'Who would have? No family here that we knew of, no permanent address. James lived like a nomad – tournament to tournament, city to city. When someone disappeared from the circuit, people just assumed they'd lost their stake somewhere and were rebuilding.'

'Tell me about the Triads.'

'Nothing to tell. It was a game a couple of months earlier. He won a hand, they lost big.'

He paused.

'That said, the gentlemen in question did believe he'd cheated them out of some personal items. Even asked me to look out for them. But I never saw anything. And then a couple of months later he was gone.'

'Did he ever mention where he stayed when he was in London? Hotels, friends?'

'Always secretive about his personal life. Claimed he preferred to keep business and pleasure separate. But there was something interesting about James that always intrigued me.'

Statham leant forward conspiratorially.

'He collected custom poker chips. Not for playing – he had special ones he claimed were lucky. Never put them in play, just kept them in a beautiful display case. I saw a photo of it once. Very protective of that collection.'

Declan and Anjli exchanged glances.

'Can you describe them?'

'They were casino chips from different casinos, always high value chips, with distinctive designs. Said each one represented a major win somewhere in the world. Part of his mystique, I suppose. He had a whole case of them. I think it was a motivator, you know? He'd look at them and it'd inspire him. Actually, there's a poker exhibition at the Museum of London Docklands now. I help out there occasionally, some of my photos are up. They've got a small display about James – that very same chip collection, some photos, other bits and pieces. Only went up a few weeks back, too.'

'At the Docklands Museum?'

'The exhibit started a couple of years ago. History of gambling in London, that sort of thing. James gets a corner of it – his story's quite popular with visitors.' Statham smiled slightly. 'People are fascinated by the idea of a cowboy poker player in London. Very romantic, I suppose.'

'How did the museum acquire his belongings?'

'That's an interesting story. Years after James disappeared, the storage company he kept a unit at decided to sell off his contents as he hadn't paid his rents. This was earlier this year, which is what, fifteen years or so after he was last seen.'

'They waited fifteen years?'

'They had to, as he'd paid for that amount of time in advance.' Statham shrugged. 'Anyway, the storage company auctioned off the contents. The museum had been given the nod and acquired the items for literal pennies.'

'What kind of things were in storage?'

'Poker memorabilia mainly. Tournament photos, newspaper clippings about his wins, the chip collection in a pretty box, I think. Some personal items too – clothes, books, that sort of thing. Nothing that gave any clues about what happened to him.'

He paused.

'Actually, there was one thing that puzzled everyone when they catalogued his belongings. James had six watches in a small wooden box – all identical *Patek Philippe Grand Complications*. Beautiful pieces, worth about twenty, maybe thirty thousand each. The storage auction people had no idea what they were, but I did; I'd seen enough Pateks on people's wrists, so I slipped them the nod and the museum got them for practically nothing.'

He paused, adjusting his reading glasses.

'Course, once the museum realised what they had, they sold four of them to collectors – used the money to buy other gambling memorabilia for the exhibition. Kept two for display. Actually, they gave me one of the four as payment for helping identify what everything was.'

Statham looked slightly embarrassed.

'Lovely watch, really. Somewhere upstairs, I think. Or maybe in the kitchen drawer? I'll have a proper look for it later.'

Anjli noted this down and, as they prepared to leave, Statham walked them to the door with careful, arthritic steps.

'There was one other thing about James that always struck me as odd,' he said. 'He always paid in cash – never cards or cheques.'

'Suggesting what?'

'That he didn't trust banks, also liked to keep things off books. Easier to keep huge profits away from the taxman and all that.'

Anjli closed her notebook.

'Thanks for your time,' she said. 'If you think of anything else, please call.'

'Of course. Though I have to say, finding out what happened to James after all these years... it's rather unsettling. Makes you wonder what other secrets that building might be hiding.'

OUTSIDE, ANJLI LOOKED AT DECLAN.

'Nobody just "loses" a twenty or thirty grand watch,' she said softly.

'Maybe he spent so much time with that kind of jewellery it's lost on him?' Declan replied. 'One thing's for sure. We need to get more information on this Triad guy, and go check out that museum.'

AT TEMPLE INN, BILLY AND JESS HAD TRANSFORMED THEIR corner into a research station, with multiple screens displaying poker forums, tournament databases, and video archives.

'Right,' Billy said, stretching in his chair. 'I've been going through D.Q. James's online presence for the past three hours. The pattern that's emerging is both fascinating and disturbing.'

Jess looked up from her laptop, where she'd been scrolling through social media posts and forum discussions.

'Disturbing how?'

'He wasn't just a poker player – he was definitely a

psychological predator who used cards as camouflage. Look at this forum post from *PokerMadness*, dated September 2007. *"Played against D.Q. James in Amsterdam last month. Somehow the bastard knew about my divorce before I'd even told my lawyer. Spent the entire evening making comments about custody arrangements and child support. Made me so angry I couldn't see straight. Lost my kids' university fund in one night. James collected his chips and actually tipped his hat at me on the way out".*'

'Jesus. How was he getting that kind of information?'

'That's what I've been trying to work out. There are dozens of similar complaints across different forums, different countries, spanning several years. All with the same pattern – James knowing impossibly personal details about opponents.'

Billy clicked through to another window showing a spreadsheet he'd been building.

'Look at this one from *CardSharp Forum*, 2008: *"D.Q. James cleaned me out in Monte Carlo. Knew my business was being investigated for tax evasion before the investigators had even contacted me. Made jokes about prison food all night. Couldn't concentrate on my hands. Lost everything."* And this one from *HighRollerLife*, also 2008: *"James destroyed me psychologically in a private game in Barcelona. Somehow knew my husband was having an affair – brought it up repeatedly during crucial hands. Even I didn't know this. When I finally confronted him afterwards, he just smiled and said business was business".*'

He leant back.

'Utter prick. But you have to admire him.'

Before Jess could respond, her phone buzzed insistently. She glanced at it and her expression changed.

'Shit. Prisha's been waiting at the cafe for half an hour.'

'Can't you text that you're working on something important?'

'That's exactly the problem.' Jess was already closing her laptop and shoving papers into her bag. 'I've been saying that for weeks. "Just finishing this research," "Five more minutes," "This case is really important." She thinks the dead are more important to me than the living.'

'Are they?'

Jess paused, her hands stilling on her bag straps. The question hung in the air between them.

'I don't know,' she said finally. 'That's what scares me. When you were just talking about a stranger's financial problems from fifteen years ago, I cared about it more than I did about missing lunch with my girlfriend.'

She shouldered her bag, looking genuinely troubled.

'I'll finish this after classes, send you everything I find. But right now I need to go convince the most important living person in my life that she matters more than dead cowboys and old poker games.'

After she left, Billy continued working alone, but her words echoed uncomfortably in his mind. *How many police officers had he known who'd lost marriages, friendships, family connections because they became too absorbed in solving other people's tragedies?*

He'd had his own fair share, that was for sure. And Jess wasn't even an official member of the police force yet, and she was already on that path.

He should tell Declan.

Yes.

But maybe later. It wasn't his problem right now, after all.

Around the former Harrison Casino, De'Geer and Cooper had spent two hours methodically canvassing businesses that had operated in the late "noughties". They'd worked their way around the entire block, speaking to shop owners, office workers, anyone who might remember activity from fifteen years ago. The picture emerging was of a casino that catered to people who preferred their business private.

'Last one,' Cooper said, nodding towards a family-run newsagent that had been operating since the eighties, but before they could continue, a man's voice spoke behind them.

'Morten?'

De'Geer turned at the sound of his name. Walking towards them across the street was a man looking considerably worse for wear. He looked as if he had recently lost weight, his clothes hung badly, and he carried the desperate air of someone whose world was collapsing.

And De'Geer recognised him.

'I'll be back in a minute,' De'Geer told Cooper, who nodded and continued towards the newsagent. Once she was gone, he crossed the street to meet the man on the pavement. 'I told you I'd think about it—'

'I can't wait any more, Morten.' The man's voice carried barely controlled panic. 'The hearing's too soon. Professional Standards are going through everything with forensic accountancy. If I don't have someone who can vouch for my whereabouts on the tenth...'

De'Geer felt his stomach tighten. The tenth of last month – he knew what the man was referring to. He'd had it explained at length on a phone call during the briefing.

'You know I can't do that.'

'You were with me that evening. We had dinner, remember? The Chinese place in Chinatown. You can verify I was nowhere near Mayfair.'

The lie hung between them. They hadn't had dinner. De'Geer had been at home with Cooper that evening, something he could easily prove. But this man was asking him to provide a false alibi, to say they'd been together...

'This is about gambling debts, isn't it?' De'Geer said quietly. 'How much do you owe this time?'

'That's not... it's complicated. The people I borrowed from, they don't accept excuses. I've got a way to pay them back, but I need to tread water. Stay above the water for a week at least. But now the professional standards department are closing in...'

The man stepped closer, desperation making him reckless.

'We're old friends, Morten. We came up through training together. And if they start digging deeper into why the case was taken from me, if they look at me more carefully... well, they might discover things about *both* of us that we'd rather keep quiet.'

There it was – the threat wrapped in a plea for help. *Help me lie, or face consequences for both of us.*

'I need time to think.'

'There is no time. The hearing's this week.' The man glanced around nervously. 'Look, I know this is difficult, but I'm fighting for my life here. And if this all comes out, if they start investigating connections...'

He didn't finish the sentence, but the implication was clear. There were deeper connections, more secrets that could surface.

The threat made, the man walked away as he saw Cooper crossing the street towards them.

'Who was that?' she asked.

'Detective Constable Paul Elliott,' De'Geer said, his voice tight. 'Works with DCI Cohen's lot. Said he'd heard about the casino case, came by to offer help.'

Cooper watched Elliott's retreating figure, noting how De'Geer's hands were trembling slightly.

'Everything alright?' she asked.

'Fine,' De'Geer replied, but his voice came out harsh and clipped. 'Just someone wanting favours.'

'What kind of favours?'

'Nothing important.' He started walking back towards their car, cutting the conversation short in a way that was completely unlike his usual steady demeanour. 'We should get back. Write up what we've found.'

Cooper followed, sensing the dramatic shift in his mood and, as they walked, she discreetly pulled out her phone and took a photo of the man who was still visible at the far end of the street. Something about that encounter had badly shaken De'Geer, and her detective instincts told her that understanding why might be crucial.

She'd run Elliott's name through the system when they got back to Temple Inn.

Whatever he'd really wanted, it was clearly more significant than offering help on their case.

And Esme Cooper was damned if someone was going to cause issues for her man.

5

MAHJONG PIECES

MONROE STOOD OUTSIDE KENNY TSANG'S IMPORT OFFICE IN Chinatown. The irony wasn't lost on him – coming to see one of the most corrupt gangland lords in London to help with a case, but Kenny had connections to London's Chinese community that the police needed, regardless of personal complications.

The brass nameplate read

TSANG – IMPORT/EXPORT INDUSTRIES

in both English and Chinese. Monroe pressed the buzzer.

'What?' An unfamiliar voice spoke.

'Tell Kenny it's Monroe. Need a word about something old.'

'Kenny who?'

'Don't be a prick, laddie.'

'Monroe who?'

'*Detective Superintendent* Alexander Monroe.'

There was a pause at this before the door buzzed open

and Monroe climbed the stairs to the offices above. A bald, vicious-looking doorman in black suit and tie stood in front of the door.

'Let me guess, "if you're not on the list, you're not coming in"?' Monroe smiled.

The doorman said nothing, simply rapping twice on the door and then opening it, revealing Kenny Tsang sitting behind his mahogany desk. Tall and imposing even while seated, his iPad open beside him, Kenny looked up as Monroe entered.

'Detective Superintendent Monroe,' Kenny said. 'To what do I owe the pleasure? Professional business, I assume?'

'Always is with us, isn't it?' Monroe replied, settling into the chair opposite without being invited. 'Unlike some people, I don't mix business with pleasure.'

Kenny's smile was knowing.

'How is Rosanna? Married life treating her well?'

'Well enough. Though I'm not here to discuss my wife.'

'Of course not. Though I do hope she's happier now than she was during her... difficult period. Suspension can be hard on people. Makes them seek comfort in unusual places.'

Monroe felt his jaw tighten. It wasn't a secret in Temple Inn that Doctor Marcos had once seen Kenny romantically, but that had been years back.

'That's ancient history. How's the bullet wound? You know, from when your old family tried to kill you?' He looked around. 'Where's Jimmy? I thought he'd taken over the reins?'

Kenny leant back in his chair.

'Itches when it rains,' he replied. 'And Jimmy? Decided London wasn't really his speed. As you said, ancient history.'

'Aye, and we're here about something even older.' Monroe

pulled out his phone, swiped to a photo of the Mahjong piece they'd found and then placed it on the desk between them. Kenny glanced at it, and as if by magic, his amused expression vanished.

'Where did you find this?'

'Body that's been buried for fifteen years. Victim called D.Q. James – American poker player, which is why we felt it strange he'd be carrying a mahjong gaming piece.'

Kenny leant forward, studying the image. When he sat back, his face had gone serious.

'This is not a gaming piece, Monroe. This is an entrance token to something very dangerous. Something that should have stayed buried along with your cowboy.'

'What kind of entrance token?'

'High-stakes gambling operation. Very exclusive, very illegal. Ran from the late nineties until the early 2010s.' Kenny's voice had lost its earlier playfulness. 'Games where people bet considerably more than money.'

'You knew about these games?'

'I knew of them. There's a difference.' Kenny stood and walked to his window. 'This wasn't me or Benny.'

'Bullshit.' Monroe shook his head. 'You ran Chinatown back then. If you didn't know, it would have been the Turk's business and he, well...'

'He was a racist prick who hated Asians.' Kenny smiled. 'This was a family he knew, who he owed, so he asked us to work with them on this. Only one location, started small, built up though. The entire operation was run by someone who called himself Wong Sei – not his real name, but he put on traditional airs to impress the mainland money.'

'Real name?'

'I think it was Barry something.' Kenny smiled. 'Seriously. I'll ask around, get it for you.'

'What kind of people played there?'

'Politicians hiding bribes, business executives laundering funds, criminals from various organisations. Anyone with serious money and flexible morals.' Kenny stroked his chin as he thought back. 'Buy-in was fifty thousand minimum. These weren't casual poker nights.'

Monroe made notes.

'And this D.Q. James would have been involved?'

'A professional player with that reputation? Absolutely. Wong Sei recruited specific players for their psychological skills. The games weren't just about gambling – they were about power, networking, information trading.'

'What shut them down?'

'November 2009, the operation hit a speed bump.' Kenny shrugged. 'Wong Sei vanished along with about half a million in-house funds and a Triad boss hunting stolen diamonds. People assumed he'd either fled to Hong Kong or been eliminated by unhappy clients. We took over for six months, but it wasn't the same.'

'Would any of these "unhappy clients" have killed D.Q. James?'

'Without question. But Monroe, these games weren't just gambling dens. They were information exchanges. State secrets, criminal intelligence, business deals – everything was currency there. D.Q. James, with his talent for gathering personal dirt on opponents, would have been extremely valuable.'

Monroe absorbed this.

'So, he might have learned something dangerous?'

'Or tried to blackmail the wrong person. Or was caught

working for competing interests.' Kenny chuckled, and Monroe wondered what the joke was. 'In that world, there were many ways to make fatal mistakes.'

Kenny returned his attention to the photo of the game piece, staring down at it, frowning as he did so.

'One more thing – if your victim had Wong Sei's token, he was either heading to a game or leaving one when he died. Tokens were only distributed a day or two before events, collected at entry. But this one feels off somehow. Hold on...'

He walked over to a side cabinet and opened it to reveal a small safe. He tapped in a number, opened it, reached in and withdrew a small felt bag.

'Here,' he said, passing it to Monroe. 'It's a keepsake. I want it back when you're done.'

Monroe opened it to find another mahjong piece, identical to the one in the image.

'Aye, thanks, we can do some comparison analysis on these,' he replied, placing it back in the bag and putting it into his pocket. 'Any idea where these games were held?'

'Various high-end locations. Never the same place twice. Wong Sei was paranoid about security, and with good reason. We agreed to help, so a couple were held at locations we knew, but mainly it was the Turk's buildings, as he liked the idea of having his own people there.'

Monroe stood to leave, then paused.

'Kenny, you mentioned he disappeared in November 2009. Do you remember the exact date?'

Kenny consulted his iPad.

'November fifteenth or sixteenth. I remember because there was concern in the community about police raids afterwards. But Monroe, if Wong Sei is still alive, and if he learns someone is investigating those old games? Then you should be very careful,' Kenny finished. 'The people involved in that operation have long memories and considerable resources. They don't appreciate police attention.'

Monroe sighed theatrically as he walked to the door.

'Nobody ever does, Kenny,' he replied. 'Nobody ever does.'

'Hey, say hi to your wife for me.' Kenny grinned.

'Not a hope in hell, Kenny,' Monroe said as he left.

AT THE MUSEUM OF LONDON DOCKLANDS, HOUSED IN A converted Georgian warehouse that had once stored sugar, rum and coffee from the West Indies, Declan and Anjli made their way through exhibits chronicling London's maritime history.

The building's red brick walls and cast-iron columns spoke of the Thames's commercial past, when these docks had been the beating heart of the British Empire's trade. Now, more a side piece to Canary Wharf, it seemed to be law firms and posh restaurants.

And a cryotherapy company that probably never want to see us again.

The curator had aimed them at one of the volunteers, Imogen Rothwell, who led them to the gambling exhibition on the second floor, a newer addition that explored London's relationship with games of chance from medieval dice to modern casinos and, in a quiet corner, Declan and Anjli stood before the D.Q. James display case.

'These were his prize possessions,' Rothwell explained, gesturing to a professional poker chip rack, black-painted wood, holding what appeared to be a complete set of one hundred chips, arranged in neat stacks of twenty. 'Each one supposedly custom made to represent a major win at a different casino. He probably had one commissioned after each big win during his career or had a hundred made and lied about it – all to boost the reputation. He was quite superstitious about the collection, though. Never played with them, just kept them as inspiration.'

'Were?' Declan studied the chips. They were clearly high quality, with intricate designs and gold detailing. Each was different – Las Vegas, Monte Carlo, Macau, London.

'Well, he's not come back for them for quite a while now, so I think "were" is valid.'

'They're heavier than normal casino chips,' Anjli observed, picking one up, feeling the weight.

'Good eye. Yes, they are unusually heavy. Most poker players prefer standard weights, but James had said in an interview once these were just for show, so he didn't care about semantics. Just another part of his theatrical personality.' Rothwell now moved to a display board showing tournament photographs. 'James was quite a character in his heyday. Always in costume, always playing a role. The cowboy persona was his trademark. The psychological aspect was crucial to his success. He'd research opponents beforehand, find out personal details, then use that information to create doubt and uncertainty. Quite ruthless, really.'

'This research he did,' Declan asked, 'how comprehensive was it?'

'Extremely thorough. Stories of him knowing about opponents' business troubles, family problems, medical issues. Information that shouldn't have been publicly available. Some players accused him of hiring private investigators.'

'In your research, did you come across anyone who lost everything to James?' Anjli made notes. 'Someone who might have held a serious grudge?'

Rothwell's face grew thoughtful.

'Well, there was one case that's become legend in poker circles. A businessman called Trevor Sullivan owned a chain of electronics stores. Happened years back, during a private tournament in London.'

She led them to another display case containing newspaper clippings and a small pewter figure.

'This is interesting,' Rothwell said, pointing to the figure. 'As you can see, it's a gunfighter in a long coat and Stetson, perfectly painted down to the finest detail. D.Q. James carried this everywhere as a good luck charm. You can see it in almost every tournament photo.'

She indicated several photographs where the tiny figure sat beside James's chip stack, regardless of his outfit.

'The painting work is exceptional. Museum-quality precision on something barely two inches tall. In several interviews, James was very passionate about miniature painting – Warhammer figures, D&D characters, military models. Incredibly skilled work. We believe this was "The Gunfighter", a limited edition figure from a never-released game based on Stephen King's *Dark Tower* series.'

Declan studied the figure closely. The detail was remarkable – individual buttons, weathering on boots, even tiny facial features perfectly rendered.

'Impressive.'

Rothwell didn't hear, as by now she'd moved to the newspaper and magazine clippings.

'I mentioned the poker game against Sullivan? Well, here's a piece on it,' she said. 'He was a recreational player, successful businessman but amateur gambler. James apparently destroyed him psychologically during a winner-takes-all game. Used personal information about Sullivan's failing marriage and business troubles to unnerve him completely.'

'What happened?'

'Sullivan lost everything. His business, his savings, even his house was part of the stake. James took the lot – about two million pounds' worth of assets. The poker community was appalled. Even by their standards, James had been unusually cruel.'

'Is Sullivan still alive?'

'I believe so, though I've never met him personally. Got divorced, pretty much ghosted his entire family and took a decade off, travelling the world as a backpacker, some say. Last I heard, he was working security for a gym somewhere in London. Quite a fall from running a successful business empire.'

'You seem to know a lot here.'

'Word travels.' Rothwell smiled.

'Does he still play?'

'Oh, God knows,' Rothwell gave an embarrassed shrug. 'Probably still trying the tables. Many of them never know when to quit.'

Anjli exchanged glances with Declan.

'Would you happen to have any contact information for Mr Sullivan?'

'I might have something in our research files. Let me check.'

While Rothwell consulted her files, Declan studied the articles on the wall but then flinched back as he saw the byline date and writer of one of the magazine articles.

August 18th 2008
By Kendis Taylor

'Shit,' Anjli said as she leant closer, reading it as well. 'You okay?'

'Kendis had a long and illustrious career,' Declan said, but there was a tightness to his eyes. 'Of course she did stuff like this. She would have still been local papers back then, so this would have been freelance.'

'You need a moment?' Anjli continued, and Declan knew why she was worried. Kendis had been his childhood sweetheart, and they'd rekindled their relationship the day before she'd been murdered for her silence. It was well before he'd got together with Anjli, but she'd been there at the time, seen how Declan had been.

'I'm good,' he said as Rothwell returned with a folder.

'I found Trevor Sullivan's last known address from about three years ago. The postal service returned our letter marked "addressee unknown," but it might give you a starting point.'

She handed Declan a slip of paper with an address in Bow.

'We'd normally require special authorisation to handle any artefacts, but given this is a murder investigation, I can arrange for you to examine items more closely if needed.'

'We appreciate that. We may need to take you up on that offer.' Declan smiled.

'Now,' Imogen Rothwell smiled, 'would you like to see our Thames mudlarking exhibition? We've found all manner of material, from a late medieval eel spear to the sawn-off barrel of a shotgun.'

Declan raised an eyebrow, and Rothwell reddened.

'We did make sure it wasn't involved in any cases,' she admitted.

OUTSIDE THE MUSEUM, DECLAN AND ANJLI WALKED ALONG THE West India Quay towpath towards their car.

'Trevor Sullivan,' Anjli said. 'Lost everything to James around a couple of months before he died, maybe. If anyone had motive...'

'Agreed. And did you see that miniature figure? The painting work was extraordinary. James had serious skills with fine detail work.'

'You think that's significant?'

'Someone with that level of precision... they could forge anything small. Documents, artwork, maybe even...' Declan paused. 'I'm not sure yet. But it feels important. Maybe we should get Billy's partner Sam in for a chat? See if he ever heard of James dabbling?'

'It's a reach but sure.' Anjli shrugged. 'Currently we have nothing.'

Declan's phone buzzed with a text from Monroe.

> Chinese gambling connection confirmed.
> Kenny says dangerous people involved.
> Briefing end of day.

'Looks like Monroe's had an interesting afternoon too,' he said. 'Maybe we have something after all.'

Anjli paused.

'Declan, the piece by Kendis...' she started, but paused as Declan grabbed her by the shoulder, pulling her close as they looked at the water.

'Is my past,' he said with a smile. 'You're my present, Anjli. And my future.'

'And don't you forget it,' Anjli smiled. 'Hey, have you heard the coppers at Bishopsgate have a name for us?'

'A name?'

'Yeah. "Declanjli",' Anjli chuckled. 'You know, like Bennifer, or Branjalina.'

'Both of those broke up,' Declan shuddered as they continued. 'Let's hope that's not an omen.'

'Yeah, that's totally how it works,' Anjli linked her arm with Declan's. 'Come on, ignore Bishopsgate until after we solve the crime, yeah?'

BACK AT TEMPLE INN, BILLY WAS HUNCHED OVER HIS LAPTOP, surrounded by printouts from the City of London council planning department. He'd spent the last hour digging through renovation records for the Harrison Casino, trying to make sense of a timeline that didn't add up.

'Bloody hell,' he muttered, cross-referencing dates between two different documents.

'Problem?'

Unaware he wasn't alone, Billy jerked up to see Bullman emerging from Monroe's office, looking restless and slightly irritated.

'Ma'am. Didn't know you were here.'

'Monroe's office is more comfortable than mine when I need to think,' Bullman said, settling into the chair beside Billy's desk. 'And it saves me having to go back to Guildhall. What's got you swearing at paperwork?'

Billy turned his laptop screen towards her.

'Katarina Kováč, the woman who bought the casino. Her planning documents don't make sense.'

'How so?'

'Original renovation plans called for the basement to remain untouched – heritage preservation area, sealed off completely. But three weeks ago, she filed an amendment requesting access to the south-facing wall for "structural assessment".'

Bullman leant forward, interested now.

'The wall where we found the body.'

'Exactly. She must have surveyed the building, discovered something about that specific wall, and then made sure she had legal permission to modify it. She didn't just happen to find a body – she knew exactly where to look.'

'So, she either knew about the murder or...'

'Or she was involved fifteen years ago.' Billy rubbed his eyes. 'Between this, Monroe's Chinese gambling connections, and the businessman who lost everything to the victim DCI Walsh texted me to find details on, we're drowning in suspects.'

Bullman was quiet for a moment, studying the documents.

'Good work, Billy.'

'Thanks. Though can I ask a question?'

'Never stopped you before.'

'A personal one?'

'Go on,' Bullman replied, but her face gave a different answer, one of *don't you bloody dare.*

'It's just... what are you doing hiding in Monroe's office? Shouldn't you be at Guildhall?'

Bullman's face shifted, becoming evasive.

'Just needed some space to think about a case.'

'Right,' Billy said, clearly not believing her. 'Nothing to do with avoiding anyone in particular?'

'I'm not avoiding anyone.'

'Ma'am, you're hiding in someone else's office, making excuses. What's going on?'

Bullman sighed.

'Bradbury wants me to move in with him. Says it's time I met his daughter properly, integrate into his family life.'

'And that's bad because...?'

'Because it's too fast, too much. We've been seeing each other for what, three months?'

'I think it's a lot more than that, Ma'am.'

'And now he wants me playing stepmother to a teenager?' Bullman shook her head. 'I'm not ready for that kind of commitment.'

Billy nodded sympathetically.

'Family complications. I know the feeling.'

'Your lot still giving you grief?'

'Always. Though to be fair, they don't want to meet any of my partners either. Apart from Uncle Chivalry, but he's...' Billy paused, smiling slightly. 'Well, you know Chivalry.'

Bullman's face softened, and Billy caught what looked suspiciously like a fond smile.

'Yes, I know Chivalry. He's quite... unique.'

'He liked you, you know. After that whole Essex Rider business, he said you were "formidable" and that I should introduce you to more of the family.'

'Did he now?' Bullman's smile became more genuine. 'Well, Chivalry has excellent taste in people.'

'He does. And he's probably the only family member who'd approve of my life choices.' Billy closed his laptop.

'Maybe you should talk to Bradbury instead of hiding from him? Tell him you need more time?'

'Perhaps. Though avoiding problems has served me well so far.'

'Has it though? You're hiding in Monroe's office instead of dealing with your own life.'

Bullman straightened, but her face wasn't annoyed – more thoughtful.

'When did you become so wise about relationships, Billy?'

'I didn't. I'm terrible at them. But sometimes talking helps more than hiding.'

'Fair point.'

As Bullman disappeared back into Monroe's office, Billy looked at his research spread across the desk. Three major suspects emerging from a fifteen-year-old murder: Chinese criminals who might have killed James for betraying their operation, a businessman destroyed by James who had serious motive for revenge, and a building owner who seemed to know exactly where to find the body.

Maybe everyone was right about his needing better life balance. But first, they needed to solve the mystery of D.Q. James and discover whether fifteen-year-old secrets were worth killing to protect.

6

OLD DEBTS

THE *FLEX-U-FIT* GYM IN BOW SMELT LIKE INDUSTRIAL disinfectant fighting a losing battle against human sweat. Monroe pushed through the glass doors past a collection of motivational posters featuring people who looked like they could bench press a small car and carried on walking. Mid-afternoon, the place was quiet except for the rhythmic clank of weights from the back room and the occasional grunt of someone discovering their physical limitations.

Trevor Sullivan sat behind the reception desk, methodically checking membership cards and handing out towels to the few afternoon regulars. He looked older than his files suggested, with grey stubble for hair over a thicker, darker beard, hollow eyes behind orange shades, likely something to do with healthiness and blue light from phones rather than trying to look cool – Monroe remembered seeing these back when they were surrounded by biohackers – and overall the sort of weariness that came from having life systematically dismantle your expectations. The expensive suits that had once marked him as a successful businessman had been replaced by a black polo shirt with *FLEX-U-FIT MANAGER* embroidered across the chest. In fact, if they hadn't been told in advance he was working there today, they wouldn't have recognised him from the Harrison Casino's member's photo on file, one that was the same as Sullivan's 2006 driving licence photo.

'Trevor Sullivan?' Monroe showed his warrant card. 'Detective Superintendent Monroe, City of London Police.'

Sullivan glanced up from his paperwork, and his expression shifted to that careful neutrality Monroe recognised from people who'd learned not to show too much to the wrong audience.

'That's me. What's this about then?'

'Someone you used to know. D.Q. James.'

The change was immediate. Sullivan's knuckles went white against the desk edge, and Monroe could see the muscles in his jaw tighten.

'That bastard's name isn't welcome here,' Sullivan said quietly. 'What's he done now? Destroyed someone else's life for entertainment?'

'He's dead.'

Sullivan blinked. Then blinked again.

Then the tension melted from his shoulders like someone had cut the strings holding him upright.

'Dead?' The word came out barely above a whisper. 'Actually dead? Not just disappeared off to fleece some other poor sods?'

'Very dead it seems, laddie. Fifteen years dead, as it happens.'

Sullivan let out a long, shuddering breath and reached under the desk, pulling out a hip flask – battered silver, looked like it had seen better decades – and unscrewed the cap.

'Jesus Christ,' he muttered, taking a long pull. 'Fifteen bloody years. Happy days.'

He wiped his mouth with the back of his hand and looked at Monroe with something approaching a smile for the first time since he'd arrived.

'You'll think I'm terrible for saying this, Detective Superintendent, but that's the best news I've had since my divorce came through.'

He offered the flask. Monroe shook his head.

'Another?' Sullivan asked himself, then took a second swig. 'I'm celebrating, you understand. First genuinely good news I've had since D.Q. James destroyed my life.'

'Tell me about that.'

Sullivan's face went hard, but there was relief mixed in with the anger now.

'Private tournament. Winner takes all. Invitation only – apparently I'd developed something of a reputation on the London recreational circuit.' He laughed bitterly. 'Thought I was decent at cards. Turns out there's a difference between being decent and being professional.'

Sullivan leant back in his chair, flask still in hand.

'James turned up looking like something out of a bloody Western film. Cowboy hat, those ridiculous glasses, acting like he'd ridden into town to clean up the saloon. Should have been a joke, except he wasn't.'

Monroe made notes, letting Sullivan talk.

'Started making comments about my wife during the second hand. Personal things – how she'd been spending money we didn't have, how she'd been seeing her tennis trainer more often than she'd actually paid for sessions. I mean, what a cliche, yeah?'

'He knew about the affair?'

'Knew about it before I did. Kept dropping little hints all evening. "Hope the home fires are still burning, Trevor." "Funny how people find comfort when their partners are working late." Completely threw me off my game, which was exactly what he wanted.'

Sullivan took another drink.

'Then he moved on to the business. Knew I was behind on supplier payments, knew about the tax investigation that hadn't even bloody started yet. Knew about loans I'd taken against shop leases that nobody should have had access to.'

'Where was he getting this information?'

'No idea. Private investigators, maybe. Hacking. Bribing clerks. James was the sort who'd do whatever it took to get an edge.'

'How much did you lose?'

'Everything.' Sullivan's voice was flat. 'Assets, business, house, savings, pension fund, kids' university money. He cleaned me out in one night, and the bastard enjoyed every minute of it.'

Sullivan stared at the flask.

'You know what he did afterwards? He actually tipped his hat and said, "Business is business, partner." Like it was all just a game to him. Like destroying my family was just another hand of cards.'

Monroe watched Sullivan's reaction carefully. The man was genuinely relieved about James's death – no question about that. *But was he a killer?*

'Interesting career change,' Monroe looked around. 'Choice or necessity?'

'After the divorce, I was lost,' Sullivan replied. 'Became a loner. Wife and kids didn't want to know me. I was a massive loser, and I didn't fight that. Then a few months after, I down-sized and went backpacking around the world. Off the beaten trail, off the grid, never hanging around more than a few months. Always found work, people always need a barman or an English teacher. Then a few years ago I came back to England. Missing it, mainly. I'd worked for the firm in Australia, so I asked for a job.'

'Family?'

'Had emigrated to Norway while I was away. Ex-wife's new husband. Anyway, They hadn't tried to contact me, I hadn't returned the favour. And here I am.'

'Here you are indeed,' Monroe nodded. 'Where were you in November 2009?'

Sullivan's laugh was bitter.

'November 2009? I was in a gambling addiction treatment centre in Wales. The Bridges Recovery Centre, if you want to check. Signed in on the tenth of November, after a bit of a post-divorce papers relapse, didn't get out until December, just in time for a solo Christmas.'

'They'll have records?'

'I'd guess so. Group therapy sessions, individual counselling, medical records, the lot. I was a complete mess when I arrived – and I was a barely functional human being when I left.'

'Okay then,' Monroe looked around the gym as he spoke. 'Any idea who might have wanted James dead?'

Sullivan's expression shifted.

'Take your pick. The man was a psychological predator who used poker as cover for sadistic entertainment. He didn't just beat people – he destroyed them systematically. There's a shit ton of us who wanted him gone. We had badges.'

He screwed the cap back on his flask.

'I heard stories over the years through what's left of the gambling community. Other players he'd ruined. Businessmen and women, politicians, even some serious criminals. James didn't discriminate – if you had money and weaknesses, he'd take both.'

'Anyone specific come to mind?' Monroe asked. 'Someone who'd actually go that step further, do what you wouldn't?'

Sullivan leant forward conspiratorially.

'There was talk that James had seriously pissed off the Triads. Couple of months before he vanished, word was he'd won half a million in diamonds off them in some high-stakes game.'

Monroe looked up from his notes.

'Diamonds?'

'Story goes that one of the Triad players suspected James of cheating, so he'd marked an ace – tiny pinprick, something only he would notice. When James laid down his last hand for the biggest pot of the night, it was aces and eights.'

'Dead man's hand. The one Wild Bill Hickok had when he died.'

'Exactly. But when the Triad player examined the cards afterwards, the ace that should have been marked wasn't. Clean card, no pinprick.'

'Meaning James had somehow switched it during play.'

'Don't know all the details – this came out after James disappeared,' Sullivan shook his head. 'But half a million in diamonds is serious money, and proving someone cheated you? That makes it personal with those people.'

He paused, frowning as he tried to remember something.

'Always wondered what happened to all the money James accumulated over the years. Tournament winnings, private games, whatever he stole from the Chinese – had to be hitting the millions. Never seemed to spend it on anything permanent though. No property, no investments. Just lived hand to mouth despite massive paydays.'

'You think he hid it somewhere?'

'Had to. Man like that, always making enemies, always on the run? He'd have had exit strategies, hidden assets, something to disappear with when the heat got too much. Go-bags in every casino.'

Sullivan stood up, suddenly looking years younger than when Monroe had arrived, almost like a different man.

'Detective Superintendent, I want you to know something. I've spent fifteen years wishing that bastard was dead. Dreaming about it, fantasising about it, hoping someone would put him in the ground where he belongs.'

He looked Monroe straight in the eye.

'But I didn't kill him. I was too broken to kill anyone in 2009. Hell, I was too broken to leave a treatment centre in Wales.'

However, Sullivan's smile was genuinely happy for the first time in their conversation.

'But now that I know he's been dead all this time? I feel like I can finally move on with what's left of my life. I feel *lucky* again. You know? I might play a game of cards.'

KOVÁČ DEVELOPMENT OCCUPIED THE TOP TWO FLOORS OF A converted Victorian warehouse on Liverpool Street, all glass and steel modernisation wrapped around original brick walls. Declan and Anjli found themselves in a conference room overlooking the station, surrounded by architectural plans and scale models of various London developments.

Katarina Kováč looked different in her business environment than she had at the construction site – more composed, more in control. She'd changed from yesterday's expensive number into a sharp business suit, but her manner remained guarded.

'So, the body we found yesterday,' she said, pouring coffee from a machine that looked like it belonged in a laboratory. 'Have you identified him yet?'

'We believe it could be a man named D.Q. James,' Declan said, watching her reaction carefully. 'American poker player. Ring any bells?'

Katarina's hand stilled on her coffee cup.

'D.Q. James is dead?' For the first time since they'd met her, she looked genuinely surprised. 'That explains a great deal.'

'You knew him?'

'Knew of him. He played at the casino several times while I was there. Always caused trouble, always made people angry. Caused me problems.'

'Why?' Anjli looked up from her notes.

Katarina realised she'd said too much, and then sighed, obviously deciding to lean into this.

'Because when he was an arsehole and pissed people off, it was when I worked at the Harrison Casino,' she nodded, settling into her chair. 'For about two years, when I first came to London. I was young, needed money, spoke several languages. Perfect for dealing with international clients who liked their privacy.'

'What kind of work?'

'Hostess. Entertainment coordinator for high-stakes players. My job was to make them comfortable, ensure they had a good time, encourage them to keep playing and losing money.'

Declan made notes.

'So, you knew the building layout well.'

'Every room, every corridor, every hidden passage. The casino was my world back then.'

'Including the basement?'

Katarina's expression shifted slightly.

'Especially the basement. That's where the serious games happened. The ones that weren't entirely legal.'

She moved to the window, looking out over the city.

'There were stories, you understand. Rumours about what happened in those basement games. Players who went down and came back up as different people. Some who didn't come back up at all. People losing more than money. Businesses, families, sometimes their sanity. The basement games weren't just gambling – they were psychological warfare.'

Katarina returned to her seat.

'I made my connections, made money and learned,' she said. 'Within a year, I'd worked out how to beat every high-stakes player in the place. I started playing there on my off-times, made more than I did as an employee, so gave my notice and carried on working on the "other side" of the table, so to speak. I didn't see him around that much, but I heard about James disappearing after winning big down there. Very dramatic, very mysterious. Made quite an impression on the other players, until his disappearance.'

'You saw him the night he disappeared?'

Katarina hesitated, then shook her head.

'I was there but didn't see him. As I said, working the basement was enough to show me I never wanted to bet in the basement. November fifteenth, 2009, last time anyone saw D.Q. James at a poker table. Private game. Very exclusive, very expensive. From what I was told by someone there, James had been winning all evening, making his usual psychological attacks, systematically destroying people.'

'Who was the person who told you?'

'Richard Statham. He was the manager then. Also the man who originally hired me. We were close. Not... well, we were friends. Nothing more.'

'Who else was playing?'

'Some Chinese businessmen, couple of Russians, few local high-rollers. The Chinese contingent was brought in by someone who called himself Wong Sei – not his real name, obviously. He ran underground gambling operations all over London and had a gentlemen's agreement with Statham.'

Anjli pulled out her phone, scrolling to a message from Monroe.

'Wong Sei was there that night?' she asked, reading it. 'November the Fifteenth? Because my boss just spoke to someone saying this was the last time Wong Sei was seen.'

'Oh yes. He'd organised the entire game, brought in the Chinese money. Very traditional, very formal, but you could tell he was someone playing a part, trying to impress the mainland investors. Even had special dominos or something to get in.'

Katarina's expression grew troubled.

'Wong Sei and D.Q. James had history. Bad history. There were rumours James had been cheating in Wong Sei's other games for months, but nobody had proof until that night. I'd even heard he'd been banned; got in with a domino nobody knew he had.'

'You mean Mahjong piece?' Declan showed an image of the one found on the body.

'Maybe.' Katarina shrugged. 'I wasn't there, remember?'

'What happened?'

'The story goes that James won the final hand around half-past three in the morning. Massive pot – maybe half a million in cash and other assets. He was collecting his winnings, making jokes about easy money, when one of the Chinese players accused him of cheating.'

Katarina's voice dropped.

'The accusation was very specific. They claimed James had been swapping cards, that his previous wins against Chinese syndicates had been fraudulent. One of them was furious he'd won their diamonds a month or two earlier – said James cheated.'

'Diamonds?'

'Half a million pounds worth, apparently. The Chinese player was extremely angry, very specific. Apparently he'd been building up to this outburst all night.'

Katarina wrapped her hands around her coffee cup.

'James denied everything, naturally. Said they were sore losers, that maybe they should learn to play poker before accusing professionals of cheating. But Richard said he could see James was nervous – first time he'd ever seen him rattled.'

'What about his winnings from that night?'

'He claimed he won cleanly, so he took everything, dared them to prove him a liar. Nobody did. And Wong Sei killed the event, kicking everyone out, never to be seen again if your boss is correct. Maybe he was taken by the Triads in payment.'

Katarina Kováč was quiet for a moment, then moved to a filing cabinet in the room's corner.

'Actually, let me show you something. I kept a few mementos from those days,' she said as she pulled out a manila folder and extracted several photographs. 'These are from various casino events over the years. High-roller parties, tournament celebrations, that sort of thing.'

She spread them across the conference table, pointing to one taken in what looked like the Harrison Casino's main gaming room.

'This one's from about six months before James disappeared. You can see him there in the background.'

Declan studied the photo. James was clearly visible in his trademark cowboy hat, but there were several other figures in the background, including what appeared to be well-dressed Asian businessmen.

'Wong Sei's in this photo too,' Katarina said, pointing to a tall figure partially obscured by shadows near the bar. 'He rarely allowed himself to be photographed, but the camera caught him here by accident.'

'Can we take this?' Anjli asked.

'Of course. It's a digital print; I can make more copies.' Katarina returned the other photos to the folder.

'In that case, can you send us the original digital image?' Declan passed across a card. 'It'd help a lot, as it'd give more definition.'

'I'll do it today.' Katarina placed the card in a pocket. 'Looking back, I remember James was always bragging about hidden assets, secret retirement funds. Said he had millions put away where nobody would think to look.'

Declan exchanged glances with Anjli.

'What happened after the cheating accusation?'

'Things got very tense very quickly. James packed up his winnings and left, but the damage was done – the accusation had been made in front of witnesses.'

'Then?'

'James left through the rear exit with his bag of cash. The Chinese players left immediately after – very angry, very organised. I never saw any of them again.'

'You didn't report this to police?'

Katarina's laugh was bitter.

'Report what? That gambling was happening in a licensed casino? That foreign criminals were losing money to an American con artist, and furious because of losing to him at another game at another time? The casino owner would have had me banned within twenty-four hours.'

'But you suspected James had been killed?'

'When someone accuses D.Q. James of cheating in front of witnesses and he disappears that same night?' Katarina Kováč shrugged. 'It didn't take genius-level deduction to work out what happened.'

'So, when you bought the building…'

'I never thought there might be a body in the basement. As I said, I had good memories there, regardless of what happened to D.Q. James.'

Anjli looked up from her notes.

'Mrs Kováč, who do you think killed D.Q. James?'

Katarina was quiet for several seconds.

'The Chinese players who left immediately after James did. I wasn't in the basement, but I watched them being escorted out before they started a fight. They were furious, very organised, very scary. And hiding at the back? Wong Sei looked like a man whose honour had been publicly challenged.'

'You think they followed James?'

'In their world, reputation is everything. Allowing a Western card sharp to humiliate them publicly would have been unacceptable.'

Katarina finished her coffee.

'Detective Chief Inspector, I didn't kill D.Q. James. But I'm not surprised someone did. And I'm certainly not sorry about it either. Is there anything else? I have a conference call with Prague in ten minutes.'

'We'll come back to you,' Declan rose, placing away his own notepad. 'And if you find any other dead bodies? Give us a call.'

As they left the building, Anjli looked at Declan.

'What do you think?'

'I think we know she had information on the wall, and she suspected exactly where that body was,' Declan replied. 'But I don't think she's telling the truth about who might have put it there, and I'm wondering if the next wall taken down will show us a mysterious Chinese man who disappeared the same night.'

7

THE FORGER

BILLY FITZWARREN WAS ALONE IN THE TEMPLE INN OFFICE, surrounded by the comfortable chaos of an active investigation. Printouts from the Harrison Casino's planning department covered his desk, cross-referenced with architectural drawings and financial records that painted an increasingly suspicious picture of Katarina Kováč's renovation project.

The afternoon light had that grey London quality that made everything look slightly ominous as he glanced at his watch. The briefing Monroe had called for was in half an hour, and would bring everyone together to share what they'd learned since splitting up that morning, and Billy wanted to have something more concrete than suspicious planning documents and a growing sense that their supposed informants might not be entirely trustworthy.

That said, he had an ace up his sleeve. A very hot and handsome ace.

His phone buzzed; a text from Sam.

Okay, arrived and on my way up. What have you gotten yourself into this time?

Billy smiled despite himself. Sam had a talent for cutting through his work obsessions and understood the demands of Billy's job without being intimidated by them.

Footsteps on the stairs made him look up from his monitors as Sam Mansfield appeared in the doorway. Mid-twenties, with tousled brown hair and wearing what Billy recognised as expensive casual clothes – the kind that cost more than most people's monthly salary but were designed to look effortless – he gave a mock tip of the cap.

'Afternoon, Detective Sergeant,' Sam said, crossing the room to give Billy a quick kiss on the cheek.

'You actually came,' Billy said, surprised but pleased. 'I thought you were struck by lightning when you entered a police station.'

'Well, when my boyfriend sends me a text saying, *"need to see you urgently about work, can you come to Temple Inn"*, I tend to assume I'm in trouble again.' Sam settled into the chair beside Billy's desk.

'You're not in trouble,' Billy assured him. 'Well, not that I know of. I need your expertise on something.'

'My reformed expertise,' Sam corrected. 'I keep telling you, I'm completely legitimate these days. Well, mostly.'

Billy grinned.

'It's the "mostly" I'm interested in.'

Sam had been Billy's boyfriend for the better part of a year now, a relationship that had begun cautiously after Billy's painful breakup with Andrade Estrada. What made it particularly interesting from a professional standpoint was

Sam's background – he was a former art forger who claimed to have gone completely legitimate, and in the last couple of months he'd been running a small gallery in Shoreditch that specialised in contemporary British artists. The keyword here was "claimed", though, because Sam's expertise in identifying forgeries had proven invaluable to the Temple Inn team on several previous cases. He'd even outsourced to Ellie Reckless and her crew recently.

'So, what's this about?' Sam asked. 'Please tell me you haven't uncovered another dodgy Picasso or something.'

'Nothing like that.' Billy reached for the evidence bag containing the mahjong piece they'd found on D.Q. James's body. 'I need you to look at this.'

Sam's demeanour changed immediately as he saw the evidence bag. His casual manner became professional and focused – the transformation Billy had seen before when Sam's expertise was required, and the "forger" took over from the "restorer".

'What am I looking at?' Sam asked, accepting the bag and holding it up to the light.

'Mahjong piece. Found in a victim's pocket. Been there for about fifteen years.'

Sam examined the piece through the clear plastic, turning it to catch the light from different angles.

'It's a Red Dragon tile,' he said. 'Look here, the vertical line with the rectangle behind? That's the character for "centre". *Red Dragon*, or *Hóng Zhōng* as the Chinese call it.'

'How do you know so much about this?' Billy frowned suspiciously. 'Some kind of gambling habit I never knew about?'

Sam looked up at Billy, surprised.

'You never played *Microsoft Mahjong?*' he asked. 'I was addicted as a kid. Got really into the real thing in my teens. Anyway, it's Chinese, probably ivory, though I'd need to examine it properly to be sure. The surface work looks good from here – painted character, proper proportions.'

He paused, frowning.

'Where did you say this came from?'

'Harrison Casino. Basement. Our victim was buried down there, possibly after a gambling dispute with Chinese organised crime.'

'Right.' Sam's expression became more serious. 'That would explain why someone modified it, then. Standard Red Dragon tiles use basic red – *hong* – for the centre character. But this one's been repainted in vermillion – *dan* – with gold flecks added.'

Billy leant forward, peering at the tile.

'You can tell the difference between red shades?'

Sam looked at him like he was an idiot.

'I'm an ex-art forger, Billy. Colour differentiation was literally my job. I can spot the difference between cadmium red and alizarin crimson from across a room.' He held the bag up again, slightly affronted. 'This vermillion has a completely different undertone to standard mahjong red. Warmer, more orange-based. And the gold flecks are sitting on top of the paint layer – they're not integrated into the original colour.'

'Right,' Billy said, realising he'd just professionally insulted his boyfriend. 'Sorry. That's significant then?'

'Very. Vermillion has a different cultural meaning than ordinary red. It's associated with masculine yang energy, fire, good fortune. Much more specific symbolism.' Sam's tone softened slightly. 'And those gold flecks definitely don't belong on any legitimate mahjong tile.'

'So, it's been altered?'

'Completely repainted. Someone scraped off the original red paint and redid it in vermillion with gold specks. The work's excellent – museum-quality precision. But once you know what to look for...' Sam pointed to a barely visible mark along one edge. 'There. You can see where the original surface wasn't disturbed, and the paint depth is different.'

Billy felt his detective instincts engaging.

'Why go to all that trouble?'

'Because to anyone casual, this looks like a normal Red Dragon tile. But to someone in the know – someone running illegal Chinese gambling operations, for example – this specific combination of vermillion and gold would be a recognition code. An invitation token.' Sam looked at Billy seriously. 'Whoever did this had serious artistic skills and detailed knowledge of Chinese cultural symbolism. I'd also say that they had a source to work from as these are seriously hard to do without the original in front of you.'

'Experience talking there?'

Sam simply gave a smile, which in a way was even more damning. Billy thought about what they'd learned about D.Q. James's miniature painting hobby.

'Our victim was apparently quite talented with detailed artwork. Miniatures painting.'

'That'd do it,' Sam agreed. 'The precision required for good miniature work translates perfectly to this kind of modification. Same attention to detail, same steady hand, same understanding of how paints behave on different surfaces.'

Before Billy could respond, Monroe's voice echoed up the stairwell, slightly out of breath.

'Billy! You up there? I've got something you need to see.'

'Up here,' Billy called back, then lowered his voice. 'That's Monroe. He'll want to hear what you've found.'

Sam nodded.

'Should be interesting. Last time I saw him, he was accusing me of that business with the Rothko authentication.'

'You were innocent,' Billy pointed out.

'I was *technically* innocent,' Sam corrected. 'There's a difference.'

Monroe appeared at the top of the stairs, looking pleased about something. He stopped when he saw Sam sitting beside Billy's desk.

'Sam,' Monroe said with a slight nod. 'Should have known you'd turn up eventually.'

'Detective Superintendent,' Sam replied, standing politely. 'Don't worry, I've not stolen anything from your office. Well, mostly.'

'Aye, mostly,' Monroe said dryly. 'That's what worries me. What's that you're looking at?'

Billy showed him the mahjong piece.

'It's the one from the basement body. Sam thinks it's been altered. Professional forgery work.'

Monroe's eyebrows rose as he processed this information, before he pulled out his own evidence bag, this one containing a very similar-looking mahjong piece, now taken from the original bag it'd been in.

'Kenny Tsang gave me this for comparison. Said it was completely authentic, from the same type of operation our victim was trying to infiltrate.'

Sam's expression changed completely as Monroe handed him the second bag. He held both pieces up to the light, comparing them side by side.

'Bloody hell,' he breathed. 'That's a genuine piece. Completely authentic.'

He positioned them so that the differences were clear.

'Look at this – natural brush variations in the calligraphy, proper aging patterns in the ivory, original construction throughout. Your victim was carrying a very sophisticated fake of the real thing.'

Billy felt pieces clicking together in his mind.

'D.Q. James used his artistic abilities to infiltrate the Chinese gambling ring.'

'Makes perfect sense,' Sam agreed. 'The precision required is exactly what you'd get from someone who painted miniature figurines to a high standard. But as I said, I could only do it if I had the original to work from – a photo wouldn't give me everything I needed. So D.Q. James may have faked a token, but he had to have a real one in his possession at one point to be able to do that.'

Monroe was already moving towards the briefing room.

'Right then. Team should be here any minute. Sam, you'd better stick around – we might have more questions about the forgery technique.'

'Wouldn't miss it,' Sam said.

As if on cue, voices and footsteps echoed from the stairwell as the rest of the team arrived. Declan and Anjli appeared first, looking like they'd had a productive afternoon for a change. They were followed by Doctor Marcos, and then finally, De'Geer and Cooper arrived from their canvassing work around the old casino site. They settled into the briefing room in their established positions and Sam took an unobtrusive chair near the door, close enough to contribute when needed but clearly not part of the official team structure.

'Right then,' Monroe began, 'before we get into what everyone's learned today, Kenny Tsang gave me a gambling piece for comparison, and said it was completely authentic, from the same type of operation our victim was trying to infiltrate. If you could tell the others what you told me and Billy, Sam?'

Sam stood, accepting both evidence bags from Monroe and holding them where everyone could see.

'The piece found on your victim has been expertly modified,' he began. 'I'd need to look properly at it, but if I were a betting man, I'd say it's a block that someone scraped off the original painted symbols and replaced them with new ones. The work is bloody good – took real skill and considerable time to pull off.'

He held the bags up to the briefing room's lighting.

'The genuine piece – the one Mister Monroe obtained from Mister Tsang – shows natural variations in the brushwork, proper aging patterns, original ivory properly seasoned. The modified piece uses the same quality base material, but the painted surface has been completely reworked.'

Doctor Marcos leant forward.

'D.Q. James used his artistic skills to fake his way into the Chinese gambling operation.'

'That's my assessment,' Sam agreed, passing the evidence bags back to Monroe and sitting down. 'And as I said to Billy, standard Red Dragon tiles, like the ones you see for sale use basic red for the centre character, while this one's been repainted in vermillion with gold flecks.'

'Which brings us to some rather interesting questions about the gambling operation itself, and about the helpful information we've been receiving,' Declan said from his chair. He gave a nod and Billy clicked through to the first image – the digital photograph Katarina Kováč had provided through email minutes earlier, showing the Harrison Casino's main gaming room during what appeared to be a high-stakes poker event. D.Q. James was clearly visible in his trademark cowboy hat and aviator sunglasses, while several well-dressed men and women occupied tables in the background.

'Declan?' Monroe looked over. 'Share with the class?'

'That's Wong Sei there,' Declan said, pointing to a tall figure partially obscured by shadows near the bar. 'Katarina identified him from this photograph, which was in her collection of memorabilia from her time at the casino. Supposedly, this is the mysterious Chinese crime boss who ran the illegal gambling operation we believed D.Q. James was invited to, but with Sam's additional intel, we know now he tried to infiltrate.'

'Kenny Tsang confirmed Wong Sei was running illegal gambling operations around that time,' Monroe continued the narrative. 'Very exclusive, very dangerous, very expensive to get into, primarily working with the Turk when he was still in control of London. He was very helpful, our Kenny was. Almost too helpful, if you ask me.'

Billy tapped his trackpad, zooming in and showing a close-up enhancement of the shadowy figure near the bar.

'Problem is,' Monroe went on, 'something about Kenny's eagerness to help doesn't sit right. He knew exactly what the mahjong piece meant, had his own authentic example ready to show me, seemed genuinely concerned about helping us solve this fifteen-year-old murder. Almost like he was ready and waiting.'

Declan leant back in his chair.

'You think he's not telling us everything?'

'I think Kenny Tsang knows considerably more about this case than he's letting on,' Monroe replied. 'The wee question is though, how much more, and why he's so interested in steering our investigation in particular directions.'

'What kind of directions?' Anjli asked.

'Away from himself,' Monroe said. 'Every piece of information he's given us points towards Wong Sei as the mysterious villain, while positioning Kenny as the helpful informant who just happens to know all about these dangerous gambling operations.'

Billy pulled up another image, now showing one of the spreadsheets he'd been working on, showing the casino's financial records.

'And then there's Katarina Kováč's planning documents,' he said as he used his mouse arrow as a pointer. 'According to these additions sent in at the last minute, she specifically targeted the basement wall where we found the body three weeks ago. She didn't just renovate – she knew exactly where to look.'

'So, we've got two people with suspiciously detailed knowledge of our fifteen-year-old murder,' Anjli observed.

Before Monroe could respond to this though, there was movement in the doorway as Johnny Lucas appeared. The surprise was immediate and genuine. Johnny rarely came to Temple Inn – their meetings usually happened on his territory, mostly at the boxing club in Globe Town where he felt more in control.

'Bloody hell,' Monroe muttered under his breath. 'Johnny.'

'Alex,' Johnny replied, entering the room. He was dressed

in his usual expensive but understated style – dark suit, crisp shirt, no tie. 'Hope you don't mind the intrusion.'

'How did you get past reception?' De'Geer asked, though not aggressively.

'I asked nicely,' Johnny said with a slight smile. 'Your desk sergeant was very accommodating once I mentioned I'd been personally invited by Detective Superintendent Monroe.'

'Did I invite you?' Monroe raised an eyebrow.

'I'm sure you must have.' Johnny smiled. 'Once or twice. Usually followed by a request not to, in case the lightning that hit me caused collateral damage.'

He looked across at Sam and smiled.

'And with two of us "wrong'uns" in the room, I hope your insurance is up to date.'

Monroe sighed.

'I suppose you'd better come in. Though I should mention, this is an active investigation briefing. Official police business.'

'Which is exactly why I'm here,' Johnny said, positioning himself near Sam. He nodded politely to the art dealer – and Declan wondered if the two had ever worked together before deciding it was best to push that thought away – as he returned his attention to Monroe. 'Remember our chat at the boxing club? I mentioned Jackie and I ran security for the Harrison Casino from the nineties?'

'You also mentioned there was a new Chinese addition sniffing around,' Monroe cocked his head, considering this. 'Connected?'

Johnny considered this for a moment.

'Maybe,' he said. 'Main face is a man named Jun Ng Kai-lok, known around as "Ironthread".'

'Ironthread?' Declan frowned.

'Stronger than silk, harder to break than wire.' Johnny smiled. 'Anyway, in his pre-"Ironthread" days, Jun was a London gambler around 2008 and 2009, mostly concentrated in Chinatown and the East End. High stakes, serious money.'

'Would he have been at these secret Chinese gatherings with mahjong invites?' Monroe asked.

'Well, considering I have no clue what the hell you're talking about—'

'Come on,' Monroe interrupted. 'We know the Harrison Casino worked with people to provide illicit games in the basement, and as you said, you ran security back then. You're telling me you never knew?'

Johnny looked genuinely pained.

'I worked for the Casino, but there were times we were waved off,' he explained. 'The Turk ran a lot of those, and he didn't trust us,' he replied. 'I think he was outsourcing to others. Maybe the Tsangs, even though they hated him more than I did, and were waiting for their shot. Literally. And I was spending a lot more time as Jackie, which even now is... well, fuzzy.'

He looked at the evidence bags still sitting on the table in front of Monroe.

'These the mahjong invites you mentioned?'

Monroe passed them over. Johnny examined both pieces, handling them like someone who'd seen similar artefacts before. His attention seemed particularly focused on the authentic piece Kenny Tsang had provided.

'I've seen these,' he nodded. 'Yeah, they ran them at the Harrison. They ran them all over the place. And according to my contacts, Jun Ng Kai-lok would have been there.'

'And D.Q. James, too,' Monroe took Kenny's token back, waving it. 'This is the real one. The other? Forgery.'

'It is? Damn,' Johnny examined it more carefully this time. 'I wouldn't have guessed it. Kenny's been helpful, then?'

Declan frowned – something in Johnny's tone suggested this wasn't necessarily good news.

'Very helpful,' Monroe replied carefully. 'Identified the piece immediately, explained the significance, seemed genuinely concerned about helping us solve the case. Why?'

Johnny's expression shifted – not quite a frown, but definitely thoughtful.

'Did he now,' he replied quietly. 'And what else did our helpful Kenny have to say about the late D.Q. James and his gambling problems?'

'Confirmed that Wong Sei was running the operation James tried to infiltrate,' Monroe continued. 'Warned us that people involved in those games tended to disappear rather than retire. Clarified that crossing the Chinese was essentially a death sentence.'

'Mm,' Johnny said, setting the evidence bags back down on the table. He looked up at the plasma screen, where the photograph from the Harrison Casino was still displayed. 'That Wong Sei there?'

Billy clicked back to the enhanced close-up of the shadowy figure.

'That's him. Only photograph we have, according to Katarina. Apparently, he rarely allowed himself to be photographed.'

Johnny stared at the screen for several long moments, his expression unreadable. Then, unexpectedly, he chuckled – a sound that started low and gradually became more pronounced, until he was actually laughing.

The team exchanged puzzled glances. Johnny's sense of

humour was usually dry and sardonic, and genuine laughter was rare, especially in the context of a murder investigation.

'Something amusing about our case, laddie?' Monroe asked, though his tone suggested he wasn't entirely sure he wanted to know the answer.

Johnny wiped his eyes, still chuckling as he looked around the room.

'Oh, this is brilliant,' he said. 'Absolutely brilliant. No wonder Kenny was so bloody helpful with your investigation.'

'Johnny,' Declan said patiently, 'would you mind sharing what's so funny about our fifteen-year-old murder case?'

Johnny stood and walked closer to the plasma screen, pointing directly at the shadowy figure they'd identified as Wong Sei.

'You said this photograph is from fifteen years ago?'

'About that, yes,' Declan confirmed. 'Around October or November 2009, according to Katarina.'

'And Kenny Tsang told you about Wong Sei, the mysterious Chinese crime boss who ran the illegal gambling operation that the victim tried to infiltrate?'

'That's correct,' Monroe said, though his tone suggested he was beginning to suspect where this was heading. 'Said he was British born, possibly named Barry.'

'Who, according to Katarina, disappeared around the same time as James,' Anjli added.

Johnny turned back to face the room, his expression now showing genuine amusement mixed with what looked like professional respect.

'Does nobody recognise this man?'

As if on cue, everyone leant forward.

'Go on...' Monroe sighed. 'You're just dying to bloody tell us.'

I'll grant you, it's terrible make-up and a terrible disguise, real *Charlie Chan* bollocks.' Johnny Lucas grinned as he looked back at the image. 'But I'm pretty much one hundred per cent convinced that this man, Wong Sei... *is* Kenny Tsang.'

8

PRESSURE POINTS

Kenny Tsang looked smaller in the Temple Inn briefing room. The usual composure that made him such a formidable figure in London's criminal landscape had cracked, replaced by something approaching relief, if Declan was being honest. They'd decided to speak to him here, mainly because the last thing they wanted him to think was that he was a suspect; Kenny Tsang wasn't one to speak to police at the best of times, after all.

'Right then, Kenny,' Monroe said, leaning back in his chair. 'You wanted to tell us about Wong Sei.'

Kenny's hands rested flat on the metal table, his expensive suit somehow diminished under the harsh fluorescent lighting.

'Wong Sei doesn't exist. Not the way you think.'

'How do you mean?' Declan asked.

'Wong Sei is me. I created him.'

Monroe raised an eyebrow.

'No way,' Monroe deadpanned, giving his best surprised expression. 'You're saying *you* are Wong Sei?'

Kenny stared at Monroe for a long moment before realisation set in.

'Ah, piss off, you prick,' he muttered. 'Who was it, Johnny bloody Lucas?'

'I don't know what you mean,' Monroe leant back on the chair with a smile. 'Perhaps it was our genius deducting skills. So, why create him?'

'So I had a sock puppet, if you like. A way to operate without dragging the Tsang name through the mud.' Kenny looked directly at Monroe. 'My cousin Jimmy's been circling my territory for years, even when it was split between me and Benny. You might think he's a pain in the arse now, but back then he was even hungrier. Wanted his cut of everything I'd built. But family politics don't allow me to tell him to piss off directly. Then you add the Turk... it was well known we hated him, so Wong Sei gave me the opportunity to play a long game on him, screw up his relationship with other Chinese.'

'So, Wong Sei does the things you can't do in real life,' Declan said.

'Exactly. Wong Sei can be territorial. Aggressive. All the things Kenny Tsang has to avoid to keep the peace with family like Jimmy or leaders like the Turk.' Kenny shifted slightly. 'I'd been using the identity for about five years. Different accent, different mannerisms when I needed to be him.'

'Yeah, we saw the make-up.' Monroe smiled. 'Very "Fu Manchu".'

'Hey, it's not cultural appropriation when I do it.' Kenny shrugged. 'Couple of cheek fillers, contacts to make my eyes blue, long hair wig – the point was to make people realise it was obviously make-up, but aim them at someone who wasn't... well, me.'

'British born Barry.'

'Exactly. Even had business cards printed.'

Monroe tapped his pen once against his notepad.

'And D.Q. James knew about this arrangement?'

'James knew Wong Sei existed, even attended a couple of games "Wong" organised. I think he thought he was a rival operator muscling in on my territory, although he never told me as much. Never worked out it was the same person, though.' Kenny's mouth twisted into something that might have been amusement. 'Which made it very confusing for him when both Kenny Tsang and Wong Sei banned him from gambling in their games at exactly the same time.'

'Why was he banned?' Declan wrote this down.

'Two reasons. First, he was marking cards. Nothing dramatic – just tiny scratches on the edges, bending corners slightly. He thought he was being subtle, but I've been in this game too long to miss that kind of thing. There was talk he was swapping cards in, even when we changed the manufacturer, but that was never proven.'

'And in your business, reputation is everything,' Declan observed.

'Word gets out that you allow cheating in your games, and you're finished. Players need to trust that the game is honest, even if everything else about the operation is illegal.'

'What was the second reason?' Monroe asked.

Kenny's expression went stony.

'The diamond match. James cost very important people a ton of money – we're talking high six figures – and nearly started a war with them.'

Monroe stopped writing.

'Tell us about this match.'

'Private game, very exclusive. I only ran maybe three of

these a year – invitation only, serious money.' Kenny paused, choosing his words carefully. 'This particular game had some Triad players who'd brought diamonds as stakes. Serious stones, small ones but family pieces, the kind of thing that's been in collections for generations.'

'We've heard it was half a million pounds worth back then,' Declan said. 'Is that about right?'

'Could have been more – some of those stones were antiques,' Kenny shrugged.

'And D.Q. James was playing in this game,' Monroe stated it as a fact rather than a question.

'Yes, but there was a confusion. He had one of my – well, Wong's – mahjong tokens, the one you showed me the photo of, Alex. And unfortunately, if you have the token, you get in. We assumed someone had given him their token, but nobody was missing from the match. I wasn't happy about it – his reputation was already questionable – but he was also spending serious money at my tables, like he wanted to prove a point now he was there.'

'What happened during the game?' Monroe leant forward.

'Everything seemed normal for the first few hours. High-stakes poker, but nothing unusual. Then came the biggest hand of the night. James was holding aces and eights. One of the Triad players – goes by the name Jun – had thought James was cheating, so had marked one of the aces earlier in the evening to check.'

'Aye, I heard this too. Is this standard practice?' Monroe asked.

'Who told you?'

'Trevor Sullivan. Apparently he was another of your players.'

'Sullivan wasn't there that night,' Kenny muttered, then sighed. 'So if he's been told this, it's second-hand news.'

'So explain it from the source itself, Monroe smiled sweetly.

'Okay, so everyone's looking for an edge, and as long as it's not blatant cheating, most players accept it as part of the game. But yes, he was marking cards, and that's what caused the issues at the end.' Kenny rubbed his temples as if the memory gave him a headache. 'When James laid down his last hand – aces and eights, full house, winning everything – Jun later checked the cards. The ace that should have been marked was clean. No pinprick. He swiped it from right under their noses. Had to have palmed the marked card earlier in the game, probably when he needed a different suit or card in his spread, and replaced it with a clean one from somewhere else in the deck at the end when he needed his Aces. Takes incredible skill and brass balls to pull off during a live hand.'

'When did they realise what had happened?'

'They suspected, and confronted him, but he simply claimed they were sore losers and left. About an hour after the game ended, so maybe four thirty in the morning, Jun got hold of the shoe, where the cards were, and was examining them more carefully, trying to work out how he'd missed the switch. When he found the marked ace still in the deck – the one that should have been in James's hand – he knew he'd been had.'

Monroe made a note.

'What was James's reaction when confronted?'

'He wasn't. By the time Jun worked it out, James had already left with the diamonds. Just walked out like nothing had happened, probably already planning his next move.'

'This Jun,' Monroe asked, checking his notes. 'I'm guessing this was Jun Ng Kai-Lok, known as "Ironthread"?'

'Well, you've mangled the pronunciations, but you're Scottish, so we expect that.' Kenny smiled. 'But yeah. Now he's Ironthread. Back then? Just a gambler with strong ties.'

'And the Triads came to you,' Declan said.

'Before the night ended, Jun and two of his associates cornered me. They were...' Kenny paused. 'Let's say they were displeased. Demanded I make it right, since the game was held in my name, under my protection.'

'What did you do?'

'Nothing. They'd admitted they'd marked cards, so they'd forfeited the round.' Kenny shrugged. 'Told them this was their issue, not mine. So, they then came to me.'

'But they'd already come to you.'

'No, sorry, they came to me as Wong, then came to me as Kenny,' Kenny sighed. 'How did Johnny Lucas manage to pretend to be Jackie all those years? It's bloody tiring. Anyway, I said it was Mayfair, and that was the Turk's area, so they needed to speak to him. This was a couple of years before he died.'

'You mean when you and your brother allegedly took the Turk out in a drive-by shooting,' Declan commented without looking up from the notebook.

'You might think that, but I couldn't possibly comment.' Kenny smiled darkly. 'The Triad went to see the Turk who effectively told them to piss off.'

'Did you ever speak to Richard Statham about this?'

'The manager? Why would I?'

'He said he was approached to keep an eye out for the diamonds.'

'Never heard that,' Kenny shook his head. 'And besides, by

then he'd come to me, me again, the Turk... weeks had gone past and the diamonds were likely long gone. I decided that the Triad would want reparations, and that would end up coming from my pocket, or from a gang war in London, so I decided it was time to retire Wong Sei. That decision was made very clear when a couple of months later, and in my last game as Wong, both Jun and James appeared, even without being given entrance chips. November fifteenth, 2009

'The same day we believe D.Q James played *his* last game,' Monroe closed his notepad. 'Kenny, I need to ask you this directly. Did you kill D.Q. James, maybe in return for him screwing you over, even if by association?'

'No.' The answer came without hesitation. 'I wanted him gone from my operations, not dead. Dead men can't be used as examples to other potential cheats.'

'And the Triads?'

'The Triads...' Kenny left it hanging for a moment. 'I think James made very dangerous enemies that night. People who don't forgive or forget. Jun lost face as well as money, and in their culture, that's often worse than the financial loss. Sure, he's a big name now, but it took him close to a decade to remove the stink.'

'You think Jun caught up with D.Q. James?'

'I think James underestimated how seriously they take betrayal. Half a million in stolen diamonds is one thing – making someone look foolish in front of their associates is quite another. And the November game, the rematch, of sorts, was the last time I saw him, in either of my identities.'

Monroe stood, indicating the interview was over.

'We'll need a formal statement, Kenny. Everything you've just told us, on the record.'

'Of course.' Kenny rose as well, straightening his jacket. 'Detective Superintendent, I hope you understand why I created the Wong Sei identity. It was about survival, not deception.'

'Aye, survival I understand. Question is whether you'll survive the fallout from this revelation.'

After Kenny was let out by Cooper, promising to pass on anything else he learned, Monroe and Declan remained in the interview room.

'So, Johnny was right, and our mysterious Chinese crime boss was Kenny playing dress-up,' Monroe said. 'Changes the entire dynamic of the case.'

'The Chinese organised crime angle wasn't entirely wrong – just not in the way we thought.' Declan stretched in his chair. 'But the diamond theft gives us a clear motive and timeline.'

'Half a million stolen from the Triads, aye. That's serious money and serious enemies.' Monroe pulled out his notepad again. 'Question is whether they caught up with him, or if someone else got there first.'

'And what happened to the diamonds? If James was killed for them, where did they go?'

'Could still be out there. Could have been fenced immediately. Could be sitting in someone's safe deposit box waiting for the heat to die down.' Monroe rested his hands on the back of his chair. 'I'll check what intelligence we have on Triad activities around late 2009.'

'What about our other suspects? Katarina still had advance knowledge of where the body was located, I'm sure of it.'

'Aye, and her renovation work was suspiciously precise.

Could be she knew about James's diamond score, waited for the right moment to claim it.'

As Monroe returned to his office – his again now Bullman had returned to Guildhall for the moment – Declan walked back into the main office to study the evidence board they'd assembled. Photos of the crime scene, the mahjong piece, James's poker victories, and their growing list of suspects told the story of their investigation so far. The diamond theft had given them motive and timeline, but it had also opened up new questions about who else might have known about James's score.

Half a million in stolen diamonds didn't just disappear.

Someone, somewhere, knew what happened to them.

Morten De'Geer was finishing his review of witness statements in the Temple Inn break room when Paul Elliott appeared in the doorway. The man looked rougher than he had earlier that day – clothes wrinkled, stubble showing, the kind of desperate edge that came from too much stress and not enough sleep.

'We need to talk,' Elliott said without preamble.

De'Geer glanced around the break room, confirming they were alone, then set down his paperwork.

'Paul, I told you I'd think about—'

'Time's up.' Elliott stepped into the room and closed the door behind him. 'My hearing's been moved to tomorrow morning. Professional Standards have found new evidence.'

'What kind of evidence?'

'The kind that proves I've been compromised.' Elliott's voice carried barely controlled panic. 'My DCI at Paddington

– Cohen – he knows about the gambling debts. That's why he's been moving me off anything important and has had me on cold files and paperwork since spring. Says he can't trust me with live investigations, won't tell me why. But I know it's because he's been tracking my finances.' Elliott moved closer, lowering his voice. 'Which is why I need your help now more than ever.'

'Paul, what exactly are you involved in?'

'I owe money to Katarina Kováč.'

The name hit De'Geer like a physical blow.

'The casino owner? She's a suspect in our case.'

'I know she's involved in your case. That's exactly why I'm here.' Elliott's desperation was becoming more apparent with each word. 'I need to know what you have on her. Every piece of evidence, every lead, everything your team has discovered.'

De'Geer stood slowly, understanding dawning.

'You're asking me to compromise an active murder investigation.'

'I'm asking you to help someone who helped you at Hendon when you needed it most.' Elliott's voice took on a pleading tone. 'Katarina works with a guy, right? He runs private games – high-stakes stuff, invitation only. I got in over my head, and now I owe thirty grand with interest climbing every week.'

'How did you even meet her?'

'Through other players. Started small – few hundred here and there, just for fun. But the games got bigger, stakes got higher, and I kept thinking I could win it back.' Elliott rubbed his face. 'Classic gambler's fallacy, I know. But by the time I realised how deep I was, she owned me.'

'Who's the guy?'

'Dunno. Never got his name. Foreign.'

'Asian? Russian?'

'Eastern European, perhaps? I'm not great with accents.'

De'Geer studied his former training partner, seeing the man he'd once known buried under layers of desperation and poor choices.

'This isn't about character references any more, is it?'

'Character references won't help if your investigation exposes my connection to her gambling operations. She's already nervous about police attention – keeps asking if I've heard anything about investigations into their business.'

'And you want me to feed you information so you can reassure her.'

'I want you to help me stay ahead of whatever's coming. If your investigation leads to her operations, if Professional Standards connects my gambling to my evidence tampering, I'm finished.' Elliott's voice grew harder. 'And if I'm going down, I won't go alone.'

De'Geer felt the familiar weight of the old secret pressing down on him. The incident at Hendon – a serious misconduct never reported – had been eating at him for years.

'What you're asking me to do isn't covering up past mistakes. This is actively obstructing justice.'

'And what I didn't report at Hendon was actively covering up justice.' Elliott's voice rose, then he caught himself and lowered it again. 'We both made choices, Morten. We both have things we don't want exposed.'

The silence stretched between them. De'Geer stared at the floor where, if he had X-ray vision, he'd have been able to look into the room below, and see Cooper at one of the desks, methodically working through case files. The thought of losing her respect, her love even, of destroying the trust he'd slowly built with this team, made his chest tight.

But the thought of betraying a murder investigation was worse.

'I can't do it, Paul.'

'You mean you won't.'

'Both. I won't compromise this investigation, and I can't help you cover up your gambling problems. I'll be there tomorrow to support you, but that's the most I can do.'

Elliott's expression went cold.

'Then let me be very clear about the alternative. If your investigation exposes my connection to Katarina, if Professional Standards connects my gambling to my evidence tampering, I will tell them everything about Hendon. Everything about what you did and what I knew.'

The threat hung in the air between them like a physical presence.

'You'd destroy both our careers over your gambling debts?'

'My career's already destroyed. Cohen's made sure of that. The question is whether I take you down with me.' Elliott moved towards the door, pausing with his hand on the handle. 'You have until tomorrow morning, Morten. Either you give me what I need on Katarina, or we both face the consequences of our past mistakes.'

After Elliott left, De'Geer remained in the break room, staring at the closed door and feeling the weight of an impossible choice settling on his shoulders. His phone buzzed with a text message from Cooper.

> Ready for the next round of interviews when you are. Found something interesting in the witness statements. xx

De'Geer looked at the message for a long moment, then typed back.

On my way.

Tomorrow morning, he would have to choose between destroying his career or destroying his integrity. Tonight, he needed to focus on the job that had given his life meaning – even if doing that job might cost him everything he'd worked to build.

9

BREADCRUMBS

The Temple Inn offices had gone quiet, half the overhead lights switched off, the hum of computers the only sound besides occasional rustling paperwork. De'Geer found Cooper at one of the empty desks, rolled-up sleeves and a desk lamp throwing shadows across witness statements. Her checked cap sat beside a forgotten sandwich. She glanced up as he approached.

'You look knackered.'

De'Geer pulled up a chair. After Elliott's visit, after the ultimatum sitting like lead in his stomach, here was Cooper. Solid. Real.

'Long day,' he said. 'And you look beautiful too. Your text said you found something?'

Cooper's face brightened.

'The newsagent near the casino. Been there since 1985, remembers D.Q. James. Said he drove the most ridiculous car he had ever seen in Mayfair, and he's seen some sights over forty years.' She checked her notes. 'A 1970s Cadillac Eldorado. Bright yellow with white leather interior, chrome everywhere, fins on the back. The guy reckoned you could spot it from the International Space Station. Although he also said it was lime green, so he could have been colour blind, but just on really obnoxious colour schemes because there's no way you'd miss that.'

'Christ.'

'Exactly. So I started wondering – what happens to a car like that? Something that distinctive doesn't just vanish.' Cooper picked up her phone, swiped the screen and an image of D.Q James, standing in front of the aforementioned affront to car style appeared. 'Interestingly, googling the colour, the car and James's name shows it – some kind of PR shot for a poker tour he did in 2007.'

She looked over at Billy, still working at his monitors.

'DS Fitzwarren, do you have a moment?'

Surprised at the official tone, Billy glanced over.

'I'm all ears,' he said suspiciously as Cooper gathered her notes and, with De'Geer following, made her way over to him.

"Need to pull up a car, 1970s Cadillac Eldorado, banana-yellow,' she said, showing the photo. 'That's the reg.'

'Classic vehicle registration; should be doable,' Billy muttered, screens flickering. 'Filtering for make and model... right.'

He whistled.

'It's not the same one, but according to a classic car forum, a 1972 Cadillac Eldorado convertible was listed recently in the UK for thirty-three grand.'

Closing the page, he opened another, typing in extra details.

'So there's an R reg, that's 1973... got it. Cadillac Eldorado, 1973, registered yellow. Current owner is a Brian Curtis in Shrewsbury.'

'Can you go back?' Cooper leant over his shoulder.

'Already on it.' More clicking. 'Curtis bought it in June 2019 for twenty-eight thousand – or, at least that was the asking price, previous owner was a Sarah Donnelly in Lewisham, who purchased it March 2015. Before that...'

He scrolled.

'Robert Taylor in Greenwich bought it August 2012, twenty grand. And before that...'

Billy paused.

'Here we go. November 2009, D.Q. James sold it to a Thomas Greaves in Hackney. Purchase price...'

He looked up.

'Two grand.'

Silence.

'Two thousand pounds?' De'Geer said. 'For a classic Cadillac? Even as a project car, it'd be no less than about eight.'

'Cash sale, minimal documentation. And you're right, comparative sites have sales of the same year in approximately the same condition for around fifteen grand in 2009, and that's even with the banking collapse the previous year.' Billy pulled up another screen. 'Either someone was desperate or—'

'Paid off,' Cooper finished. 'Car as payment for something worth two grand.'

'Who's Thomas Greaves?' De'Geer asked. 'I'm guessing he's not some random buyer at that cost.'

Billy was already typing.

'Denham address, fifty-three years old, no criminal record. Employment history shows…'

Billy leant back in his chair, looking around at the others.

'Well bloody hell. Thomas Greaves, croupier at the Harrison Casino from August 2005 until December 2009. Left the job the month after James disappeared.'

'Quit or fired?'

'Not mentioned on his file,' Billy pursed his lips. 'I'll dig deeper.'

'Someone needs to tell Monroe,' Cooper said.

'Aye lassie, you call the devil, and he shall appear,' Monroe appeared from his office, Declan and Anjli following. 'Has wee Billy found us a clue?'

'Actually wee Cooper did—' Billy started but then stopped abruptly as he realised what he'd just said. 'I mean…'

'Don't sweat it, wee Billy.' Cooper smiled. 'I am the smallest here after all. And when I stand next to Morten, I look even shorter.'

She frowned.

'But Guv, do you spend your days hovering around your office door, waiting for a moment to appear like a genie?'

'Ach, no, lassie. I was getting away from these two because I heard a far more interesting conversation out here,' Monroe thumbed at Declan and Anjli as the team formed a semicircle around Billy's monitors, the DVLA trail still displayed.

'Thomas Greaves,' Monroe said, reading the screen. 'Casino croupier who got James's Godawful-looking banana car for two bags.'

'Bags of what?' Anjli frowned.

'Two bags, four monkeys—' Monroe paused as Anjli chuckled. 'That's what I get for using London rhyming slang, is it? Fine.'

He stood back, arms folded, trying hard not to reveal he was sulking.

'That's a payoff,' Declan said. 'Has to be.'

'And he worked at the Harrison until a month after James disappeared,' Billy continued. 'He'd have known the casino layout, had access after hours, could move around without raising suspicion.'

Monroe scratched at his beard.

'So we've got a casino employee who gets James's car for almost nothing, right when our victim disappears, then leaves.' He made notes. 'There's something wrong here, and it's not just why anyone would want that bloody day-glo car at any cost.'

'He could have helped build that wall,' Anjli said. 'Someone who knew the casino, had access to the basement, could explain being there if anyone asked.'

'But if he bought the car from James, would he help kill the man?' De'Geer frowned. 'He had to buy the car, and that cost makes me feel he did a service and this was a laundering money kind of thing.'

'You don't need to personally vouch when you sell one, just send the V5 document in,' Anjli mused. 'As long as someone had that, they could have sold the car to Greaves, pretending to be James. So, James is killed, Greaves helps hide the body, the killer gives him the car for a steal. He gets it for two grand, sells it three years later, once the heat's died down for twenty... that's a ten-times upsell.'

'Where is he now?' Declan asked.

'Denham,' Billy pulled up a street view. 'Works private events, corporate poker nights. Done alright for himself, actually.

'Aye, with twenty grand in his pocket, tax free, too.'

'We visit him tomorrow,' Monroe decided, pulling out his phone. 'First thing. Billy, text me that address. Declan, you're with me.'

'What about Katarina?' Declan asked. 'We should speak to her again, too.'

'Aye, but now we've got someone who was actually working at the casino when James died. Someone who got paid off with a car.' Monroe looked across at the briefing room and at their evidence board. 'Thomas Greaves may be our best shot at finding out what really happened.'

'There's something else,' Billy said, and his tone made everyone pay attention. 'Before PC Cooper—'

'Wee PC Cooper,' Monroe gave a slight smile as Billy reddened.

'Before she asked me to look into this, I was also looking into these diamonds mentioned. Half a million in stolen gems – serious money, serious motive, especially fifteen years back. But we don't actually know what they looked like.'

'Kenny said they were family pieces,' Declan offered. 'Antiques, serious quality.'

'Right, but how big? Because if we're looking for them – and we probably should be – it'd help to know whether we're talking about a bag full of rocks or something small enough to fit in your pocket.' Billy pulled up a new screen. 'I can't find any records of diamonds being sold on books or confiscated in the UK since 2009 – especially ones with links to Triads. Nothing matching the description. Either they've never surfaced, been sold abroad or under the counter, or whoever has them has been very careful.'

Anjli flipped through her notebook.

'When we interviewed Richard Statham, he mentioned

the Triads came to him after James won the game, trying to get stolen items back. Maybe they gave him something more than a threat?'

'If it's a family thing it could mean photographs,' Billy said.

Declan pulled out his notebook, flipping through the pages.

'Statham gave me his mobile.' He stepped away, phone to his ear. The others watched as he spoke, his face shifting from inquiry to satisfaction.

'He's got it,' Declan said, covering the phone. 'The Triads gave him a photograph of the diamonds in case they turned up at the casino. He kept it in his records.'

'Why didn't he show it when we met?' Anjli narrowed her eyes.

'Apparently we "didn't ask for it", so he assumed we didn't want it,' Declan shrugged. 'Probably was hoping we, and this, would all go away if he kept quiet.'

'Can he send it?' Monroe asked.

Declan relayed the question, then shook his head.

'Physical photograph – original from the Triads. But he has it there, can either scan and send it to us, or show us on video call.'

'Video call it is,' Monroe said, already moving towards the briefing room. 'That way we can have a wee chat with him too. Put him on the big screen.'

Declan followed, tapping at his phone.

'Right, so if I just...' He frowned. 'How do you—'

'Guv,' Billy said, appearing beside him. 'AirPlay. Top right.'

'I know that,' Declan muttered. 'It's not showing the—'

Billy reached over and tapped the screen once, and the plasma in the briefing room flickered to life.

'Cheers,' Declan said dryly.

He started the call, and a moment later, Richard Statham appeared on screen, his home office behind him, looking tired in the lamplight.

'Mister Statham,' Monroe said. 'Appreciate you doing this.'

'It's no trouble... but who said that?' Statham's voice carried through the screen, slightly tinny.

'It's me,' Monroe waved at the screen. 'Detective Superintendent Monroe.'

'Guv, he can't see you,' Billy muttered, almost apologetically. 'The screen's mirroring Declan's phone, so it's Declan's front camera he can see. It's not magic.'

'Of course,' Monroe said, walking to Declan and leaning over the camera. 'It's me.'

He grinned back at Billy as he returned to his usual spot.

'Isn't technology great,' he said.

'I'm trapped in a room filled with Uncle Chivalries,' Billy muttered. 'Every FaceTime call I get from him, all I see is the top of his head.'

'Can we get on with the matter in hand?' Anjli gently encouraged.

'Yes, please, sorry, Mister Statham, you were saying?' Declan asked.

'I was saying that to be honest, I'm relieved you're finally looking into this properly. I've wondered for fifteen years what really happened to D.Q. James.'

The team had gathered around the plasma screen, watching as Statham adjusted his position, a manila envelope visible on his desk.

'So when we met, you said the Triad came to you after they were conned,' Declan prompted. 'Was this after they spoke to Wong Sei, Kenny Tsang and the Turk?'

'Actually no, they came two days after the game,' Statham confirmed. 'Jun – the man whose diamonds were stolen – came to my office. Very angry, but very controlled. Said James had humiliated him, cheated him, stolen property that had been in his family for three generations. He made it clear he was going through higher channels – the names you mentioned, but in the meantime if the diamonds surfaced at the casino, I needed to contact him immediately.'

Statham opened the envelope on camera, pulling out a photograph.

'He gave me this. Said I needed to know exactly what I was looking for.'

He held it up to the camera. The resolution wasn't perfect, but clear enough. Six diamonds arranged on black velvet; each photographed separately with a ruler beside it. They weren't enormous – the largest perhaps two centimetres across, the smallest barely a centimetre – but even through the video call, the quality was obvious. Perfect cuts, absolute clarity.

'Jesus,' Billy breathed.

'Jun's great-grandfather won them in Shanghai in the 1920s,' Statham said. 'He never explained why he had them, but I'd heard he'd used them in the past to scare off rival players. They weren't just valuable – they were family heritage.'

'But they're small,' Anjli observed. 'All six together, you could fit them in your jacket pocket.'

'Which is exactly what James did,' Statham confirmed. 'He won the final hand – cash, some other valuables, and the diamonds. James scooped everything up, dropped them into his jacket pocket like loose change, and walked out.'

'Did Jun try anything else to get them back?' Monroe asked.

Statham's face grew troubled.

'He came three times between August and November. By the third visit, he just said the matter was being handled, and I shouldn't expect to hear from him again. Then he turned up on the fifteenth of November game and even though he confronted James he never did anything. But then James was never seen again after that, so...'

'You thought he'd killed James,' Declan said.

'I thought it was possible. Half a million in diamonds, family heritage, public humiliation? That's not something Jun would forgive.'

'But you never reported this to the police,' Monroe observed.

Statham's shoulders sagged.

'And say what? That illegal high-stakes gambling was happening in my casino? That Chinese organised crime was involved?' He shook his head. 'The casino would have been shut down immediately. My career finished over a game of – excuse the pun – Chinese whispers. I convinced myself James had probably left London, that he'd realised his life was in danger, that it would all blow over.'

'Instead,' Declan said quietly, 'he ended up dead in your basement.'

Statham flinched.

'I didn't know. I swear, I had absolutely no idea he was down there until the builders found him.'

'Why didn't you explain this to us when we spoke to you? Show us the photo?'

'You never asked if I had it, and I felt it prudent to stay quiet,' Statham explained. 'Let's be honest. I mentioned the Triad had been involved, but you don't go throwing around accusations until you know you won't be getting a knock on the door, or worse still, a figure at the end of your bed.'

'Can you scan and send the image?' Billy called across, and as Declan thanked Statham and ended the call, the briefing room went quiet.

'Right,' Billy said, pulling up his laptop. 'Half a million in 2009. Diamond prices have...' His fingers typed in web page after web page, as he checked historical numbers. 'Accounting for market fluctuations, quality premium, provenance value... We're talking close to a million pounds now.'

'So, we're looking for six small diamonds,' Declan said, 'worth approximately a million pounds, that have never surfaced in fifteen years.'

'Whoever has them has kept them very quiet,' Monroe added. 'Too quiet. Even careful fencing leaves traces. But these? Nothing.'

'Three possibilities,' Anjli said. 'One, D.Q. James hid them before he was killed, and they're still hidden. Two, the killer took them and still has them, too scared to sell, because the Triads are probably still looking, even after all this time, and Jun the gambler is now Ironthreads the Marvel supervillain, if we go on name alone. Three, the killer took them and sold them so carefully we can't trace it.'

'If D.Q. James hid them,' Cooper said, 'why kill him before finding out where? You'd need him alive.'

'Unless they tortured it out of him first,' De'Geer said quietly.

The room went silent.

'Made him talk, found out where they were, then killed

him to keep it quiet,' Monroe mused coldly. 'Jesus, that's not the way I want to go.'

'You say it as if that's the kind of way *anyone* would like to go, Guv,' Declan replied.

'I think we might be looking at number one,' Anjli said slowly, and everyone turned to look at her. 'Basically, they're still hidden, James never said anything, and someone's still hunting them.'

'Katarina,' Monroe said.

'Think about it,' Anjli continued. 'She worked at the casino when James disappeared. She knew about the diamond theft. Then fifteen years later, she buys the entire building. Claims it's for development, but she knew exactly where to renovate. Her contractors found the body after her plans said where to break through the wall.'

'She wasn't trying to develop the building,' Declan said. 'She was searching for the diamonds. Fifteen years, waiting for the casino to go up for sale, buying it the moment she could, tearing apart the basement looking for where James hid them.'

'Maybe she didn't know there was a body there?' De'Geer observed. 'Maybe she knew there was a new wall built and assumed it was the perfect hiding place for the winnings.'

'Either way, fifteen years? That's a long obsession,' Cooper observed.

'That's what a million pounds does,' Monroe countered.

'Actually, I want to talk to the contractors again, too,' Declan added. 'When we spoke to them at the casino, there was a moment, a look between Katarina and Terry, the foreman. Felt like there was something more going on there.'

Monroe nodded at this.

'Right then. Tomorrow we bring all of this together – the

car sale to Greaves, the diamonds, Katarina's possible involvement, and the contractors' place in this. Work out who killed D.Q. James and where those stones ended up.'

'Priorities?' Declan asked.

'Greaves first,' Monroe decided. 'He's our eyewitness, whether he knows it or not. Someone who was there, who got paid off with James's car. We find out what he knows. Then we look harder at Katarina – her finances, her movements, any sign she's been searching for or selling diamonds.'

'If they're still in the casino,' Billy said, 'there are a lot of places to hide something that small.'

'Or she has,' Anjli countered, 'and she's just very good at keeping quiet about it. Either way, let's bring her in and chat.'

The team began gathering their things, the briefing room emptying as people headed home, but De'Geer remained at the table.

Six stones, small enough to hide, valuable enough to kill for.

Tomorrow they'd get into that, but before then he had Elliott's Professional Standards hearing.

'Morten?' Cooper stood in the doorway, jacket on. 'You coming? It's late.'

'Yeah.' He stood. 'Just thinking about tomorrow.'

'Big day,' Cooper agreed. 'Feels like we're finally getting somewhere.'

'Yeah,' De'Geer said. 'Somewhere.'

He followed her out, through the darkened office and down to Temple Inn itself. London at night had its own rhythm – quieter, more intimate, the kind of city where secrets felt closer to the surface.

Somewhere out there, diamonds waited, and a killer thought themselves safe after fifteen years, while a casino croupier who'd been paid off with a bright-yellow Cadillac would have questions to answer. But before all that, tomorrow morning, De'Geer would have to decide whether being a good police officer meant destroying yourself to protect the truth.

Tomorrow, they'd bring it all together.

Tomorrow, everything would change.

10

SPINJACK

MORTEN DE'GEER ARRIVED AT GUILDHALL JUST BEFORE NINE, uniform pressed, trying to look like someone attending official business rather than someone about to make the worst decision of his career. The planning meeting was scheduled for nine sharp, and he'd told Cooper he was supporting an old friend at a Professional Standards hearing. Not technically a lie, but the omission sat heavily on his conscience.

The Guildhall foyer bustled with its usual morning activity – councillors heading to committees, staff carrying files, the echo of footsteps on marble floors. De'Geer had always found the place intimidating; all that history and power concentrated in one building.

'Sergeant De'Geer?'

Bullman stood near the information desk, coffee in hand, case files under her arm. Her short white hair was spiked as always, grey suit immaculate.

Damn. I forgot she was here today.

'Ma'am.' De'Geer's stomach dropped. 'I didn't expect to see you here.'

'I work here, Morten,' Bullman said. 'Why are *you* here?'

'Supporting an old friend. Professional Standards hearing.'

'Character reference?'

'Something like that.'

Bullman's eyes narrowed, but before she could press, DCI Cohen from Paddington walked over, looking like he'd been up all night. Closely cropped grey hair, and still slim like a stick, he pushed his glasses up his nose as he saw the Sergeant.

'Sergeant De'Geer? You here for Elliott?'

'Yes, Guv. I knew him at Hendon.'

'Ah, well you wasted your time, the Cohen meeting's been postponed for two days. DC Elliott was attacked last night, ended up in hospital.'

'Attacked?'

'Knife wound to the abdomen. Made his own way to A&E around four this morning.' Cohen glanced at Bullman nervously. 'Said it was a mugging, but something's off.'

'How so?' she asked.

'He's pissed a lot of local scum off since he's been at Paddington,' Cohen replied. 'We all have. Goes with the warrant card. One of them might have seen an opportunity for payback. Either way, we're rescheduled for the day after tomorrow.'

Bullman watched this exchange like a cat watching mice.

'And DC Elliott's from your unit?' she asked Cohen.

'That's right. He's been having difficulties for a few months.'

'What kind?'

'Personal issues. Let's just say some concerns about his judgement.'

Bullman's gaze settled on De'Geer.

'Which hospital, Guv?' he asked, trying to ignore this.

'St Thomas's. Should be discharged by now.' Cohen checked his watch. 'Anyway, I need to get back. Good to see you standing up for a fellow officer. How's the case going?'

'It's a little all over the place, Guv.'

Cohen grinned.

'Exactly how I know Monroe likes 'em,' he said, nodding to Bullman and leaving the reception out of the main entrance.

After Cohen left, Bullman took a sip of coffee.

'Old friend having difficulties?'

'It's complicated.'

'It always is.' Bullman's tone was flat. 'Sort it before it becomes my problem, Morten. You're a good copper. Don't let someone else's mess drag you down.'

She glanced out of the doors, watching Cohen walk across the courtyard.

'And don't be like that prick,' she growled. 'Dumping your mess onto someone else and walking off with a whistle. Met me once, thinks I'm a "pal" and that I don't mind him unloading the cases he's too thick to solve on my best team.'

'So, we're your best team now?' De'Geer smiled.

'Sergeant, Temple Inn is my *only* team.' Bullman gave a smile back, but hers felt way more menacing. 'Until I get bored and have you all fired. Or shot out of a cannon. Or hand you over to Charles Baker for security.'

'Point taken, Ma'am.'

'Be wary of friends calling for character witnesses.' With a nod and a far more warmer smile, Bullman walked towards the lifts, leaving De'Geer with the uncomfortable certainty that Bullman suspected more than she was letting on.

He pulled out his phone and called St Thomas's Hospital.

The A&E department had that morning chaos De'Geer recognised – overnight patients being discharged, day staff arriving, exhausted night team handing over cases. He found Paul Elliott in a cubicle near the back, pale, one hand pressed against his bandaged midsection.

'Morten. What are you doing here?' Elliott asked as he half rose.

'I was at Guildhall, Paul. Cohen said you were attacked.'

'Nothing more than wrong place, wrong time.' Elliott's voice was flat. 'Bloke wanted my wallet; I didn't want him to have it.'

De'Geer pulled up the visitor's chair.

'Was it someone with a grudge against you? Cohen seems to think it was.'

'Nah, it was random.'

'Was it... them? The people you owe money to?'

'No. Just random.'

'Paul, if they're threatening you—'

'It *wasn't them,*' Elliott snapped, then winced. 'Just drop it. I'm fine, the hearing's postponed, you've got another couple of days to think.'

De'Geer studied his former training partner.

Something about this wasn't right.

'Did the doctors say when you can leave?'

'Any minute. Just waiting for discharge papers.' Elliott shifted uncomfortably. 'You should go, Morten. This isn't your problem. You have a case to solve, after all.'

'You made it my problem when you asked me to compromise a murder investigation.'

Elliott's jaw tightened.

'And you made it mine when you didn't report what happened at Hendon.'

They sat in tense silence until a doctor appeared, a young South Asian woman with tired eyes and a tablet computer.

'Mister Elliott?' she said, glancing at her notes. 'I just need to go over your discharge instructions.'

'I'll wait outside,' De'Geer said, standing.

'No need,' the doctor replied, pulling up Elliott's chart on the tablet. 'This won't take long. The wound is clean and stitched. You were lucky – another centimetre to the left, and we'd be having a very different conversation. Keep it dry, change the dressing daily, watch for signs of infection.'

'Will do,' Elliott said.

'And Mister Elliott?' The doctor's tone became more serious. 'If there are ongoing domestic or personal safety issues, we have resources that can help.'

'It was a mugging,' Elliott insisted.

The doctor didn't look convinced, but she nodded and left.

After Elliott had his discharge papers and was pulling on his jacket with obvious discomfort, De'Geer walked with him towards the exit. However, as they reached the hospital entrance, Elliott turned to him.

'Day after tomorrow, Morten. That's when you need to decide. Either you help me, or we both go down.'

De'Geer watched Elliott walk away with that careful, pained gait, then turned back into the hospital. He found the young South Asian doctor at the nurses' station, finishing her notes.

'Excuse me, Doctor,' De'Geer said, showing his warrant card. 'I need to ask you about DC Elliott's wound.'

The doctor glanced at the card, then at him.

'Are you investigating the assault?'

'Possibly. Can you describe the wound for me? Location, angle, depth?'

She pulled up Elliott's chart on her tablet, though her expression suggested she was already suspicious, as De'Geer started writing in his notepad.

'Single incision, lower left quadrant of the abdomen, approximately eight centimetres lateral to the midline. Penetration depth of roughly four centimetres angled slightly upward and medial. Clean edges, minimal tearing.'

'Defensive wounds?'

'None. No bruising on the torso consistent with a struggle, no cuts or abrasions on the hands or forearms.'

'And he walked here himself?'

'Arrived around four this morning, on foot apparently. Applied pressure with his own shirt to control bleeding.' The doctor set down her tablet. 'Sergeant, I've treated dozens of stab wounds from assaults. If I'm being honest, this doesn't feel like one. If your colleague is in that much trouble, he needs help. Not the kind I can provide.'

De'Geer thanked her and walked outside, pulling out his phone and dialling the Temple Inn morgue.

'Doctor Marcos.' The voice on the other end sounded tired, likely because Doctor Marcos had been up all night.

'Doc, it's De'Geer.'

'What were you doing in Guildhall?'

De'Geer paused, surprised.

'I—'

'It's okay, I'm not tracking you. That's Billy's kink,' Doctor

Marcos chuckled down the phone. 'Bullman just spoke to me about her chat with you.'

'Ah, right. I went to see an old colleague, and heard from DCI Cohen he'd been stabbed,' De'Geer replied, deciding to avoid the question as long as he could. 'Just saw him at the hospital and, if I'm being honest, I need your professional opinion off the record.'

'You mean don't tell Monroe?'

'At least until I arrive, please.'

'Go on.'

'Knife wound, lower left quadrant of the abdomen, eight centimetres lateral to midline,' De'Geer read from his notes. 'Penetration depth four centimetres angled slightly upward and medial. Clean edges, minimal tearing. No defensive wounds, no signs of struggle. Victim walked himself to A&E.'

Long pause.

'That's self-inflicted,' Doctor Marcos said flatly. 'The angle and location are textbook for someone who knows enough anatomy to avoid major damage. Left-handed person would naturally use their right hand to access that area. Upward and medial angle suggests they were controlling the depth.'

'Could it be from an attack?'

'Morten, you train under me. You know what assault wounds look like.' Her tone became more serious. 'Who is this?'

'Someone who was supposed to attend a Professional Standards hearing this morning,' De'Geer said quietly. 'Someone desperate enough to stab himself to delay it.'

'Christ. Whatever this is, don't let it drag you down.'

'That's just what Bullman said, too. The problem is I think it might have a connection to the case, too. I'll be in shortly.'

De'Geer ended the call and stared at the hospital entrance. Paul Elliott had been so desperate to delay the hearing that he'd stabbed himself. Not just desperate – terrified.

And, in two days' time, De'Geer would have to decide whether his loyalty to an old friend was worth destroying his career and compromising a murder investigation.

DECLAN WALSH STOOD IN THE EXHIBITION HALL OF THE EXCEL Centre, surrounded by casino expo chaos. Electronic chimes from slot machines, dice clattering, sales reps who'd been on their feet since seven.

Monroe looked thoroughly unimpressed by a nearby demonstration of *"Blackjack Lightning"* – apparently regular blackjack, but with LED lights.

'Remind me why we're here instead of bringing Greaves in for a proper interview?'

'Because Billy found him via social media posting about *"exciting first day at the expo"*,' Declan replied, scanning the booths. 'And because as there's two more days of this, he's less likely to be at home right now.'

Billy had tracked Thomas Greaves to the expo after finding his Facebook posts from yesterday – enthusiastic photos of casino equipment and hashtags about *#GamingInnovation* and *#StartupLife.* According to Billy's research, Greaves had recently tired of his croupier life and had begun investing in a startup gaming company.

'There,' Declan said, pointing.

The banner read *"LUCKY LOTUS GAMING"* in gold letters on red, with a smaller tagline: *"Revolutionising Casino*

Entertainment". Behind a demonstration table stood Thomas Greaves – or at least a man that matched the driving licence photo they had on record. He was early fifties, greying hair neatly trimmed, wearing a crisp white shirt and burgundy waistcoat that gave him the air of a professional croupier, even in a sales environment, currently demonstrating something to a small crowd.

'Ladies and gentlemen,' Greaves was saying, 'I give you the future of casino gaming – *SpinJack!*'

Declan and Monroe exchanged glances.

'Did he just say—'

'SpinJack.'

'Aye, I thought I heard that.'

They moved closer. On the table was a modified roulette wheel, but instead of numbers, each segment was labelled with blackjack actions:

HIT - STAND - DOUBLE DOWN - SPLIT - BUST - BLACKJACK - INSURANCE - SURRENDER

'The concept is simple,' Greaves continued. 'Play the game where *the wheel meets the deal!* Players are dealt standard blackjack hands, but instead of choosing their own actions, the wheel decides for them! One spin affects every hand at the table simultaneously!'

'So, you have no control over your own hand?' someone in the crowd asked.

'Exactly! That's the genius of it. It combines the excitement of roulette with the strategy of blackjack. The house edge is significantly improved because players can't make optimal decisions. If you're sitting on twenty and the wheel lands on *HIT*, well, that's the game!'

'That's mental,' another attendee muttered.

'We prefer to call it "revolutionary engagement through randomised agency",' Greaves said, the smile not quite reaching his eyes. 'We've run the mathematics, and the house edge is roughly forty-two per cent.'

The patter lasted another five minutes, with a couple of people passing Greaves business cards, but eventually the crowd dispersed, clearly unconvinced.

Monroe leant close to Declan.

'I've seen some shite in my time, but that might take the biscuit.'

'Mister Greaves?' Ignoring the comment, Declan approached as the last attendees wandered off. 'Could we have a word?'

Greaves looked up, professional smile faltering as he took in their bearing – that instant recognition that police had arrived, even in plain clothes.

'Of course. Are you gentlemen interested in our product?'

'DCI Walsh, Detective Superintendent Monroe, City of London Police.' Declan showed his warrant card. 'We'd like to ask you some questions about D.Q. James.'

The colour drained from Greaves' face. For a moment, he looked like he might bolt.

'I wondered when someone would come asking,' he eventually said quietly. 'It's been fifteen years. Thought maybe it was buried for good.'

'Things have a way of surfacing,' Monroe said. 'Especially when they're walled up in casino basements.'

Greaves frowned at this, but then glanced around the expo hall, clearly aware they were in a public space.

'Not here,' he said, and there was almost an element of pleading in the tone. 'I talk to police here? I'm screwed for bookings as that becomes the story for the rest of the week. There's a cafe outside on the main thoroughfare. Let me get someone to watch the booth.'

Then Thomas Greaves walked – although it felt more like he almost ran – over to a young woman passing flyers out for SpinJack, pointing at the booth before joining them.

'Okay we have about ten minutes,' he said. 'Is that enough time?'

'Depends how lucky you feel when you spin that wheel.' Monroe smiled. 'SpinJack!'

11

CAR SALES

The Excel café Greaves took them to was nothing more than some seats in a cordoned off area of the main thoroughfare next to an expensive coffee counter, but at ten in the morning, it was still relatively quiet. Greaves sat across from Declan and Monroe; hands wrapped around a coffee cup he wasn't drinking.

'How did you find me?'

'Your car,' Declan said. 'The 1973 Cadillac Eldorado you bought from D.Q. James in November 2009 for two thousand pounds.'

Greaves closed his eyes.

'That bloody car. I should have scrapped it.'

'Why didn't you?'

'Because I loved it. I'd admired that car for two years. Every time James drove up to the casino, I'd be out front just to see it. Ridiculous thing, completely impractical for London, but it was beautiful.'

'So, when he offered to sell it to you for two grand, you jumped at it,' Monroe said.

'He didn't offer at first. I'd been asking him for months if he'd ever want to sell. He always laughed it off, said it was worth way more than I made, and he'd drive that car until it killed him.' He paused. 'Ironic, I suppose.'

'What changed?' Declan asked.

'Late August 2009, he just showed up at my apartment one evening. Said he needed to sell the car quickly, needed little money for it, just wanted to cover a recent repair to the exhaust system. Said it should go to someone who'd appreciate it properly.'

'And you believed him?' Monroe's tone was sceptical.

'Why wouldn't I? He seemed genuine, even sad about it. He had like three cars, so I assumed he was downsizing. Said he was leaving London later that year, starting fresh somewhere, and the car would just be a reminder of old mistakes.'

Declan made notes.

'How much was the exhaust repair?'

'He said about two grand, hence the cost. I had that much in savings, handed it over in cash the next day. He signed over the registration documents, gave me the keys, and that was that.'

'Did he say where he was going?'

'No, and I didn't ask. D.Q. James wasn't the kind of man you pressed for personal details.' Greaves finally took a sip of coffee. 'Look, I know how this looks. Casino employee gets paid off with a car a couple of months before the owner of it disappears. But I swear, I had no idea anything had happened to him. I thought he'd just left London like he said.'

'Why did you leave the casino a month after his disappearance?' Monroe asked.

'Because the place was falling apart. The Harrison had

been struggling for years, and after the Chinese gambling ring got exposed – all the issues with James winning diamonds and that, we knew it was only a matter of time. I got out whilst I could still find another job. If I'm being honest, I'm stunned it limped along as long as it did.'

'But that aside, a professional gambler suddenly came to you, desperate to offload a valuable classic car for a pittance, and you never wondered why?'

'I thought he was in trouble. I thought maybe he owed money to the wrong people, needed to liquidate assets quickly. Possibly even seed money for a big game.'

'He'd just won a massive hand of diamonds,' Declan reminded.

'Yeah, but they're hard to sell, right? I mean I assume so. Perhaps he needed money while he waited? But I also thought it was none of my business.'

'And when he disappeared?'

'I assumed he'd run. Assumed the people he owed caught up with him, or he'd gone into hiding...' Greaves trailed off.

Declan studied the man across the table. Everything Greaves said was plausible, but there was something off about it.

Monroe leant back.

'Mister Greaves, we're going to need you to come to Temple Inn for a formal statement. And we'll need access to any documents you still have related to that car purchase.'

'Am I under arrest?'

'Not yet,' Declan said. 'But we need to establish exactly when D.Q. James came to see you, and whether you're remembering this correctly, because right now something feels off, and it's not SpinJack.'

Greaves sighed, leaning back in the seat.

'I can't leave,' he muttered. 'If I do, I'll miss sales. And I need it.'

'So, tell me something that keeps you here, then?' Monroe suggested. 'Something that saves us time taking you to the interview room?'

Greaves bit at his lip.

'He sold another car,' he said eventually. 'Same as mine, but in this hideous lime green. Same price, two grand.'

'Who to?'

'Barman at the club, guy named Carrigan. Ronnie Carrigan.'

Monroe and Declan said nothing, waiting. Greaves seemed to want to say more, and right now they were happy to let him.

'We paid for the cars knowing they were worth ten times the cost, sure,' he eventually said, slumping back into the chair. 'But there was more to it. He gave these as payment for work.'

'What kind of work?' Declan looked up.

'We drove around London in them, dressed like him.' Greaves had given up being cautious now. 'Stupid hat, glasses, one of his Rolex watches, the lot.'

'Did he ever say why?' Monroe asked.

'Didn't need to. I knew he had issues with other players, especially the Chinese. They were so pissed at him they'd banned him from games. He'd had someone try to kill him, apparently, shot through a pub window in a driveway so he was using us as decoys, especially after he got the diamonds.'

'Dangerous work,' Declan raised an eyebrow.

'Damn right. I did it a couple of times and then thought "screw this". I already had the car. I gave him back the Rolex and told him he could go whistle.' Greaves shrugged. 'Ronnie was still doing it, and he was closer to James anyway.'

Declan noted this down.

'Anyone else involved in this whole "fake James" game?' he asked.

'How do you mean?'

'He means do you have anyone else who could agree to this story?' Monroe gave a slight smile, but there was no humour there.

Greaves considered this for a moment.

'Moir,' he replied. 'Dunno the first name. He was the investigator D.Q. James used on his rivals.'

'To work out their weaknesses?' Declan noted the surname down. Moir wasn't as common as Smith, per se, but it'd still be a long journey to find him.

'Yeah. I don't remember anyone else being involved, but I know people were looking for him,' Greaves continued. 'That Sullivan guy, the Chinese, the manager, Statham—'

'Why?'

'He was being leaned on by the Chinese.' Greaves shrugged. 'He helped James fix the game that cost them the diamonds, and they pressured him to find them. As I said though, once it got like that, I left.'

'But you still stayed in the business.'

'I was a croupier.' Greaves shrugged again. 'You don't get many changes in jobs doing that.'

'Until now, it seems,' Declan waved around the convention centre. 'That game you're demonstrating – SpinJack. Who created it?'

'I did. I've been working on casino game concepts for years. Passion project.'

'And how's it going?'

Greaves gave a weak smile.

'Not well. Turns out people don't want a roulette wheel making their blackjack decisions for them. But we keep hoping someone will see the potential.'

'Who's we?' Declan asked automatically, and at the question, he saw the slightest tightness around Greaves' eyes.

'It's an entrepreneur,' he said, as if this answered the question.

'Name?'

'Marek,' Greaves replied, almost reluctantly, and Declan understood why the moment he continued. 'Marek Kováč.'

This brought a whistle from Monroe.

'That's a rare sounding surname,' he said.

'Common in Slovakia,' Greaves argued half-heartedly.

'We spoke to another Kováč recently,' Declan said. 'Katarina. You know her?'

Greaves let out an almost theatrical sigh this time.

'Of course I do,' he muttered. 'Bloody chip chaser.'

'Chip chaser?' Declan wrote it down as he asked.

'Someone who hangs around winning players at a casino, hoping to latch on to their luck, or their wallet.' Monroe smiled. 'We heard Katarina was a player, a serious one.'

'Maybe at the end, once her sugar daddy covered her buy-in,' Greaves was obviously not a fan. 'Katarina Havel – that's her maiden name – leeched the tables for a year or two before snaring Marek. Then, with his backing, she became a player. She made more than she spent, so she was profitable, but she was never a name, if you know what I mean.'

'And Marek was?'

'Oh, he was a massive whale in the casino,' Greaves nodded. 'Comes from East European money, doubled it and then doubled it again. He made more in a night playing poker than I made in a year, and it was just his hobby. We got talking though, I did some events for him over the year, even worked on a yacht he part-owned for a summer, and when I came up with the idea for SpinJack, he put in the seed money.'

'He thought it was a good idea?'

'He probably thought it was a good tax loss,' Greaves pursed his lips. 'Well, it will be if we don't make sales.'

'Is Katarina involved?'

'Christ no!' Greaves actually laughed at this. 'They split a couple of years back. She gained a couple of million in the divorce so she did okay, but he's well shot of her.'

'Did you know she'd bought the Harrison Casino?'

Greaves frowned.

'No. Why? That place is a money pit. Even the land it's on is overvalued. That crazy bitch is her own worst enemy.'

He straightened in the chair now.

'Have I said enough? Can I go now?'

'One more thing,' Declan closed his notebook. 'Marek Kováč. Did he have beef with D.Q James?'

'Didn't you hear what I said?' Greaves chuckled. 'D.Q. bloody James is a guy who gave away two expensive cars with gold Rolexes to create doubles – just to stay alive. He had beef with everyone.'

'Enough for Marek to kill him, and bury him in the Harrison's basement?'

Greaves' eyes widened. Declan and Monroe had deliberately not mentioned this part of the story, and the look of shock was genuine.

'He died?'

'It seems so. But you haven't answered the question.'

Greaves looked back at the entrance to the gaming convention, as if seeing his booth through the wall.

'Yeah,' he whispered. 'Yeah, I reckon he could have.'

'Do you know where we can find Mister Carrigan?' Monroe rose from the chair now as Greaves matched him.

'No, sorry, we weren't that close,' he replied. 'I got on better with his sister, Imogen. Never saw him after he quit, and that was around the same time as D.Q. James. I assumed he sold the car and the watch and buggered off with the money.'

Declan felt a tingle at the back of his neck.

'Imogen? Do you mean Imogen Rothwell?' he asked.

'Nah, Carrigan,' Greaves paused. 'Though she might have married. Sorry I can't help more.'

As they walked back through the expo hall, Monroe shook his head.

'That man's story has more holes than Swiss cheese.'

'Let's find Ronnie Carrigan and see if it's just as bad,' Declan suggested. 'And let's see if Billy can find us an investigator based on a surname.'

'It's George,' Monroe replied. 'Georgie Moir, to be exact, I'd bet my rep on it. He was a guttersnipe toadie back when your father ran Mile End, usually caught taking photos of affairs. How James found him, however, is anyone's guess.'

He stopped.

'Bloody Johnny Lucas,' he muttered. 'They ran security for the casinos. I bet he put them in touch.'

'Well then we're talking to Johnny again, too, and this Moir fellow.'

'Aye,' Monroe replied, 'but the problem with that, laddie, is that Moir had a minor stroke a couple of years back, and last I heard, he's not been that responsive.'

They headed for the exit, leaving behind the casino expo with its flashing lights, desperate sales pitches, and one particularly terrible game called SpinJack that would almost certainly never see the inside of an actual casino.

INTERVIEW ROOM TWO AT TEMPLE INN HAD THE STARK DESIGN of all police interview rooms – plain walls, metal table, recording equipment, uncomfortable chairs that discouraged people from getting too comfortable with their lies.

Katarina Kováč sat on one side, talking to them for the second time in two days, looking less composed than before. Tailored business suit, but her hair was pulled back in a simple ponytail rather than the elegant styling from their previous meeting. And no solicitor, which Anjli found interesting.

Cooper sat beside Anjli, notepad ready.

'Mrs Kováč. Thank you for coming in voluntarily.'

'I want to help,' Katarina said, though her hands were clasped tightly. 'I want to clear this up.'

'Good. Then let's start with what you knew about the diamonds.'

Katarina took a breath.

'I knew D.Q. James had them. Everyone at the casino knew.'

'And when you bought the building fifteen years later, did you think about those diamonds?'

Katarina hesitated, then nodded.

'Because James always bragged about hidden assets, about insurance policies. He used to say he'd never trust banks, never trust anyone. Said he kept his valuables where only he could find them. Made a joke about them being under everyone's noses. I thought if the diamonds were anywhere, they'd be hidden.'

'So, when you bought it—'

'The spa development is real,' Katarina interrupted. 'My husband's money, legitimate business plan, proper planning permission. But yes, I hoped I might find the diamonds as well. A bonus.'

'Did you know where they were hidden?'

'No. I thought maybe in the walls, under floorboards. That's why the renovation was so thorough.'

'But you knew exactly where to tell your contractors to break through that basement wall.' Cooper spoke up.

'I'm not stupid,' Katarina replied haughtily. 'When you "renovate" a room that, when people come back in, looks exactly the same but about three foot shorter? I thought he'd made a deal with the owner, and someone had built a false wall, created a hidden space. Perfect place to hide something valuable.'

'Or a body,' Anjli observed.

'I never imagined that. I thought I'd find diamonds, not a corpse.'

There was a buzz from Anjli's phone, and she checked her messages as Cooper leant in.

'What else did D.Q. James tell you about the diamonds?'

'That the moment he tried to move them, he'd have people after him.'

Anjli sat back, studying Katarina's face. The woman was

nervous, but her story had internal consistency. Either she was telling the truth, or she was very well prepared.

'Mrs Kováč, I need to ask you directly. Did you kill D.Q. James?'

'No.'

'Did you have anything to do with his death?'

'No. He was just another player at the casino.'

'But you knew enough to wait fifteen years for the casino to go up for sale, then buy it specifically to search for those diamonds.'

Katarina's jaw tightened.

'I've already bloody said the spa development is real. Check my business plans, my financing, my contractors. This is a legitimate project that might also have had an additional benefit. That doesn't make me a murderer.'

'No,' Anjli agreed. 'But it makes you someone with strong financial motivation to find those diamonds. And when you bought that building, it feels very much like you knew exactly where to look.'

'Because I'd researched the building's history.'

'Or because you knew where the body was buried.'

The room went quiet. Katarina stared at Anjli, expression shifting from defensive to something that might have been genuine offence.

'You think I killed him, then bought his tomb fifteen years later to search it? My husband—'

'Yes, let's talk about Marek.' Anjli smiled darkly. 'He's not your husband any more, is he?'

Katarina opened and shut her mouth.

'It's true, we are in the process of taking time apart—'

'Divorcing two years ago is a little more permanent than that,' Anjli checked her messages again. 'So, when you mention your husband's money, did you mean the money he gave you in the settlement?'

Katarina seemed to diminish at the question, her shoulders slumping as she retreated into the chair.

'I never thought that David – D.Q – was dead,' she whispered. 'I seriously believed that he'd gone into hiding, taking the millions he'd made, and was living his life out in some Arizona redlands, spending his days playing poker for beer money.'

'But you don't know this for sure.' Anjli made a note. 'Did you ever speak to Thomas Greaves or Ronnie Carrigan about this?'

'Greaves? He's a snake. Always hated me. He was pissed that Marek picked me, that I gained my Prince Charming while all he could find was octogenarian frogs.' Katarina rose back up in her chair now, the arrogance returned. 'And Ronnie? He was a flake. He even started dressing like David at the end, even found a knock-off Rolex. Pitiful.'

'Do you know what happened to him?'

'Ronnie? Probably in prison for something. He was never going to add up to anything. Kept sucking up to the Triad.'

'How so?'

'They had money, they bought drinks, he was a barman.' Katarina shrugged. 'I think he honestly thought he could "network" there.'

Anjli closed her notebook.

'We'll need access to all your documentation, even the ones you've kept from us.'

'You can have whatever you need. I want this solved. I want to know who killed a man in my building.'

'Our building,' Anjli corrected. 'Right now, it's a crime scene.'

After Katarina was led out by another constable, Anjli and Cooper followed her out, heading along the corridor, down the stairs and towards the main office, where Billy would be working at his monitors. Cooper was checking her notes.

'What do you think, Guv?'

'I think her story's almost too convenient. Knew about the diamonds, bought the building, her ex-husband apparently also had issues with James.'

They emerged down the stairs into the office, as Billy looked up at them.

'Saw Katarina just walk past,' he said. 'She looks pissed off. You definitely riled her.'

'Good. Anything new?' Anjli asked, sitting down at her desk.

'Checking more hideous cars.' Billy grinned. However, before he could continue, the door from the stairs burst open and Doctor Marcos stormed in, waving a sheet of paper in one hand while holding her tablet in the other.

'We have a problem,' she announced.

Billy looked up. Anjli and Cooper turned.

'What kind of problem?' Anjli asked.

'The kind where we've been investigating the wrong bloody victim.' Doctor Marcos slapped the paper down on Billy's desk. 'I just got the dental records back early. They don't match.'

'What do you mean they don't match?' Anjli moved closer.

'I mean the body in that basement isn't D.Q. James.' Doctor Marcos pulled up images on her tablet, waving them around too fast for anyone to truly read the X-rays and skeletal measurements she wasn't even attempting to show properly in her anger. 'The dental work is completely different. Wrong fillings, wrong configuration, wrong everything.'

She swiped to another image.

'And there's more – I found evidence of a healed ulnar fracture on the right arm, radius and ulna both broken, roughly two to three months before death. Major break, would have needed a cast for weeks.'

Billy was already pulling up photos.

'I've got photos of D.Q. James from September and October 2009—'

'Look there, see!' Doctor Marcos rapped her finger on the screen. 'No cast. Both arms completely functional. He's even got that Rolex on his right wrist in every photo.'

'And our body?' Cooper asked quietly.

'Rolex on the left wrist.' Doctor Marcos crossed her arms. 'Height's wrong too. Our victim is five-ten. James was six-dead according to his passport.'

'So, someone else was dressed up to look like him,' Anjli said slowly.

'Someone wearing his clothes, his hat, his sunglasses, even his Rolex,' Doctor Marcos confirmed. 'Question is – who? And *where the hell is D.Q. James?*'

12

DOOM SCROLLING

BILLY FITZWARREN STARED AT THE MISSING PERSON REPORT until the name stopped looking like letters and started looking like an answer.

Ronald Carrigan. November 2009. Five foot ten. Bartender at the Harrison Casino.

Sister: Imogen Carrigan.

He hadn't started looking for a missing person, he was simply looking up the owner of the lime-green 1973 Cadillac Eldorado, one sold to a Ronald Carrigan and then found burnt out by the side of a road a year later, having apparently been left there for months.

Which never boded well. Especially when this missing person's report appeared.

He pulled up Imogen Carrigan's details next; Declan had commented on the phone call that Imogen wasn't, in his opinion, that common a name, and even though Billy knew several Imogens, he was very aware this was because of the social circles he ran in rather than the probabilities of names. That said, Declan had been right. Imogen Carrigan became

Imogen Rothwell in April 2012, in a registry office in Islington.

The museum curator who ran the Poker Exhibit, and therefore the D.Q. James section, was Ronnie Carrigan's sister.

Billy needed more than a suspicion as to Ronnie's disappearing, though. He opened Imogen Rothwell's Facebook – he didn't intend to hack it or anything, just check through the public posts – and as he scrolled back he saw professional posts about exhibitions, and the occasional photo of museum events. Scrolling back through years of content, he found a post from 2011; it was one of those "memories" throwback photos, and of Imogen with her arm around a bloke in his thirties.

Missing you every day little brother.

The caption wasn't ambiguous in the least, but the man had been tagged, and the link led to the profile of Ronnie Carrigan. The profile hadn't been updated since 2009, but the photos were still there. Billy clicked through – Ronnie at pubs, Ronnie with mates, Ronnie in rugby kit. Then a shared post from the *Henley Hawks RFC* page, dated August twentieth, 2009.

It was a team photo, with Ronnie on the far right, grinning despite the splint across his right arm. Underneath simply read:

Gutted to lose our flanker for the rest of the year. Get well soon Carrigan! See you in the New Year!

It was followed by a dozen rugby ball emojis – although honestly, Billy wasn't sure if they were American Football ones – and had a variety of comments from teammates wishing him well, saying the tackle was mental, worth it for the try, etc.

Opening the image in a new browser to get the full size, Billy zoomed in on the splint. Not a full cast – this was more the kind for an ulnar fracture that needed support but allowed some movement.

He checked Doctor Marcos's report.

Healed right ulnar and radius fracture, two to three months before death.

August to November. Six to eight weeks for a splint. Billy did the maths. Eight weeks from August twentieth would be mid-to-late October, a couple of weeks before D.Q. James disappeared.

Now for the tedious part.

Billy opened a new search and started pulling every image of D.Q. James from September to November 2009. These weren't that common, but many of them were tournament photos, candid shots, and publicity stills he'd looked at already, many bookmarked. Now, however, he was checking a wider date.

He arranged them chronologically; September had James at a private game, trademark cowboy hat and aviators, both arms visible holding cards. No sign of injury. October had blurry casino shots, long sleeves, hat, glasses. Right arm visible with Rolex on right wrist. Left arm mostly hidden by angle and body position. November was the last known photo and in this James was in full regalia, arms crossed but positioned so the right wrist with the Rolex stayed visible.

Billy leant closer to the screen. Every distance shot photo

from September onwards had long sleeves, sunglasses never off, not even indoors, and hat always on, and not a single clear view of both wrists simultaneously.

Clever, he considered. *If you were doubling as someone and hiding an injury, you'd dress to conceal it. Long sleeves, strategic positioning, always keeping the injured arm partially obscured. And if you were impersonating someone who always wore long sleeves, a hat, and sunglasses anyway...*

He pulled up the crime scene photos, staring at the Rolex on the left wrist, clearly visible despite fifteen years of decomposition.

Billy sat back, fitting it together.

D.Q. James always wore his watch on the right wrist. Every photo, every interview, every tournament. It was one of his quirks – poker forums discussed it. Most people wore watches on their non-dominant hand, but James was right-handed, believed to be ambidextrous, but there was no actual proof of this, but wore his on the right, anyway. Weirdly, only near the end did he wear a Rolex – before that it was a Patek Phillipe. Which made sense if Richard Statham was correct about the watches found.

But the body had the watch on the left wrist.

Ronnie Carrigan breaks his right arm in August. Gets a splint, keeps it on through October. The injury heals but it's still uncomfortable, still weak. When he's impersonating D.Q. James in November, wearing the Rolex on the right-hand wrist would be painful, awkward. So, he wears it on the left – his good hand, his strong hand.

Probably meant to swap it over before anyone noticed. Never got the chance.

Billy pulled up the forensic report again, double-checking.

'I know who the body is,' he said aloud to the empty office.

THE AFTERNOON BRIEFING ROOM FELT DIFFERENT WITH WHAT they now knew. Monroe stood at the front, Billy controlling the plasma screen. Declan and Anjli right side, Doctor Marcos and De'Geer at the back. Cooper was still out canvassing.

'Right,' Monroe said. 'Billy's worked out who's in our basement, and thanks to Doctor Marcos as well, we know it's not the cowboy.'

Billy clicked to the rugby photo, appearing on the screen behind Monroe.

'Ronnie Carrigan. Thirty-four in 2009, five-ten, bartender at the Harrison. Disappeared same weekend as D.Q. James. Sister Imogen – now Rothwell – filed a missing person report three days after the infamous poker game. Police response was minimal. Adult male, no signs of foul play, probably left town.'

He zoomed in on the splint.

'August twentieth; breaks his right arm playing rugby. Standard healing time, six-to-eight weeks. Takes us to mid-to late October to fully heal.'

'And our body?' Monroe prompted.

'Healed right ulnar and radius fracture, two to three months before death,' Doctor Marcos confirmed. 'Healing pattern matches that timeline.'

Billy pulled up the next series of images.

'Every photo of D.Q. James from September through November shows long sleeves, hat, sunglasses – even indoors.

Right wrist visible in some shots with the Rolex, but never a clear view of both wrists. If you're hiding a healing injury whilst maintaining your public persona—'

'You dress to cover it,' Declan said.

Billy clicked to the crime scene photo.

'The Rolex is on the left wrist. James always wore his on the right – documented in photos, mentioned in interviews, discussed on poker forums. But if your right arm was still weak from a recent fracture—'

'You'd wear it on your stronger hand,' Anjli finished. 'Your left.'

'So, someone killed Ronnie Carrigan,' Declan said, 'thinking they were killing D.Q. James. Which explains why he looked older than the body when we first saw his photo, as there's a good ten years difference.'

'Which means D.Q. James has been alive this whole time,' Anjli added.

'Or was,' Doctor Marcos said. 'Fifteen years is a long time. Could have died naturally, been killed elsewhere, left the country.'

'But he's not in our basement, and that's what matters right now,' Monroe said firmly. 'That's Ronnie Carrigan. Doctor Marcos, can we confirm with DNA?'

'If Imogen gives us a sample, yes. Sibling DNA should give us a solid match or exclusion. Also, we can now compare the dental records we have to his, and with Carrigan being UK based it should be easier.'

De'Geer raised a hand.

'Laddie...' Monroe sighed, and De'Geer smiled sheepishly – it was still a habit he couldn't drop.

'So, I'm guessing that dressed like that, someone thought they were killing D.Q. James,' he said, looking around. 'But what if they actually meant to kill Carrigan and this was by chance?'

'Well then we start from scratch,' Monroe mused. 'So, let's hope we don't do that.'

He looked at Declan.

'You and Anjli speak to Imogen Rothwell. Get DNA, get her statement, find out what she knows, even De'Geer's idea – see if anyone hated Ronnie Carrigan enough to kill. Billy, everything you can find on Ronnie – where he lived, who he knew, what he did before he disappeared.'

'On it.'

'This changes everything,' Monroe continued. 'If James is alive, he's got at least half a million in diamonds hidden somewhere, and he's been too scared to come back for them.'

'Or he can't come back,' Declan said. 'Prison, dead, hiding—'

'Or he knows whoever killed Ronnie is still out there,' Anjli said. 'Thinks he's safe because someone thinks he's dead.'

'Until we found the body,' Declan said.

'Aye,' Monroe agreed. 'So, if D.Q. James is alive, the moment that body gets identified as someone else, the killer knows they got the wrong man. We'd better find him before they do. Move.'

Imogen Rothwell was adjusting lighting on a display case when Declan and Anjli approached, and something in her expression once she looked up said she'd been waiting for them.

'DCI Walsh,' she said, setting down her cloth. 'Back so soon?'

'We need to talk about your brother,' Declan said. 'Ronald Carrigan.'

Her hands stilled on the display case. For a moment she didn't move. Then, carefully, she walked to a bench against the wall and sat down.

'Wondered when you'd work it out,' she said quietly.

Anjli sat beside her whilst Declan remained standing. 'You knew we would?'

'The moment you told me about the body in the casino basement.' Rothwell looked at the D.Q. James display. 'Been waiting fifteen years for someone to ask the right questions.'

'Tell us about Ronnie.'

Rothwell took a breath.

'My little brother. Three years younger. Hopeless at everything except making people laugh and mixing drinks. Got the bartending job at the Harrison in 2007, said it was the best gig he'd ever had. Good tips, interesting people.'

'When did you last see him?'

'November 2009. Came to my flat in that stupid car he'd bought. Lime-green Cadillac, ridiculous thing. Said he'd got it for a steal from one of the casino regulars a few weeks earlier.'

'D.Q. James,' Anjli said.

'Ronnie was obsessed with him. Thought he was the coolest person he'd ever met – the hat, the sunglasses, the whole persona. Started dressing like him sometimes, bought fake aviators from Camden Market.' Rothwell smiled sadly. 'I told him he looked daft. He just laughed, said he was "method acting", said it was the easiest money he'd ever made.' Rothwell's voice cracked. 'I told him it sounded dodgy.

He said it was fine, that James just wanted to confuse some people who were bothering him.'

'And that was the last time you saw him?'

'Last time in person. He called a day or so later. I was doing a roast. He rang at half twelve, said he couldn't make it, something came up with work.'

'What did he sound like?'

'Scared,' Rothwell said immediately. 'Trying to play it off, but I could tell. I've known my brother his entire life. He was frightened. I asked what was wrong and he said—'

She paused, collecting herself.

'He said, "I'm in too deep, Immie. James is into something properly dangerous. The Chinese are after him, some Russian bloke too. I need to get out".'

Declan made notes.

'Did he mention any names?'

'No. Just said there were people looking for James and they weren't the kind you wanted to meet. Said he was going to tell James he was done with the decoy thing, get his head down, maybe visit Mum in Manchester until it blew over.'

'But he never made it to Manchester.'

Rothwell shook her head.

'Few days after that, I went to his apartment. Landlord said he hadn't seen him since the weekend. That's when I filed the missing person report.'

'And the police response?'

'Useless,' Rothwell said bluntly. 'They took the report, asked questions, said he'd probably just taken off. Adult male, no signs of violence, probably got scared and left. Said people disappear all the time and most turn up eventually. But Ronnie wouldn't have just left without telling me. We were close. Lost our dad when we were young – it was always just the two of us looking out for each other. He wouldn't vanish without a word.'

Anjli pulled out her phone and showed Imogen the rugby photo.

'Is this your brother?'

Rothwell's face softened.

'That's him. The Henley match – so pleased with himself. Said the tackle was worth the broken arm. Daft sod kept going on about scoring before he went down. Wouldn't shut up about it for weeks.'

'When did the splint come off?'

'Start of November, I think. He posted something on Facebook about finally showering properly again. The splint had driven him mad, kept getting in the way of everything.'

'Did it still bother him? The arm?'

'He said it was fine, but I could tell it was still weak. Kept favouring it, being careful. I thought he shouldn't be doing that decoy driving thing with a recently healed break, but he said it was just driving, not manual labour.' Her voice dropped. 'I should have pushed harder. Should have made him stop.'

'Mrs Rothwell, there's nothing you could have done,' Anjli said gently. 'Whatever happened to Ronnie wasn't your fault.'

Declan looked at the D.Q. James display.

'How long have you worked here?'

'Since 2018. Started as a volunteer, got hired full-time when a position opened.'

'The museum acquired D.Q. James's collection a few months back, right?'

'Yes.'

'Did you know it was coming up for auction?'

A pause.

'I found out through a contact at the storage company. They handle entertainment memorabilia. Over the years I'd made it known I was interested in anything related to poker history. When D.Q. James's unit came up, they gave me the heads up.'

'So, you made sure the museum bought it.'

'I suggested we bid. Told the board it would be valuable for our gambling exhibition. Which it was. It's been one of our most popular displays over the last three months.'

'And personally?'

Imogen Rothwell stood and walked to the display case. She opened a drawer beneath it and pulled out a silver lighter with an engraving.

RC – Good luck at Henley. Love always, Immie.

'I gave that to Ronnie for his birthday in 2009,' she said quietly. 'March seventeenth. He always had it with him, even though he didn't smoke any more. Paranoid about losing it, kept it in his front right pocket. Always.' Her voice tightened. 'When I was cataloguing the collection and found it in a box with D.Q. James's personal effects, I knew that whatever happened to my brother, James was involved. That Ronnie hadn't just left – something terrible had happened.'

Anjli took the lighter carefully.

'Why didn't you come to the police?'

'And tell them what? I found my brother's lighter in a storage unit sealed for over a decade? With no body, no evidence of a crime, nothing but a lighter James could have got a hundred different ways?' Rothwell's frustration showed. 'The missing person case had been closed years ago. Ronnie was legally an adult who'd left of his own accord. Anyway, I did try. I went to the police station, explained about the lighter. They were polite but made it clear – without actual evidence of foul play, there was nothing they could do. One officer even suggested Ronnie might have given James the lighter as a gift or sold it to him.'

Her voice hardened.

'As if my brother would have done that. Is it? Is it my brother?'

'We don't know for certain yet,' Declan said carefully. 'But the body has several indicators that suggest it could be. Height matches, age matches, evidence of a healed right-arm fracture that occurred before death. Timeline fits with Ronnie's rugby injury.'

'We need a DNA sample from you to confirm it,' Anjli added. 'Would you be willing to come to Temple Inn?'

'Of course. Anything. Just tell me the truth. Whatever it is, I need to know. Even if it's the worst news, at least it's an answer. At least I can stop wondering.'

'We will,' Anjli promised. 'But first, I need to ask – you found the lighter a few months ago. What else did you do with that information?'

Rothwell looked at her for a long moment.

'I contacted Katarina Kováč.'

'Why Katarina?'

'Because she used to work at the Harrison. Because she'd known D.Q. James, had been there during the time he disappeared. And because I heard she'd been looking to buy the casino, and I thought…' She paused. 'I thought if there were answers anywhere about what happened to Ronnie, they'd be in that building. In the basement, maybe, or in old records. Somewhere. There was an event here for the poker exhibit, she turned up, had a couple too many wines. When Katarina said she thought there might be something hidden in the casino's basement, I saw it as a chance to finally get answers.'

'Did you know Katarina would find a body?'

'No! God, no. I thought maybe we'd find records, or evidence James had been there that night, or something that explained what happened. Maybe Ronnie's wallet, or his phone, or something proving he'd been there. I never imagined—'

She stopped, collecting herself. Declan closed his notebook.

'Mrs Rothwell, we need you to tell us everything Katarina said about her plans for the casino. Everything she mentioned about D.Q. James, about the basement, about what she was looking for.'

Rothwell nodded.

'She was obsessed with the diamonds. That's why she was so keen on the renovation. Said she'd strip the place to the foundations if necessary.'

'Did she mention anyone else who might have known about the diamonds?'

'She said Marek – her ex-husband – used to play high-stakes games at the Harrison. That he'd lost money to James too, though not as much as some of the others. She didn't think he'd have killed James over it, but she said he'd been interested when she mentioned buying the casino.'

She paused.

'And going on Marek's rep? I could believe *he'd* kill.'

13

TAPED CONVERSATIONS

As soon as they returned to Temple Inn and reached Declan's office, he went to the side cabinet, opened up the base, and pulled out a cardboard box filled with microcassettes. They'd been retrieved from Kendis Taylor's estranged husband, now widower, when Declan needed to stop Malcolm Gladwell releasing a tell-all book, finding a smoking gun within the recordings, and had sat on the box since then.

The problem Declan had, however, was that there were so *many* cassettes. In frustration, and for ease of scanning, he upended the box onto his desk, the cassette cases tumbling out in a clatter of noise.

'Jesus, laddie,' Monroe said from the doorway, Anjli beside him, 'if you wanted to make a mess of your office, you could've asked me to come and play as well.'

Declan smiled, already rummaging through the cassettes.

'There was an article from a magazine Kendis had written for on the wall of the museum,' he said. 'I don't know if it was about poker or D.Q. James or anything, but...'

He paused.

'I just have a feeling there might be something there.'

Monroe said nothing. He'd known Declan long enough to know how Declan had felt about Kendis; had even met her frequently before she was murdered, and Anjli had been beside him every step of that journey.

After a moment, Declan triumphantly held up three cassettes.

'All of these are recorded in the same year,' he announced. 'Hopefully one of these might give us some information.'

'Aye, well you can pass them to Cooper to re-listen through,' Monroe suggested. 'Or maybe Billy has some kind of device, as we need to carry on with our interviews.'

'I've got a better idea.' Declan looked out of his office and saw a new arrival placing her bag down. Reaching into his drawer, he pulled out a Dictaphone tape recorder, placing the first of the microcassettes in. With the others in hand, he exited into the main office, where his daughter looked up expectantly.

'You look like you have a job for me,' she observed.

'Actually, yes,' Declan replied, passing her the player and the two spare cassettes. 'Listen through these and see if you can find anything that talks about D.Q. James. There's a chance the interview was recorded before a magazine article was written.'

Jess glanced down at the cassettes, but then she paused as she recognised the handwriting.

'Oh,' she looked back at Declan. 'I'll do my best, Dad.'

'I never expected anything else,' Declan gave a smile. 'Billy! What do we have?'

Working at the monitor station, Billy glanced back at him.

'I've got the Guv an address for Moir,' he replied. 'It's a couple of years old, but it'll do.'

Declan leant over and saw the address.

'Mile End,' he said to Monroe. 'Looks like the apple hasn't fallen far from the tree.'

Monroe glanced at Anjli.

'You worked Mile End for a couple of years before Ford had you removed,' he said. 'Fancy a trip down memory lane?'

Anjli shrugged, a wry smile crossing her face.

'If we're visiting Georgie Moir, I'd hardly call it memory lane,' she replied. 'More like a trip down the sewers.'

'Aye, well, the sewers are where we find the rats,' Monroe said. 'And Moir's a rat who knows things. Come on. Declan, speak to this Marek guy. Rattle his leaves.'

As Monroe walked off, Declan noticed Cooper standing near the stairs – no, more loitering with intent. He walked over, noting her guilty expression.

'You okay?'

'I'm not sure,' Cooper replied. 'It's Morten. He had this guy turn up yesterday, a DC at Paddington. Paul Elliott. Anyway they trained at Hendon together and I got the impression there was something suss going on. This morning Morten went to Guildhall, for something to do with him.'

'Go on,' Declan glanced around, but there was no De'Geer around.

'Well, I was talking to Detective Superintendent Bullman when she passed through... she knows Morten and I, well...'

'We all know you're well, you know.' Declan smiled. 'What did Bullman say?'

'She said she saw Morten at Guildhall, at some hearing

for Paul Elliott. But then DCI Cohen turned up and said it'd been delayed because he'd been stabbed. I'm a little worried about De'Geer being caught up in something.'

Declan nodded. He understood exactly why Cooper was concerned. And if Morten was being pushed by someone in Paddington...

Was this why Cohen passed the case on? He knew his people were corrupt?

'I'll look into it,' he said, patting Cooper on the shoulder. 'You did right in bringing it to me.'

'I feel like I betrayed my boyfriend.'

'Sometimes,' Declan gave a reassuring smile, 'that's the only way to save them.'

MONROE AND ANJLI STOOD OUTSIDE A SIMPLE TWO-UP, TWO-down terraced house to the east of Victoria Park. Monroe hadn't called ahead; he wanted it to be a surprise. And when the door opened, the man who faced him did *not* look happy to see him.

'Afternoon, Georgie.' Monroe smiled. 'Can we come in and have a chat?'

Georgie Moir was a man in his late sixties. Slim, although with the look more of illness than fitness, with thinning grey hair, combed back, slightly greasy or still wet from the shower, perhaps. He had narrow, suspicious eyes and a pug nose that did not fit his face at all. It was almost like someone had placed the wrong pieces onto his body at some point, or he'd got bored and had really bad plastic surgery.

'I told you, Monroe, I'm legit,' he said. 'I don't appreciate...'

'Georgie, I've not seen you for years,' Monroe replied. 'Why in God's name would you think that I'm *hassling* you?'

Georgie paused, and as he looked at Anjli, she saw the slight downturn of his lip, possibly from the stroke he'd had a couple of years earlier.

'Your people have been calling me,' he said.

'And who would that be exactly?'

'Some guy named Walsh. You telling me you don't know a Walsh?'

'Aye, I know a Walsh,' Monroe replied. 'But I can tell you now, I was talking to him no more than twenty minutes ago, and that man didn't have a clue who you were. So, if he's been calling you...'

He trailed off as he realised what was being said.

Someone was using Declan's name to gain information.

'What exactly was he asking?'

'Wanted anything I had on David James,' Moir replied. 'Knew that I'd been working with him back in the day. Knew I'd worked in connection with him after.'

'After what?' Anjli asked.

'After he ran away,' Moir said. 'It was my contacts he used to change his passport.'

Monroe nodded past the doorway.

'I really think we need to have a chat, laddie,' he said, 'because we've not called you by phone any time recently. If someone's speaking to you, there's a different game being played, and you're currently the pawn on the board.'

MOIR'S HOUSE WAS SMALL, HIS LIVING ROOM CLUTTERED WITH pictures on the wall and articles from newspapers, most of which were tell-all pieces or stories about the fall from grace of various celebrities.

'Let me guess, your work?' Anjli asked as she looked around.

'Well, I can't take the credit publicly.' Moir shrugged. 'So, I just keep them. Reminds me of what I've done. I've taken down some real bastards in my time. I've done good work.'

'And yet you've also broken up marriages and caused strife between couples—' Monroe paused as Moir spun to face him, his eyes flashing angrily.

'Every case I took on had a reason,' he spat. 'If I found that someone was having an affair, it's their fault for having the bloody affair, isn't it? Don't start saying that I'm the bad guy here.'

Monroe raised a hand to calm Moir down, and Anjli frowned, noticing the tension between the two men.

'Okay,' she said, 'let's stop this bullshit. What aren't you two telling me?'

Monroe sighed.

'Moir here worked for Johnny Lucas back in the day,' he said, 'as well as half a dozen grubby tabloids. When Emilia disappeared—'

'When she went to work for the spooks, you mean.' Moir smiled.

'When she *disappeared*, there were rumours that I'd killed her.' Monroe shrugged. 'They didn't last long and they weren't really taken seriously. But Mister Moir here dug deep, trying to find something on me. Started going around my childhood areas in Glasgow. Started checking into my past.'

'Oh,' Anjli replied, understanding exactly what Monroe was talking about. He hadn't exactly been an angel as a teenager in Glasgow, and one of the reasons he'd moved down to London was to avenge his brother's death, after he'd been killed by a vicious Glaswegian gangster family.

'Yeah,' Monroe nodded. 'Anyway, it's all over and done with and old news.'

He turned his attention back to Moir.

'You still haven't told us what you were asked.'

'So, I had a call this morning from a guy claiming he was called Detective Inspector Walsh.'

'Well, that's wrong for a start,' Anjli said. 'He's a Detective Chief Inspector now.'

'Oh, I know,' Moir replied. 'I checked into it – it's not as if the guy's kept a low profile over the years. I assumed Monroe had got one of his smaller people out there using Walsh's name to gain a bit of cred. Anyway, he wanted "everything I had on D.Q. James, especially the last few months of his life", so to speak.'

'Did you give it to him?'

'Of course I bloody didn't,' Moir said. 'I told him if he wanted it, he had to come in with a court order or a warrant or whatever it was I thought he needed. Guy sounded young on the phone. Didn't really know what to say. Sounded a little desperate, if you ask me. He was a copper, though.'

'How do you know that?'

'Because he called from a landline,' Moir chuckled, shaking his head. 'Genuinely. What kind of police officer tries to pretend to be someone else and then phones from the Paddington Nick?'

'Paddington?' Monroe looked at Anjli before returning to Moir. 'DCI Cohen of Paddington passed this case to us.'

'Well, he obviously didn't tell everybody in the office.' Moir had sat down now and was continuing to drink a cup of tea. He hadn't offered any to the others. 'Whoever it was didn't know that much.'

Anjli scratched at her chin.

'The last time we really worked with Cohen's lot was on Justice,' she said. 'And back then, DCI Walsh was a DI. Maybe they checked the old notes and thought he still was?'

'Aye,' Monroe said. 'We'll have a chat with DCI Cohen when we're done here.'

He settled back on the sofa, staring across at Georgie Moir.

'So, why don't you tell me what you did for David Quincey James?' he asked.

'I think you'll find, like a doctor or a lawyer, I have client confidentiality.'

'Bullshit,' Monroe snapped. 'Private investigators don't have that luxury. When was the last time you saw D.Q. James?'

Moir smiled.

'Well, that's the question, isn't it?' he said. 'Because let's face it, you *really* want me to say the middle of November, 2009.'

He sipped at his tea as he waited for some kind of response, but neither Monroe nor Anjli humoured him.

'I know there was a body found,' he continued. 'Your fake Declan told me. Claimed it was D.Q. James. Wanted to know what I knew about it.'

'And what do you know about it?' Monroe asked.

'I know it's not David Quincey James.'

'Aye,' Monroe nodded. 'Ronnie Carrigan.'

At the name, Moir's eyebrows rose.

'Ronald? Shit. I didn't think of him, but it makes sense. The duplicates were a bloody stupid idea at the best of times.'

'You knew about his idea?'

'What, to sell his cars for stupid money and have people pretend to be him?' Moir nodded and then sighed. 'So, you want to know about the diamonds, I'm guessing?'

'We'd like to know anything you can give us,' Monroe said in response. 'We've got a dead body that we think was killed because whoever did it believed he was D.Q. James. We have a D.Q. James who, the moment this happened, disappeared off the grid so well that when the body was found, everyone thought it was him.'

Moir nodded at this.

'So, carry on,' Anjli suggested.

'Look, the Triads were really kicking off at the time,' Moir explained. 'Someone like me, I get through the cracks, but I don't make myself known, you know? The last thing I want to do is piss off someone with a meat cleaver. Yeah, that's what they used to play with. Bollocks to knives or anything else. Giant sodding meat cleaver. Terrifying. Anyway. David was bored.'

'What do you mean, bored?' Monroe asked.

'I mean, he'd got tired of doing everything he wanted to do. He'd spent months planning one big revenge, and now it was over. He was looking for something new.'

'This revenge, what was it?'

'Trevor Sullivan,' Moir said. 'He'd wanted to take him down for months. It wasn't just a gaming thing. This was personal. He wanted to remove this guy completely. Destroy his life. Destroy his reputation. There was more here than just rivalry; it was a genuine hatred. He had me go in on Sullivan, find out everything I could. Family, debts, problems with his company. And all that time he would press the buttons, keep Sullivan gambling, make him want to do more, win little games, lose hands so Sullivan thought he had a chance, generally piss him off. And then one night he came in and took everything. Used every piece of information I had to put Sullivan off so badly that he lost the lot.'

'Aye, we've heard,' Monroe said. 'We spoke to Sullivan about it. Carry on.'

'Sullivan was furious about what had happened. Swore he'd kill David if he ever got the chance, and then the next thing I know he's pissed off into a gambling rehab clinic to try to get himself clean. I think it was a last chance to try to save his marriage, but it didn't work.' Moir shrugged. 'Anyway, this had been burning David up for months, and when we knew this was building up to the last act, he wanted something new to start on. At an earlier event, he'd met Jun Ng Kai-lok for the first time. He'd been playing in a big game David had been banned from, but he heard Jun had a bag of diamonds that he would use as a last resort. If he was losing badly, he would push them down and effectively outbid anyone. It's bad playing, but I got the impression Jun didn't care about sportsmanship. So, a month or so before he destroyed Sullivan, David contacted me. Said he really wanted to work out how to get these diamonds; had a great idea of what to do.'

Moir ran his hand through his thinning hair as he placed his teacup down.

'I did what I do. I asked around. I found out the truth. Half a million pounds' worth of diamonds. Jun Ng Kai-lok wheeled them around like gangsters wear their gold. This was his Rolex watch. This was his *"look at me, aren't I big?"* moment. Once David knew what was going on, he started to find ways to niggle at Jun, appearing at events, snapping at his heels.'

Moir shook his head sadly.

'The problem with Jun Ng Kai-lok, he was a wannabe Triad. Kenny Tsang tried to stop it. He could see it happening before it even did. And then David turned up to a poker night that Jun was at and cleaned him out. Once more, took everything I knew. His tells, his wins, his losses. Used it against him. Forced Jun to put the diamonds down on a hand. But he'd fixed the deck, so he won.'

'And how did he do that?'

'I couldn't possibly tell you.' Moir smiled. 'Maybe you should speak to the manager at the time.'

Anjli noted that down.

'What happened then?'

'Then the Triads decided they were going to cut his balls off.' Moir laughed. 'He realised he was in trouble. Started this stupid idea of having doubles driving around. Basically, they were nothing more than meat shields.'

He pursed his lips as he looked away.

'Poor bloody Ronnie Carrigan showed how much they were worth to him. Anyway, he couldn't help himself. He should have stayed hidden, but he hadn't finished with Sullivan yet. So he carried on playing. And during the games he heard Jun had been trying to gain back his money, so couldn't resist turning up after he'd finished off Sullivan and waving those diamonds in Jun's face.'

'Was he always like that?' Anjli asked.

'No, but he'd just had the biggest win of his life and I don't mean the diamonds,' Moir replied. 'He'd removed Sullivan completely, so there was still adrenaline in his system, he hadn't had the "come down" yet when he turned up.'

'So, he was more of a dick than usual?' Monroe asked.

'Exactly. It was strongly suggested that David disappeared, which he did, but two days later he knocks on my door, unshaven, terrified. Tells me that the Triads have stopped playing games now and that he needs to get out of town. Asked me if I could sort him a new passport from the guy who did the last one. I said I could, put him in touch. Never heard back from him again. Gained my payment in the post. Moved on.'

'When you say gained your payment in the post, what do you mean?' Monroe asked.

At the question, Moir laughed, getting up and walking over to his side cabinet. Crouching down, he opened it up and inside Monroe could see a small desk safe, the kind you'd see in hotels. Moir tapped a couple of numbers into the pad and opened it up; inside there were various folders, what looked to be photos, and a little box. Moir pulled the box out, placing it down on the coffee table.

'David didn't like to pay me in cash. He didn't carry it,' he explained. 'Cash for him was gambling money. He didn't like using bank accounts either.'

'Aye, we've heard,' Monroe said. 'He used to put it all into gold.'

'Which, if you look at prices now, was a bloody good idea. Anyway, every time I did a good job, I'd get a gold coin.'

He opened up the box and Monroe could see seven gold pieces.

'Arr.' He smiled. 'Pirate booty.'

Anjli picked up one coin, looking at it.

'It's not a Britannia,' she said. 'That's usually what you see, because of the lack of capital gains tax.'

'No, these are Mexican fifty-peso coins,' Moir said, and there was an almost proud tone to his voice. 'They're slightly more than a Britannia with one-point-two ounces.'

'And you've never wanted to spend them?'

'Oh, this is all I've got left,' Moir replied. 'Over the years, I probably got twenty or thirty of these, and a watch. Recently, with the prices going up, I've been selling them off. As your friend there said, there's no capital gains tax, so I just wander into a gold merchant in London and sell them when I need a bit of extra money. Right now? One of these is around three and a half grand.'

Monroe took the coin from Anjli, hefting it in his hand. The theatricality of the gold coin matched D.Q. James exactly.

'I'll need to take one of these as evidence,' he said, holding the coin up.

Moir's eyes narrowed suspiciously.

'Evidence of what, exactly?'

'Evidence that D.Q. James paid you with gold,' Monroe replied evenly. 'Part of establishing his financial patterns, his methods. Standard procedure.'

'Bollocks to that,' Moir said, reaching for the box. 'You're Scottish. I know how you lot work. You'll pocket that and I'll never see it again.'

Monroe raised an eyebrow.

'Are you suggesting I'd steal evidence, Georgie?'

'I'm suggesting you're a Scotsman who sees a piece of gold and suddenly finds himself with sticky fingers,' Moir said. 'No offence, but I know your type.'

'My type?' Monroe's voice carried a dangerous edge now.

'Aye, your type,' Moir said, mimicking Monroe's accent poorly. 'The kind who'd nick a coin worth three grand and claim it got lost in evidence. I want a receipt. Signed. Dated. With your badge number on it.'

Anjli bit back a smile as Monroe's jaw tightened.

'You'll get your receipt, laddie,' Monroe said, the word "laddie" sounding particularly Scottish and particularly threatening. 'And when this case is closed, you'll get your coin back. Assuming, of course, that it's not needed for prosecution.'

'Prosecution of who? David's probably dead by now or hiding in a caravan in the Midwest.'

'Prosecution of whoever killed Ronald Carrigan, then,' Monroe said, slipping the coin into an evidence bag he'd pulled from his jacket. 'Or did you forget that's why we're here?'

Moir watched the coin disappear into Monroe's pocket with the expression of a man watching his wallet being stolen.

'I want that receipt before you leave,' he muttered.

'You'll get it,' Monroe assured him, though the smile on his face suggested he was enjoying Moir's discomfort. But then something that Moir said earlier made him pause, and he turned his attention back to the conversation.

'You mentioned you put him in touch with a forger,' he said. 'A man who was able to sort his passport out?'

'Yeah, I can give you the name. I haven't spoken to the guy for years. I don't even know if he's in the business any more.'

'That's not what I'm curious about,' Monroe said, placing the other coins back in the box. 'You mentioned you'd done it *before*.'

'Oh, sure. That's how we met,' Moir explained. 'D.Q. James needed a passport in his name so he could travel back and forth from America. We're talking five or six years earlier. This is like 2002, 2003, maybe.'

'I don't understand,' Monroe frowned. 'Everything we've heard said he was over in America for years before that.'

'He was.' Moir grinned. 'But he wasn't D.Q. James back then.'

'What name was he using then?' Anjli looked up from her notebook.

'That I don't know,' Moir replied. 'You'd have to ask the guy who put me in touch with him back then. Your friend and mine; Johnny Lucas.'

14

THE EX-HUSBAND

Marek Kováč had an office just off Liverpool Street, and when Declan arrived he realised it was less of an office and more of an entire floor. The man was minted, but whether or not he still gambled, however, was up for debate.

The receptionist nodded as he arrived, motioning for him to take a seat. And even though he'd explained who he was, showed his warrant card and expressed the urgency of the situation, there seemed to be no urgency in bringing him in to talk to Marek himself. If anything, he felt he was being given the runaround. Still, it gave him a chance to go through his messages, including one from Monroe who was asking if he'd been calling George Moir recently. Declan replied in the negative, but no explanation for the question came.

Eventually, however, the door opened, and Declan rose, stopping as he saw who was leaving.

Kenny Tsang stared in horror at Declan.

'What are you doing here?' he demanded.

'I think the question's more, what are *you* doing here,

Kenny?' Declan countered. 'It wouldn't be to do with the body that was found, would it?'

At least Kenny had the decency to look embarrassed as he hurried past and headed out through the main glass entrance. Declan glanced back at the receptionist who, if she'd noticed the confrontation, hadn't bothered paying much attention to it.

'He'll see you now,' she murmured.

Declan entered the office to find Marek Kováč sitting behind a modernist chrome and glass desk with full-length windows behind him that looked out across London. It was a fifth-floor office, so the view was quite good, but it was marred by cranes and building works, although most of London had that these days. Marek himself was in his sixties, broad-shouldered and thick through the chest, with greying hair swept back from a weathered, olive-toned face, a face that didn't match the surname. Deep-set eyes, a strong nose, and a kind of rugged, Javier Bardem look that made people notice – and think twice before crossing him.

'DCI Walsh,' Marek said with a smile. 'Are you here to tell me what my ex-wife's doing?'

'In part,' Declan replied. 'I'm also here to ask about your movements fifteen years ago.'

'Oh good.' Marek smiled, seemingly enjoying the conversation. 'Although I have to say I was kind of expecting this. You'd have noticed my previous meeting.'

'I'm guessing Kenny gave you a big heads-up,' Declan surmised.

'Kenny and I have worked together often over the years,' Marek elaborated. 'I put my money into a lot of various enterprises; some work, some don't. We've had a few wins over time.'

'I heard you like to invest in strange things,' Declan stated, sitting down in the chair facing him. 'SpinJack, for example.'

'Yes, Thomas also mentioned that you'd spoken to him.' Marek's accent was clipped, British, even though the name didn't match. Declan wondered whether this was partly because of his education, as he gave the impression of a man who'd spent years in a higher echelon of society.

'Ask your questions. I've got nothing to hide,' Marek offered.

'Did you kill D.Q. James?'

'No,' Marek stated flatly. 'That body has nothing to do with me.'

Declan went to ask if Marek had a problem with Ronnie Carrigan and then paused.

That body. Not "the" body or "James's" body.

'Hold on one second,' he said, pulling out his phone and sending a quick message to Billy.

> Check whether anyone knows the found body was Carrigan, not James. Timeline important.

'What about Ronnie Carrigan?' he now asked.

'Carrigan?' Marek scoffed, then shrugged. 'Christ, that's a name from the past. He was just a barman. I never really dealt with him.'

Declan noted it down, aware that there was every chance this was just something said to deflect the conversation.

'Let's talk about D.Q. James, then,' he said. 'You played against him.'

'Everyone played against him,' Marek leant back in his

chair. 'He was at every high-stakes game in London for about three years. Hard to avoid the man.'

'And you lost to him.'

'I lost to a lot of people. That's poker. Sometimes you're the winner, sometimes you're the one funding everyone else's night.'

'Thomas Greaves said you had a beef with James. That you could've killed him.'

Marek's smile didn't falter, but something shifted in his eyes.

'Thomas has a habit of exaggerating. Makes his boring life seem more interesting.' He stood and walked to the window. 'Did I dislike D.Q. James? Absolutely. The man was a psychological bully who enjoyed destroying people at the table. Did I want him dead? No more than any other player who'd lost to him.'

'How much did you lose?'

'To James specifically? Maybe seventy, eighty thousand over the years. Not enough to bankrupt me, but enough to sting. Especially the way he did it.'

'How *did* he do it?'

Marek turned back from the window.

'He researched me. Used some East End gutter-dweller investigator, found out about business troubles I was having with a property development in Prague. Started needling me about it during a game, making jokes about Eastern European corruption, about whether I'd bribed the right officials. Made jokes that I was a spy.'

'Were you a spy?' Declan asked. 'We heard there were more than profits being passed around those games.'

'Spy is such a dirty word,' Marek replied with no further explanation. 'But James persisted with his spurious tales. Got so far under my skin I played emotionally instead of logically. Lost thirty grand in one night because I was trying to prove something to a man wearing a bloody cowboy hat.'

'When was this?'

'Mid 2009. Right before everything kicked off with the Chinese and he started fixating on sparkly things.'

'You knew about the diamonds?'

'Everyone knew about the diamonds,' Marek said. 'James made sure of it. Bragged about outsmarting the Triads, waved those stones around like trophies. Stupid thing to do, really. You don't humiliate people like that and expect to walk away clean.'

Declan wrote this down.

'Where were you on November fifteenth, 2009?'

'No idea. That was fifteen years ago.'

'Think harder.'

Marek returned to his desk, pulling out his phone and tapping at it.

'I keep all my old calendars backed up. Business habit – never know when you'll need to verify where you were.' He scrolled through. 'November fifteenth, 2009... I was in Vienna. Three-day trip for a development project, back on the seventeenth. Hotel receipts, flight records, meeting notes – all documented.'

'Can you send those to me?'

'Of course. Give me your email.'

Declan passed over a card. Marek photographed it with his phone.

'You'll have them within the hour.' He sat back down. 'I assume you've already worked out why Katarina bought the Harrison Casino?'

'Why don't you tell me?'

'Because she thinks the diamonds are still there,' Marek said simply. 'She became obsessed with them after James disappeared. Convinced herself he'd hidden them somewhere in the casino before he died or ran. When the building came up for sale, she saw her chance.'

'You didn't try to stop her?'

'We were divorced by then. What she does with her money isn't my concern, even if it used to be my bloody money. Besides, I told her it was a terrible investment even without the diamond hunting. The housing market's one cough away from a collapse and there's already three spas down that street.'

'But you're still in contact with her.'

'Occasionally. Business matters, mostly. The divorce was relatively amicable, considering.' Marek's expression hardened slightly. 'Though I imagine that's about to change, now you've found a body in her basement.'

'Did Katarina ever mention knowing where the body might be?'

'No. But she did mention targeting that specific wall in the basement two weeks ago. Said something about it being added later, not part of the original construction. She'd studied the building plans obsessively before buying, but I think her contractor gave her the nod.'

Declan made a note of this. Then a name came to mind, a Paddington copper Cooper had mentioned.

'What about Paul Elliott? Know that name?'

Marek's face remained neutral, but Declan caught the briefest hesitation.

'Should I?'

'Police officer. Works for DCI Cohen at Paddington. Might have gambling debts.'

'I don't know every gambler in London, Detective. If he plays in private games, I might have seen him around, but the name doesn't ring bells.'

'What about the private games? You still play?'

'Occasionally. Lower stakes these days. I've got too much legitimate business to risk the kind of money I used to throw around.' Marek leant forward. 'Is there anything else? I have a meeting in five minutes.'

'Just one more thing,' Declan said. 'Kenny Tsang. What was he doing here today?'

'Business discussion. As I said, Kenny's connected to several profitable ventures in Chinatown. I'm always looking for investment opportunities.'

'Nothing to do with D.Q. James or the Harrison Casino?'

'Everything's connected in London, Detective.' Marek smiled. 'But no, we didn't discuss your murder case. Though I imagine Kenny's feeling rather exposed right now, given his Wong Sei persona has been revealed. That can't be good for business.'

'You knew?'

Marek chuckled.

'Poor sod genuinely thought nobody knew, but it's been the worst kept secret in Soho for the last ten years.'

Declan stood.

'I'll need you to come to Temple Inn for a formal statement. Tomorrow afternoon?'

'I'll have my solicitor arrange it.' Marek stood as well, extending his hand. 'For what it's worth, I hope you catch whoever killed D.Q. James. Not because I liked the man, but because whoever did it let the body sit there for fifteen years. That takes a particular kind of cold bastard.'

As they shook hands, Declan studied Marek's face. The

man was polished, professional, seemingly cooperative. But something about the timing bothered him. Kenny Tsang visiting just before Declan arrived. Marek's immediate knowledge of the case details. The convenience of having documented alibis from fifteen years ago, the lack of any confirmation on whether he'd conducted any espionage there and the mention of the body being James's, while being more nascent earlier on in the conversation.

'One last question,' Declan said at the door. 'We've kept the story under wraps right now, so was it Kenny who told you we'd found a body at the Harrison?'

Marek's smile didn't waver.

'Katarina called me. She called yesterday, quite upset.'

'So, you spoke to her two weeks ago and yesterday.' Declan noted this. 'Doesn't sound that "occasional".'

'Horses for courses.' Marek smiled. 'How often do you speak to your ex-wife?'

At the question, Declan froze.

'I looked you up,' Marek continued. 'Nothing sinister. Just noticed we had things in common.'

'I didn't give my wife millions of pounds.' Declan smiled darkly. 'So, I'm not sure how common these things are. I'll be in touch.'

Walking out of Marek Kováč's office, Declan considered what he'd just been told. On paper, Marek sounded as if he was simply caught in the same gravity as the others, someone who had faced D.Q. James in the past and lost money but not enough to kill over. He had alibis, business documentation, a seemingly reasonable explanation for everything.

But there was something more there.

It wasn't just that Katarina, his ex-wife, had now bought the casino. It wasn't that he'd paid a high five-figure advance to Thomas Greaves for a roulette–blackjack game that was never going to make him money.

It was the way Kenny Tsang had looked when Declan caught him leaving.

The way Marek had possibly known about the actual body's identity before it was public knowledge.

The way everything was just a little too neat, a little too prepared.

Declan couldn't quite put a finger on it, but his instincts were screaming that Marek Kováč knew considerably more than he was saying.

As he reached the upstairs lobby and the elevator doors opened, he stopped. In front of him was a group of men, Chinese, and when they saw Declan, they stepped back in surprise. For a moment, Declan wondered if these were the bodyguards of Kenny Tsang, and perhaps Kenny had waited around to speak to him, but the leader, the only man who didn't flinch back when the doors opened, nodded.

'You are DCI Walsh,' he murmured.

'And you're blocking my way,' Declan replied. He'd had enough by now, and didn't really want to kick off an argument, but the tone was calm, arrogant, like Declan should know him as well. He was older than the others but not by much, maybe in his forties, slick suit, short black hair spiked out in a "tussled" way. The other men didn't step aside to let him pass; instead, as he entered they stayed in the elevator, surrounding him. Now with six people in the carriage – Declan, the leader and the four lieutenants – things felt a little crowded.

'We've never met,' the leader observed, 'although you've stepped on my turf many times. My name is—'

'Jun Ng Kai-lok,' Declan replied. 'Or do you want to be called Ironthread?'

The leader's eyes widened slightly.

'How do you know?' he asked.

'Calculated guess. You're going to see Marek. You've waited until Kenny Tsang wasn't around. You have bodyguards, and you know me more than I know you,' Declan replied. 'And the only Triad leader I don't seem to know is this mysterious Ironthread.'

Jun moved closer now, uncomfortable in the lift.

'You should leave these things well alone,' he said gently, almost like a lover's whisper. 'You should walk away and be grateful that you still can.'

'Are you threatening an officer of the law?'

'I don't threaten, Declan,' Jun returned softly. 'I state facts.'

'If you're stating facts, you can call me by my title,' Declan countered. 'Detective Chief Inspector Walsh.'

'But we're just two men having a conversation, aren't we?' Jun raised an eyebrow. 'Nothing more. And I'm giving you a friendly warning, a fact, that to continue down this line will get in the way of my family regaining their diamonds.'

'How do you even know the diamonds are still around?' Declan asked.

Jun Ng Kai-lok paused, thrown by the question.

'What do you mean?'

'I mean, it's been fifteen years,' Declan said. 'They could've been split up, sold around the world by now. Half a million in diamonds doesn't just sit in a basement waiting to be found.'

He trailed off as he noticed the expression that Jun had on his face was matched now by his lieutenants.

'You've been told something different, haven't you?' he pressed.

Jun looked at his men and they shifted slightly – Declan wondered if they were actually about to try to attack an officer of the law in the middle of a crowded elevator. Visions of that *Captain America* film where the same thing happened came to mind, but in this situation, he didn't have a magic shield that could bounce off walls and defy physics.

One of the men reached into his pocket and Declan saw the bulge of what looked to be a weapon. Quickly, he moved in, grabbing the arm, yanking it free, seeing it held a folding knife. This seemed to be a tacit invitation for the others to react, but the space was tight, and Declan wasn't the simple police officer they thought he was. He was ex-military police. His military years had been spent tracking down and arresting people who'd been trained how to kill. He didn't need to use those skills as much these days, but Declan still knew how to take aspects of Krav Maga, judo, karate, and a dozen other counter-insurgency fighting styles and use them to his advantage, especially in close quarters.

The scuffle took seconds: a sharp strike to disable the knife hand, a knee to the solar plexus of a second attacker, and a twist that sent the third stumbling into his companions. Declan backed into the corner, his extendable baton now out and ready.

'This is a misunderstanding,' Jun warned, looking at the others. 'They reacted. You started this.'

Declan looked at the men, all of whom were nursing minor injuries and glaring at him.

'That knife's illegal.'

'Will you arrest him for it?' Jun's tone was almost incredulous.

'I'm leaving now,' Declan stated. 'Open the door.'

The door was opened and, using the man he'd grabbed as a shield, Declan moved around, stepping outside until he was facing Jun.

'I'd like you to come and have a chat with us at Temple Inn,' Declan said evenly. 'Explain to me exactly how you think the diamonds still exist.'

'I assumed you knew. Your colleagues know.'

'My colleagues?'

'Cohen. The DCI at Paddington.'

Declan started to understand now.

'You think I work for Paddington,' he said.

'Well, you're working with them on this case.'

'I think you need to check your information,' Declan said, pushing the man he'd used as a shield back inside. 'DCI Cohen passed this case to us at Temple Inn. I don't work for him.'

Jun's expression shifted to something between anger and confusion.

'Then you don't know about the game being set up?'

'What poker game?'

'The one being set up at the Harrison,' Jun said, his voice tight with frustration. 'The one where we were supposed to learn everything about what happened to our diamonds.'

The elevator door closed.

'Wait,' Declan said, but Jun made no move to stop it.

'Be careful, Detective Chief Inspector,' Jun called as the doors shut. 'Someone's playing a much bigger game than you realise.'

The doors now closed, the elevator headed upwards, and Declan stood in the downstairs lobby, stretching as the adrenaline drained from his system. Jun Ng Kai-lok believed there was a poker game happening at the Harrison Casino, a game where the diamonds would be revealed. Which meant somebody was setting up an elaborate trap or con, and somehow DCI Cohen at Paddington was involved.

In addition to this, Cohen was apparently telling people that Declan was under him, which explained the fake phone call to Georgie Moir using Declan's name that Monroe had texted him about.

Things were moving quicker than Declan had expected.

He pulled out his phone and called Monroe.

'We've got a problem,' he said when Monroe answered. 'DCI Cohen's running a parallel operation, and Jun Ng Kai-lok thinks there's a poker game being set up at the Harrison Casino. Someone's playing us, and I think they've been playing us from the start.'

15

FINDERS FEE

Cooper had been checking through property records when the call came from the desk sergeant at Charing Cross.

'We've got someone you might be interested in,' he murmured down the line. 'Apparently he's one of the contractors you'd spoken to in relation to a dead body found in a casino? Does that mean anything, or is he just pissed?'

'I can take that,' Cooper replied. 'Go on.'

'Well, let's just say he had a very liquid lunch today. Managed to cause himself some trouble and now he's begging to speak to somebody connected to the case because he wants to make a deal.'

'He wants to make a deal?' Cooper was surprised at the statement.

'Yeah. He seems to think he's in major trouble and unless he cuts himself a deal he's going down for a while.' The desk sergeant started laughing. 'I did mention he was utterly pissed, right?'

'What's he arrested for?'

'Just causing an affray, nothing more. Usually we just let them sleep it off and tell them to bugger off, but he's paranoid he's gonna be dumped in prison and someone'll "take him out". His own words, too. I think he's watched too many movies.'

'What's his name?'

'Michael Baker,' the desk sergeant replied. 'Says he's known as Mickey to his friends.'

'I'll come and pick him up.' Cooper smiled. 'Let's see what deal he wants to give us.'

MICHAEL BAKER, OR RATHER MICKEY THE CONTRACTOR, hunched over the desk. When Cooper had arrived, the desk sergeant she'd spoken to had pointed out there was no point even taking him elsewhere, allowing her to sit down with Mickey in an empty interview room with a cup of lukewarm tea while he sobered up.

'So, what do you want to tell me, Mickey?' Cooper asked, giving her best *I'm-on-your-side* smile.

Mickey looked up and his eyes were haunted.

'I keep seeing the body,' he whispered. 'Whenever I shut my eyes, it's still there. I didn't sign up to see a body.'

'No one ever does,' Cooper replied. 'So, what do you want to tell us?'

'It wasn't an accident.'

'Accident? What wasn't an accident?'

'Finding the body.' Mickey shuffled on his chair, uncomfortable about what he was saying. 'Look, they're my friends, okay? I've worked with them every day, but I can't go to prison.'

'I totally understand,' Cooper responded, resisting hard the urge to tell him that he *wouldn't* be going to prison. She'd now found out the extent of his affray, and in her experience, she reckoned an apology to a shop owner and offering to clean up the vomit he'd left all over the floor seemed to be the extent of what he'd need to do.

This, however, wasn't going to be said right now.

Mickey was almost in tears and his head kept doing that weird swirly motion that drunks had when they were trying to focus, but the world kept spinning out of reach.

'Dave took the wall down,' he muttered, 'but it wasn't because it was our job, it was because Terry had been told there was something behind there worth getting.'

'What do you mean?'

'I don't know the full story, because Terry wouldn't tell me, but he gave us the impression he'd spoken to somebody who'd told him about it, someone he knew, probably from his gym,' Mickey explained, the words now tumbling out as he gave his confession. 'Anyway, they mentioned there was a chance that there were diamonds or something hidden behind the wall. Terry had looked into the casino when we took the job and he knew that there was a story there, some gambler losing money, disappearing. His contact had said that the wall had been built up to hide the treasures. He'd spoken to the owner—'

'Katarina Kováč?'

'Kováč? Yeah, I think that was the name. He said what he'd heard and they told him that if he took it out he could keep half.'

'This was fine with Terry?'

'He wasn't happy about this,' Mickey muttered. 'Muttered he should've just kept quiet and claimed it was an accident, because he now had to pay us percentages because we knew about it too.'

'He was unhappy at paying you?'

Mickey nodded.

'He was trying to convince us to go off to lunch. I think the plan was for him to go through the wall on his own. Then, when we got back, he'd just inform us that there was an empty space behind the wall, and there'd be sod all to see because he'd have already removed whatever gold and diamonds and whatever was hidden there. But we worked it out something was going on, and so he had to basically pay us a percentage of whatever we found, and then ten per cent to this guy in the gym—'

'In the gym?'

'Yeah, the guy who told him about it in the first place.'

Cooper noted this down.

'So, let me get this right,' she said, making sure that she'd got the information correct. 'Terry, your foreman, was told by someone in his gym that there was a false wall in the basement of the Harrison Casino that, when punched through, would provide treasure – of which this contact in the gym wanted ten per cent of what was found. Your client found out and demanded fifty per cent, and then when you found out, you all demanded a percentage as well...'

There was a snore. Mickey had fallen asleep.

'Mickey!'

Jerking awake, Mickey nodded, although Cooper wasn't a hundred per cent sure he knew what he was nodding to.

'We weren't told there was a body,' was his only comment.

'I bet you weren't,' Cooper observed. 'Tell me, do you know what gym your boss goes to?'

'I don't know the branch, but I know it's somewhere in London and called *Flex-U-Fit*, if that helps,' Mickey muttered.

'Actually,' Cooper said, noting this down in her book, 'that means a lot. So, let's talk about the deal.'

JOHNNY LUCAS WASN'T AT THE BOXING CLUB WHEN MONROE and Anjli found him. He was holding court at the *Angel & Crown Pub* on the Roman Road, near Globe Town. Anjli had been there before, back when Johnny still had the Jackie persona. In fact, she'd been witness to Johnny turning into Jackie in the middle of a conversation. At the time it'd had been a traditional pub with a blue and white, recently painted frontage, but this had now been replaced by a blue and almost orange colour scheme, with the traditional copperplate font pub name replaced by a funky style in orange and red. In fact, if it hadn't been a particularly recognisable corner pub, Anjli would have been convinced she was at the wrong place.

He was having a late lunch, but it felt more that he was holding court, something that Monroe knew Johnny had started getting back into since leaving Westminster.

The pub was seventies themed, and a complete change from the older look, and Anjli couldn't help noticing the opening hours on the door stating that the pub wouldn't be open until four p.m.

Obviously Johnny kept different rules.

'Have you come for more information?' Johnny grinned, as he demolished a plate of light bites. 'Want one? They're deep-fried mac and cheese arancini balls. Not quite the old fare, but you move with the times.'

'Why the bloody hell are you here?' Monroe looked horrified at the interior. 'I mean, I know you did business here for years, but Christ, man, what if someone takes a photo of you? I'd die of embarrassment.'

'You're just a fossil.' Johnny grinned. 'This is exciting, new, funky even.'

'You're not Bethnal Green and Bow's MP any more,' Monroe replied sullenly. 'You're allowed to dislike things.'

Pete, Johnny's trainer but also right-hand man, looked suspicious and frowned.

'They're unhappy, boss,' he muttered.

'Of course they are, they're always bloody unhappy.' Johnny smiled. 'You could've called, Alex, I would've come to you.'

'Aye, well, we wanted to have a quicker chat with you that wasn't on your timescale,' Monroe replied, looking around. 'That said, maybe we should have. Would you like to explain to me why a private eye who I know you worked with on a regular basis also worked with D.Q. James?'

Johnny sighed, wiping his mouth with a paper napkin.

'Look,' he replied, 'I've said to you before, the Jackie side of me, it's fuzzy. And sometimes there are things that I did that I simply don't remember.'

'Aye, and this is conveniently one of those times, I'm guessing.'

'There was a kid who I worked with,' Johnny said. 'We're talking back in the day, you know, when Jackie was here and in the flesh. I didn't really pay much attention to him, but Jackie had a soft spot for the kid's mum. She'd been screwed around, husband had cheated on her, beaten the kids. Jackie took that kind of thing personally.'

'Aye, and where is this story going?'

'Anyway, the older of the two boys wanted to be a boxer,' Johnny ignored the interruption. 'Would come by the gym every now and then. This was when we were still quite new in the area, having just bought the boxing club. Jackie saw nothing in him, didn't think there was enough passion, but this kid? He knew how to out-think his opponent. Very good at the psychological side. He could have any boxer facing him within a minute convinced he was going to lose.'

Johnny chuckled to himself.

'The problem was, once they started fighting that all disappeared, because he didn't have the skills to match what he was saying, and had the shit smacked out of him on a regular basis.'

'So, this kid, the expert in psychological warfare... Are you telling us that Jackie Lucas taught him how to box?' Anjli asked.

'No.' Johnny shook his head. 'I'm not. I'm telling you that my brother took this kid under his wing and taught him how to play *poker*.'

He held a finger up to pause Anjli's next question.

'No, not D.Q. James, before you ask. A boy by the name of Trevor Sullivan.'

Monroe straightened at the name.

'The rival,' he said. 'The one who lost everything.'

'Yeah.' Johnny nodded. 'That's the exact one.'

'Tell me about the fake passport.' Monroe felt he already knew where this was going, but he still asked the question. 'Moir was led to a forger, someone who could help D.Q. James disappear.'

Johnny nodded.

'I only put it together about an hour ago,' he said. 'Georgie contacted me earlier today, mentioned he'd had someone contact him claiming to be Declan Walsh. And before you carry on at me, I was going to contact you and let you know that someone's pretending to be Declan.'

'Aye. We'll be getting to that in a minute,' Monroe snapped. 'Carry on.'

'D.Q. James is like a pen name,' Johnny said. 'I always knew that, but I never knew what the original name was. I assumed it was David something. Or maybe James was his first name and he liked it as a surname. Perhaps he'd decided to do that thing where you pick your first dog and your mother's maiden name.'

'That's your porn star name,' Monroe added.

'Maybe he decided he liked that for his poker name.' Johnny shrugged. 'All I know is that it's not his real name and that my guy helped him get a passport for it.'

He picked up a paper napkin and scribbled on it, passing it across.

'Finch. That's the name of the forger,' he said. 'Please be aware, I don't deal with him because I would never deal with criminal types any more. But if you tell him I sent you, he'll give you the name. I never asked.'

'Bullshit,' Monroe snapped. 'You mightn't have known when we first spoke about this, but you would've made it your business to learn about it. So, how about you stop us running around, which, let's be honest, is purely so you can gain yourself some time, and just tell us what we need to know. What I think I already know.'

'And what do you think you already know?'

'This Trevor Sullivan. You said *kids* and *boys*, so he had a brother. What was *his* name?'

'I can't recall.'

'Don't give me this stupid bloody runaround, Johnny!'

Johnny sighed.

'Darren,' he admitted. 'Darren Sullivan.'

'Younger or older?'

'Younger.'

'And what happened to Darren Sullivan?'

Johnny paused, looked as if he was going to try to change the subject... and then sighed.

'Parents split up when they were kids. This was before we really got to know them. Jackie had taken Trevor under his wing and was teaching him poker. The brother turned up here and there. I couldn't tell you if he was good or bad at it, I was too busy actually doing my job. Had a bit of a concern at the time that Jackie was either feeling paternal or he had a thing for little kids.'

Johnny shuddered.

'Of course, there's always the option that he might've been the dad. He did get around. Either way, when the family quit, the mum? she went to America. Rejoined her family. Younger son went with her. Older son stayed in London with the abusive dad. Never understood why.'

'Do you remember where she went?'

'I don't remember anything. Did you not listen to what I was saying?' Johnny muttered. 'This was Jackie's game. You want to ask Jackie, go get yourself a Ouija board. But, I can tell you now, if that younger brother had the same skill set as his older brother did...'

He shrugged.

'I can't give you anything more. I simply don't know.'

'You've given us enough,' Monroe said. 'I'll leave you to your weird fried ball things.'

'You should hang around.' Johnny grinned. 'I'm having a bacon jam double smash burger next.'

'You're just saying random words at me now,' Monroe muttered as he walked back to the main door. 'I'm heading back to the station. Maybe I'll get a truffle-dusted waffle sausage melt on the way. Or perhaps a maple-bacon kimchi croissant wrap.'

'Everyone's a bloody food critic,' Johnny shouted mournfully after them.

As they walked back to Anjli's car, Monroe was spitting feathers in anger.

'We're being led by our bloody noses,' he growled as he spun and glared at her. 'D.Q. James isn't dead. He's not even bloody D.Q. James. We were hired to sort out a body, to solve a murder. And now we're not only bouncing around, but we're finding that Paddington are actively asking questions about us on the same thing. What the bloody hell is going on here?'

He was already dialling a number as he spoke, not expecting Anjli to answer.

'Billy, it's Monroe. I need you to do me something. Look into Trevor Sullivan. Find out who his parents were. Find out his mother's name. Find out where she went to live. And find out everything you can about his younger brother, Darren.'

Disconnecting the call, he returned his attention to Anjli, as she was opening the driver's side and climbing in.

'If D.Q. James turns out to be Darren Sullivan,' she murmured, 'that makes his game against Trevor way more personal.'

'Aye, it does,' Monroe nodded. 'And it also means that we were lied to when we spoke to Mister Sullivan himself.'

He checked his watch.

'Gather the chickens, lassie. I'm done playing around. And stop off at a service station on the way back. I'm hungry for a wee toffee scotch egg sundae right now.'

16

RSVP

Richard Statham was watching some baking show on daytime television when his front doorbell rang. However, by the time he reached it and opened it, whoever had pressed it had gone.

They had, however, placed a small envelope on the floor.

Picking it up, Richard glanced around, unable to see anyone. He stepped back into his house and closed the door before opening the envelope – inside was a single mahjong piece. It wasn't specially designed; it was mass-produced, but Richard understood the significance. The card itself looked impressive but was likely knocked off quickly on a card printer.

You are invited to attend the Harrison Casino's memorial poker game. Play one last hand in memory of D.Q. James. Thursday, ten p.m.

At the bottom was a signature – or at least one of those fake signatures you can buy online that makes your name look really cool – of Katarina Kováč. Richard read the card three times before placing it down. Thursday was tomorrow night. For somebody who'd done her best to remove anything to do with the casino, it sounded like Katarina had changed her mind. Nostalgia was one thing, but he wasn't an idiot. If she wanted him there, it was because she wanted people who remembered D.Q. James. And by that, he knew damn well what she wanted – people who remembered where the gold was, where the diamonds were, and maybe even where D.Q. himself was.

They wanted to know the answers to the secrets.

At the bottom was an email with the letters *RSVP* next to it. Richard picked up his phone. He didn't bother replying via email. Instead, he sent three words by text message.

I'll be there.

This done, he returned to the television, but his mind wasn't on the show any more. This would be the first time in years that he'd be attending as a guest rather than as an employee, and he wondered what he'd make of it. Absently, he stroked his wrist where, until a couple of months ago, a Patek Philippe Grand Complication watch had rested. He'd lied to the police, he knew exactly where that watch was, and he hadn't been given it by the museum. He had suggested to them they buy the others when they'd been found; that was true. But the Patek Philippe watch he wore had been his for over a decade, given to him the night that D.Q. James cheated the Triad out of half a million.

Turning off the television, he stared blankly at the wall.

Did she know? Did she know who the body really was?

And did she understand – had she been told – why Ronnie Carrigan had to die?

He shuddered, leant forwards and began to sob into his hands. He'd always hoped he'd run the clock out before it came to light but now it seemed that, by the weekend, everything would change.

THOMAS GREAVES WAS FINISHING A PITCH AT THE BOOTH AS THE Excel event slowly came to a close, convincing yet another group of mildly unimpressed attendees about the joys of *SpinJack*. If he was being honest, it had gone better than he'd expected; the biggest problem people had was the introduction of randomness into a game of skill as far as they were concerned. He didn't have the heart to tell them that Blackjack was one of those games where, unless you could count the cards or had a system, the house would *always* win. At least this way, the randomness gave you a fighting chance.

Kate, the "booth babe" they'd hired to be beside him – who, in fairness, was actually quite a nice person – tapped him on the shoulder.

'While you were talking, someone left this for you,' she said, passing him an envelope.

'Did you see who it was?'

'Woman, long hair, looked like money. Hopefully it's an offer.'

Thomas didn't think that it would be, but that someone had passed him anything was an optimistic sign. He opened the letter and pulled the cardstock out, reading it. Attached to it was a post-it note where, in a familiar handwriting script, read the words:

Fancy a night at your old job? I need a croupier for a very special game. Five per cent of all takings for one night's work. Ten p.m. tomorrow.

Pulling the note off, he read the card and smiled when he saw Katarina's artificial signature that looked nothing like the scribbled mess on the post-it note. He placed it back into the envelope and looked back at Kate.

'It's not quite the message we were hoping for,' he remarked. 'But it is money. And interestingly, it's connected to SpinJack.'

Kate smiled.

'How so?'

'You know the guy who gave you the job? Marek? Well, this is a party his ex-wife is running. And if it all goes well, there could be a lot of money coming our way.'

He realised he'd said, 'our way', but Kate had already walked off. She was paid by the hour on a three-day contract, and the moment she'd heard that it was something to do with the guy who'd hired her, she'd lost all interest. She was, after all, based on commission, and this wouldn't be anything she could make money from.

Greaves read the card once more, folded it, and was about to toss the envelope aside when he realised there was something else in it. Dropping it into his hand, he stared at the mahjong piece and then started to laugh. If Katarina thought she was being clever, she hadn't realised just how insulting she was being. By throwing a random mahjong piece in, she was proving she had no idea what the pieces actually meant.

Greaves did, however. Greaves remembered very clearly what those mahjong pieces had meant and what had happened the night that somebody had thought it was clever to make their own.

TREVOR SULLIVAN HAD FINISHED HIS SHIFT AT *FLEX-U-FIT* AND was leaving for the day, walking out into the car park when he noticed the expensive-looking Mercedes with the driver inside. This wasn't really a chauffeur-driven area, if he was being brutally honest. The entire infrastructure was tired and could do with an injection of cash, but to many of the locals, an injection of cash meant taking someone at knifepoint and demanding their money.

Trevor didn't look like money. Trevor's car was battered and old. He had no worries about anybody trying to take anything from him, and he didn't have any savings in banks.

Nobody would give him credit. Not that he asked.

But he knew somehow, following on from the detectives turning up yesterday and asking him about D.Q. James, that this car was there for him.

He walked towards it and had gained four steps before the door opened and Katarina Kováč emerged. She paused, looking at him.

'I came in,' she said. 'I asked for you. They said you were finishing in five minutes and that I might as well wait here.'

Trevor had paused, keeping his distance.

'What do you want, Katarina?' he asked.

'Is that any way to say hello to an old friend?' Katarina enquired.

'We were never friends. Is Marek with you?' Trevor looked around to see if anybody else was there. He wasn't moving closer, and Katarina wasn't trying to approach him.

Instead, she reached back into the car, pulled out an envelope, and threw it across the car park, allowing it to land at his feet.

'I'm guessing you've heard the news,' she stated, ignoring his comment about her ex-husband. 'D.Q. James is dead.'

Trevor nodded.

'Detectives came and told me yesterday. Did you come here to gloat? Or to inform me they'd got it wrong and it's actually *Ronnie Carrigan?*'

At the name, Katarina winced, but she didn't deny it. Instead, she pointed at the envelope.

'Tomorrow night,' she announced. 'I'm having a wake, so to speak, for D.Q. James. I'm inviting the people who knew him. One last game of poker.'

'I don't know if you've heard the rumour mill, Katarina, but I don't play any more.'

'Bullshit.' Katarina smiled. 'Just because I haven't come to see you recently doesn't mean I haven't kept tabs on you. I've kept tabs on *all* of you. All that time you travelled I was waiting for you to try to fence the diamonds or spend money you didn't have.'

At this, Trevor laughed.

'You think I've got the diamonds and the gold?' he scoffed, shifting position, relaxing a little now.

'Hypothetically, okay? D.Q. James and Trevor Sullivan meet up. Do you think Trevor Sullivan is going to A, befriend D.Q. James, or B, try to kill that son of a bitch?'

Katarina shrugged.

'Either way, you might want to come,' she suggested. 'There'll be a party upstairs, and a more personal event in the basement.'

'Depends. How large is the buy-in?'

'Free, as you've already paid it.' Katarina smiled now. 'To get an invite to the basement event, the buy-in is being screwed over by D.Q. James.'

'And the pot?'

'There'll be something to win.' Katarina smiled. 'It's being sorted right now. It's going to be a real party. The kind of thing you'd just *die* for.'

With that said, she clambered back into the car, and her driver eased the Mercedes past Trevor, heading off back towards the city. Only now did Trevor pick up the envelope, opening it, seeing the mahjong piece, and tossing it away.

'Amateurs,' he muttered as he read the card, tore it in half, tossed it after the mahjong piece, and continued to his car.

Trevor Sullivan would be there, if only to see the ending of a hand that had been dealt fifteen years earlier.

A hand *he'd* dealt out three weeks earlier.

Katarina Kováč sat in the back of her Mercedes and stared at the two remaining envelopes in her hand. This could have been the worst mistake she'd ever made, but she knew without a doubt that one of the people invited on Thursday night knew where the gold and, more importantly, half a million pounds' worth of diamonds were.

Somebody would slip up. Maybe even D.Q. James himself would appear, unable to resist the spotlight.

Because that was the plan.

She'd realised the body wasn't James the moment she'd seen the Rolex on the wrong hand as they bagged it up, a hand she'd seen wearing a Rolex, and not a Patek Phillipe, a week before D.Q. James had disappeared. She'd spoken to

Ronnie Carrigan's sister many times over the years, never knowing where her brother was. However, it seemed that now people did. And if Ronnie Carrigan was believed to be D.Q. James, that meant the real D.Q. James wasn't dead. He was out there, and there was every chance he'd be wanting to either show off the diamonds he'd stolen, or fight whoever found the diamonds, purely to gain them back.

Either way, Katarina would get the revenge, and the answers, she needed.

Terry Callahan was working through some blueprints when Declan arrived at the basement of the Harrison Casino. Looking up, he gave a nod and then rolled them up, placed them in a tube, and repositioned it beside a cabinet.

'Come to see the clown show?' he asked, with a hint of amusement in his voice.

'How so?'

'Boss tells us to take the place apart, turn it into something different, and then in the space of two days decides instead to return it to what it was like. Chandeliers and all.'

They started walking back up the steps into the main hallway, where, behind a pair of double doors, the one-time Harrison Casino was being returned to its former glory.

'Waste of two weeks' bloody work, that was,' Terry muttered. 'All because somebody was found in a wall.'

'You think that's a joke?' Declan asked.

'Not at all,' Terry shook his head. 'I'm being serious. If we hadn't found that body, we wouldn't be having this stupid poker game. We wouldn't be returning this casino, which by the way *failed* at being a casino, into, well, a casino again, before tearing it back down on Monday.' He sighed, running a hand through his hair. 'Still, I suppose we're being paid for it, so I can't complain.'

Declan walked through the main casino floor, noticing that the chandeliers were being replaced into the ceiling sockets. It filled out the room far more than he'd realised when he first walked through the empty shell, as under them, contractors were putting together a couple of poker tables and roulette areas.

'So, what's the plan?' he asked.

'One night, maybe a weekend.' Terry shrugged. 'I think this is Katarina trying to make some money. House always wins and all that. Rumour mill says D.Q. James is the body – I know a bit of poker, and James was a definite name. Now? He's dead. People will always find ways to profit from it.'

'What if he's not dead?' Declan asked.

This was a question that Terry hadn't expected.

'I saw the body.'

'We haven't been able to do any DNA tests,' Declan replied carefully. 'All we have is a body wearing a hat, glasses, and a Rolex that was owned by him, and that he's not been around for fifteen years.'

He paused, letting this sink in before continuing.

'Neither had Ronnie Carrigan.'

'Who the bloody hell is Ronnie Carrigan?'

'Another possible name for the body.' Declan stretched his back. 'We won't know until we get the information through. But that's not why I'm here today. I'd like to talk to you about the gambler.'

'You know, I know a lot of gamblers.' Terry smiled, walking over to one of the contractors, tapping him on the shoulder and pointing out something he'd missed. 'I do a lot of casino rebuilds, you know. It's one of the reasons we were hired.'

'I'm on about the one that you spoke to in your gym,' Declan said. 'The one Mickey says told you there was treasure behind this wall.'

At the statement, Terry paused in what he was doing, slowly turning to face Declan.

'I didn't know there was a body,' he said, as if this explained everything.

'I never said you did, but I would like to know what you were told.'

Terry nodded, walking Declan away from the other contractors.

'Look,' he replied, 'all I know is three, four weeks back I was at my gym, and I talked about the job I was on. One guy there is an ex-gambler, knows the story of this place. Mentioned there had been rumours that a big score had been taken. Diamonds, gold, you know, that kind of thing. No one ever found it because it had been buried behind a wall in the basement. Even said which wall it was rumoured to be.'

'And so you decided to take out the wall for yourself?'

'Well, no.' Terry shook his head vehemently. 'I'd get fired if I started knocking walls down. I went to the owners. I told them what I'd been informed about, mentioned there was a definite discrepancy in the dimensions down there. Said there was every chance that there was a hidden wall and, if so, there was something there. Katarina agreed that we should look, and if I found something, we'd split it.'

'Did Katarina say what she thought it could have been?'

'No.' Terry shook his head. 'And I realise this is a bit of a pun here, but if I were a betting man, I'd say she knew there was something. And her partner definitely did. Or, at least, he didn't want me buggering around there.'

'The partner?'

'Her ex-husband, I think. Only ever dealt with her.'

Declan noted this down. If it were true, then Marek had been a little more cavalier with the truth than they'd first suspected.

'And this man in the gym told you this out of the goodness of his own heart?'

'Christ, no,' Terry laughed at this. 'He wanted ten per cent of the findings. A finder's fee, so to speak.'

'Katarina told us that she'd known about the wall from the start.'

'Only if she was psychic,' Terry replied. 'That woman didn't have a bloody clue what the blueprints said. Half of them were signed off by her ex-husband.'

'And he was definitely her partner?'

'Well, she bought it with his money – divorce money or something like that, but I think there was a further injection on the condition he was a silent partner.'

Declan noted this down. This was definitely not the impression he'd gained from Marek earlier that day. However, Terry took his silence for accusation.

'Look, all I'm saying is I was told that it was worth taking out that wall. Katarina wasn't going to use it anyway, and well…'

He trailed off.

'At best, she would've made fifty per cent of a broken Rolex.'

'And you?' Declan asked.

'I would've given ten per cent to my friend at the gym and split the rest with the others, to be honest. I think Dave could've done with it right now, although I think he would've asked us to hold it until after the divorce – stop his wife getting her hands onto that as well.'

'This gym rat, the gambler,' Declan said. 'How long have you known him?'

'Oh, a few years now,' Terry replied. 'Ever since he started working there.'

'Working?' Declan paused, writing in the notebook. 'So, he's not a gym member?'

'Oh, I mean, he works out at the gym as well, but he's mainly behind the counter.'

Declan stared at Terry for a long moment.

'The Flex-U-Fit gym in Bow,' he said, more a statement than a question, even though Terry hadn't mentioned the location.

'Well, yeah,' Terry replied, as if it was the most obvious thing in the world. 'I assumed you knew that.'

Declan stared at the man in front of him.

'Trevor Sullivan told you about this, didn't he?' he asked. 'Did he say anything else?'

'No, just that he knew the stories and I should look,' Terry replied. 'I'm sorry, but if there's something I need to know here...'

'No.' Declan shook his head, looking around. 'This poker event, are you attending?'

'I've been given an invite, but I don't gamble,' Terry shook his head. 'Katarina said I could pass it on to anyone I wanted to.'

'But, let me guess,' Declan said. 'Now it wasn't as much of a shot in the dark as it was before, you offered it to Mister Sullivan.'

'I felt it was the least I could do,' Terry replied. 'He

thought he'd found a place where millions of pounds were, and all he found was trouble and a body. I thought if he could make some money from the poker, we'd kind of be quits. Funny enough, I just called him.'

'And did he accept?'

Terry shook his head.

'Said he was already invited,' he replied, and there was almost a hint of annoyance in his voice. 'Which was bloody weird because he doesn't gamble any more.'

'Oh I think Trevor Sullivan has been gambling for fifteen years now,' Declan replied coldly. 'I'll leave you to your work.'

'And if I see Trevor, do you need me to say anything?'

'Oh no,' Declan replied, his eyes narrowed. 'I think we'll be chatting to Trevor Sullivan before you do.'

'Here,' Terry said as a final comment, reaching into his pocket and pulling out what looked to be a Mahjong piece. 'Katarina dropped this when she was offering me the invite. I don't know if it's relevant or not.'

Declan took the piece, pocketing it.

'Honestly, right now? I've no idea.' He smiled.

17

IDENTITIES

THE TEMPLE INN OFFICE HAD THAT LATE-EVENING ENERGY THAT came with a case accelerating faster than anyone liked, or even potentially wanted right now. It was one thing to be ahead of the game, but another to be spinning so many plates one could easily fall as Declan walked in from the casino visit to find Billy at his desk, three monitors glowing, Jess talking to him animatedly and Anjli going through statements at her workspace.

Monroe emerged from his office, took one look at Declan's expression, and gestured him inside.

'How's our crime scene looking?' Monroe asked, closing the door.

'Like someone's preparing for the world's worst memorial service,' Declan replied, settling into the chair across from Monroe's desk. 'Katarina's having the casino restored to how it looked before it closed. Chandeliers, poker tables, the lot. One night only, then it all gets torn down Monday.'

'She's that confident people will show up?'

'She's sending invitations, and some of them are for a very exclusive audience. Terry the foreman? He mentioned there's some kind of memorial poker game tomorrow night. He said Trevor Sullivan got invited.'

Monroe leant back in his chair.

'The same Trevor Sullivan who lost everything to D.Q. James.'

'And who conveniently pointed Terry towards the exact wall where we found our body.' Declan nodded. 'Terry said Sullivan told him he was already invited before Terry offered to pass his invite on. Which means Katarina wants Sullivan there specifically.'

'Someone's setting something up,' Monroe said. 'Question is whether it's Katarina laying a trap, or someone else entirely.'

'Might be Marek, as apparently he's a silent partner in the business,' Declan replied. 'Either way, we need to know who we're dealing with. Speaking of which, Cooper mentioned something earlier. De'Geer's got an old mate from Paddington who's in trouble. Paul Elliott, DC. Apparently, according to Bullman—'

'You said Cooper.'

'Yeah. Cooper spoke to Bullman, and what she said to Cooper was that this Elliott guy claimed he was mugged, gained a stab wound. However Doctor Marcos—'

'You mean Cooper.'

'No, apparently even Doctor Marcos was involved in this, said he likely stabbed himself to avoid a Professional Standards hearing this morning.'

'Aye?'

'She's worried. Said Elliott turned up asking De'Geer for

character references, then stabbed himself to delay the hearing. De'Geer was seen there by Bullman, but when Cooper looked into this, it seems Cohen's been keeping this guy off active cases for months.'

Monroe's expression darkened.

'Cohen dumps this case on us, one of his DCs is compromised enough to stab himself, and now we've got a memorial poker game brewing at the murder scene. I'm thinking Cohen knew exactly what he was handing over.'

'You think Paul Elliott's connected to our case?'

'I think Cohen wouldn't have dumped this on us unless he had a bloody good reason. Come on, we'll talk to De'Geer about this later. Until then, let's see what Billy's found.'

They walked back into the main office as Billy looked up from his screens, and Declan could tell immediately that Billy and Jess had found something significant.

'What?' he asked.

'So, I went through the tapes.' Jess turned to face her father. 'Nothing much there, standard puff piece interview, getting the bones for a PR piece for a trade magazine. However, there's one moment when, talking about his misspent youth, he says he did a stint in a "Juvie detention centre" for drugs, but then backtracks, saying he doesn't want this in the piece. Kendis agrees and strikes it from the story, but it's still on tape.'

'Okay.' Declan noted this down. 'So, he did time in a young offenders—'

'Not young offenders, Dad, juvenile detention centre. That's American, not British.'

'You think he slipped that he was in America earlier than his official story?' Declan understood now. 'Billy?'

'Looking now for any mention of a David Quincey James in the American justice system.' Billy smiled. 'It could be nothing, or it could be a smoking gun.'

'Good catch.' Declan ruffled his daughter's hair, ignoring her wince. 'What else?'

'Trevor Sullivan's family history,' Billy said, pulling up a timeline on his centre monitor. 'Parents divorced when he was fourteen. Mother was American – Margaret Jameson, originally from Boston. She moved back to the States in the late eighties, taking the younger son with her.'

'Darren Sullivan?' Anjli said, joining them at Billy's desk. 'As per Johnny's admission?'

'Exactly. Darren was twelve when they left. Trevor stayed in London with his father, who according to the divorce notes was an abusive drunk, and who eventually died in 1995. By all accounts, Trevor and Darren lost contact after the split, as the mum felt he'd betrayed her by staying with the dad.'

Monroe studied the screen.

'So, we've got two brothers, separated by an ocean when they were kids. Trevor stays in London, becomes a recreational poker player. Darren goes to America with his mother. And then what?'

'That's where it gets interesting,' Billy said. 'I can't find any record of Darren Sullivan after 2000. No employment records, no tax returns in the US, nothing. It's like he vanished.'

'Or changed his name,' Declan said quietly. 'Maybe changed it to Jameson...'

'No Darren Jameson, either,' Billy added.

'But he might have changed it to James,' Anjli replied. 'David Quincey James, in fact. A poker player who appears on the London scene in the early 2000s, claims to be American, and has an obsession with taking down Trevor Sullivan specifically, after they meet a few years later.'

'And who may have been in a detention centre as a teen.' Billy pulled up another screen. 'It fits the timeline. D.Q. James starts appearing at American poker tournaments around 2001. No previous history before that – he just appears, fully formed, with a cowboy persona and a talent for psychological warfare.'

'So, he builds a rep in the States, then comes here,' Monroe mused. 'And he eventually targets his own brother, the one who got to stay in London while he was shipped off to America.'

He frowned.

'But why wait? If it was revenge, Darren's back in London by 2003, maybe 2005 at the latest. He doesn't destroy Trevor until 2009. That's several years. What changed?'

'Building reputation,' Declan suggested. 'You can't psychologically destroy someone at poker unless you're good enough to beat them. Trevor was the one trained. Maybe Darren spent those years getting better, making a name for himself.'

'Or building up to it,' Anjli added. 'Making sure when he took Trevor down, it would be complete. Total destruction, not just a win.'

'That's one hell of a grudge,' Declan observed.

'Sullivan wasn't big on the scene until 2008,' Billy was looking at records. 'Never did the showbiz games, just played the London scene, more as a hobby. Maybe they didn't cross paths?'

'Aye, possibly. But either way, this could explain why James was so focused on destroying Sullivan completely. This wasn't just poker – it was family revenge,' Monroe said, almost to himself before returning his gaze to Billy. 'Can you prove it? Find something that connects Darren Sullivan to D.Q. James?'

'I'm working on it, but it'll take time. Your investigator said he gained a forged passport in 2003, but that never appeared on records.'

'We don't have time,' Monroe said. 'Tomorrow night, someone's gathering everyone who knew D.Q. James in one room. Including Trevor Sullivan. If Sullivan worked out his brother was D.Q. James back then—'

'Then he had motive to kill him, especially with the humiliation...' Anjli continued, but paused as the door to the stairwell opened and Doctor Marcos walked in, still wearing her lab coat. She was carrying an evidence bag with something small and gold inside.

'Alex, darling, got a moment?' she asked.

'I didn't do it.' Monroe turned to look at her. 'It was Declan he made me. Whatever it was.'

Doctor Marcos ignored the joke.

'This coin you took from George Moir.' She held up the evidence bag. 'The Mexican fifty-peso. I've logged it, photographed it, verified the gold content.'

'But?'

'But there's something off about it.' She walked to Billy's desk, setting the bag down under his desk lamp. 'The weight's correct, the gold content tests properly, and it's definitely the real thing, minted in 2006, but the surface texture feels wrong. There's a slight roughness in the recessed areas, and when I was examining it under magnification, I noticed what might be discolouration.'

'What, like some kind of residue?' Declan asked.

'Chemical, possibly. Or organic compound of some kind.

I can't say for certain without running proper tests.' She picked up the bag again. 'I'm taking it to the lab tonight. Whatever's on this coin, it wasn't there when it was minted. Someone's done something to it. I'm letting you know in case you think I've sold it to buy the handbag you never bought me.'

'You've never asked for a handbag,' Monroe protested.

'Well then, it's a good job I'm not selling it for one. Give me until tomorrow. I'll run a full spectroscopy analysis, check for organic compounds, see what we're dealing with.'

'D.Q. James paid Moir with these coins,' Monroe said. 'If there's something unusual about them, let us know as soon as you can.'

'I'll prioritise it.' Doctor Marcos headed for the door, pausing. 'Whatever you've got brewing here – be careful. People don't alter gold coins unless they're hiding something.'

After she left, the team stood in silence for a moment. Monroe walked back towards his office, then stopped.

'I need to have a conversation with Cohen,' he muttered. 'See if the wee bastard's willing to admit why he really dumped this case on us.'

'Want company?' Declan asked.

'No. If his station's compromised, the fewer of us poking around there, the better.' Monroe grabbed his jacket from the coat hanger by the door. 'Billy, keep digging into the Sullivan brothers connection. Anjli, go through everything we have on the poker game attendees.'

'We don't have anything on—'

'Then start *finding* some,' Monroe cut her off. 'Declan, write up what you learned at the casino. I want everything documented before tomorrow night.'

'And if Cohen won't talk?' Anjli asked.

Monroe's expression was grim.

'Then we go into that poker game blind, and hope nobody else ends up behind a wall for the next fifteen years.'

THE PADDINGTON ARMS WAS ONE OF THOSE LONDON PUBS that had survived gentrification through sheer bloody-mindedness. Dark wood, brass fittings, and a clientele that still remembered when the area was working-class rather than boutique. Monroe had called Cohen's mobile, suggested they meet for a pint somewhere nobody from Paddington Green would think to look, and Cohen had named this place without hesitation.

Monroe arrived first, ordered a gin and tonic, and claimed a corner booth that gave him a clear view of the entrance. The early evening crowd was thin – a few regulars at the bar, a couple having a quiet argument near the dartboard, nobody paying attention to anything except their own business.

Cohen walked in ten minutes later, tie loosened, looking like a man who'd been carrying the weight of the world on his shoulders and had finally decided it was time to set it down. He spotted Monroe, ordered something at the bar, and made his way over with a pint of bitter.

'Monroe.' Cohen slid into the booth across from him, taking a long drink before setting the glass down. 'Wondered how long it would take you to work it out.'

'Work what out?' Monroe asked evenly.

Cohen's smile didn't reach his eyes.

'Why I gave you the case. Why I've been keeping certain

officers off active investigations. Why Paul Elliott stabbed himself rather than face a Professional Standards hearing.'

Monroe leant forward.

'You gave us the case because you can't trust your own team,' he said coldly. 'So, how about you stop playing games and tell me exactly what we're walking into tomorrow night, and what the merry hell is going on here.'

The silence stretched. Cohen glanced around the pub, confirming nobody was within earshot, then sighed heavily.

'Six months ago,' he mumbled, 'I started noticing irregularities. Cases that should have progressed suddenly going cold. Evidence that should have been logged never quite making it to the system. Small things, easy to miss if you weren't looking.'

'But you were looking.'

'Yeah, because three of those cases involved gambling operations in Mayfair and Soho. High-stakes private games, invitation only, the kind of thing that attracts serious money and serious criminals. Every time we got close to making arrests, something would go wrong. Witnesses would recant. Evidence would be compromised. Suspects would know exactly when we were planning raids.'

Monroe understood where this was going.

'Someone on your team was feeding information.'

'Not just feeding – actively sabotaging. I couldn't work out who at first. Could've been anyone with access to the case files. Kenny Tsang was involved, but it was like he was one step ahead. Some loser Triad guy who'd never amounted to much made moves someone with his rep – or, rather, lack of one – shouldn't have been making. Even Whitehall turned up, believing someone was passing secrets in our patch.'

'Marek Kováč?'

'Unsure. But then I started tracking financial records, looking for unexplained income, expensive purchases, lifestyle changes.' Cohen took another drink. 'Paul Elliott. Detective Constable, good man, solid copper. However, I found out through some contacts he was down thirty grand in gambling debts, all to private games.'

'And you think he's been providing intelligence in exchange for debt forgiveness,' Monroe stated this as fact. 'How long have you known?'

'Long enough to document everything, not long enough to move on it officially. Professional Standards moves at the speed of bureaucratic treacle, and if I tipped my hand too early, Elliott would have time to cover his tracks.' Cohen's expression darkened. 'But then that body turned up in the Harrison Casino basement, and suddenly Elliott's compromise became relevant to an active murder investigation.'

'So, you dumped it on us.'

'I gave it to the one team in London I knew I could trust,' Cohen corrected. 'Temple Inn. No connections to my station, no officers who could be compromised, and Detective Superintendent Monroe – a man who'd rather eat glass than cover for a corrupt copper.'

'Flattery doesn't make up for dropping us in the shite without warning.'

'I know. But I couldn't risk Elliott finding out what we had. The woman running these games – Katarina Kováč – we believe she's the one he owes the money to, who he's been feeding information to, but it could be the husband too.'

'Ex-husband, apparently.'

'Ex-husband, then. He only used the surname, so it could be either. Details about our investigations, surveillance plans, arrest timings, all being passed over. I started moving backwards through Katarina Kováč's timeline, and when I saw she bought that casino a few months ago, I knew she was looking for something.'

'The diamonds,' Monroe said. 'Half a million in stolen gems that D.Q. James took from the Triads fifteen years ago.'

Cohen's eyebrows rose.

'You've been busy.'

'We're good at our jobs. Unlike some units I could mention.'

'Touché.' Cohen finished his pint. 'But, that said, there's something else. Elliott knows things he shouldn't about your investigation. Specific details that haven't gone through official channels. He's been putting pressure on one of your team – the Viking. Old training mate from Hendon, apparently; caught him looking like a deer in headlights at Guildhall. Heard later he went to visit Elliott in hospital. I think Elliott's been using him to get information about what you've found.'

Monroe's jaw tightened, but he said nothing.

'And now,' Cohen continued, 'Katarina's planning something for Thursday night. A memorial party, and an exclusive poker game at the casino. One last hand in honour of D.Q. James. Elliott's on medical leave but we're watching him. He had a man at his door today demanding he provide intelligence about any police presence at the event, make sure no one interferes with whatever's planned. Reckons his debts will be wiped if the "right outcome is gained".'

'Which is?'

'No idea,' Cohen replied with a shrug.

'Did you get a picture of this man?'

'I'll have it sent over.'

'No offence, laddie, but you should have kept us looped in

here, and have already sent us this,' Monroe snapped. 'We're already on the back foot.'

'I know. All I can do is apologise.'

'She thinks the game will flush out whoever has the diamonds,' Monroe realised. 'Or reveal who knows where they are.'

'Either way, it's going to be a bloodbath.' Cohen leant closer. 'Chinese Triads, and this Jun guy in particular are muttering about wanting their property back. I'm guessing that's the diamonds?'

'Aye, we believe so.'

'Well, then he'll be there, and various criminal elements who lost money to James will be there. As well as Katarina herself, who's obsessed with finding whatever treasure James hid.' Cohen pulled out a card, wrote something on the back, and slid it across the table. 'That's my mobile. Direct line, no station switchboard. If you need backup tomorrow night and can't trust who you're calling, use that. I'll come myself if I have to.'

Monroe pocketed the card.

'One more question. Who do you think killed D.Q. James?'

Cohen was quiet for a moment, staring into his empty glass.

'Honestly? I think it was an accident. I think someone meant to kill James, got someone else instead, and by the time they realised their mistake, it was too late to do anything except wall up the body and hope it never surfaced. But whoever did it had access to the casino basement, had the skills to build a false wall, and had a motive to want James dead.'

'That could be almost anyone who knew him.'

'Yeah. Which is why if you get the right people in the same room and apply enough pressure, someone will crack.'

'It's not James,' Monroe replied softly. 'It's a guy named Ronald Carrigan.'

'The body?' Cohen raised his eyebrows, but as quick as they rose, they narrowed. 'Wait. I've seen that name across my desk recently. I'll look into it; let you know off books.'

'I'd appreciate it.'

Cohen stood, extending his hand.

'Good luck, Monroe. You're going to need it. And I really am sorry I threw you in the shit here.'

'I get it.' Monroe smiled. 'We had a similar issue a while back with detectives we couldn't trust. Luckily for me, I was out of action with a head wound at the time.'

Monroe shook his hand, watching as Cohen made his way out of the pub and disappeared into the London evening. He sat there a moment longer, finishing his gin and tonic, thinking about compromised stations, desperate officers and murders that had been hidden for over a decade.

And in the middle of it all, Temple Inn, trying to solve it without getting anyone else killed.

By the time Monroe left the pub, the London night had settled in properly, street lights reflecting off damp pavements. He pulled out his phone and sent a quick text to the team.

Meeting first thing tomorrow. We need to be ready.

Three replies came back almost immediately. Billy's was typically efficient, Anjli's was practical and Declan's was characteristically dry:

Should I bring my poker face?

Monroe smiled despite himself as he called for a taxi. Tomorrow was coming, whether they were ready or not.

And somewhere in London, someone who'd kept a secret for fifteen years was about to discover that some walls, once broken, could never be rebuilt.

18

EXCESSIVE FORCE

Everybody arrived at the briefing, bright and early. With the apparent poker game hours away, it felt important to finish this case. But, before the briefing, Monroe and Declan brought De'Geer aside, closing the door to Declan's office behind him.

'Laddie,' Monroe said gently, and as De'Geer stared from boss to even bigger boss, he continued. 'Is there something you'd like to share?'

De'Geer had no poker face, and within seconds he slumped, nodding.

'I passed an old police friend some information about the case,' he said softly.

'Would this be Detective Constable Elliott of Paddington and Mayfair?' Monroe asked.

'Yes, Guv.'

'And what did you tell him exactly?'

'Just keeping him in the loop on the case, you know, what we're trying to find out,' De'Geer replied. 'I didn't give major information. I kept him at arm's length.'

'Go on,' Declan prompted. 'Because right now there's no reason you'd do what you've done that I can see.'

De'Geer was silent for a long moment, staring at his hands.

'Paul and I came up through Hendon together,' he said finally. 'Same cohort. We got on well – both of us were outsiders in different ways. We looked out for each other.'

'And?'

'There was another trainee. Tristan Vaughn.' De'Geer's jaw tightened. 'Aggressive type, enjoyed the power side of policing more than the justice side. Picked fights during training exercises, pushed people harder than necessary during restraint practise. Made it personal. He targeted both of us.'

'What happened?' Monroe asked.

'During a scenario exercise – one of those role-play situations where we're supposed to demonstrate proper arrest procedure – Vaughn came at me hard. Threw real punches, not pulled ones. Said afterwards it was to "test my reactions under pressure".' De'Geer met Monroe's eyes. 'I defended myself. Put him down. But I didn't stop when the instructor called time. I was angry. Tired of his games. I held the restraint position too long, applied too much pressure. Dislocated his shoulder.'

The silence stretched.

'The instructor saw it,' De'Geer continued. 'Wrote up an incident report. Said I'd used excessive force, lost control. Should have been disciplinary action, possibly dismissal. But Vaughn was scared. Realised he'd pushed too far and didn't want his own conduct examined. So he agreed not to press charges if the incident was handled "informally".'

'Meaning the report disappeared,' Declan said.

'Meaning the report was filed away somewhere and I was given a warning. One chance to prove I could control myself under pressure. The instructor made it clear – one more incident, and I was out.'

Monroe leant forward.

'And Elliott?'

De'Geer took a breath.

'Paul saw what happened. Vaughn had been bullying both of us for weeks. A few days after my incident, we were doing a vehicle search exercise. Paul was my partner that day. Standard scenario – search a training vehicle, log what you find. But this time the car we were supposed to use had gone missing, so the instructor said for the "suspect" to use their own vehicle for the exercise.'

He paused, looking between them.

'Vaughn was the "suspect". He was pissed about using his car, but there wasn't much he could do. However, when we did it, Paul found a bag of pills in the vehicle. Controlled substances. Called the instructor over, made a big show of the discovery.'

'Let me guess, Vaughn claimed innocence?'

'The pills were logged as evidence,' De'Geer nodded. 'But they weren't part of the training scenario – Paul planted them. The instructor worked it out within an hour, as the pills weren't from the training stock, but they also weren't personal supply as they were from one a couple of weeks earlier. The instructor started asking questions.'

De'Geer's voice was flat as he continued.

'Problem was, the staged car disappearing and these being found? Made it very suspicious. And I already had history with Vaughn, and it was me and Paul who found this. Paul claimed they must have been left over from a previous exercise, and that Vaughn hadn't realised. But I knew what he'd done. He'd planted evidence on Vaughn to get him kicked out.'

'Revenge for what Vaughn did to you,' Declan said quietly.

'Exactly. The instructor couldn't prove it – no witnesses to the actual planting, just suspicion. But Vaughn was finished anyway. The pills being "found" during his scenario, combined with his history of aggressive behaviour... he was quietly withdrawn from the programme.'

Monroe studied De'Geer's face.

'You knew Paul had planted them.'

'I saw him slip them into the boot while we were setting up the vehicle. He looked at me after, and I understood what he was doing. He was protecting me – making sure Vaughn couldn't come back at me later.' De'Geer's hands clenched. 'I said nothing. I should have reported it, but I didn't. I let Paul frame someone, let him plant evidence, because I was grateful Vaughn was gone.'

'So, you're both compromised,' Declan said. 'Your excessive force incident, and Paul's planted evidence that you witnessed and didn't report.'

'That's not all. Paul kept the original incident report about my excessive force. Took a copy before it was filed away. And he knew I saw him plant those pills.' De'Geer met Monroe's eyes. 'When he came to me asking for help, he reminded me about Hendon. Said if I didn't help him, he'd send my excessive force report to Professional Standards. And if I tried to claim he planted the drugs on Vaughn, he'd say I was part of it – that we'd worked together to frame Vaughn as revenge.'

'Would that stick?' Monroe asked.

'Doesn't matter, Guv. It'd ruin us both. But Paul's already

facing a Professional Standards hearing. He's got nothing to lose. I do.' De'Geer's voice was barely above a whisper. 'Every case I've worked, every arrest, every testimony – all of it gets questioned if Professional Standards sees that excessive force report. And if they investigate Hendon, they'll find out I witnessed Paul planting evidence and said nothing. That makes me complicit. I'd likely have been kicked out of the force. My police work, everything I've done is because of his silence.'

'Aye, that's stupid, and you know it, laddie,' Monroe snapped, his accent stronger with anger. 'Your work stands up because you're an outstanding officer. Wouldn't have brought you to Temple Inn if we didn't think so.'

'Hindsight is twenty-twenty, sergeant,' Declan added. 'Look at me. If I hadn't punched a priest, I'd still be at Tottenham and wouldn't have met you.'

'It was on live TV, sir.' De'Geer gave a small half smile. 'If you just punched priests away from cameras, you might stay in the job.'

'Well, if I hadn't been accused of corrupt things at Mile End,' Monroe replied calmly, 'I'd be gone, too. Let's be honest – the only reason I'm telling you what to do here is because a Prime Minister pardoned me to keep me in my job. And the only reason Declan has his rank is blackmail against the previous City Commander. None of us are angels, laddie. None of us.'

De'Geer nodded.

'You should have told us,' Declan said.

'I didn't realise it was connected,' De'Geer replied. 'And I tried to sort it myself.'

'Luckily, your girlfriend is more intelligent than you,' Declan murmured. 'Now, how much does Elliott know?'

'Only what I've told him.'

'Unfortunately, sergeant, that's not the case,' Monroe replied. 'We believe your buddy Elliott – whether from the office, hospital, or wherever – has been phoning people pretending to be Declan.'

At this, De'Geer paled.

'I only told him Declan was running the case,' he explained.

'We know,' Monroe replied. 'Believe it or not, we don't think you're as idiotic as you seem. But we now have a situation where a corrupt officer, who owes a potential suspect a lot of money, is keeping them informed on our investigation. Someone who apparently has also been asked to provide some kind of police overview of an event tonight – a poker game purely for people involved with D.Q. James.'

'I understand, sir,' he said. 'If you need me to step down or return—'

'Oh, don't be an idiot,' Monroe replied. 'You're seven feet tall. If a fight's kicking off, I'm standing behind you. I'm saying we need you to perhaps play a part in this.'

He looked over at Declan.

'Do you remember when he played Little John?'

'At that Robin Hood convention.' Declan grinned. 'Such a nice sheepskin top he had. Do you remember when he thought he was some kind of Viking axe wielder, or the time he was using reenactment spears?'

De'Geer stared at both of them in confusion.

'Don't fret, laddie, we just need you to play along with Mister Elliot. Convince him you've decided to work with him. Perhaps even attend tonight as a buddy. I mean, from the sounds of things, he's not going to be that great in a fight, if he's stabbed himself already.'

De'Geer, obviously relieved, nodded.

'Absolutely, Guv,' he said. 'Whatever you need.'

'What I need is for you to tell us these things before it gets too important,' Monroe replied. 'I shouldn't have found out about this *after* my wife, for example. I know you work for her and do all her little minion jobs – like digging up bodies for her to weld together and all that – but I'd really appreciate it if, from now on, you kept us in the loop when a corrupt officer is trying to stop a murder investigation.'

THE BRIEFING ROOM HAD THE USUAL MORNING FEELING – coffee going cold in mugs, Billy hunched over his laptop, Anjli flipping through notes from yesterday, Cooper by the evidence board with a fresh cup. Jess had also returned and sat at the table with her own laptop, helping Billy cross-reference databases. The only person missing was Doctor Marcos, who'd said she'd come up when she was finished with what she was doing.

Monroe and Declan walked in with De'Geer following, looking like a man who'd just had a weight lifted but wasn't entirely sure what came next.

'Right then,' Monroe said, not bothering to sit. 'Quick update for those who don't know – one of Cohen's lot at Paddington is compromised. De'Geer's helping us sort that particular mess, which is why he's been having quiet chats with people who shouldn't exist.'

Nobody asked for details. The team had learned when Monroe was being deliberately vague, it was for good reason.

'Tonight's poker game,' Monroe continued. 'Billy, what do we have?'

'We don't have a list for the more exclusive game yet, but we can make educated guesses based on who she'd probably want there,' Billy replied, still staring at his screen. 'In my hypothetical game here I've got four players so far – Richard Statham, former casino manager, as I feel he has more going on than just his job. Thomas Greaves, former croupier who bought a car off James for tuppence would probably be brought back to work the table. Trevor Sullivan, who lost everything to James and now works at a gym. And Marek Kováč, Katarina's ex-husband and the man who had all the casino building plans.'

'And apparently owns the casino too, and might even be a spy,' Declan said. 'Anything on that?'

'I called Trix Preston,' Billy said. 'She's back in MI5's good books apparently, so she's checking with the more shadowy figures in Whitehall, looking into Marek's name popping up.'

'Remember when she tried to screw us over, pretending to be work experience?' Monroe asked innocently. 'Good times.'

'What about Jun Ng Kai-lok?' Anjli asked.

'Unsure. There's a part of me that thinks he'll be there but won't be playing, maybe watching. Kenny Tsang might be there too.'

'Christ, that's going to be a fun evening,' Cooper muttered.

'Aye, well, fun's what we do here,' Monroe replied. 'Billy, where are we—'

The door to the main office opened, and once more Johnny Lucas walked in as if he owned the place, carrying a large paper bag that smelled distinctly of fresh pastries.

Monroe stopped mid-sentence.

'Christ, Johnny. Twice in one week? People will talk.'

'Morning, Alex,' Johnny said pleasantly, nodding to the room. 'Declan. Ladies. Billy. And Jess, I hope they're not keeping you from your boxing training.'

'What brings you to our humble station?' Declan asked. 'Again?'

'I didn't know if you lived the trope or not, so I didn't bring donuts, I brought more palatable items.' Johnny set the paper bag on the table – croissants, by the smell of them. 'Two things. First, I reckon you're wondering who's actually going to this poker game tonight.'

'Billy has a hypothetical list,' Monroe replied.

'Well, I've got an actual one.' Johnny smiled as he pulled his phone out. 'Katarina's not exactly subtle when she wants something, and she invited me out of the blue. So, I made a few calls.'

'And?' Monroe prompted.

'There's a public event, all ex-members and their connections, created as a "last hurrah" but probably testing the waters for other options, maybe even selling the new building's plans, while in the "VIP room" – and by that I think we're talking the basement – we have Richard Statham, Thomas Greaves, Corey Moore, Tony Norton and Linda Burrell. Also Trevor Sullivan, a few others I've not gained names yet for and Marek Kováč,' Johnny said. 'All confirmed. Some woman from a D.Q. James museum or something will be there—'

'Imogen Rothwell?' Declan asked.

'Name sounds about right but I don't know her. Oh, and Jun Ng Kai-lok will be there and apparently so will Kenny Tsang – but whether this is because Katarina knows he's Wong Sei, or she's just completely clueless remains to be seen.'

'Marek knows, and he's apparently part of this, he might have told his wife, you know, when she was like still his wife.' Billy was already updating his notes.

'How'd you find that out?' Declan asked Johnny.

'Let's just say Katarina's not as careful as she thinks she is.' Johnny smiled slightly. 'Plus, I know people who know people. Statham's been talking about it at his club, Greaves mentioned it to his assistant at the ExCeL, a lovely young lady who owes me a few favours, and Trevor Sullivan was apparently shouting across a gym car park at her. Subtle lot, these poker players.'

'That's more than we had,' Monroe admitted.

'Which brings me to my second reason for being here.' Johnny pulled a slip of paper from his jacket pocket. 'Remember you asked about the forger who did D.Q. James's passport? The one who gave him the David Quincey James identity?'

Monroe's attention sharpened.

'This mysterious Finch you named in the disco pub?'

'Arthur Finch,' Johnny said, handing the paper to Billy. 'Died three years ago. Stroke, apparently, though I've heard rumours it was more self-inflicted than that. Either way, he's not talking any more.'

'Dead forger's not much use to us,' Monroe said.

'No, but his ledgers are.' Johnny tapped the paper. 'Arthur was paranoid. Kept detailed records of every job he ever did – names, dates, fees paid. His insurance policy against clients who might decide he knew too much.'

'And where are these ledgers now?' Billy asked, already reaching for his laptop.

'Police seized them when he died. Part of some Westminster fraud investigation – Arthur got sloppy towards the end, forged documents for a benefits scam. Nothing to do with passports, just regular fraud.' Johnny gestured at the paper. 'That's the case number and reference. Thought you might want to track them down.'

Billy was already typing, pulling up the Westminster evidence database as Johnny picked up his pastry bag.

'Anyway, croissants are for you lot. Consider it payment for putting up with my family's mess over the years.'

He headed for the door, then paused.

'One more thing. Arthur's ledgers – if they're as detailed as I remember him being, they'll have everything. Not just the David Quincey James passport. Everything Arthur ever did. You'll be pulling a lot of skeletons out of that closet, so be wary.'

With that, Johnny left. The room was quiet for a moment.

'Can you find them?' Monroe asked.

'Already on it.' Billy was already on the phone to Westminster evidence storage.

'Good,' Monroe said as he picked up a phone, calling front desk. 'Sergeant Mastakin? Can you do me a favour? Can you stop letting Johnny bloody Lucas swan in here as if he's some kind of VIP contest winner?'

He paused.

'He's not an MP any more,' he added. 'Make him wait in reception. He needs to be more humble.'

The door to the office opened again, and for a moment Declan wondered if Johnny Lucas had returned, but it was Doctor Marcos who walked in, holding the evidence bag with the Mexican fifty-peso gold coin from George Moir inside.

'I've been up most of the night with this,' she said, connecting her phone to the room's display screen. 'There's paint on it.'

The magnified image appeared – the coin's surface in sharp detail – and, in the recessed areas of the engraving, they could see tiny traces of something that didn't belong.

'We thought there was discolouration due to some cleaner or oil, but actually there's incredibly minute traces of acrylic paint,' Doctor Marcos continued. 'The type used for miniature figure painting. Someone painted this gold coin, then tried to clean it off.'

'Why paint a gold coin?' Anjli asked.

'That's a hell of a test palette,' Monroe replied.

'I think in this case it was to hide what it was,' Doctor Marcos said simply. 'Paint over gold and it no longer looks like gold. The work was professional – whoever did this knew exactly what they were doing.'

Anjli had gone very still, her notebook open in front of her.

'The poker chips,' she said quietly. 'At the museum. When I picked one up, it was too heavy. Way too heavy for a normal chip.'

Monroe looked at her. 'You think they're gold coins?'

'I think D.Q. James was an expert miniature painter,' Anjli said. 'We saw his work. Museum-quality detail on figures smaller than your thumb. If he could paint Warhammer figures that precisely and fake up Mahjong pieces to get into high-level games...'

'He could paint gold coins to look like poker chips,' Declan finished.

The room was quiet for a moment.

'Billy,' Monroe said, 'call the museum. Tell Imogen Rothwell we need those poker chips brought here for examination. Don't explain why yet, just say they're potential evidence.'

'On it.'

'Doctor Marcos, when those chips arrive, I want you here to examine them.'

'I'll clear my afternoon.'

'You think she knows?' Declan asked.

'I think she's the sister of a man who died pretending to be D.Q. James,' Monroe nodded. 'There's every chance she's bought the coins, via the museum, purely to wait for D.Q James to appear...'

'And get her revenge on him.' Anjli nodded.

Monroe turned back to the team.

'Right. Until those ledgers arrive and we can confirm who D.Q. James became after 2009, we've got work to do. Anjli, Declan – bring Richard Statham in. Voluntary interview, nice and polite, but I want to know everything about his relationship with Jun and those basement poker games. I know he's told us "everything he knows" and all that, so let's point out that we know more than he reckons.'

'You think he knows about the coins?' Declan asked.

'I think Richard Statham ran that casino long enough to know where the bodies are buried,' Monroe said. 'Literally, as it's turned out. Cooper, you're with me. We're going to the Harrison Casino to gain us some wee invites for this shindig and maybe see why Katarina never mentioned her ex-husband is on the papers. Billy, chase up Preston.'

He looked around the briefing room.

'Unless you've bugged this bloody room again, Trix,' he said loudly. 'If so, you can bloody come visit.'

'What about me?' De'Geer asked.

'You're going to visit your mate Paul,' Monroe said. 'Tell him I'm putting pressure on everyone, see what he says. Let's get on his good side, see if we can slip him up, gain something from him we weren't supposed to know.'

De'Geer nodded.

'And then I get to punch him, yes?'

'Laddie, if we solve this case? You can do whatever you want to him.' Monroe added. 'And Jess? When's your boxing session?'

'Whenever I want.'

'Good. Go there in about an hour, say you're at a loose end, get some training in. But keep an eye on everyone and anyone visiting Johnny today who you don't recognise.'

'You're sending her in alone?' Declan was surprised.

'No, I'm sending her off to box.' Monroe smiled as he headed for the door but then paused.

'One more thing. Tonight's going to be messy, so let's try to have all our facts straight before we walk into that casino, aye?'

19

OLD NAMES

If Paul Elliott had been expecting De'Geer to arrive at his doorstep, he made a pretty good act of surprise, stepping back from the doorway and letting the seven-foot-tall Viking enter.

'I guessed you wouldn't be at work today,' De'Geer said, shaking off the morning rain as he entered. 'How's the stab wound?'

'It hurts.' Elliott shrugged. 'What can you do? You have to get on with life, don't you? I'm sure they'll catch the bastard who did it.'

'Oh, I know they will,' De'Geer replied coldly. 'Especially as it was you.'

As Elliott went to reply, likely to deny this or find some other excuse, De'Geer raised a finger, almost as if testing the air for wind direction.

'You know what I do at the Last Chance Saloon, right?' he asked.

'You're a sergeant, a beat copper?' It was a guess, which showed Elliott wasn't actually too sure about this.

'I work under Doctor Rosanna Marcos,' De'Geer replied. 'I might have been a motorcycle cop the last time we spoke but, since Maidenhead, I've learned forensics and I understand a whole lot more about it than you thought I did. So, when you're telling me about this terrible knife attack, I'm looking at angles and depths and realising that you did it with your offhand.'

He looked down at Elliott's likely bandaged torso, hidden under a *Megadeth* T-Shirt.

'I know you did this yourself, Paul,' he said. 'And I know you did it to make sure that you didn't have your tribunal, because the moment that happened, you were screwed.'

'I think you'll find that *we're* screwed, Morten,' Paul said. And for the first time since De'Geer had arrived, Paul Elliott's mask slipped. 'Are you here to arrest me? Shout at me? Tell me off in your *holier-than-thou* voice?'

'I could be here to beat the living shit out of you,' De'Geer replied. 'We both know how well I did the last time you saw me fight.'

'You wouldn't dare,' Elliott replied.

'You don't think so?' De'Geer moved closer, and his size, compared to Paul's not-inconspicuous six foot two, still dwarfed the man. 'You came demanding things of me in front of a fellow officer, who then started looking into you, idiot.'

'What?'

'The woman? Cooper? She was suspicious. Learned who you are and checked you out. And now, because you couldn't do "subtle", my boss is talking to your boss about what's going on and why *you're phoning people up pretending to be one of my other bosses.*'

There was an awkward moment of silence.

'I'm sorry about that,' Elliott replied. 'But you didn't give me anything. I wasn't in the room where it was happening, so I decided to check things out. I used Walsh's name as I thought people would ask if I pretended to be a female DI and my Glaswegian accent is bollocks.'

'You should have trusted me to help you!' De'Geer almost shouted now. 'Because of this, right now, DI Kapoor and *DCI* Walsh are interviewing Richard Statham again. You know, the ex-manager of the Harrison Casino?'

Elliott paled considerably.

'They're... they're talking to Statham?'

'Brought him in twenty minutes ago,' De'Geer said, watching Elliott's reaction carefully. 'Funny thing about Statham – turns out he's got connections all over the place. To Katarina Kováč. To Kenny Tsang. To Jun Ng Kai-lok and his Triad buddies. Probably Trevor Sullivan, definitely the late D.Q. James and Marek Kováč. And from what Monroe's been saying, to you as well.'

'So, the body was James's?' Elliott replied. 'I heard it could have been—'

'Ronnie Carrigan?' De'Geer sneered. 'Yeah, we put that out the moment my bosses realised someone was sniffing around. Hold that, let me change that, I mean when they realised *you* were sniffing around.'

'I don't know what you're—'

'Don't,' De'Geer cut him off. 'I've worked it out, Paul. I understand that you've got your gambling debt, and Katarina Kováč is pulling your strings. I know that Statham connects you to her operation, probably some kind of off-books handler. And I know that tonight you're going to be providing security or interference or whatever for a very special poker night. One where Katarina hopefully finds out, after all these years, who took five hundred grands worth of diamonds and about a million dollars' worth of winnings from D.Q. James, before killing him and bricking him up in a wall.'

Paul Elliott looked like he might be sick.

'How much does Monroe know?'

'Enough to be planning surveillance tonight. Maybe even a raid.' De'Geer leaned against the wall, arms crossed. 'If Statham's panicking in that interview room right now, do you think he's going to protect you? Or is he going to give Monroe everything he needs to save his own skin?'

'Christ.' Elliott's breathing had gone shallow. 'If Statham talks, if he tells them about the watch—'

'What bloody watch?'

'The Patek Phillipe that D.Q. James owned,' Elliott crumpled now. 'He had it for years. One of many D.Q. James had, but the others were all in the lockup.'

'So, how did Statham get them?'

'He was keeping the lockup payments going.' Elliott shrugged. 'I have no idea why. Then, a few months back, he stops paying, puts the whole lockup up for auction. Minus a couple of things he nicked from inside it first, over the years.'

'And that's when the museum bought it?'

At this, Elliott started to laugh, and De'Geer wondered if he'd overplayed his hand.

'The museum bought nothing,' he replied. 'Some watches, a couple of trinkets. Most of the good things were already gone by the time they bought the items.'

'But Walsh and Kapoor saw the exhibition,' De'Geer frowned. 'They saw the poker chips, the figurine...'

'Oh the figure he played with? Yeah, that was in the sale.' Elliott nodded. 'But those chips? They were never in the sale. They were never in the lockup.'

'Then where did Imogen Rothwell get them?'

'No idea.' Elliott shrugged. 'Ask her tonight, she'll be at the event, for sure.'

'What time does it start, Paul?'

Elliott hesitated, then seemed to decide it wasn't a secret worth keeping.

'Event starts at eight, downstairs game starts at ten. I'm supposed to be there at nine.'

'And what exactly are you supposed to be doing there?'

'Katarina wants police presence. Off-duty, plainclothes, just stand around looking official.' Elliott's voice cracked. 'She thinks one of the people she's invited knows where James hid the diamonds. Everyone who knew him back in 2009 – the casino manager, the croupier, that businessman who lost everything, all invited. And she's worried about Jun.'

'Jun Ng Kai-lok? She's worried about him or the Triad he runs with?'

'Both. They've been watching the casino for weeks, all the way through the build. I also know Jun's been talking to Marek about buying his percentage of the building off him. If Jun Ng Kai-lok thinks someone at that game knows where his family's diamonds are, it's going to kick off. That's why Katarina wants protection.' Elliott looked up at De'Geer. 'She'll wipe my debt clean if I do this. Thirty grand, Morten. Gone.'

'And if Monroe sends people in tonight and you're standing there as Katarina's hired security, you're finished.'

'I'm finished anyway!' Elliott's desperation finally broke through completely. 'If I don't show up, she'll come after me, and the Triad will think I've turned informant. If I do show up and there's a raid, my career's over. And now Statham's in there talking to your bosses, and I'm telling you—'

'Sit down,' De'Geer said quietly.

Elliott stared at him.

'I said *sit down*.' De'Geer pointed towards the chair.

Elliott moved slowly, lowering himself into the seat, confusion and fear warring on his face.

'You weren't telling me what was going on,' De'Geer said. 'I knew most of this already. But you see, the problem you've got, Paul, is I now understand the full picture. And here's what I think – I think you've got me into deep shit because of your selfish nature. You think I *wanted* to be here? You think I wanted to keep in touch with you after Hendon? I owed you – and you almost got us both screwed over.'

'I was your only friend—' Elliott began to protest, but De'Geer held up a hand.

'You know what else I know? I know that come Monday morning, I'm probably going to be out on my arse. PC Cooper talking to my boss about what happened in Hendon means they now know what's going on. The chances are my time at the Last Chance Saloon is finished. So, do the maths. At a place called the Last Chance Saloon, what do you think happens when you *use up* that last chance?'

He moved closer, his massive frame looming over Elliott's seated form.

'So, here's what's going to happen. You're going to call your friend – Statham, Kováč – I don't give a shit who your real handler is. And you're going to tell them that I'll be helping you. I'll stand beside you tonight to make sure nobody gets out of line. But, to do so, I want a cut of the profits. Whatever Katarina's offering you, I want the same.'

'I can't do that,' Elliott replied.

'You *will* do that,' De'Geer snarled. 'You've got me into deep shit because of your selfish nature. Good coppers don't take reports, photocopy them and then hold them over someone for years. You're nothing but scum, Paul. And when this evening's finished, and when you've made me my money – of which I expect to equal what you've had removed from your debt – we will never talk to each other again. I will leave the force, and I will go do something else with the money I've made. And if I ever see you again, I will rip off your arms and beat you to death with the squishy ends. Do you honestly think I can't?'

Paul Elliott shook his head silently. De'Geer nodded with a smile on his face, as if they were just bantering about.

'Nine o'clock.' De'Geer checked his watch. 'It's ten now – eleven hours until your thing starts. I'll be back at eight, and we'll go in together. And between now and then, you're going to decide I'm right, call me up and tell me everything. Who else is involved, what Statham's actual role is, how he connects to both Jun and James. Everything.'

'And if I tell you to piss off?'

'Then I walk out that door and tell Monroe exactly how to stop your payout. Your choice, Paul. Partner up with me and maybe we both get out of this as I divert everyone to a different location or face a potential raid with no warning and no backup.' De'Geer's expression hardened. 'What's it going to be?'

Elliott stared at him for a long moment, then seemed to deflate completely.

'Statham set up the whole thing,' he whispered. 'He's been running Katarina's operation for years. He's also the one who introduced D.Q. James to Jun's games back in 2009 – that's how James got into the basement poker night where he won the diamonds.'

'So, Statham connects to both Jun and James?'

'Yeah. And to Marek Kováč, Katarina's ex. They go way

back, used to work together. He used to put Marek in rooms with the diplomats. I guess for trade deals and all that.'

'Did you consider Marek might have been a spy?' De'Geer shook his head in disbelief.

At this, Elliott paused.

'If they're interviewing Statham now, he's going to panic. He might warn Katarina, and then the entire game gets called off.'

'Then you'd better hope he doesn't talk too much,' De'Geer said. 'I'll check in every hour. Keep your phone on. If there's a raid planned, I'll warn you. But if you try to back out, if you try to run or warn Katarina yourself, I'll make that stab wound you gave yourself look like a paper cut. Understood?'

'Understood.'

'Good.' De'Geer headed towards the door, leaving Elliott sitting alone in the chair, looking like a man who'd just realised he was trapped between multiple bad choices with no way out.

OUTSIDE, DE'GEER TOOK A DEEP BREATH. HE NEEDED A shower; he felt filthy inside. Still, if it helped, it was worth it.

Pulling out his phone, he sent a text to Billy, summarising what he'd learned there; Paul Elliott had effectively just confessed to corruption, leaking police information, and conspiracy to obstruct justice, while Imogen Rothwell seemed full of even more secrets than before. He knew Billy would pass it around the team as he climbed back on his motorcycle and headed back to Temple Inn. He hadn't lied when he said there was every chance he could be fired by Monday, but that was next week.

This week they had to catch a murderer.

20

RETCONNED

THE HARRISON CASINO HAD BEEN DRESSED UP TO LOOK AS IT had in its heyday - or at least Monroe assumed, based from the photos of the casino he'd seen. That said, for the fact this had been created in less than a day, it was pretty impressive. Chandeliers were sparkling, and poker and roulette tables covered the floor. It was only one floor, however, that had been made to look so; obviously the budget wasn't extending to an entire building for just a weekend.

The bar was being restocked, and staff, likely rehired for the night only, were already setting things up as Monroe and Cooper entered through the main door.

A familiar face waited for them.

'I wondered when we'd get a visit.' Thomas Greaves smiled. He wasn't wearing the SpinJack clothing he'd had on the previous day but instead wore a Harrison Casino waist-coat and a white shirt – no bow tie, however. That said, the event still wasn't on for another eight or so hours, so there was every chance he was playing it casual until he needed to dress for the part.

'Thought we'd pop in, see how the party we've not been invited to is going.' Monroe gave a smile. 'Care to give us a tour?'

'Of course.' Greaves motioned across the floor. 'Open to all ex-members of the casino and their guests for one night. We were expecting fewer people, so it's scaled down. Only roulette, Texas Hold 'Em, and blackjack.'

Greaves smiled.

'And of course, a SpinJack table. No self-respecting casino would be without a SpinJack table.'

'Of course,' Monroe deadpanned. 'I would expect nothing less. No manager?'

'You mean Statham? Apparently he's "guest" status tonight,' Greaves replied. 'No idea who'll they'll have as floor manager.'

'Not vying for the spot?'

'Hell no.' Greaves shook his head. 'There's fireworks tonight and I won't want to get burned.'

Monroe nodded, understanding exactly what Greaves was insinuating.

'And the basement?'

Greaves, to his credit, didn't change his expression.

'It's being set up right now,' he said. 'If you want to see it, I think you'd have to ask—'

'Oh, it's okay, Thomas.' A woman's voice spoke across the hall as Katarina Kováč appeared. She was wearing jogging bottoms and a hooded sweater and looked more like she'd come from her Pilates session than preparing for a night out. Again, however, the chances were her party dress wouldn't be put on for many hours, and she was taking the opportunity to wear something comfortable while working. 'I'll take over from here.'

She led Monroe and Cooper to a back-room door, which, when opened, led down some stairs. It was a route Monroe had taken before, the day they'd found a body hidden behind a wall.

'I'm guessing you were told about the invites,' she said.

'Aye, we were told there was something small going on, but this seems a lot bigger than we expected.'

'D.Q. James dying is a big thing.'

'Well, he's not really dying, is he?' Monroe replied. 'More having died a long time ago.'

'Well, it's still a memorial, a wake of sorts.' Katarina wasn't really playing along, keeping her voice light as she continued. 'There's a lot of people who still want to pay their respects.'

'And they can do it while giving your casino some last-ditch money.' Monroe smiled. 'Get some drinks, food, a few tables, allow the house to always win... you can make a fair amount tonight.'

'Going out in style,' Katarina replied. 'I think it's only fair. Considering the history of this place, the last night at the Harrison Casino was a bit of a damp squib. Five or six people resolutely holding out that things wouldn't change. My plan today is to give it a bit of pizzazz one last time.'

'Aye, lassie, before you decide to turn it into what? Houses and a spa, I believe?'

'Among other things.' Katarina opened the door to the basement, and Monroe was surprised at what he saw. The last time he'd been in here, it had been a construction site with table saws and demolition equipment, but now it had been cleaned up and shined to a squeaky clean level. In the centre of the room, a giant poker table had been set up. It was well lit, with a small bar to the right-hand side – but opposite, where only days earlier a body had been found, the hole in the wall was still visible.

'You decided not to clean up that section?'

'It would have taken too long to fix up or fully remove, and I felt it made a statement for tonight's event,' Katarina replied. 'After all, everybody in this invite-only area of the event will have had a personal connection to D.Q. James.'

'Oh aye, and what's that then?'

'They will have been screwed over by him at some point,' Katarina replied. 'I'm guessing you already know who's turning up.'

'We have an idea,' Monroe said.

'Every single person who D.Q. James ever screwed over is coming along.' Katarina smiled. 'A chance to raise a toast, remember him, and then spit on that memory.'

'I get that, but that's not what this is about, is it?'

'What else would it be?'

'It's all about you looking for five hundred grand's worth of diamonds, which in this day and age are probably close to a million by now,' Monroe started. 'It's about Ironthread, the Triad leader, looking for the jewels that he lost fifteen years ago. It's about a manager who worked all sides and betrayed everybody. A rival who lost everything, including possibly his own brother. A woman who built her way up from hostess to full-level player, who it seemed married the wrong person – an East European spy for example – and has spent the last couple of years looking for the money.'

There was a long, uncomfortable pause in the conversation, one that Monroe seemed to revel in.

'Tell me,' he asked, 'did you know Richard Statham controlled D.Q. James's storage facility?'

'Not until recently. I learned when it went up for sale.'

'Aye. And what happened to the money made in that sale?' Monroe asked. 'You see, we'd been told it was to cover debts of unpaid bills, but it sounds like Mister Statham had been *paying* the bills.'

'You'd have to ask Mister Statham that.'

'Oh, don't worry, we will,' Monroe said. 'So, will you also be bringing Mrs Rothwell to the event?'

'I don't know a—'

'Please, Miss Kováč, don't pretend you have no idea who that is,' Monroe interrupted. 'For a start, we know you've been to the museum a couple of times, especially after the storage locker was bought. And we also know that you're likely aware through your own private investigations that she's the sister of Ronnie Carrigan.'

'Has Ronald Carrigan been invited to the event?' Cooper now asked, looking up from her notebook.

'Ronald Carrigan disappeared fifteen years ago,' Katarina replied coldly. 'He's been a little hard to tie down.'

'Well, if you have an invitation for him, we can pass it on,' Monroe said darkly. 'You see, we know exactly where he is right now. We can literally place it in his hand. Well, what's left of it.'

Before Katarina could ask what he meant, he straightened, looking around the room.

'We'd like some invites,' he said. 'If that's okay with you.'

'The more the merrier,' Katarina replied, her face not giving away anything. 'I can provide you with some access. I can't give you chips or anything – you'd have to pay your own money for gambling – but I am more than happy to have law enforcement officers here, especially with such gambling going on.'

'And what about down here?' Monroe asked. 'Do we get an invite to the special room?'

Katarina stopped, turned and fully faced Monroe now.

'Did you get screwed over by David Quincey James?' she asked.

'Can't say I did, I think.'

'Then no,' Katarina replied simply. 'No, you won't get an invite down here, and no token, no entrance. You have to deserve the invite, have a personal connection, I'm afraid. I wouldn't try to sneak in, either.'

'Oh, aye, we heard what happened to the last guy who faked a piece to get in.' Monroe gave a slight tip of an imaginary hat, glancing meaningfully at the hole in the wall before leaving Katarina Kováč to her own devices in the basement.

BILLY WAS AT HIS DESK WHEN THE MESSAGE CAME FROM reception; someone wanted to see him, wouldn't give a name, told him to meet her in the car park.

Aware that time was running out, but also curious as to whether these were the expected ledgers, Billy made his way down to the main entrance of the Temple Inn crime unit... where, in the middle of the car park, leaning against a tree, he saw Trix Preston.

She was young, early to mid-twenties, with long blonde hair pulled into a ponytail. She wore a slightly battered olive Barbour jacket and jeans, and if you walked past her in the street you would never have picked her out as anything special. This, however, was Trix Preston's ability. The first time Billy had met her, she pretended to be nothing more than a simple intern scrolling through Instagram and listening to music on her ear pods. It was later found out that she'd been working for Francine Pierce of *Pierce Associates*, one of the suspects in a decades-old murder case they were working on, and that the earphones were actually providing her with the bugged conversation footage. She'd then cut a deal with the government and, through the Prime Minister Charles Baker, had next popped up monitoring Temple Inn. In fact, it was her monitoring that had helped save Monroe's life when he was attacked and who had also assisted Declan in escaping when he was being set up on terrorism charges.

Over the years, here and there, she and Billy had shared information – more on her lines than his – and she'd even shown him a few back doors and tricks he could use, as the hacker in her was better than the cyber expert in him.

She was a friend, as much as Trix Preston had friends.

She nodded as he approached.

'You can come up if you want.' He nodded back at the building.

'No, I'm fine,' Trix replied with a smile. 'But I needed to pass some information, and I didn't really want to be in the office.'

'Go on.'

'Your bloke Marek Kováč.' Trix nodded. 'Hungarian security. Used to work for the Információs Hivatal, which is Hungary's version of MI6 back in the nineties. Came over to London in 1998. The official story is that he came from money and doubled it – there's an element of truth in that. His parents were rich, but he was more funded than entrepreneuristic.'

She shrugged.

'Late nineties, a lot of the Eastern Bloc was breaking up

and people were trying to work out who was worth talking to. Marek was aimed at diplomats – brought in a lot of information. The problem was that in 2007 he was turned by MI5 and MI6. He would provide *them* with information, you know, here and there.'

She pulled out a flash drive and passed it to him.

'Your body died in November 2009, right? Shortly before that, Marek Kováč had been attacked by FSB operatives.'

Billy whistled. Russian security was not somebody you wanted to piss off. Ask any Russians living in Salisbury about that.

'They tried to kill him. He escaped, brokered some kind of deal that kept him alive. However, the promise was that he would step away from the limelight – no longer would he be seen in the places he'd been.'

'Death or retirement.' Billy nodded. 'And the drive?'

'Everything we have on him,' Trix said. 'Which, to be honest, isn't much. For the last ten to fifteen years, he's provided occasional intel to MI5 and MI6 when things have crossed his path, but most of the time he's done nothing.'

'Thanks,' Billy replied, pocketing the drive. But then he paused. 'You know, this could have been a phone call and a courier.'

'Yeah, about that.' Trix looked around. 'You need to pass a message to Declan and Monroe. An old friend has resurfaced. I'm heading to Edinburgh right now to speak to her.'

'What kind of old friend?'

'Someone who we all believed was dead.'

'There aren't many people who fit that bill,' Billy said, an icy shiver of realisation sliding down his spine. 'Are we talking Francine Pierce?'

Trix paused, and Billy understood the hesitation. Francine Pierce was, after all, the woman who had brought her into Temple Inn's sphere of orbit.

'All I'm saying is there's something going on. Francine's in the middle, and it might be worth your boss's time, if they're still hunting her – to take a quick trip to Edinburgh in the next day or two.'

She tapped Billy's pocket – the one he'd placed the flash drive in.

'That's on there as well,' she said, turning and walking off. 'I'll let you know when I'm around next. We should go for a drink – it's been too long. And I like your forger.'

'You only like my forger because you know you can use him for work.' Billy smiled. 'Hey, who do you use as your go-to ID person?'

Trix paused and turned, a smile on her face.

'Go-to ID person?'

'Yeah.' Billy nodded. 'When Marlowe wasn't playing with MI5, you two were still travelling around and you wouldn't have done it on your IDs. Who made them for you?'

'Woman named Helen Bonneville,' Trix replied. 'Why?'

'Could you ask her – are you in contact with her?' Billy asked hesitantly. 'Can you ask her if she ever knew a guy called Finch?'

'I can check. Any particular reason?'

'Crossing T's and dotting I's.' Billy smiled. 'Good to see you, Trix. Don't be a stranger.'

Trix left just as the courier arrived with three leather-bound notebooks, and Billy signed for them at the door, and brought them back to the briefing room where Jess was still working.

'You should be in Globe Town by now,' he said.

'Johnny's not there,' Jess replied, not looking up from her screen. 'Leroy said he'll be arriving at one, so I'll leave in a minute. What are those?'

'Arthur Finch's ledgers,' Billy said, pulling on evidence gloves before opening the first one. The entries were cramped handwriting, meticulously detailed. Dates, names, documents created, and here and there fees paid. Billy flipped through 1995, 1996, 1997 – hundreds of ID forgeries, each one catalogued like a business ledger.

'Jesus,' he muttered. 'I can't show this to Sam. He thinks he's a big fish in the forging community. This'd kill him.'

'Here,' Jess said, pointing. 'March 2000.'

Client: Darren Jameson, DOB 15/08/1972.
New identity created: David Quincey James, DOB 15/08/1972.
Passport, driver's licence, National Insurance number.

'No fee written,' Jess said, scratching at her chin. 'It was done for free?'

'Might have been a favour, Ellie Reckless-style, or maybe a cost that wasn't able to be numerically explained,' Billy replied as he continued through the pages.

'So, Darren Jameson became D.Q. James,' Jess said. 'That's Johnny's story confirmed.'

Billy stopped at January 2010.

Client: David Quincey James, DOB 15/08/1972.
New identity created: Trevor Michael Sullivan, DOB 02/03/1970.
Passport, driver's licence, National Insurance number.
Fee: One Patek Philippe Grand Complications in box – estimated at £20,000

'Trevor Michael Sullivan,' Jess whispered. 'I'm guessing that's the real Trevor Sullivan's name and date of birth.'

Billy kept reading Finch's notes.

'Listen to this,' he said. '"*Client insisted on exact DOB and personal details of original Trevor Sullivan. Confirmed original deceased, no family to identify discrepancy. Paid extra for current photo rather than using original's documentation. Client appearance significantly different from original – longer beard, different hair*".'

'Original deceased? Does that mean...'

'That Darren Sullivan – who'd been D.Q. James for a decade – either killed his brother, or found him dead,' Billy said quietly. 'He did more than just take everything. He took his very identity.'

'January 2010,' Jess shook her head in disbelief. 'Two months after Ronnie Carrigan was murdered. D.Q. James waited for things to cool down, then became his brother.'

They sat there for a moment, the implications settling in.

'So, Trevor Sullivan...'

'Isn't Trevor Sullivan,' Billy finished. 'It's D.Q. James. It's been him for fifteen years. The question is, did he kill his brother or find him dead?'

'If he destroyed his life and Trevor committed suicide, does that mean technically James killed him by default?'

Billy pulled out his phone and called Monroe. It rang twice before Monroe answered.

'What've you got?'

'The ledgers,' Billy said. 'Darren Jameson became David Quincey James in March 2000. Then in January 2010, David Quincey James became Trevor Michael Sullivan – using the real Trevor's name, date of birth, everything. However, Finch's notes say the original was deceased, no family. So, the man working at that gym, who Katarina invited tonight...'

'Is D.Q. James himself,' Monroe said. 'And he doesn't know we've worked it out yet.'

21

ARRESTED DEVELOPMENTS

Billy had been staring at Finch's ledgers for twenty minutes, cross-referencing dates and names, when Bullman appeared at his desk with two mugs of coffee.

'Thought you could use this,' she said, setting one down beside his keyboard. 'You've been at it for hours.'

'Thanks, ma'am.' Billy took a grateful sip. Bullman settled into the chair beside him, looking at the pages displaying Finch's cramped handwriting.

'So, Trevor Sullivan is actually D.Q. James,' she said. 'That's a hell of a twist. Takes some nerve, too.'

'Or desperation. Someone killed the wrong man. James knew they'd come for him if they realised their mistake.'

He whistled.

'Finch's ledgers could burn a lot of people,' he said. 'I've got Triad members, a couple of bank robbers we've been looking for... I'm stunned Westminster did nothing with this.'

'Compartmentalised.' Bullman shrugged. 'Sure, there might be names they can use here, but with the forger dead, how do you prove things aren't just fiction?'

Bullman leant back, hands wrapped around her mug.

'Georgie Moir, the man who led us here. He's a seasoned investigator, right? Monroe claims he's dodgy as hell, but competent, and it sounds like he worked for James for years.'

She leant forward, staring down at the books.

'Did he ever work out that Trevor Sullivan was actually his old client? Or did he work it out and get paid to keep quiet?'

Billy sipped at his coffee, considering this.

'Moir would have known what James looked like. Known his habits, his patterns. If he ever crossed paths with "Trevor Sullivan"—'

'He'd have recognised him,' Bullman finished. 'So, either he never looked, or he did look and said nothing. And given Moir's track record, I know which one I'd bet on.'

Billy was already reaching for his phone.

'I need to call him.'

'Let me know what you find.' Bullman stood. 'And Billy? If Moir's been sitting on this for years, there's a reason. Be careful.'

The phone rang three times before Moir answered.

'Yeah?'

'Mister Moir, it's DS Fitzwarren from Temple Inn. You spoke with us the other day about D.Q. James.'

'I remember. I also remember Monroe stealing my gold. What d'you want now?'

Billy paused. If he gave away too much now, there was a chance Moir could pass it on. If he gave too little, Moir might keep quiet.

'We've discovered that David Quincey James wasn't the body found. We also know that from 2010, James was using the ID of Trevor Sullivan, thanks to the forger you provided him.'

There was a long silence.

'Moir? You still there?'

'Yeah. I'm here.' Moir's voice was careful now.

'This is the same Trevor Sullivan you were hired to investigate every aspect of his life.'

'I see that,' Moir replied carefully. 'But I gave James everything. I never kept copies.'

'You worked for D.Q. James for years. You'd have known what he looked like. His habits, his patterns. You told my boss you'd never known the new name Mister Finch gave him with his fake ID, but did you ever cross paths with Trevor Sullivan *after* James destroyed his life? Ever think he looked familiar?'

Another pause.

'Because if you recognised him and didn't tell anyone, that's obstruction. But if you recognised him and told someone else – maybe sold that information – that's a different problem entirely.'

Moir let out a long breath.

'I didn't sell it,' he said. 'I was hired to find him.'

Billy stopped.

'What?'

'March 2020. Woman came to me asking about Trevor Sullivan. Wanted to know where he was, what he was doing. Said she believed Sullivan was responsible for her brother's death. I took the job, tracked him down – which, considering what I'd learnt a decade or so earlier wasn't difficult—'

'You said you gave the notes to James.'

'Still had the basics in my head though,' Moir replied irritably. 'Anyway, I followed him for six months.'

'Who hired you?'

'Imogen Rothwell. Ronnie Carrigan's sister.'

Billy felt his stomach drop.

'She hired you to find Trevor Sullivan?'

'Yeah. She thought Sullivan orchestrated Ronnie's death.'

'How?'

'Word on the street was he wound up some Triad bloke to kill who he believed was D.Q. James – but instead they killed the decoy. She'd spent years on her own looking into this, had it all worked out. Just wanted me to confirm Sullivan's location.'

'And you recognised Trevor as James.'

'Course I bloody did. Beard, grey hair, fifteen years older – but it was him. Same height, same build, same way of moving. I worked for the man for years. I knew.'

'And you didn't tell Imogen?'

'She paid me to find Trevor Sullivan and report on his movements. That's what I did. What I recognised wasn't part of the job. I took her money to do surveillance work. What she did with that information was her business, not mine.'

Billy's mind was racing. *Imogen had been tracking Trevor for five years, believing he'd orchestrated her brother's death. Not knowing Trevor was actually D.Q. James.*

'What did she say she was going to do with the information?'

'Said she'd handle it from there. I assumed she meant lawyers or something. Civil case, maybe.' Moir paused. 'Why? What's she done?'

'I can't discuss an ongoing investigation,' Billy said. 'But I need copies of everything you gave her. Reports, surveillance photos, the lot.'

'That'll cost you.'

'Mister Moir, this is a murder investigation. You can either cooperate voluntarily or I can have DCS Bullman get a warrant and we'll take the rest of your gold. Your choice.'

Another pause.

'Fine. I'll email what I've got. Same address as before?'

'Please. Today.'

'Will do.'

Bullman had emerged, watching Billy as he disconnected the call.

'Imogen thinks she's been tracking her brother's killer,' he said. 'She doesn't know she's been following the man Ronnie died impersonating.'

'Where's Anjli?' Bullman looked around.

'Museum. She was going to speak to Rothwell.'

'Well that's going to be an interesting conversation,' Bullman muttered.

ANJLI STOOD IN THE D.Q. JAMES POKER EXHIBIT, STARING AT the empty display case.

The curator – a woman in her fifties with greying hair pulled into a practical bun – looked apologetic.

'Mrs Rothwell took them first thing this morning,' she explained. 'Said they were needed for something. Didn't say much else, just signed them out and left.'

'What time was this?'

'Around ten o'clock. She seemed quite determined about it.'

Anjli felt something cold settle in her stomach.

'Did she say where she was taking them? Who she was giving them to?'

'No.' The curator looked worried. 'Should I not have let her take them? They're not technically museum property, and Mrs Rothwell is connected to the donor, so I assumed...'

'And the donor is?'

'Oh, you'd have to ask Mrs Rothwell that.'

Anjli pulled out her phone, already walking out of the museum, texting Monroe.

> Chips are gone. Imogen took them from the museum, and she's in the wind.

A second later, a response from Monroe replied.

> I was just texting you. Rothwell just arrested trying to buy an illegal firearm in Hackney.

Anjli stopped walking as a second message came through.

> Glock 17. Being brought here so get your wee arse back.

Anjli climbed into her car and headed back immediately.

IMOGEN ROTHWELL SAT IN THE INTERVIEW ROOM SILENTLY AS Anjli entered and sat down, Bullman behind her. She didn't feel she needed the extra power of a heavyweight Detective Chief Superintendent, but Bullman was there anyway, and Anjli felt that having two people there might gain the information quicker, especially with the clock ticking.

Anjli leant closer, tapping the recorder.

'Interview with Imogen Rothwell, Thursday, four p.m. In attendance, Detective Inspector Anjli Kapoor, Detective Chief Superintendent Sophie Bullman.'

She looked at Imogen.

'Are you aware of your rights? Have they been explained to you?'

Rothwell nodded.

'For the record, Mrs Rothwell has nodded to the question,' Anjli added.

'I'm not going to fight this,' Rothwell said. 'I did what you accused me of. Fifteen years ago my brother was murdered.'

Anjli placed the gun, now in an evidence bag, on the table.

'Did you feel that this was the way to fix that?' she asked. 'How were you paying for this?'

Rothwell kept quiet.

Anjli shook her head and then reached into her pocket, pulling out the golden Mexican fifty-peso coin that Georgie Moir had allowed them to examine.

'If we go back and speak to the person you bought this from,' she asked, 'will we find you paid them with one of these?'

Imogen stared at the coin.

'Where did you get that?' she asked.

'Georgie Moir, who you've been working with.' Anjli leant forwards. 'Please, Imogen, we're trying to help. Explain to us why you bought an unregistered gun from an illegal back alley, using contacts likely gained by a gutter-scum investigator, hours before a poker game to commemorate a dead gambler who had a connection to your late brother. You can see why we have concerns.'

Rothwell sighed and nodded.

'I've said to you before I've always believed that Ronnie was murdered,' she replied. 'And I was angry at him for taking James's stupid deal. But he wasn't the only person who had an issue with him.'

'Go on,' Anjli encouraged. 'What exactly do you mean by that?'

'Well, he was a bit of a ladies' man,' Rothwell replied. 'It's one of the reasons he'd leapt at the opportunity to pretend to be D.Q. James. Rolex watch, fast car, he was in love with that lifestyle. But he'd been trying to live that life even before he bought the car. Ever since he started working in the casino, he'd been looking at these gamblers and thinking he was one of them rather than the guy who served them drinks. I suppose when you've opened your thirtieth expensive four-figure bottle of champagne, you start to believe that surely a sip can't hurt.'

She shook her head.

'The problem was he'd got himself caught up in that world. And he'd started trying to create his own blackmail folders on a few of the gamblers.'

'What kind of blackmail?' Anjli enquired.

'I don't know, I never found out,' Rothwell replied. 'However, when James utterly destroyed Trevor Sullivan, nobody knew how he'd done it. Sure, there was talk of private investigators, but people reached for the low-hanging fruit first, and that was the barman. A few weeks earlier, Sullivan had a bad day and lost a few thousand on the tables, and then got drunk at the bar, giving a sob story to my brother. Much of the information given out there was used by James in that later game. So, Sullivan assumed – whether incorrectly or not – that Ronnie was the one who had fed D.Q. James the information that destroyed his life.'

She shook her head.

'There was more to it as well. There was something

personal between the two of them. Something that nobody really understood, from what I can work out. I never saw it. I didn't hang in those circles, but I got it second hand. Trevor Sullivan was angry, and Ronnie had told me he'd had a confrontation with the man a week or two after the conversation he'd been accused of overhearing. Sullivan had been following him.'

She shrugged.

'But then he was also dressing as D.Q. James, so we don't know if Sullivan was following James or Carrigan, if you get what I mean...'

She started to cry. Anjli reached into her pocket and pulled out a small travel pack of tissues, passing one across.

'Please, I know it's hard, but can you continue?' she asked. 'We still need to understand why you needed this.'

She tapped at the weapon, and Rothwell nodded.

'On the night my Ronnie disappeared I'd had a call from Trevor Sullivan in the afternoon asking where my brother was. I didn't know where he was, but Ronnie had specifically asked me not to say anything to Trevor if he ever called, so when Trevor asked if Ronnie was anywhere near Islington, I said no. I later found out that he *had* been there, pretending to be D.Q. James again. It was only a couple of weeks later I started to put it together.'

Anjli frowned, looking up.

'How did Sullivan contact you on that day?' she asked. 'If we're talking about the middle of November, Sullivan has an alibi. He was in rehab from the tenth.'

'It wasn't the middle of November,' Rothwell frowned. 'It was November eighth, a Sunday.'

'November eighth? You're sure?'

'Positive. It was my niece's birthday party that afternoon. I remember because Sullivan's call interrupted the cake cutting.'

Bullman leant forward.

'Miss Rothwell, everyone's been looking at November fifteenth as the crucial date. That's when D.Q. James was last seen publicly. But you're saying Ronnie disappeared a week earlier?'

'He did,' Rothwell nodded. 'I assumed he was just doing his thing or had gone off the rails a little. Then when D.Q. James disappeared on the fifteenth, I assumed they were connected, but...'

She trailed off. Anjli was already texting Billy.

> Check construction timeline. When was basement wall actually built? Rothwell says Ronnie disappeared Nov 8th, not 15th, James's last public appearance.

'Anyway, I didn't know what was happening. I didn't know what had gone on. Then, by pure chance, I met Georgie Moir. He'd been working with D.Q. James; when I was trying to understand why both D.Q. James and my brother disappeared at the same time, he arrived at my doorstep.'

'Why would he do that?'

'Because he wanted to know about the casino chips.' Rothwell shrugged. 'You see, Ronnie gave a box to me before he disappeared. Asked me to look after them, said he had gained them, but wouldn't explain how. I got the impression he'd stolen them but I didn't know why. I think he was trying to find his lighter, maybe thought James had stolen it, so he'd steal something back.'

'Did you know they were something else?'

'Not at the time. But when Moir turned up at my door

and asked me if I knew where they were, I explained that I wasn't part of the plot. I hadn't seen my brother.'

'So, you lied.'

'Of course I lied! When a stranger turns up at your doorstep and asks about something that's hidden in a box around the corner of the hallway, you don't tell them unless you know what's going on,' Rothwell snapped. 'Anyway, we started to talk. Moir explained what he'd been doing, and I realised that Moir felt guilty in relation to my brother, because he was the one who had found the information out for D.Q. James.'

'The information your brother had been accused of,' Bullman stated.

Rothwell nodded.

'He offered to help however he could, and I explained that I believed D.Q. James wasn't dead, that it was my brother who had been killed, because he hadn't called me back. I just didn't know where or when. Moir offered to help, said he'd look into it.'

She gave out a shuddering sigh, the memory probably vivid in her mind now.

'Then, a couple of weeks later, he contacted me and told me that D.Q. James had gone on the run. Moir had sorted him a passport through a third party, didn't know what his identity was, but he got the impression that D.Q. James was scared. Around the same time, Sullivan was divorced, had lost everything, and decided to go on a backpacking tour around the world over the next ten years. I assumed this was a story to explain some kind of longwinded global hunt of James.'

'You also thought Trevor Sullivan had killed your brother?'

'Yeah. Killed Ronnie, and now James was running because he didn't know if it was deliberate or accidental. Either way, I didn't trust him. Especially when there were no more sightings or mentions at all about D.Q. James,' Rothwell explained. 'So, I tried to play detective. At first, I used savings, but then one day I was moving things around in the house, and I dropped one of the casino chips on the floor. I noticed it had chipped where it hit, some of the paint had come off, and when I examined it, I realised it was gold.'

She looked up.

'I'm not an idiot. I realised immediately what it was. And when I checked every other coin in the pack, I realised they were all Mexican fifty-peso coins – these are thirty-seven millimetres in diameter, and two-point-seven millimetres deep. A casino chip? Thirty-nine millimetres and three-point-three deep. Almost the same size, even if the weight's off by a factor of four. However, I now had a hundred gold coins in my pocket. Hundreds of thousands of pounds, which made me a very strong suspect for the murder. But, with that money, I suddenly realised I had opportunities.'

'You could spend more on finding Trevor Sullivan.'

Imogen Rothwell nodded.

'I followed him,' she explained. 'By proxy. Hunting him as he travelled around the world. I saw the games he played at while I spoke to various people. I used the coins to bring in other investigators, anyone who could find out what I needed. Then, a few years ago, Trevor came back home, decided he was going to live a normal life again and rebuild his life. By this point, I'd run out of reasons to follow him, but I still had a need to know what he was doing, so I brought Moir back in.'

'So, the gun,' Anjli said carefully. 'Who was it for?'

Imogen Rothwell's hands had stopped shaking. She looked tired now, fifteen years of anger draining out of her.

'When you said about the body, I knew it had to be Ronnie. I was going to confront Sullivan at the poker game, accuse him of the murder, and make sure he knew Ronnie's name before I pulled the trigger.'

She looked up, meeting Anjli's eyes.

'I thought... I thought I could finally get answers. Find out why Ronnie had to die. And then...'

She didn't finish.

Bullman leant forward slightly.

'Marek said it would be my only chance,' Rothwell muttered.

'Marek Kováč knew you wanted to kill Trevor Sullivan?'

'No, just confront him,' Rothwell shook her head. 'I hadn't decided on the weapon at that point. I'd donated the rest of the chip collection, filled the empty spots with some random chips at the back, said they could have it as part of the event, but only if they told everyone about it, made a big deal.'

'Because whoever knew the truth about the chips would definitely appear,' Bullman nodded in understanding. 'Miss Rothwell, you're being charged with attempted illegal firearms purchase. Given the circumstances and your cooperation, we'll be recommending bail with conditions. You'll need a solicitor.'

'I don't want bail,' Rothwell said quietly. 'I want my brother back. But since I can't have that...'

She gestured at the coin on the table.

'At least someone found him. At least he's not alone any more in that basement. But Trevor Sullivan needs to die.'

'Actually, I have a feeling someone may have beaten you

there,' Anjli replied. 'We have reason to believe Trevor Sullivan passed away a long time ago.'

OUTSIDE IN THE CORRIDOR, BULLMAN PULLED ANJLI ASIDE.

'You think she would have gone through with it?' Bullman asked. 'Killing Sullivan?'

Anjli thought about Imogen Rothwell's face when she'd talked about her brother. The years of searching, the fortune spent, the obsession that had consumed fifteen years of her life, the utter breakdown the moment she heard the real Trevor Sullivan might be dead.

'Yeah,' she said. 'I think she would have.'

Anjli's phone buzzed; a text from Billy.

> Building records show work done in November 2009 – Harrison Casino closed on two Sun/Mons during this time, 8 – 9 / 22 – 23. If wall built first dates, both Marek and Sullivan alibis are void.

Bullman read over her shoulder.

'Christ. We've been checking alibis for the wrong bloody date.'

'Everyone assumed the wall was built after the fifteenth because that's when James vanished,' Anjli said. 'But if Ronnie was killed on the eighth...'

'Then the killer had a week to seal him in before anyone even noticed James was gone,' Bullman said, checking her watch. 'We need to find conclusive proof of this, as Monroe's going to have his hands full with that poker game as it is.'

'Speaking of which,' Anjli replied, 'I have a thought about that. Let's gather the troops.'

22

SPY GAME

KENNY WAS IN THE MIDDLE OF A MEETING WITH HIS lieutenants when Monroe and Declan appeared at the door. There hadn't been any issues this time getting through, and it almost felt as if Kenny Tsang had been waiting for them, as the men filtered back into the shadows and Kenny sat back in his chair, his arms out.

'Gentlemen,' he said, 'have you come to arrest me again?'

Monroe walked over to the chair facing the desk and sat heavily in it, kicking his feet onto the desk, relaxing as he did so.

'Make yourself at home,' Kenny added, almost with amusement.

'You know, this whole case seems to be about identity,' Monroe said, as a way of introduction. 'There's you, Kenny Tsang, living under another identity – Wong Sei. And then you've got D.Q. James, a man who lives his own fake identity of gambler and poker player.'

He kicked his feet off the desk and leant closer.

'Tell me, Kenny,' he said, 'and be honest here... so D.Q. James never realised that you were both people?'

'Not that I know of,' Kenny replied, but now his tone was more defensive, as if aware that something was happening that he wasn't fully in charge of.

Monroe nodded.

'After you decided to lose your fake character,' he continued, 'did you ever keep in contact with the gambler Trevor Sullivan?'

Kenny shrugged, shaking his head.

'Man lost everything,' he said. 'Never saw him again after that.'

'Are you sure about that?' Monroe asked.

'What exactly are you implying?' Kenny had tired of this now, but it was Declan who responded.

'Forger named Finch,' he said. 'Passed away a couple of years ago. Used to work with you, I've been told. We've been going through his ledgers. Man provided passports and other items for the Chinese triad. Fresh identities that, if I was a suspicious man, I'd think they could use for legitimate companies.'

'What about it?' Kenny replied. 'You just told me this Mister Finch is dead, so he could never contradict anything I say.'

'No, I get that,' Declan replied. 'But I can also tell you that your name pops up in them.'

'I'd be very surprised to see that.' Kenny smiled now. And Declan knew it was the smile of a man who believed he'd covered all aspects.

'Oh no, sorry, I didn't explain properly,' Declan replied. 'You're not in them. But Wong Sei is. Did business with him a couple of times, too. You see, it would have been fine for you to claim you didn't know him... if it wasn't for the fact that we knew your *other* name.'

Kenny kept quiet.

'Now, luckily for you, this isn't our problem. And I'm sure you can find a way of getting out of it when the relevant people find you. The problem we have right now, is that you were in discussion with Finch at the same time that he was in discussion with D.Q. James.'

'I wasn't talking to Finch until 2010,' Kenny replied. 'Sure, I worked with him. I was introduced to him through a mutual friend.'

'Johnny Lucas?' Monroe asked.

Kenny just gave a smile.

'Johnny and Jackie used him at the time,' he said. 'I was looking for someone, and, well, Benny never got on with Johnny – but I did. Benny was more a Jackie guy.'

'Surely in 2010 he was the same man with different identities?'

'Who knows.' Kenny shrugged. 'But I'm afraid, detectives, I can't really help you. You see, I started talking to Finch after D.Q. James died.'

'But here's the problem with your story,' Declan replied. 'You were talking to Finch at the same time D.Q. James was, because the body found in the wall was that of Ronald Carrigan, who had been playing the part of D.Q. James as a decoy.'

Kenny did not look surprised by what had been said.

'But you already knew that, didn't you?' Declan continued.

'Suspected,' Kenny replied. 'We had people looking for Carrigan, and it wasn't exactly a secret that Carrigan and the croupier had been pretending to be D.Q. James—'

Kenny went to continue but then stopped himself

momentarily – Declan had the definite feeling this was a change of tack.

'So, D.Q. James is still alive?'

'Yes.' Declan smiled. 'And you'll be meeting him tonight at your little poker game.'

'Really?'

'That is... if we actually allow you to attend,' Monroe replied. 'You see, you've not exactly been helping us, have you, Kenny? We're having to find all these things out without your assistance, and I'll be honest, laddie, you're pissing me off now.'

Kenny sighed.

'You want something?' he said. 'Okay, I'll give you something. Have you spoken to the other decoy? Greaves?'

'Yes,' Declan replied. 'We know he was given a car. We know he pretended to be D.Q. James as well.'

'Did he tell you why he stopped?'

'Why don't *you* tell us why he stopped,' Monroe replied. 'Let's stop doing the "what information do you know that I can tell" game and just give us something we can use.'

He looked at his watch.

'We've got a couple of hours until they all meet up, and I have yet to work out why exactly Marek Kováč has such an issue with this.'

'Because Katarina was sleeping with Ronald Carrigan,' Kenny replied. 'It was well known. Carrigan was a player. He'd slept with Trevor Sullivan's wife. He'd slept with Linda. I think even Corey had had a moment with him. And then there was Katarina. Fell for him quite hard until he dumped her. It got quite violent.'

'He hit her?'

'Christ, no.' Kenny laughed. 'She hit him. And then, immediately after he disappeared, she married Marek.'

BILLY SIGHED, STRETCHING HIS NECK AS HE WORKED THROUGH the files Trix had given him. Most of it was standard intelligence reports – surveillance logs, financial records, diplomatic movements, bureaucratic detail that painted a picture of Marek Kováč as a man who existed in the shadows between nations.

But one folder had caught his attention.

'Ma'am?' he called across to Monroe's office, currently borrowed and returned to its old form as Bullman's office. 'You'll want to see this.'

Bullman appeared in the doorway, coffee in hand.

'Tell me it's good news.'

'Depends on your definition of good.' Billy gestured at his screen. 'Trix's flash drive has surveillance reports from November 2009. MI6 was watching Marek Kováč because they suspected he'd been compromised.'

'Compromised how?'

Billy clicked through to a scanned document – handwritten surveillance notes, dated November 2nd, 2009.

'The FSB tried to kill him,' Billy said. 'Late October, early November timeframe. There was an incident – details are redacted – but Marek survived. Then, on November 2nd, he was spotted meeting with a known FSB operative at the Harrison Casino bar.'

'Who was the operative?' Bullman moved closer, reading over Billy's shoulder.

'Konstantin Belov.' Billy pulled up another file – a grainy photograph of two men sitting at a bar. One was definitely Marek, younger but recognisable. The other was a stocky man in his thirties, with dark hair, expensive suit. 'According to this, Belov was one of the FSB's London station chiefs in 2009. Heavy hitter. The kind of person you only meet with if you're brokering something serious.'

'A deal to keep himself alive,' Bullman said quietly.

'That's what MI6 thought.' Billy clicked to the next page – more surveillance notes. 'The meet lasted forty minutes. No physical exchange. Just talking. But Ronald Carrigan was working as bartender that night. And, according to this, the surveillance team noted that Carrigan was "positioned close enough to overhear conversation" and "appeared to be paying attention to subjects".'

'Bloody hell.' Bullman let out a long breath.

'It gets better.' Billy opened another file. 'Three days later, November 5th, Carrigan called in sick. Didn't show for his shift. MI6 noted it as potentially significant but didn't follow up – they were focused on Marek, not the bartender.'

'Because they didn't know Carrigan would end up dead three days after that,' Bullman said.

'Exactly.' Billy leaned back in his chair. 'If Marek thought Carrigan had overheard him making a deal with Russian intelligence – especially while he was supposed to be working for MI6 – that's the sort of problem that gets people killed.'

'And we know Trevor Sullivan had his own reasons to want Carrigan dead, and likely knew he was doubling as James back then. Put them together...'

'Two men with two different reasons to kill the same bartender, both at the same place at the same time.' Billy clicked back to the photograph of Marek and Belov. 'This puts Marek at the casino, meeting with the FSB, with Carrigan in earshot. It's motive. It's opportunity.'

Bullman studied the screen for a long moment.

'Can we use this in court?'

'Trix reckons she gained it through official channels,' Billy said. 'She's been cleared to share intelligence when it relates to active investigations. The provenance is clean, but you'll probably find they'd prefer it if we found another way to get him.'

'Good.' Bullman straightened up. 'Print everything. I want hard copies for the briefing. Everyone needs to see this before we go into that poker game tonight.'

'Already on it.' Billy sent the files to the printer. 'There's one more thing, though. The surveillance notes mention that after the meeting, Belov left immediately. But Marek stayed at the casino for another hour. Just sitting at the bar. Drinking.'

'Processing what he'd just agreed to,' Bullman said.

'Or working up the courage to do something about the bartender who'd heard too much,' Billy replied. 'Carrigan was a threat to him personally. Not to his property development or his business interests. To his actual survival. If word got out that he'd brokered a deal with the FSB after being turned by MI6...'

'He'd be a dead man walking,' Bullman finished. 'Either MI6 would burn him or the FSB would finish what they started.'

Billy closed the files on his screen, ejecting the flash drive.

'You think he'll admit it?'

'Not a chance. But we don't need him to. We just need to prove he had reason to want Carrigan dead.' Bullman tucked the papers under her arm. 'Good work, Billy. This is exactly what we needed.'

'Thank Trix,' Billy replied. 'She's the one who pulled the files.'

'I will,' Bullman said. 'Right after I thank her for giving us enough rope to hang a double agent.'

23

FINISH THE JIGSAW

THE BRIEFING ROOM HAD THAT LATE AFTERNOON TENSION OF A case either about to break wide open, or else find out something was so incorrect that the entire thing fell back to the start, and everything they'd learned would have to be re-examined again.

Monroe stood by the plasma screen, arms crossed, while the team settled into their usual spots. Declan and Anjli to the right, Billy with his laptop to the left, De'Geer and Cooper at the back, Bullman by the door. Sam Mansfield had returned and sat beside Billy's desk, looking like he was reconsidering his life choices.

'Right,' Monroe said. 'We all know where we stand. Trevor Sullivan – the man working at Flex-U-Fit, the man Katarina's invited to tonight's poker game – is actually D.Q. James. Has been for fifteen years. Billy and Jess found the proof in Finch's ledgers this afternoon.'

'Paid for his new identity with one of those expensive watches,' Billy added, pulling up the relevant document on screen.

'Aye, we'll come to those watches in a moment,' Monroe replied, looking back at Declan, who held up the Mahjong piece that he'd been given by Terry Callaghan. 'Before that, what we need are invites to this exclusive gathering. How hard are those to forge?'

'Let me have a look.' Sam smiled, reaching over and taking the Mahjong piece. He stared at it, turned on his phone camera, zooming in on sections, and nodded to himself.

'Let me speak to a couple of people,' he said mysteriously. 'I'll see what I can do. How long do I have?'

Monroe looked at his watch.

'A couple of hours? Can this be done?'

'I wouldn't be able to keep my reputation as a miracle worker if I couldn't.' Sam smiled, blowing a reddening Billy a kiss as he left the office. Instead of commenting on this, Billy decided to furiously focus on an email that had just appeared.

'How many watches do we know of?' he asked. 'The Patek Philippe Grand Complications?'

'Richard Statham was given one,' Monroe started. 'He reckoned there was about six that were sold to the museum.'

'So – and if one of those was given to him – so, you would think six, maybe seven.'

'Aye,' Monroe said. 'Why do you ask?'

'Because I've found the purchase receipt for the first time they were bought,' Billy said. 'Paid for in cash by David Quincey James. Amount: a quarter of a million dollars. Bought in America.'

Declan frowned.

'Okay, so that's what, forty grand each? That's a hell of a lot, isn't it?'

'Yes and no.' Billy smiled. 'Invoice says they were Patek Philippe 5146Js, the annual calendar with moon phase in yellow gold. Looking on sites, these retailed in 2009 for around twenty-five grand. However, this price wasn't for six Patek Philippe watches. According to the receipt, there were twelve.'

'Twelve.' Declan leaned back in his chair. 'Christ.'

'Watch collecting is a good investment,' Billy added as he waved his Omega Black Lacquered Seamaster. 'I've got a fair few myself. This Aqua Terra is my everyday watch.'

'Aye, but that's because you're a super-rich lord of the manor.' Monroe smiled, waving his own watch. 'There's nothing wrong with a Seiko.'

'Never said there was, Guv.' Billy smiled back, knowing that this was yet another class-level conversation about to kick off. 'What I'm trying to say is that if I was given a quarter of a million and told to put it into something back then, I'd be sticking it in gold, or probably watches.'

'Not stocks?'

'Wouldn't have considered it back then. We're talking here a year after the crash of 2008. People still weren't that happy about using money in long-term investments. Maybe D.Q. James felt that expensive watches were more worth it, and the lack of high paying customers after the crash is probably why he got twelve for effectively the price of ten.'

He checked a website.

'Especially as it looks like they're averaging fifty thousand dollars right now, depending on provenance and condition. That's double the purchase price.'

'But surely if he's spending two hundred and fifty grand on watches, he should have just bought an expensive Rolex – that would've made more money?' Declan frowned.

'Okay, so here's a hypothetical.' Billy turned to face him. 'A man buys a bar of gold. It's got ten ounces in it. Cost him – I don't know – thirty grand now, maybe more? That gold price will go up. But if he has a Britannia coin? One ounce, around three grand? Well, when he needs to gain a couple of grand for spending money, that's far easier for him to sell on. That giant chunk of gold can't be cut up. It can't be adapted.'

'It's the million dollar bill,' Monroe muttered. 'You've heard that one, eh? It's an old story. Bloke gets handed a real, honest-to-God banknote worth a million dollars. Not fake, no trick to it. Legal tender, right enough. So, he walks into a shop, wants a loaf of bread or a new coat, and he pulls out this thing like he's the King of bloody America. And the shopkeeper just stares at it, eyes wide, and says, "I can't change that." So, he tries somewhere else, and it's the same again. Too big to spend, too much to touch. Nobody wants it, because nobody can handle it. Some folk give him what he asks for, just assuming he's rich enough to pay later, others chase him out thinking it's fake. Either way, he's walking about with a fortune in his pocket and he cannae buy a sandwich. And that's the point, isn't it? Value's useless if you can't move it.'

There was a moment's silence as everyone took in the story.

'Okay, but if this was some kind of investment, where did the Patek Philippes go, then?' Anjli asked.

'Well, we know where half of them went.' Billy smiled. 'The others – that's a little more interesting. It seems every two years, one of them would appear on the market.'

He pointed at a list of numbers.

'They all have unique markings and numbers, you see –

so you can trace them if lost. And you can see here that every two years, almost like clockwork, a Patek Philippe Grand Complication from the same list is sold.'

'Who by?' Declan asked. 'Because it sure as hell isn't James.'

'Richard Statham.' Billy looked up from the list. 'Apart from the last one, which was sold a month ago. This one, however, was used – not in box – but it's still from the same list.'

'And who sold that?'

'No name given.' Billy shrugged. 'Some of these watch companies – they have levels: A, B and C. A is mint in box, never touched – that's what most of these Pateks were sold as. This was a grade C. The watch shop was one stop higher than the pawnbroker's. Whoever went in had a watch with nothing else, was given ten grand in cash and told to piss off.'

Anjli looked over at Monroe.

'Statham didn't have his watch on – claimed he'd mislaid it in the house. You even commented on the fact that nobody would be so calm about that. Could he have pawned it?'

'Why bother when you could sell it mint in box for four times the cost?' Billy replied, checking the numbers against a spreadsheet. 'Each of these payments match the cost of two years rental, give or take. Richard Statham had them and was using this to fund D.Q. James's storage locker, while probably giving a large backhand so people didn't give out his name or ask questions.'

Declan went to reply, but was interrupted by a smiling Sam Mansfield, already returning through the door of the main office. Stopping by the desk beside Monroe, he pulled out the Mahjong piece, placing it on the surface in an almost ritualistic fashion. He then reached into his pockets and pulled out around a dozen more Mahjong dragon tiles.

'How the bloody hell?' Declan muttered.

'This isn't forged in any way.' Sam smiled, as he held up the tile. 'Mass-produced, part of a game deck. Obviously, Katarina Kováč isn't bothering to go the full mile with her homage to the Triad.'

He twitched his head towards the window as if motioning at the outside world.

'There's a bar just outside the boundaries of Temple Inn that I'd meet Billy at sometimes. I've noticed in the past they have a few board games; you know, *Cluedo, Backgammon, Scrabble,* things like that. I went to check if they had a Mahjong box. They did, and they were thrilled to pass you these tiles for police usage. The average game box has about ten or twelve dragon tiles, so I think that should be enough for you.'

He held up one of his recently gained tiles.

'And as you can see, there's literally no difference.'

Declan's phone rang. He glanced at the caller ID and frowned.

'It's Johnny Lucas,' he said.

'Put him on speaker,' Monroe replied. 'Let's hear what the wee bugger wants now.'

Declan pressed the button. Johnny's voice filled the briefing room, smooth and amused.

'Evening, all. Hope I'm not interrupting anything important.'

'What do you want, Johnny?' Monroe asked.

'Just wanted to give you a heads up about tonight's casino guest list,' Johnny said. 'I've added two names. Hope you don't mind.'

'Who?'

'Jess and her friend Prisha.'

The room went quiet. Declan sat up straighter.

'My daughter is not attending a potential crime scene,' he said flatly.

'Your daughter has been watching my boxing gym, pretending to work on a heavy bag for the past three hours,' Johnny replied, still sounding amused. 'Did you think I wouldn't notice? Come on, Declan. I've been in this game longer than she's been alive.'

'Then why didn't you—' Declan started.

'Because I'm not bothered by it,' Johnny interrupted. 'She's thorough, I'll give her that. Better tradecraft than half the surveillance teams I've had on me over the years. But she's also obviously not experienced enough to know when she's been made. So I'm inviting her and her girlfriend to the party. Public event, perfectly safe, they can watch the posh people pretend to care about poker history while you lot do whatever you're planning in the basement.'

'Absolutely not,' Declan said.

'Already invited them,' Johnny replied cheerfully. 'Jess accepted two minutes ago. Said she'd love to bring Prisha, actually. Apparently they've been having some relationship issues about how much time Jess spends on "this case stuff" and thought this might be a nice gesture. You're welcome, by the way.'

Monroe was trying not to smile.

'Johnny,' he said carefully, 'why are you doing this?'

'Because I like Jess. She's got potential. And because you lot will be more careful if you know she's in the building.' There was a pause. 'Plus, Katarina's invited some very boring people and the party needs better "youth" energy. Those two will liven things up.'

'If anything happens to my daughter—' Declan began.

'Then you'll arrest the people who do it, because you're all going to be there anyway,' Johnny finished. 'Relax, Declan. She'll be upstairs at a champagne reception. You'll be downstairs playing cops and robbers. Never the twain shall meet.'

'Unless something goes wrong,' Anjli said quietly.

'Which is why you won't let it go wrong,' Johnny said. 'Right then. See you tonight. Oh, and Declan? Jess told me to tell you she's wearing something nice, so don't embarrass her.'

The line went dead.

Declan looked at Monroe.

'I'm pulling her out,' he said.

'You're not,' Monroe replied. 'Johnny's right. She's already invited, already going. Better she's there where we can keep an eye on her.'

'She's my daughter.'

'Aye, and she's eighteen years old and has been working this case,' Monroe said, not unkindly. 'She's going to be upstairs at a party. We'll have Cooper monitor things up there, make sure nobody wanders down. Jess will be fine.'

Declan didn't look convinced, but he nodded. But then he paused, staring at the phone.

'He bloody knew,' he said.

'He knew what?' Monroe asked confused. 'Is this a new thread? Are we continuing the conversation, laddie?'

'Johnny.' Declan snarled. 'A couple of days ago, you and me, boxing ring, Johnny talking about the Triad, right before we found out about the case. He started talking about my dad, and how he'd looked at a night watchman case, realising that the timing wasn't right. That he was being aimed at the wrong story.'

'What about it?'

'Ronnie Carrigan, the 8th of November, not the 15th,' Declan shook his head. 'We've been looking at the wrong story. Sure, we know that now – but what if Johnny already knew about this and he was leading us there slowly?'

Declan stared out of the window into the office.

'If I find Johnny Lucas knew about this and he's been screwing us around, I won't be happy, Guv.'

'It's a question for later,' Monroe replied, looking around the room. 'Perhaps in the middle of a boxing ring. Anything else?'

'One thing.' Billy opened up an image on the plasma screen, and an arrest report appeared. 'This just came through from our friends in the FBI. Remember how Jess found a comment by D.Q. James in the Kendis tapes mentioning being locked away in juvie? We couldn't find anything under David Quincey James in the records, but in 1988, Darren Jameson was arrested for possession. He wasn't legally an adult, so did time in juvenile detention.'

'Smoking gun.' Declan smiled. 'And maybe this was why he needed a new, clean passport?'

'That's a possibility, but we can look into that later,' Monroe mused. 'Right. Before we plan tonight's operation, we need to sort one more thing. Bring her in.'

De'Geer and Cooper left the briefing room and a few moments later returned, Imogen Rothwell between them, Cooper guiding her to a chair. She looked exhausted, fifteen years of anger and grief etched into her face.

'Mrs Rothwell,' Monroe said, not unkindly. 'The poker chips that we now know are painted gold-coins – where are they?'

Rothwell looked up, meeting his eyes.

'At the casino,' she said quietly.

'And why would the wee chips be there?'

'I offered them to Katarina, so that she invited me to the event.' Rothwell shrugged. 'I knew she couldn't resist it, and I knew neither would anyone else.'

'You brought a fortune in gold coins to Katarina Kováč, known as such or not, all so you could confront the man you think killed your brother,' Anjli said.

'In fairness, I think her plan wasn't to confront him, but to shoot him,' Monroe replied.

'They were Ronnie's,' Rothwell ignored the comment. 'He died for them.'

'You said he stole them.'

'Yes, but the fact Sullivan wanted them, meant he knew what they were,' Rothwell replied angrily. 'It had to be that. I wanted Sullivan to see them before I pulled the trigger. Wanted him to know what this was about.'

Monroe and Declan exchanged glances.

'Well,' Monroe said, 'you're not pulling any triggers tonight. But you're coming with us anyway.'

Rothwell's head snapped up.

'What?'

'You wanted answers about your brother,' Monroe continued. 'You wanted to know what happened that night in 2009. Well, tonight's the night we find out. You'll be there, as per your agreement with Katarina. She won't know you spoke to us, and with a little luck, lassie, you get your answers, we get our arrests. Everyone wins.'

'Except I go to prison afterwards.'

'Aye, well that depends on how things go,' Monroe admitted. 'All you're currently guilty of is making a terrible decision, one we stopped you from making. But at least you'll know the truth first.'

Rothwell considered this, then nodded slowly.

'Alright.'

After Rothwell was returned to holding, Monroe turned back to the team.

'Right then. Operational plan. Billy, put up the casino layout.'

The plasma screen shifted to show the Harrison Casino's floor plans: ground floor with the public event space, basement with the private poker room.

'Two operations running simultaneously,' Monroe began. 'Upstairs, Katarina's hosting a public memorial event. Champagne, canapes, probably some bloody awful gushing speeches about D.Q. James. Would they do one of those memorial video montages with the saccharine music? I bloody hope they don't do one of those memorial video montages with the saccharine music. Either way, that's where Jess and Prisha will be, along with Johnny and about fifty to a hundred other guests. Cooper, you're upstairs in plainclothes. Monitor the crowd, make sure nobody leaves the public areas and wanders downstairs.'

Cooper nodded.

'Billy, Sam, if you could, I'd prefer a couple of bodies near Jess and her girlfriend, purely so Declan doesn't spend the next ten years telling me "I told you so".'

'That's fine,' Billy nodded. 'I got her into this; I should keep an eye on her.'

'Besides, I really want to see the place.' Sam smiled. 'And I look damned good in a tuxedo.'

'We need tuxes?' Declan groaned. 'Bloody marvellous.'

'Downstairs,' Monroe continued, 'private poker game. Invitation only, Mahjong pieces required for entry. Thanks to Sam's initiative, Declan, Anjli and I have those pieces. We go in as guests, observe, wait for our moment.'

'What's the legal justification?' Bullman asked. 'You can't just arrest people at a private poker game without cause.'

'We've got reasonable suspicion that Trevor Sullivan is actually D.Q. James, wanted for identity fraud and potentially connected to Ronnie Carrigan's murder fifteen years ago,' Declan replied. 'Plus we have Marek possibly compromising national security, hidden gold in the form of poker chips, stolen diamonds and DC Elliott's current status means we have legitimate concerns about the event's security. DCI Cohen's given us the green light.'

'Speaking of Elliott,' Monroe looked at De'Geer. 'You're his handler tonight. He thinks you're on his side, thinks you're going to help him get out of his mess. You let him think that. Get him to the casino, stay close, and when things go sideways – and they will – you make sure he doesn't do anything stupid.'

'Like stealing diamonds from a crime scene?' De'Geer asked dryly.

'Exactly like that.'

'And if he tries to run?'

'You're seven feet tall, laddie,' Monroe replied. '*Stop* him.'

De'Geer's expression was unreadable, but he nodded.

'Armed response will be staged two streets over,' Monroe continued. 'Cohen's providing backup from Paddington Green, but he'll also be in the building as he has a wee chat he wants to have with Elliott first. Again, De'Geer, if he starts swinging, stop him. Soon as we give the signal, he'll bring them in.'

'And Rothwell?' Billy asked.

'Stays at the back, makes sure the chips don't walk off.' Monroe looked around the room. 'This is going to be messy. We've got D.Q. James thinking he's safe, Katarina and Marek playing their own games, Jun Ng Kai-lok potentially bringing Triad muscle, Elliott desperate enough to do something stupid, and a ton of ex-casino member civilians upstairs who have no idea what's happening below them.'

'So, a normal Thursday,' Declan muttered.

'Pretty much.' Monroe checked his watch. 'Event starts at eight. Poker game at ten. We need to be in position by quarter to. That gives us—' he calculated quickly, '—about two hours. Go get changed, look like you belong at a posh casino event. Declan, I assume you've got a decent suit?'

'He'll manage.' Anjli smiled.

'Good. Because if we're walking into a room full of poker players and criminals, we'd better look the part.' Monroe's expression hardened. 'And remember – we're there to observe and arrest when the moment's right. Not before. We need them to show their cards first.'

'And if they don't?' Cooper asked.

'Then we'll make them,' Monroe replied.

The team dispersed. Declan lingered by the door.

'Monroe,' he whispered. 'If anything happens to Jess—'

'It won't,' Monroe interrupted. 'Billy and Cooper are watching upstairs, you and I are downstairs. Your daughter will be fine. Now go find a suit that doesn't look like you've been crawling through tunnels in it.'

Declan managed a slight smile and left.

Monroe stood alone in the briefing room, looking at the casino floor plans on the screen. Somewhere in that building tonight, fifteen years of secrets were going to come spilling out. And, when they did, the Last Chance Saloon would be there to catch them.

'Right then,' he said to the empty room. 'Let's go play some poker.'

24

PARTY TIME

The main floor of the Harrison Casino had been transformed into something between a museum exhibit and a wake. Display cases lined the walls showing the casino's glory days – photographs of celebrities at the tables, vintage poker chips, newspaper clippings about legendary games, much of which had likely been removed from Richard Statham's personal collection. A small crowd mingled with champagne glasses, examining the displays with the polite interest of people attending a function they didn't quite understand.

Declan Walsh stood near the entrance, scanning the room with the casualness of a copper who'd spent twenty-odd years learning how not to look like he was casing a joint. The suit Monroe had insisted on felt wrong – too clean, too expensive, the sort of thing Billy would wear without thinking twice. He tugged at the collar and tried to look like he belonged.

'Stop fidgeting,' Anjli murmured beside him, accepting a champagne flute from a passing server. 'You look fine.'

'I look like I'm wearing someone else's clothes.'

'You are. That's Billy's suit.'

Declan glanced down at the jacket.

'Christ, is it? No wonder it fits like I'm playing dress-up.'

'It's Savile Row,' Anjli said, taking a sip of champagne. 'Be grateful he didn't lend you the shoes as well. You'd be limping within an hour.'

Monroe approached from the left, his own suit looking considerably more lived-in. The Detective Superintendent had the advantage of actually owning formal wear that he'd worn to enough functions to break in properly. He nodded towards the far corner.

'Katarina's holding court by the primary display,' he whispered. 'Marek's with her. Jun Ng Kai-lok arrived five minutes ago with two gentlemen who look like they could pull your arms off.'

'Triad muscle?'

'Or personal trainers. Hard to tell these days.' Monroe accepted his own glass of champagne and didn't drink it. 'No sign of Sullivan yet. Billy's got eyes on Jess and Prisha – they're over by the bar, looking like they're actually enjoying themselves.'

Declan resisted the urge to look.

'Cooper with them?'

'Aye, blending in with the crowd. She's got a clear view of all the exits.' Monroe's expression was carefully neutral. 'Your daughter's fine, Declan. Stop looking like you're about to arrest someone.'

'I am about to arrest someone.'

'Aye, but they don't know that yet.' Monroe gestured with his glass towards the displays. 'Let's have a wander. Look interested in the memorabilia. We're here to pay our respects to a dead poker legend, remember?'

'Rothwell?'

'Already in the basement, probably setting up the casino coins,' Anjli replied. 'No weapons down there.'

'There's a poker table and a card shoe,' Declan reminded her. 'We know at least one of these was used as one.'

A woman Declan recognised as Linda Burrell stood near one of the display cases, studying a photograph of herself from fifteen years ago. She looked different now – harder, the kind of difference that came from losing badly and having to live with it. She glanced up as they passed, her eyes narrowing slightly as if trying to place them, then returned to her contemplation of past glories.

'That's most of the invite list accounted for,' Monroe said under his breath. 'Richard Statham's near the back, keeping his head down. And there—'

'Sullivan,' Declan finished, spotting the man near the entrance to the toilets. Trevor Sullivan wore a sleek black suit and moved with the careful precision of someone who'd spent fifteen years not being noticed, scanning the room with quick, nervous glances.

'He knows something's off,' Anjli observed. 'Look at his hands.'

Sullivan's fingers kept moving, tapping against his thigh in what might have been a nervous habit or might have been counting cards in his head. Declan had seen enough poker players over the years to recognise the type – the ones who couldn't stop calculating odds even when they weren't at a table.

'He's looking for an exit,' Declan said.

'There isn't one,' Monroe replied. 'Not unless he wants to make a scene.'

He checked his watch.

'Poker game starts in twenty minutes. We need to position ourselves to arrive after they start moving downstairs. Maybe halfway through the first hand.'

A loud burst of laughter drew Declan's attention to the bar. Jess stood with Prisha, both holding cocktails that looked expensive and completely unsuitable for eighteen-year-olds. Billy hovered nearby, pretending to examine a painting whilst keeping them firmly in his peripheral vision. Sam Mansfield stood on the other side, chatting with what looked like a minor celebrity Declan vaguely recognised from something.

'She's fine,' Anjli said, reading his expression. 'Billy won't let anything happen to her.'

'I know.' Declan sighed. It didn't stop the familiar weight in his chest, the one that showed up whenever Jess was anywhere near police business. 'Doesn't mean I have to like it.'

'Welcome to parenthood,' Monroe said dryly. 'Where you spend twenty years worrying and then die anyway.'

'Cheerful thought.'

'I'm Scottish. We do fatalism well. I also don't have a kiddie, so I can spout as much "wisdom" as I want.'

Monroe's expression shifted slightly, his eyes tracking something across the room.

'Katarina's moving. Looks like she's getting ready to make a speech.'

They watched as Katarina Kováč stepped up onto a small, raised platform near the main display case. She wore black –

appropriate for a memorial. A microphone stand had been set up, professional and out of place in the casual gathering.

'Ladies and gentlemen,' Katarina's voice carried across the room, amplified and confident. 'Thank you all for coming tonight. We gather here to remember a legend of the game – a man who changed poker forever, who brought excitement and drama to every table he sat at. David Quincey James – D.Q. James – was more than just a player. He was an artist.'

'He was a bastard,' someone shouted, and there was a smattering of laughter.

'Whatever he was, saint or sinner, tonight, we celebrate his memory.'

There was polite applause. Declan noticed Sullivan hadn't joined in. Neither had Jun Ng Kai-lok, whose expression suggested he was remembering something considerably less celebratory.

'In honour of D.Q.'s memory,' Katarina continued, 'please enjoy the evening. There's an open bar, and we'll be sharing stories about D.Q. throughout the night. Thank you.'

She stepped down, immediately surrounded by well-wishers and hangers-on. Marek appeared at her side, his expression unreadable, and Declan watched them for a moment, trying to work out the dynamic. For someone who'd claimed he'd been better off away from her after the divorce, Marek seemed to be stuck to her like Velcro.

'Right,' Monroe said quietly. 'Time to crash the party properly.'

He glanced at Anjli.

'You ready?'

'Born ready,' she replied, which was something she only said when she was nervous and hiding it.

They made their way towards the door marked "Private" – the one that led downstairs to the basement poker room. The small group of familiar faces had already formed, clutching their Mahjong pieces like golden tickets. Declan pulled his own tile from his pocket, feeling the weight, still amused by the knowledge that Sam Mansfield had plucked it from a boardgame box in a pub near Temple Inn.

Paul Elliott stood beside the door, his uniform pressed and professional, his expression carefully neutral. Morten De'Geer loomed on the other side, seven feet of theatrical copper playing the role of building security. Elliott's eyes flicked towards Declan and away again, the movement so quick it might have been nothing.

But it wasn't nothing. Elliott knew they were here. And Elliott knew exactly why.

Declan started towards the door, Anjli beside him, Monroe a few steps behind. Somewhere in the crowd behind them, Jess was safe with Billy and Cooper watching over her. Somewhere below them, fifteen years of secrets waited to spill across green felt.

The game was about to begin.

However, they were halfway to the basement door when a man Declan didn't recognise blocked their path. Late fifties, expensive suit that had seen better days, the flushed face of someone three drinks past sensible. He squinted at Declan with the intense focus of the pleasantly drunk.

'I know you,' he announced, pointing with his champagne flute. 'Don't I know you?'

'I don't think so,' Declan said politely.

'No, no, I definitely know you.' The man circled slightly, studying Declan's face. 'Monte Carlo, 2006? The baccarat tables?'

'Never been to Monte Carlo.'

'Atlantic City then. Had to be Atlantic City.' He snapped his fingers. 'You were at the craps table with that Russian bloke, the one who kept betting on snake eyes—'

'Wrong person,' Declan said, trying to step around him.

The man grabbed his arm, undeterred.

'Wait, wait. You're that poker player from Dublin. The one who got barred from the Merrion for counting cards—'

'He's never been to Dublin either,' Anjli said, amusement clear in her voice.

'Are you sure? Because I could swear—' The man leaned in closer, eyes narrowing. 'Macau. You were definitely in Macau.'

'Never left the UK for gambling,' Declan said.

'Bloody hell, you look exactly like this bloke I played against in... where was it...?' He turned to Monroe. 'You know him, right? Tell him we've met.'

'Sorry, pal,' Monroe said with a grin. 'He's just got one of those faces.'

'One of those faces,' the man repeated, disappointed. He studied Declan one more time, then shrugged and wandered off, muttering about Macau.

Anjli was still smiling.

'You do have one of those faces.'

'Cheers for that.'

Monroe checked his watch.

'Right. The players are in, so time to make an entrance.'

De'Geer was standing beside the door to the basement as Declan walked up to him. Paul Elliott stood on the other side, and Declan wasn't sure, but he believed he saw the man flinch slightly as he approached.

'Detective Constable Elliott,' Declan said with the

slightest of smiles. 'I understand you've been throwing my name around a lot recently.'

'Don't know what you mean, sir,' Elliott replied calmly.

Declan looked over at De'Geer.

'Do *you* know what I mean?'

'Unsure, sir,' De'Geer deadpanned, and Declan noticed the smallest curl of a smile on Elliott's lips. *Elliott still believed that De'Geer was on his side.*

'I'm going to need to go downstairs now,' Declan said. 'I'd like you to open the door for me.'

'Sorry, sir. You need a pass,' Elliott replied.

'Would that be a mahjong piece?' Declan asked, pulling one out of his pocket and holding it up. 'I think you'll find that's the correct one.'

At the sight of the piece, Declan saw Elliott freeze. He was now caught between a rock and a hard place – blocking the police, but also aware that anyone with a piece was supposed to be allowed downstairs.

'I'm sorry, sir, I don't believe that Miss Kováč gave you that,' he said.

'Does it matter who gave it to me?'

'Yes, it does, sir.'

'Did you ever use these pieces?' Declan asked. 'You know, when you lost all that money playing poker?'

'I don't understand what you're saying, sir,' Elliott replied coldly. 'I'm being honest – I don't think you do either.'

Declan nodded to himself.

'I hope your injury's doing better,' he continued. 'I understand you've got a very early morning tomorrow. Nine o'clock at Guildhall.'

'Yes, sir,' Paul said, giving the slightest of smiles. 'I'm looking forward to clearing my name.'

Declan sighed.

'Look, I've tried to be nice,' he said, 'but I really do need to go past you. Morten?'

De'Geer didn't react at first. Elliott didn't understand what Declan meant, but then everything became clear as Morten De'Geer turned slowly to face him.

'I think it's time for you to take a break,' he said. 'Don't worry, I'll look after the door.'

'Oh, you son of a bitch!' Elliott now understood what was happening. 'You do this? You go down.'

He turned back to Declan.

'I've got stuff on him—'

'Yeah, I know all about what happened. We've already spoken to Mister Vaughn.' Declan gave a smile. 'You've got nothing on my sergeant, and I suggest you back down before you make it worse for yourself.'

Elliott went to reply, but with Declan on one side, De'Geer on the other, and the approaching Monroe and Anjli, he knew he was outnumbered and outmatched. Reluctantly, he stood aside as De'Geer took the pass from his hand and opened the door.

'Enjoy the show, sir,' he said to Declan. 'I hope you're very lucky tonight.'

'You'll be letting my party in as well, I'm guessing?' Declan said, motioning to Monroe and Anjli, who now arrived to the side, DCI Cohen beside her. 'They all have pieces too.'

To emphasise this, Monroe and Anjli happily waved their Mahjong tiles.

'Of course,' Elliott said, with a weak smile. 'Whoever you want, Guv.'

'Excellent.' Monroe grinned. 'We'll leave you with Mister

Cohen here. I'm sure you have a lot to discuss.'

Declan led Monroe, Anjli and De'Geer down the stairs but at the bottom of the stairs stood another man – someone Declan didn't recognise. He had an Eastern European look, and Declan wondered whether he'd been brought in by the Kovác̆s. But if he'd got past the top door, and De'Geer was with him, then it was clear Declan was permitted entry. A quick show of their mahjong pieces was enough to let him and his guests through, and Declan made a mental note to thank Sam when he saw him next, as De'Geer headed back up the stairs, likely to return his attention to Paul.

Walking into the main poker room, he realised the basement, even now cleaned... looked completely different. The poker table was surrounded by guests; the bar was busy; and there, standing, looking furious, was Marek Kováč.

'Detective Chief Inspector Walsh. I don't believe you're on the invite list,' he said. 'This is for people who were screwed over by D.Q. James.'

'Oh, I think we count,' Declan replied, as Anjli and Monroe entered behind him. 'You see, we've been lied to just as much as you were by D.Q. James.'

'And how do you see that?' Katarina asked from the other side of the room, walking forward.

'Well, I can tell you if you'd like. I understand poker's all about the story, and we have a story to tell.'

He nodded to the others as he moved to the table, noticing the chips in a box to the side.

'I'm guessing you're playing for the chips tonight,' he said. 'Winner takes all, including that?'

There was a rumbling of agreement, and Declan grinned.

'I wonder how many of you know what you'd truly be winning if you did.'

He couldn't help but glance at Trevor Sullivan, who quickly turned his attention away.

'I thought you'd given up gambling.'

'I felt lucky,' Sullivan replied. 'Tell us your bloody story and then piss off. This is a private game.'

'Well then, you'll love this one. I'd like to tell you a story of two boys,' Declan explained. 'By the names of *Darren and Trevor Sullivan*.'

25

SHOW YOUR CARDS

TREVOR SAID NOTHING, STARING DOWN AT HIS FRESHLY DEALT cards face down on the baize, no chips bet as yet.

'You see, Trevor and Darren were East End kids – hung out with Johnny and Jackie Lucas in their gym. However, Jackie took a bit of a shine to them – taught them how to play poker rather than box,' Declan continued. 'But Darren and Trevor's dad – he was a bit abusive. Drank a lot. Worked for Johnny here and there. Caused issues. Their mum filed for divorce, moved back home to America, changed her name back to Jameson, and took the younger of the two sons with her – leaving Trevor here stuck in the UK.'

'I chose to stay,' Trevor replied. 'My dad wasn't that bad to me. I never saw the problems.'

'We'll come back to that in a minute,' Declan said with a smile. 'Anyway, Trevor makes a name for himself, marries, has kids, opens up a whole ton of shops – very popular. Meanwhile, Darren Sullivan – or now Darren Jameson, rather – he's a little pissed off about all this. Feels that Trevor's had the success that he should have had, that he was dragged away by his mother. He's bitter at the family, and so he takes the one thing he was taught – his psychological skills – and he starts to use them at the poker table. And over the years, he makes a name for himself.'

'So much so that he gets somebody to provide him a fake passport under a new name,' Monroe took over now. 'You see, he spent time in juvenile while in the US for drug possession and maybe needed a nice clean passport to travel. So, he contacted the only person he knew could do such a thing – Johnny Lucas – or, rather, Johnny in the "Jackie" persona back then, possibly why he doesn't clearly remember, who put him in touch with a man who put him in touch with another man... you know how it goes. Darren Jameson became David Quincey James – D.Q. James.'

There was a hush at this, and suddenly Trevor Sullivan was the centre of attention.

'News to me,' he said again.

Declan smiled.

'I see your answer, and I raise,' he continued. 'You see, D.Q. James was very good at this – more so than most others – and one reason was because he understood how to play the player rather than the cards. He hired a private investigator – George Moir – to find out everything he could about his rivals. Took out people all over the world because of this. Knew things no one else would. At the same time, he'd sleep around, have affairs – anything that would give him an advantage in a match.'

He looked over at Marek.

'But he was getting confident – arrogant, even. He was having magazine articles written on him and was the golden child of the poker world – flamboyant with his cowboy hat and aviator glasses. He was becoming famous – and sometimes that's the last thing you want, especially when you're playing under a new name.'

'But he couldn't stop himself,' Anjli took over now. 'He found himself in Trevor Sullivan's orbit – maybe by choice, maybe accidentally – and at this point, he found out everything he could about his brother. Things he probably already knew, but enough to sit down and face him – and take away everything.'

Sullivan leant back in his chair, the cards now ignored.

'So, you're telling me that D.Q. James was my brother,' he said. 'I haven't spoken to my brother since he left for America. I couldn't have told you if he was or wasn't – and this was fifteen years ago. Besides, if you're going to blame me for his death, some kind of brotherly revenge – I think you'll find I wasn't in town.'

'Oh yes, you were "at a retreat, being treated for gambling",' Declan said, using finger quotes for emphasis. 'Don't worry – we'll get to that as well. Because D.Q. James also managed to piss off *other* people. For a start, everybody around this table has a reason to dislike the man. But one more than the others – isn't that right, Jun? Mister Ironthread? The man who managed to lose five hundred grand of family jewels because he was outsmarted psychologically, or, rather, because D.Q. James was better at swapping cards than you were?'

Jun looked as if he was about to rise, but then simply gave the slightest of nods – an acceptance that Declan was correct.

'You see, D.Q. James cheated,' Declan went on. 'Paid off Richard Statham to help him, possibly swapping a crap hand for a better one, in the process providing a fresh Ace that was a problem, as the deck already held an Ace, one marked by Jun there earlier in the game, once he suspected James of cheating. Gave him a Patek Philippe watch off his own wrist as payment, promising nobody would ever know. In fact, this is why after that match, he never wore the Patek Philippe again – only the Rolex that he bought in its place. A Rolex he bought three of, by the way.'

'This is important?' Jun asked.

'Oh, absolutely,' Monroe now said. 'You see, laddie, he took you for five hundred grand. But more than that – he took your pride and your family jewellery. He knew you weren't going to take that lightly. He understood you were looking for him – trying to find a time when you could get to him. And so he started bringing in doubles.'

'Ronnie Carrigan and Thomas Greaves,' Declan added. 'They were sold two of his cars at a steal and given two of the three Rolex watches – and spent the days driving around London, pretending to be the famous D.Q. James.'

Anjli was walking slowly around the poker table now.

'Thomas Greaves got cold feet – gave the watch back. Said he'd rather walk away from everything. Ronald Carrigan, however, was very much into it – even after he broke his arm playing rugby, which meant he had to wear his watch on the wrong arm.'

'I'm sure this is fascinating,' Marek now replied, 'but we're playing a game – and you're boring us now. Also, it's only people who were screwed over by James who get to be here. You never met the guy.'

'Oh, am I boring you? I do apologise.' Monroe gave a theatrical bow. 'But that's okay because this is where *you* come into the story. Because we're not here to discuss the murder of D.Q. James – because D.Q. James never died. This is why we have an invitation to this event – because D.Q. James screwed us around by *not being the body*.'

He looked around the room.

'The body we found was dressed as D.Q. James – but wore the Rolex wristwatch on the left wrist rather than the right – which, as you all know, having faced him across the table, D.Q. James always wore his watch on his right-hand wrist. The ulnar had also been broken – the result of a rugby injury, one James never had. Basically, kiddies, the body we found just over there – behind that wall – *wasn't* D.Q. James.'

He paused, almost as if for dramatic effect.

'It was Ronald Carrigan.'

This had not been expected. People started muttering.

'You see, we thought it was you, Jun – that you'd found D.Q. James and tortured him for your diamonds – maybe killed him afterwards. Maybe went too far.' Monroe shrugged apologetically. 'The problem was you would have realised it wasn't D.Q. James pretty much immediately. In fact, anybody who tortured him or killed him, once those glasses came off, would have known. There's also another wee problem we have – and that's the dates.'

'The wall could only have been built on two occasions,' Declan explained. 'A week before the last time that D.Q. James was seen – or the week after. If D.Q. James *had* been murdered and hidden behind that wall? Well, this would have therefore been around the twentieth of November, and both Marek and Trevor here would have had cast-iron alibis. But now we know that Ronald Carrigan was likely murdered on the eighth of November – a full week beforehand. Which kind of removes those alibis.'

'Ronald Carrigan was a well-liked bar staff member of the team,' Monroe said. 'Fewer people would want to kill him than kill D.Q. James, but he still had people who weren't happy with him. Trevor Sullivan, for example, had gotten drunk a couple of weeks before his big loss. He'd had divorce issues and was pouring out his woes to the barman. When D.Q. James used the same information to destroy him, he didn't consider a private investigator knowing this, he assumed that Carrigan, the barman himself had given D.Q. James every piece of information he'd given in confidence.'

'It's amazing what a barman can pick up,' Declan added. 'You see, Marek here had also been caught talking to a Russian operative by the name of Konstantin Belov.'

He held a hand up to stop Marek's inevitable response.

'We got the MI6 notes, Marek. We know you were a double agent during that time, possibly still. We know the FSB were trying to take you out, and we know that you met with Belov at the very beginning of November, in a way to broker a deal to keep yourself alive. The problem was, you did it at the bar, and you were convinced that Ronnie Carrigan had overheard you.'

'You can't prove this.'

'Actually, we can.' Declan smiled. 'You see, we've got friends in Whitehall. One of them passed me the full report of the night you were watched down here.'

'But it wasn't just that, was it, laddie?' Monroe smiled. 'You see, at this time, you were dating Katarina there. You were getting quite serious. Possibly even engaged, or at least talking about it. And then you found out Ronnie had been sleeping with her behind your back. That must have pissed you off. So, you teamed up with Trevor – and you found Ronnie, killed him in anger, and then realised what you'd done. You took the body, hiding it behind the wall. This wasn't something you could have just done yourselves; you would have needed a member of staff, and this is where you pulled in Richard Statham – who already knew that he was living on borrowed time as the Triad would eventually find out that he'd assisted D.Q. James – and when confronted and given the option of helping or not, he agreed. There wasn't much more he could say.'

Richard Statham's silence damned him, as the others around the table found themselves unable to look at him.

'And so, Ronnie Carrigan was murdered,' Declan continued. 'Something blunt to the head – a hammer, maybe, or even a card shoe, carrying the same cards he'd watched dealt across the room. Either way, he was dead. He was gone. And no one knew.'

'But D.Q. James knew,' Anjli now added. 'Or at least suspected, when Carrigan disappeared. This was the reason he'd created his doppelgangers. But D.Q. James didn't know *who* did it and was scared. So scared, he decided that this was it. No more. He went back to his lockup to gather his items – and then he realised that this was missing.'

She pointed across at the poker chip box.

'You see, each of these chips are more than just special victories. They're gold fifty-peso pieces, painted by D.Q. James himself. Now he realised that his entire fortune was missing – including the diamonds.'

'How?' Jun asked.

'All things in time,' Anjli smiled. 'We're not there yet. We're where the clock was ticking, and his life was in danger.'

'And then something happened he wasn't expecting.' Declan turned his attention now to Sullivan. 'Trevor Sullivan found him. He'd got out of his rehab centre – the one he'd gone into directly after killing Ronnie Carrigan. Maybe he felt guilty. Maybe he realised he'd gone too far. It doesn't matter. What matters is that Trevor Sullivan found his brother – and confronted him. We'll likely never know where it happened or when, but the fact of the matter was, Trevor Sullivan died that night.'

Sullivan stared at the cards, saying nothing. Which, in a way was exactly what a dead man would do.

'We've got Finch's ledgers,' Declan said to him. 'It shows that you took Trevor's identity in January 2010. You were similar enough – you were brothers, and Moir provided you with identity pieces from his extensive deep dive. Then, as Trevor Sullivan, you left everything – your wife, your family, the job that had been destroyed. None of that mattered to you, because... well, it wasn't you. And so, "Trevor Sullivan" travelled the world for ten years – hiding out, waiting for a moment to return, waiting for the coins to be found, the diamonds to be recovered – but they never were. And, after ten years, you started to think that you were safe. Maybe you could come back. Maybe you could start again. So, you returned, taking a job in Bow.'

'But it wasn't the world you wanted,' Monroe took over. 'You tried to find a way to return to the scene, but the Harrison Casino was a shell of its old self. Then, a couple of months back you'd visited the D.Q. James exhibit and saw your items, your custom-made poker chips. But how could you get to them? The only way was to get everybody together – to mourn D.Q. James, perhaps even play for the chips. And so you started an audacious plan.'

'I thought Katarina had the plan?' Sullivan asked.

'She did, but we think you somehow convinced her to arrange it. Like a magician, you "forced the card" on her somehow, *Mister James*.'

It was as if Sullivan pulled off a mask – he reached into his pocket, pulled out a pair of aviator glasses, and placed them on, looking around at everyone as he smiled, showing his hands.

'D.Q. James has entered the building,' he said to the table, reaching into his other pocket and pulling out a new pewter gunfighter figure, freshly painted, carefully positioning it onto the cards he held, currently face down on the baize. 'And he's here to take everything.'

26

GATECRASHERS

Jess Walsh stood near one of the display cases with Prisha beside her, their fingers intertwined as they looked at a photograph of the casino in its heyday. It felt good to be out together properly for the first time in weeks – even if it was at one of her dad's crime scenes.

'That chip's a fake,' Prisha said, pointing at one in the display. 'The weight's wrong. You can tell by how it sits.'

'How can you possibly tell that from looking at it through glass?' Jess asked, smiling, but then the smile faltered. 'Wait, you can tell that by looking through glass?'

'I can't. But Sam can.' Prisha grinned and nodded towards the bar where Sam was examining another display case, shaking his head with the resigned expression of someone who'd spotted amateur forgery work. 'Billy's boyfriend's been muttering about it for ten minutes.'

'Of course he has,' Jess laughed as she squeezed Prisha's hand. 'I've missed this. Just... being out. Being normal.'

'Normal is overrated,' Prisha replied, squeezing back. 'But

I've missed it too. Even if your idea of a date night is a casino party where you've been working the case all week.'

'In my defence, the party bit was supposed to be fun.'

'I'm having fun.' Prisha smiled. 'The question is, are you having fun?'

NEAR THE BAR, SAM WAS IN CONVERSATION WITH DOCTOR Marcos and Johnny Lucas. Both men examined the display cases like professional forgers spotting amateur work, while Doctor Marcos seemed to be enjoying the wine more than the discussion.

'That painting's dodgy,' Sam said, pointing. 'The signature's wrong.'

'Yeah, I noticed that,' Johnny agreed. 'Though, to be fair, it's supposed to be an exhibit about the casino, not an art gallery.'

'The anatomy's bollocks too,' Doctor Marcos muttered. 'No leg can do that.'

'I hope you're not corrupting him,' Billy muttered as he approached. 'That's my job.'

Johnny smiled, holding his hands up in surrender.

'How's your great uncle these days?' he asked.

'Oh no.' Billy waggled a finger. 'We are *not* going down that path tonight.'

COOPER STOOD NEAR THE ENTRANCE IN A DRESS THAT SHE KEPT tugging at uncomfortably. She'd been assigned to keep an eye on the upstairs guests, but the dress code had been "smart casual" and she felt profoundly uncomfortable in anything that wasn't her uniform or workout gear. She caught Jess watching and gave a slight grimace.

'Don't say it,' Cooper mouthed.

Jess grinned and turned back to Prisha as, through the door, Cooper saw a new car pull up outside. A black Mercedes, tinted windows, parking directly in front of the entrance. Several well-dressed Asian men got out, heading for the door.

Seeing this, Johnny's posture changed – nothing obvious, but Jess noticed – especially as immediately after this more cars arrived. Another Mercedes. A BMW. Men emerging, all heading for the entrance.

'That's a lot of guests arriving at once,' Prisha observed quietly.

Jess felt something tighten in her chest. The way they moved, the way they scanned the area before entering.

This wasn't normal.

She caught Johnny's eye across the room. He gave the smallest shake of his head – a warning. *Stay back. Don't get involved.*

But she was already heading towards De'Geer, standing at the door, pulling Prisha with her.

'Sergeant,' she whispered as they reached him. 'Those men coming in...'

'I see them,' De'Geer murmured. 'Cooper?'

Cooper had already noticed. She'd stopped tugging at her dress and was watching the entrance.

The Asian men entered in a group – ten, maybe twelve of them. Well-dressed, polite, but something about them set off every warning bell. They moved as a unit, like they'd trained together.

Elliott's clipboard slipped from his fingers when he saw them. Papers scattered across the floor as they approached.

One man said something to him in Cantonese. Elliott shook his head.

'Sorry, I-I don't speak...' he stammered.

The man smiled pleasantly and walked past him towards the basement door.

De'Geer stepped into his path, casual but firm.

'Sorry, gents. Private game downstairs. Invitation only.'

The man looked at De'Geer, then said something in Cantonese to his companions. However, before he could say anything further, Doctor Marcos was already there, Johnny Lucas beside her, that amiable smile in place.

'Lovely evening isn't it?' he said. 'The exhibit here is fascinating. Might I interest you gentlemen in some champagne while we sort out the guest list situation?'

The lead man looked at Johnny for a long moment. Recognition flickered in his eyes – not of Johnny specifically, but of what he represented. East End. Connected. Dangerous in his own right.

He spoke rapidly to his friends in Cantonese, but before he could get half a dozen words out, Doctor Marcos interrupted, her own Cantonese flawless.

The man stopped, gave a slight nod to whatever Doctor Marcos had said, and returned his attention to Elliott and De'Geer.

'We're here for the game,' the man said in perfect accented English. 'Jun Ng Kai-lok invited us.'

'We'll have to confirm that,' De'Geer replied. 'Do you have a token to enter?'

This brought on more rapid and likely angry Cantonese, but with a last look at Doctor Marcos, the men walked away, grabbing champagne from passing servers. The men weren't doing anything threatening. They were just... present. Waiting. But the tension in the room had ratcheted up considerably.

EVERYONE WAS STARING AT TREVOR SULLIVAN – NO, THE NOW outed D.Q. James – and he seemed to drink the attention in, glancing back at Declan.

'For the record, I didn't kill my brother,' he said calmly. 'I had a message to meet Trevor, he said he was leaving, wanted to clear the air. It was in a warehouse in Deptford. But when I arrived, he was beyond angry, tried to kill me. He'd worked out who I was, didn't want to reconnect or anything, he just wanted to beat me to death. He would have, too, but he knocked a lamp over near some tarp, soaked in God knows what, and it went up in flames. I think he'd planned it for me, but he'd not wiped himself down and he went up too. I ran, expecting to be arrested as soon as I woke up, but the news just said about the fire, and that a body was found – never identified, too burned beyond any possibility of identifying. Even dental records were inconclusive. It was believed it was a homeless man who had slept there had simply perished in a freak accident. I took this as a sign and ran the very next day.'

He played with the pewter figure for a moment.

'You're right about the plan, though. I heard Katarina bought the place through one of my bloody gym members – the construction foreman on the job – which I have to admit was luck rather than skill. Once I knew he was in the basement, I told him about the strange wall, told him there could be riches there. I knew there weren't riches, I'd guessed it was just Ronnie Carrigan's body. Maybe Trevor told me this before he died? I can't recall.'

He gave a smile as looked around the table, pausing at Katarina.

'And, when the body was found, and people said, "Oh my God, it's D.Q. James" – because of the hat and the glasses and everything – I kept quiet, waiting. I knew it was just a matter of time until someone suggested something like this.'

He now looked across at Imogen Rothwell.

'It was you who gave her the idea, right?' he asked. 'When she came to your museum exhibit?'

'You should be careful speaking to Mrs Rothwell,' Monroe stated. 'When we picked her up today, she was buying a gun to shoot you. Well, "Trevor", anyway. We stopped her. But more importantly – she'd spent years following you, checking on you. Do you know what she used to fund that?'

Paling now, and suddenly not in control, Sullivan-James looked over at the chip box.

'How many did you take?' he croaked.

'At least half,' Rothwell replied. 'Ronnie took them from your lockup before he died, them and a couple of other items, in payment for a lighter you took of his. I held on to them. And then when I heard you – well, "Trevor" – was back, I wondered how I could convince you to appear.'

'How did you manage it?' Statham asked, confused.

'When the body was found, I told Katarina that perhaps there should be some kind of memorial – not for my brother, of course. I didn't tell them it was my brother they'd found. I let them believe it was D.Q. James, because people would come for that, if only to spit on the corpse. No offence.'

'None taken,' Sullivan–James – *well, it was easier to still think of him as such,* Declan had decided – smiled.

'As the curator of the museum exhibit, I suggested perhaps we could do something – an event upstairs where percentages of profits could go to the museum and charity. And a party down here where the victims of D.Q. James could reminisce – and maybe play for one last pot.'

She smiled.

'Because I knew you would come. I knew you would be here. I didn't know it was *you*. I thought it was Trevor. But either way, I wanted to see you lose.'

There was a really awkward moment of silence at this. And then...

'It wasn't my idea,' Richard Statham suddenly spoke out, looking around fearfully. 'They called me. They told me they'd meant to rough Carrigan up, that things had got out of control, that he'd been hit by a card shoe in a back-room poker room in Islington and had died. They didn't know what to do. They needed to clean up. I pointed out that the casino was empty, and they brought him in through the back entrance.'

'And then?' Monroe asked softly.

'And, well, then we stuck him behind the wall. By that point, he'd bled out, and he still looked like D.Q. James, all the way down to the bloody hat.'

Richard stared down at the baize.

'Marek told me that Trevor did it. Trevor told me that Marek did it. Neither would admit the truth. But we all believed the Triad had killed and dismembered the real D.Q. James, so this was a convenient place. If years later someone found the body, they'd look at the Triad, not us.'

He shrugged.

'Yeah, it wasn't the most thought out of plans. But the three of us spent the next day bricking up the wall, plasterboarding it, painting it. By Tuesday, nobody knew. And no game was booked down here for another week, so the paint smell dispersed.'

He started to sob.

'The only person who suspected something was wrong was Wong Sei, and he said he wasn't going to run any more games down there.'

'Where's the watch?' Declan asked. 'The one they gave you as payment for your soul?'

'Paul Elliott took it,' Richard replied. 'He found out what was going on, worked it out.'

'How?'

Richard nodded his head at Imogen Rothwell.

'Because when she found the lighter in the storage locker sale, she went to the police about it, and the DC she spoke to in Paddington was Elliott. He realised what was going on, killed the case so nobody looked, and instead of going to his superiors like he should have, he blackmailed me. Took my watch. Sold it. Took the profits – and immediately lost them. Goddamn idiot.'

Declan looked upstairs, as if looking through the ceiling at Paul Elliott. The man had caused even more problems in this case than they'd thought, and if De'Geer knew about this, he'd throw him off the roof.

'This is all a lie,' Marek snapped, half rising. 'I wasn't there at the time—'

'I think you'll find,' Declan smiled, 'we know exactly where you were on the eighth. As I said, MI6 had been keeping quite close tabs on you. I got your movements for the entirety of November, and you were definitely in Islington on the eighth of November. You disappeared for a couple of hours, but you were found the following morning.'

He looked back at Sullivan–James.

'We'll never know whether Trevor was involved – and unfortunately, it does mean that we'll never know who performed the killing blow. Because you, D.Q. James, can only be guilty of leading a poor man to his death.'

'Bullshit!' Sullivan–James now snapped. 'I gave him items and paid him to pretend to be me – and he took it gladly. I didn't know he'd screwed around with Katarina. I didn't know he'd had issues with Trevor. All I knew was he was somebody who could be a double. And that was all I did!'

Suddenly realising he wasn't as safe as he thought, Sullivan–James looked around the room.

'Trevor came at me. He wanted to see me burn and die. I escaped. You can't prove that I killed him. You can't. All you can prove is I took his identity. And to be perfectly honest, all I did was change my first name – because I am a Sullivan!'

'You took the identity of a dead man.'

'Who tried to kill me! I think you'll find that most people will argue the toss and say I paid for my sins – having waited for fifteen years looking over my shoulder for that man *there* to kill me!'

The finger was now pointed at Jun, who started to laugh.

'So, where are the diamonds, then?' he asked.

'We wondered that for a while.' Declan smiled, walking to the chip box and emptying the chips onto the table – the metallic clattering audibly less than should be. 'You see, we couldn't understand why the diamonds hadn't turned up over the last fifteen years. We suspected D.Q. James hadn't been able to take them when he ran but couldn't work out why. And then we realised this.'

He held the box up.

'Ronnie Carrigan stole the chips, but he also stole the box they were in.'

Without giving any advanced warning, Declan hurled the box to the floor, where it smashed open into four pieces.

There, embedded into one of the pieces was a plastic bag – and inside it a line of glittering diamonds.

'And here's your problem.' Declan smiled. 'You all wanted the diamonds. But you didn't know where D.Q. James put them or that Ronnie Carrigan had stolen them, or that Marek or Trevor killed him. Which meant that for fifteen years, these coins and this box sat ignored.'

He looked up at Imogen Rothwell.

'You could have had way more than a few thousand pounds' worth of gold spent over the years.'

'It was never about the money,' Rothwell replied.

'Look, this is a misunderstanding—' Marek said.

'Aye, I think the understanding here was all yours, and all on point,' Monroe snapped. 'You divorced your wife, but then helped her buy this place? We couldn't work out why... until we realised you needed control. You needed to make sure that wee wall was never broken through.'

He smiled.

'Tell me, how's that plan working out for you?'

Declan picked up the bag, turning to Jun.

'Make a claim,' he said. 'If enough people can prove that you were cheated at this and that these are your family items, then we can make sure you get reparation.'

He glanced over at Richard Statham.

'But don't think you'll be getting your finder's fee – considering the fact that you were the one who made sure he lost them in the first place.'

The silence that followed was absolute. Every person in the basement stared at the glittering diamonds in Declan's hand, now almost a million pounds' worth of stolen family jewels that had been hidden for fifteen years, before looking at the potential hundreds of thousands in gold coins on the poker table...

And then all hell broke loose.

SEVERAL OF THE GENUINE GUESTS HAD NOTICED SOMETHING was wrong and were edging towards the exits. Cooper intercepted them, keeping her voice calm and reassuring even as her eyes never left the group at the door.

Sam had drifted closer to Jess and Prisha, positioning himself between them and the newcomers without making it obvious.

'Maybe you two should head outside,' he suggested quietly. 'Get some air.'

'We're fine,' Jess replied, but she could feel her heart hammering.

The lead man was pacing, staring down at a phone, as if waiting for orders. More of his companions were spreading out through the room, not threatening anyone, just... positioning themselves.

De'Geer kept his hand near the basement door, but he didn't try to block it again. Whatever was happening, it was bigger than him trying to physically stop them.

Elliott had disappeared towards the service corridor. *Running, most likely.* DCI Cohen appeared from somewhere, his face tight with concern, speaking urgently into his radio, probably calling for backup. And if he was clever, he was calling for the armed backup.

And then, from below, raised voices.

Shouting.

The unmistakable sound of violence erupting.

And the polite fiction that everything was fine... evaporated instantly.

27

52 PICKUP

IN THE BASEMENT, JUN NG KAI-LOK MOVED FIRST.

Not towards the diamonds in Declan's hand, but towards his jacket – his hand disappearing inside. Kenny Tsang saw it happening and grabbed Jun's wrist before it could emerge.

'Don't,' Kenny said quietly. But the damage was done. The movement had triggered something primal in the room—

Marek Kováč lunged across the poker table towards Declan, his hand reaching for the bag of diamonds. Painted gold-coin poker chips scattered everywhere, rolling across the baize, dropping to the floor with metallic clatters.

Monroe stepped between Marek and Declan, one hand coming up to block Marek's arm.

'Back off,' he warned.

Sullivan-James didn't go for the diamonds. He went for the chips. His hands swept across the table, scooping up fistfuls of painted Mexican gold as they rolled and scattered. Others saw him and surged forward.

'Everyone stay where you are!' Anjli's voice cut through

the chaos, her warrant card held high, but nobody was listening any more. Richard Statham dropped to his knees, grabbing chips from the floor. Both Linda Burrell and Tony Norton shoved past Imogen Rothwell to reach the table.

Katarina stood frozen, watching the civilised poker game dissolve into a scramble for treasure.

'Enough!' Monroe's voice boomed across the basement.

For a moment, it worked. People stopped mid-grab, chips still clutched in their hands. Then Jun twisted free of Kenny's grip and pulled his hand from his jacket.

He was holding a phone.

'I made a call before I came tonight,' Jun said, his voice shaking. 'Insurance. The kind that's waiting outside right now.'

Declan felt his stomach drop.

'What kind of insurance?'

'The kind that doesn't care about your British police procedures,' Jun replied, his thumb moving across the phone screen. 'The kind that only cares about family honour and stolen property.'

'Christ,' Monroe muttered. 'You brought Triad enforcement.'

'I brought my uncles,' Jun corrected, pressing send on whatever message he'd typed. 'And they're very interested in meeting the people who've kept our family's diamonds for fifteen years.'

The implications rippled through the room. Several people paled. Sullivan-James, still clutching a handful of chips, started edging towards the bar.

'How many?' Declan asked quietly.

'Enough.' Jun smiled without humour.

At his ominous words, there was the sound of shouting – angry voices – in Cantonese.

'They're coming through!' De'Geer's shout echoed down the stairwell, followed by the unmistakable crack of gunfire.

Everyone in the basement froze. The sound echoed down, followed by more shouting, the heavy thud of something – or someone – hitting the floor, and the basement once more erupted into chaos. People screamed, diving under tables or behind the bar. Richard Statham simply dropped flat to the floor, coins spilling from his hands. Imogen Rothwell grabbed one of the overturned chairs and pulled it in front of her like a shield.

Kenny Tsang headed towards the back of the room, pulling Katarina with him, while Sullivan–James had already disappeared behind the bar. Marek used the distraction to make another grab for the diamonds. His hand closed around Declan's wrist in an iron grip, twisting hard. Declan felt the bag slipping from his fingers, but his free hand, now a fist, connected with Marek's jaw in a short, sharp jab that snapped the spy's head back. Marek staggered but didn't let go.

'Anjli!' Declan shouted, and with a final yank free tossed the bag of diamonds towards her. She caught it one-handed and immediately headed towards the back wall, away from the stairs and the gunfire that was getting louder by the second.

'We need to secure this room,' Monroe said, his voice steady despite the chaos. 'Declan, get everyone to the back. Anjli—'

The door at the top of the stairs exploded inward.

Two men came through, both young and Asian, both

holding semi-automatic pistols. Their eyes swept the room, found Jun, then fixed on Anjli and the diamonds in her hand.

The first one said something sharp in Cantonese. Jun responded, pointing at Anjli.

The man raised his pistol—

But then DC Elliott came out of nowhere, diving forward beside the poker table, knocking it to the side and slamming into Anjli. They both went down behind the overturned poker table as the shot cracked out above them. The bullet hit the wall, sending plaster dust exploding outward.

'Everyone down!' Declan shouted, but most people were already on the floor.

The second gunman was scanning the room, his weapon tracking across the scattered bodies. Looking for threats. Looking for the diamonds.

Then De'Geer appeared in the doorway behind them, blood running from a cut above his eye. He grabbed the first gunman's weapon arm and yanked it upward just as another shot fired into the ceiling.

The man twisted, trying to break free, but De'Geer's size advantage counted for everything in close quarters. He slammed the gunman's arm against the doorframe once, twice, and the pistol clattered to the floor.

The second gunman spun towards De'Geer, raising his weapon – but then Cooper appeared from the side, her X75 taser already out. She fired at close range; the man convulsed and dropped his pistol, collapsing to his knees.

But more footsteps were coming down the stairs. More voices shouting in Cantonese.

'We need to contain this!' Monroe shouted. He'd pulled

his own baton and was heading towards the stairs. 'Declan, get these civilians secure!'

Behind the overturned table, Anjli pushed herself up.

'Thank you,' she said to Elliott, breathless. 'You saved...'

She stopped as she looked down at her empty hands.

'The diamonds,' she said. 'Where are the—'

But Elliott was already moving. He'd scrambled to his feet and ran for the stairs; the bag of diamonds clutched to his chest with one hand while he fed three stolen "peso" chips into the bag's top opening with his other.

'Elliott's got them!' Anjli shouted. 'He's running!'

De'Geer's head snapped around just in time to see Elliott disappearing up the stairwell, shoving past him.

'Bastard!' De'Geer started after him immediately.

Declan grabbed the nearest person – Richard Statham, still on the floor – and dragged him towards the back wall where Kenny and Katarina had taken cover.

'Everyone, move! Back of the room, now!'

Sullivan-James emerged from behind the bar, his hands raised.

'I'm not part of this! I'm not—'

'Shut up and move!' Declan shoved him towards the wall.

Marek had already disappeared. Declan caught a glimpse of him heading towards a side door – probably a service entrance. *Of course he'd know all the exits.*

'Marek's running!' he called to Monroe.

'Let him! We've got bigger problems!'

Three more men were coming down the stairs now. Cohen, Billy, Sam and Cooper were wrestling the first two gunmen to the floor, and Declan wasn't sure, but for a second he thought he saw his daughter in the mix. The new arrivals saw this and raised their weapons.

Jun Ng Kai-lok stood up from behind the poker table.

'Stop!' he shouted. 'Stop shooting!'

The men hesitated.

Jun said something else in rapid Cantonese. Declan couldn't understand the words, but the tone was clear – this wasn't what Jun had wanted. Whatever he'd expected his "uncles" to do, it wasn't this.

One of the men responded, gesturing angrily. Jun shook his head, said something else.

The man raised his pistol again, pointing it directly at Jun. The message was clear: they weren't here on Jun's orders. They were here for the diamonds, and they didn't care who got in the way.

However, Kenny Tsang stepped forward, his hands raised, speaking in Cantonese. His voice was calm, measured, carrying weight.

The gunman's aim wavered, moving between Kenny and Jun.

Then, in the distance, everyone heard sirens getting rapidly closer.

The gunmen heard it too. One of them said something sharp. The others started backing towards the stairs.

'They're not leaving without the diamonds,' Kenny said quietly to Monroe. 'If they run now, they lose face. They'll come back harder next time.'

'The diamonds just left with a bent copper,' Monroe replied grimly.

'Then we'd better hope your sergeant catches him,' Kenny said.

De'Geer emerged onto the top floor to find the roof access door swinging open, cold November air rushing in. He climbed through and out onto the flat roof of the Harrison Casino, the London skyline spread out around them, blue lights from police vehicles flashing below.

Paul Elliott was cornered near the edge, clutching the bag of diamonds to his chest.

'Paul, don't be stupid,' De'Geer said. 'There's nowhere to go. Put the diamonds down.'

'They're our way out,' Elliott said desperately. 'Don't you see? We take these, we disappear. New identities. New lives. No more gambling debts. No more blackmail. No more looking over our shoulders.'

'Our way out?' De'Geer's voice was flat. 'There is no "our way", Paul. There never was.'

'Because of Hendon?' Elliott laughed bitterly. 'That was years ago. We were kids. We made a mistake—'

'You made a mistake,' De'Geer corrected. 'And you've been making them ever since. The gambling. The debts. Compromising yourself. Stealing evidence. And now this.'

'You could have reported me back then!' Elliott's voice cracked. 'You could have ended it all before it started. But you didn't. That makes you part of this. That makes you—'

'Guilty?' De'Geer finished. 'Yeah. I know. I've been carrying that guilt for years. But I'm done carrying yours too.'

He started moving forward. Elliott backed up towards the roof edge.

'Stay back!' Elliott warned. 'I'll throw them over. I swear I will.'

'No, you won't,' De'Geer said quietly. 'Because those diamonds are all you've got left. Your career's over. Your life's over. But you think those diamonds will save you. They won't. The Triad will find you. They always do.'

'Then what do I have to lose?' Elliott's eyes were wild now.

'Your life,' De'Geer replied. 'Whatever's left of it. Or your fingers, toes, arms, whatever they decide to cut off first. Don't make it worse.'

Elliott looked at the bag in his hands, then at De'Geer, then at the drop behind him. For a moment, De'Geer thought he might actually jump.

Then Elliott lunged forward, not towards escape, but towards De'Geer, swinging the bag of diamonds, with the three heavy gold coins added to it, like a weapon.

De'Geer blocked the swing, grabbed Elliott's arm, and twisted. The bag flew from Elliott's grip, landing with a thud on the roof. Both men grappled, years of friendship and betrayal spilling out in desperate violence. Elliott fought with the desperation of a man with nothing left to lose. De'Geer fought with controlled strength.

It didn't last long. De'Geer was bigger, stronger, and not weakened by months of stress and gambling addiction. He got Elliott face-down on the roof, one knee in his back, pulling his arms behind him.

'It's over, Paul,' De'Geer said quietly, clicking the handcuffs closed. 'It's been over for a long time. You just didn't want to see it.'

Elliott's shoulders shook. He might have been crying. It was hard to tell in the darkness. De'Geer retrieved the bag of diamonds, then helped Elliott to his feet. His face was blank, but anyone watching could see the cost of what he'd just done.

'I'm done,' De'Geer said quietly. 'After this. After tonight. I can't... I can't keep covering for you. Not even in my head. I should have reported what happened at Hendon years ago. Maybe if I had, none of this would have happened. Maybe you'd have got help instead of...' He gestured around the roof. 'This.'

The roof access door opened again. DCI Cohen emerged, two armed response officers behind him.

'Well done, Sergeant,' Cohen said, looking at Elliott with undisguised disgust. 'I'll take him from here.'

De'Geer kept hold of both Elliott and the diamonds.

'These need to go back into evidence. Proper chain of custody. I'm bringing both down.'

'I think you'll find—'

'I think you'll find, Guv, that you gave us this case, and so we'll be finishing it,' De'Geer replied, his voice emotionless and strangely, even more terrifying than any other way he could have spoken the words.

'Of course,' Cohen agreed. He moved closer to Elliott, his voice dropping. 'You know what you've done, don't you? You didn't just steal from a murder scene. You stole from the Triad. Jun Ng Kai-lok's family. They don't forgive. They don't forget.'

Elliott's eyes widened.

'But,' Cohen continued quietly, 'if you keep your mouth shut about certain things – about who knew what, about who might have looked the other way back at Hendon – then maybe, just maybe, nobody needs to know you ever touched these diamonds. Maybe you just tried to flee. Maybe the diamonds stayed secure the whole time.'

He glanced at De'Geer.

'For everyone's sake,' Cohen said meaningfully.

Elliott understood. His mouth closed. Whatever he'd

been about to say – whatever threats or bargains or revelations he'd planned – died unspoken.

Cohen nodded to his armed officers.

'Escort them back down. Sergeant De'Geer has an arrest to process.'

They headed back towards the roof access.

'You know?' De'Geer asked.

'Monroe explained,' Cohen replied. 'I needed to know why you were listening to that piece of shit, willing to speak out for him. You've risked your career by taking him down. That was brave. And it was the right thing to do.'

'Doesn't feel like it,' De'Geer said quietly.

'It never does,' Cohen replied. 'But you did it anyway. That's what counts.'

Marek Kováč burst through the service door into the alley behind the casino. Guests were milling about, confused, some smoking, others just trying to get away from the chaos inside.

It was a perfect cover.

He straightened his jacket, slowed his pace to a casual walk; just another guest leaving early. Nothing to see. He was almost on the street when he heard someone call out.

'Marek Kováč?'

He turned instinctively. A young woman stood there, late teens, phone in hand. Another woman, Indian, stood beside her.

'Do I know you?' he asked, confused.

'I'm Jess Walsh,' the woman said, looking around at the

scattered guests. 'DCI Walsh's daughter. I'm making a citizen's arrest. You need to—'

Ah, shit.

'I've no time for this!' Marek pushed past her, heading for the street—

Then something hit his face like liquid fire.

Marek screamed, dropping to his knees, hands clawing at his eyes. Through the burning agony, he heard footsteps running, voices shouting, then hands grabbing his arms and forcing them behind his back.

'Stay down! Don't move!'

Through streaming eyes, he could barely make out uniformed officers surrounding him. And beyond them, the two women – the Walsh daughter staring in shock at her girlfriend, who was calmly putting a small canister back in her handbag.

Taken down by a woman. How embarrassing.

'Did you just—' Jess started.

'Pepper spray,' Prisha said matter-of-factly. 'I bought it ages ago. Figured any date with your family would probably end up needing it – after all, it's not my first rodeo.'

Jess stared at her for a moment. Then she started laughing.

'I love you,' she said. 'You're amazing.'

Prisha smiled.

'I know.'

THE SIRENS WERE RIGHT OUTSIDE NOW. BLUE LIGHTS FLASHING through the windows above.

'Armed police! Everyone stay where you are!' The shout came from upstairs, followed by heavy boots.

The Triad gunmen dropped their weapons without resistance. They knew when they were outgunned.

Within thirty seconds, the basement was full of armed response officers in black, weapons trained, voices shouting commands. The gunmen went to their knees without protest, hands behind their heads.

Jun Ng Kai-lok stood still, watching. Monroe waited until the armed officers had cleared the immediate area, then turned to Declan.

'Right. Secure this lot. I'm going after—'

He paused as they all heard footsteps on the stairs. Heavy. Deliberate. De'Geer appeared in the doorway, blood still streaming from the cut above his eye. In one hand he held the bag of diamonds and coins. In the other, he gripped Paul Elliott by the arm. Elliott's hands were cuffed behind his back, his face streaked with tears.

'Found him on the roof,' De'Geer said quietly. 'Thought he could jump to the next building. He couldn't.'

'The diamonds?' Monroe saw Jun watching intently as he asked.

'He grabbed the bag to throw these coins into,' De'Geer deadpanned, removing them out. 'I don't think he even realised he had them. I'm sure he'd never have done anything that stupid. You know, to piss off the Triad or anything.'

Declan saw Jun nod slightly, accepting this as De'Geer walked Elliott down the stairs and over to where Monroe stood. His face was blank, but Declan could see the cost of what he'd just done.

'Paul Elliott,' De'Geer said, his voice steady, 'I'm arresting you on suspicion of theft, conspiracy, and corruption. You do not have to say anything, but it may harm your defence if you do not mention when questioned something which you later rely on in court. Anything you do say may be given in evidence.'

Elliott didn't respond. He just stood there, handcuffed and defeated as De'Geer handed him over to the nearest armed response officer.

'Get him out of here.'

As Elliott was led away, De'Geer wiped blood from his face and looked around the basement.

'Anyone else need arresting,' he said flatly. 'Or can we call it a night?'

With no answer forthcoming, De'Geer walked over to Anjli and held out the diamonds.

'These need to go back into evidence,' he said. 'Proper documentation. Proper chain of custody.'

Anjli took them carefully, then looked at Jun, at Kenny, at Monroe. Jun stepped forward, his hands still raised peacefully.

'I apologise for what happened here,' he said, looking at Monroe. 'I didn't... I thought they would just make their presence known. Apply pressure. I didn't expect them to come in shooting.'

'You brought armed criminals to an active crime scene,' Monroe said coldly. 'People could have been killed.'

'I know.' Jun's voice was quiet. 'I know. And I'll accept whatever charges you bring. But please... my family has suffered fifteen years of shame over this. If there's a way to return what was stolen while still following your procedures...'

Monroe looked at Declan. Declan looked at the bag of diamonds in Anjli's hand. Then at Kenny. Then at Jun.

'We'll work something out to save face for everyone,' Monroe finally said. 'But you're still getting charged. Conspiracy, at minimum. Maybe more once we've sorted through this mess.'

Jun nodded, accepting it.

'And you,' Monroe turned to Kenny, 'you're coming in for a formal statement about your involvement in all of this. Wong Sei and Kenny Tsang and whatever other wee bloody identities you've been running.'

'Wouldn't have it any other way, Detective Superintendent.' Kenny smiled slightly.

'I'll handle it personally,' Anjli said, holding the diamonds. 'Jun's family will have a representative present when we log them. We'll do this right.'

'Right then,' Monroe said. 'Let's get everyone back to Temple Inn. We've got about three hundred hours of paperwork ahead of us, and I want to get started before I forget what actually happened here tonight.'

He looked at Declan.

'You realise we're going to be in meetings about this for weeks? Shootings. Triad involvement. Compromised officers. Bradbury's going to have our heads.'

'Worth it though,' Declan said. 'We solved a fifteen-year-old murder. Found out what happened to D.Q. James. Recovered stolen diamonds. And arrested a killer.'

'Aye,' Monroe agreed. 'Though explaining how Darren Sullivan became Jameson, then became D.Q. James, then allegedly killed his brother Trevor Sullivan and took his identity, is going to give the CPS a bloody headache.'

'They'll work it out,' Declan said. 'They always do.'

Declan looked around the basement. Painted gold-coins were scattered everywhere, scuffed, scarred and glittering in the overhead lights. The poker table was overturned. Chairs were broken. Several people were still cowering against the back wall.

'Trevor Sullivan, also known as David Quincey James and Darren Sullivan,' Declan said, pulling out his handcuffs and heading towards Sullivan–James. 'I'm arresting you on suspicion of identity fraud, conspiracy to pervert the course of justice, and we'll add more once we've sorted through this mess.'

'Marek?' Declan asked.

'Apparently your daughter and her girlfriend took him down.' Monroe grinned. 'Explain why I hire you, and not *her* again?'

They started walking back towards the stairs to begin the long process of securing the scene, taking statements, and starting the paperwork that would consume the next several days. Behind them, the Harrison Casino stood empty, its secrets finally revealed, its poker game finally over.

The painted gold-coins would likely become part of a longwinded legal battle, although D.Q. James had a case for them, if he could confirm original ownership.

The diamonds would return to Jun's family after the courts confirmed what everyone already knew – they'd been stolen through cheating and manipulation.

Richard Statham was also being cuffed downstairs, beside Katarina – he would face charges for his role in concealing a murder, and likely spend his life in witness relocation, hiding from the Triad. She would face different ones.

Marek Kováč would likely disappear into MI6's shadowy world of foreign agents and diplomatic negotiations.

Darren Sullivan, AKA D.Q. James, the man who'd lived as his dead brother for fifteen years, would face justice for identity fraud and conspiracy, also spending his life watching over his shoulder for a Triad blade.

And Ronnie Carrigan, the bartender who'd played at being a poker legend and paid for it with his life, would finally be laid to rest with his real name on his headstone.

The poker game was finally finished.

Everyone had shown their cards.

And, in the end, just like in the old Western stories that D.Q. James had loved so much, nobody had really won at all.

EPILOGUE

FOLLOWING ON FROM THE THURSDAY NIGHT, FRIDAY MORNING was a bit of an anti-climax if Declan was being honest. With Paul Elliot now in custody, there was no reason for his inquest at Guildhall, and as such Paul Elliot had stabbed himself, effectively, for twenty-four hours' worth of escape.

However, he had also decided to keep quiet about his past with De'Geer, which was lucky for the Viking. That said, Declan still wasn't sure whether De'Geer would be his own worst enemy and demand to fall on his sword.

Still, that was what the Last Chance Saloon was for – people who were one step away from sword falling and all that.

Friday morning also found Declan nursing a coffee at his desk, staring at the mountain of paperwork that came with arresting half a dozen people and solving a fifteen-year-old murder. Monroe appeared in the doorway, looking equally exhausted.

'Bradbury wants us at Guildhall in an hour,' Monroe said. 'Something about explaining last night's operation.'

'Looking forward to that,' Declan muttered. 'How's De'Geer?'

Monroe settled into the chair across from Declan's desk.

'Suspended pending investigation. Standard procedure when an officer's involved in a rooftop confrontation that ends with another officer arrested.' He paused. 'Cohen's pushing for leniency. Says De'Geer did the right thing bringing Elliott down, regardless of their history.'

'And will he get it?'

'Professional Standards are treating it as an undercover operation gone right rather than years of covering for a mate. The fact he immediately arrested Elliott and secured the diamonds helps.' Monroe's expression darkened. 'Still looking at a formal warning at minimum. Depends on how generous they're feeling.'

'Cooper's furious.'

'Aye. Already spoken to a union rep about character witnesses.' Monroe shifted in his seat. 'Speaking of Elliott, his solicitor tried to claim duress this morning. Said his client was being blackmailed by organised crime.'

'The diamonds in his hand say otherwise.'

'True, but we told everyone it was an accident to save his life, didn't we, so now they're pushing to dump out the full menu – theft from a crime scene, corruption, conspiracy, attempting to pervert the course of justice.' Monroe stood. 'Billy's also been coordinating with Jun's solicitor about the diamonds. Apparently there's some ceremony required when they're returned, having been missing for so long. Venerable ancestors and all that.'

'After what happened in that basement, Jun's lucky we're returning them at all.'

'Anjli worked out a compromise. Diamonds stay in

evidence until trial, then are returned through proper legal channels. Jun gets charged with conspiracy, but his family's honour is restored.' Monroe shook his head as if in disbelief. 'Kenny Tsang's cooperating – full statement about his role, his identities, the lot. Claiming he did it because he was in fear for his life, and it was the Turk's plan.'

'Who's been conveniently dead for almost as long as Ronnie Carrigan.'

After Monroe left, Declan turned to his computer and pulled up the file on the man legally known as Trevor Sullivan, because that's who his passport said he was. But that identity had been stolen from the real Trevor Sullivan, who'd died in a warehouse fire in Deptford in January 2010. Proving identity fraud when your victim is dead and you've been living as them for fifteen years was complicated enough; the CPS were considering charges of identity fraud, conspiracy to pervert the course of justice, and obtaining property by deception. Apparently Darren Sullivan – D.Q. James had already gone back to his original name – was claiming PTSD after years of an abusive father and alcoholic mother, split from his family, all the usual greatest hits.

The worst thing was he'd probably get away with it.

Ronnie Carrigan's murder was clearer. Trevor Sullivan – the real one – had killed him in a drunken rage after losing everything. This was claimed by Marek Kováč, who was apparently nothing more than a witness here. The forensic evidence was solid, but the problem was that Trevor Sullivan was dead, dying in a fire – whether by his estranged brother's hand or not – shortly after.

Which meant that nobody could counter Marek's claims, and more importantly Darren Sullivan would face justice for stealing his brother's life, but the two deaths that set everything in motion were legally unprosecutable.

Billy appeared in the doorway, laptop under his arm.

'Got the final inventory from the casino,' he said, settling into the chair Monroe had vacated. 'Forty-seven painted gold-coins. Imogen Rothwell used the others over years tracking Sullivan.'

'What about the chips themselves?'

'D.Q. James's work,' Billy replied. 'The museum's already requesting them for the exhibit, and Rothwell's agreed, but Darren Sullivan's made a claim that as his winnings, he should have them back. Doctor Marcos confirmed every coin was authentic, but it'll be someone else's headache.'

'Well, they're evidence for now.'

'Oh, and Katarina Kováč has been released pending investigation. Her solicitor's arguing she didn't know of any criminal activity, just hosted a memorial game, a woman who didn't realise her ex-husband had manipulated her like an asset into buying the casino. She's even trying to get out of that deal, too.'

'Well, that's all bollocks, too.'

'Naturally. But, without evidence showing she knew about the murder or the identity fraud, we can't charge her with much. She'll probably face charges for conspiracy, depending on what Statham gives them.' Billy looked up. 'Speaking of whom, Statham's cooperating. Full statement about helping brick up Carrigan's body, his role managing the casino, all of it.'

'He's facing serious charges then.'

'Accessory after the fact, conspiracy to conceal a murder, perverting the course of justice. His solicitor's trying to argue coercion but given he kept quiet for fifteen years...' Billy trailed off. 'And Marek Kováč is officially MI6's problem now. Bullman got a very polite call this morning about "matters of national security".'

'So, he walks.'

'No idea, but if we look at previous times we've seen this, we're talking debriefed, assessed, quietly relocated. We'll never see him again.' Billy stood. 'Jess is in the canteen, by the way. Brought coffee and pastries.'

Declan smiled despite himself.

His daughter and her girlfriend, taking down a foreign intelligence asset with pepper spray.

UPSTAIRS IN THE CANTEEN, JESS WAS HOLDING COURT, PRISHA beside her, both surrounded by Cooper and Anjli. Cooper was examining the small canister of pepper spray.

'I'm not saying you should carry this on every date,' Cooper was saying, 'but maybe every date with this family?'

'That's what I said!' Prisha replied.

Jess spotted Declan and grinned.

'Dad! I was just explaining proper citizen's arrest procedure.'

'The pepper spray wasn't procedure,' Declan said, accepting a coffee.

'No, but it was effective.' Jess's grin widened. 'Prisha's already given a statement. Apparently "defensive action in support of lawful arrest" is the official term.'

'You're both very lucky you weren't hurt,' Declan said seriously. 'Kováč could have been armed.'

'Could have,' Jess agreed. 'Wasn't.'

There wasn't much Declan could say to that. His daughter

had inherited his stubborn streak and his terrible habit of walking into dangerous situations.

The rest of the morning would likely disappear into meetings at the Guildhall and paperwork. By the time Declan emerged, it would likely be past noon. But first, there was one more thing to do. Imogen Rothwell had asked if she could see her brother's remains before the funeral, and the request had been approved. She'd spent fifteen years not knowing if he'd abandoned her, of suspecting, but not confirming he was dead. Learning he'd been a victim, not a villain, had brought relief mixed with grief.

The funeral would be next week. A proper one, with his real name on the headstone. Ronald Carrigan would finally be at peace… under his real name.

But first, a grieving sister wanted to look at a long-dead skeleton. And Declan would stand beside her as she did so. It was the least he could do.

By mid-afternoon, Declan needed air; the paperwork would still be there tomorrow, as murder investigations generated mountains of it, and this one – with Triads, foreign intelligence, corrupt officers, and a fifteen-year identity swap – would probably keep them buried for weeks.

He found himself driving east without really deciding to, pulling up outside the Globe Town boxing club as the afternoon light faded.

The gym was quiet. A couple of regulars worked the heavy bags, their rhythmic thuds providing a steady percussion. Near the back, a trainer, one Declan didn't recognise, was working with a young lad on footwork. The ring itself stood empty.

As Declan stood in the doorway, Johnny emerged from the office at the back, dressed in his usual black suit and shirt. He spotted Declan and walked over, two bottles of water in hand.

'Wondered if you'd show up,' Johnny said, handing one over. 'Thought you might be drowning in paperwork.'

'Taking a break from it.' Declan accepted the water.

'No Monroe?'

'I think his back gave out after last night.' Declan smiled. 'I think he needs a day or two of rest.'

They walked towards the ring. Johnny climbed up onto the apron, sitting with his legs dangling, and Declan leaned against the ropes beside him. For a moment, neither spoke, just watched the gym's activity.

'Hell of a night at the Harrison,' Johnny took a sip of water. 'Jun's not happy, naturally. But he'll survive. Always does.'

'Couldn't help but notice you stayed at the party, decided not to go down to the poker game,' Declan said.

'Katarina extended invitations. I declined.' Johnny's tone was light, but something flickered behind his eyes. 'Too many ghosts in that building. And besides, I felt guilty about bringing your daughter there, thought I should keep an eye on her. You know, like you asked her to keep an eye on me yesterday.'

Declan said nothing for a long moment, and then Johnny let out a sigh.

'Brothers,' he whispered. 'Be grateful you don't have one.'

Johnny rose, entering the ring, staring at the canvas as if watching an imaginary fight happening.

'Darren was better at it than Trevor. Not the boxing, but better at reading people, understanding what made them tick. Trevor was too honest for poker. Wore his heart on his sleeve.'

'Honest enough to kill someone.' Declan joined him in the ring.

'Anger does strange things to honest men.' Johnny's voice was quiet. 'Trevor destroyed his own life trying to win back everything. When that failed, he killed Ronnie Carrigan thinking he was killing his brother.'

Declan studied Johnny's profile. The man wasn't giving anything away.

'So you do remember him?'

'With hindsight, and I remember the kid, not the man.'

Across the gym, one of the young boxers called out a question to his trainer. The trainer responded with patient instruction, demonstrating a combination. The normality felt surreal against the conversation they were having.

'That story you told me earlier a few days back about my father,' Declan eventually said. 'The one about the night watchman found dead in the fire?'

'What about it?' Johnny asked.

'That wasn't just a story, was it?' Declan said. 'You were trying to tell me about Ronnie Carrigan, pointing out that it isn't about the timing and I should look around at all things.'

Johnny Lucas said nothing for a moment, and then slowly the tension eased in his shoulders.

'There are things I can't tell you outright,' he explained, tapping the side of his head. 'Things even I wasn't sure about. You've got to remember; Jackie was around back then. I couldn't be sure if I was correct, and while it is a good story—'

'You could have just bloody told me,' Declan snapped. 'It would have saved us a lot of time.'

'And how would that have worked?' Johnny asked. 'At the time I told you the story, I didn't even know about the body.'

'But you knew they were about to build in the casino,' Declan said... and then realisation halted him.

'You knew they were about to find a body.'

'I suspected,' Johnny replied. 'That's completely different from knowing.'

'Don't throw semantics at me,' Declan snapped. 'You knew that Carrigan was there. You've known for years.'

Johnny stared at him.

'Declan,' he asked gently, 'do you really want me to tell you all my secrets? Because the moment I do, the chances are I won't be staying here any more. I'll be in one of His Majesty's establishments. And I don't know about you, but I'd rather not go there, especially at a time when the Triad are on a knife edge.'

'You're right,' Declan replied coldly. 'But I'm sick to death of the double talk and half-truths, Johnny. You either help us or you don't but know this: if you're not going to bother helping us, if you're going to play with these stupid half-truths and rumours, you don't get to talk to my daughter any more. The last thing I want is another Walsh in your pocket.'

'Another? You think you or your father were in my pocket? *Are* in my pocket? I'm disheartened to hear that you would think such a thing,' Johnny replied, and turned to leave the ring, but Declan moved quickly, grabbing him by the arm.

'My daughter is off limits,' he said. 'She's not going to be part of your firm. She's not going to be your contact in the force after I go.'

Johnny Lucas nodded, looking back at him.

'You forget that I still owe you debts,' he said. 'You saved me when nobody else even considered doing so. If you genuinely don't think that I would have your daughter's best interests at heart, then I suggest you leave this boxing ring right now.'

'If I didn't think you had my daughter's best interests at heart,' Declan gave a dark, humourless smile, 'you wouldn't be *leaving* this boxing ring.'

He gently relaxed his grip and turned, walking back across and climbing out.

'You're not an MP any more,' he said. 'In fact, I don't really know what you are. I'm unsure if *you* even know what you are, Johnny. I think you might want to start thinking about this.'

Johnny Lucas said nothing, simply climbing out of the ring and walking back to his office in the rear of the boxing club. Declan felt bad about the harsh words, but it was quickly interrupted by a text from Billy.

Reading it, he took a deep breath and started for the door.

It seemed for the moment he was needed back at Temple Inn.

DECLAN FOUND HIMSELF MATCHING MONROE STEP FOR STEP AS he walked up the stairs to the main entrance of the Temple Inn unit.

'Text from Billy?' he asked.

'Aye, and I'm curious as to what it is,' Monroe muttered. 'I thought we'd get at least a day before all hell broke loose.'

Through the main door and up the stairs, entering the

main office together, Declan and Monroe approached Billy's monitors as he looked up from them.

'We got your message,' Declan said. 'What's the problem?'

'I didn't want to say anything until the case was over, but now the case is over, I wanted to speak to you both about a mutual friend. Trix Preston.'

'Aye, she helped us out.' Monroe narrowed his eyes. 'Does she already want us to repay the wee favour?'

'Not quite.'

'Billy, what did Trix Preston tell you?' Declan, ever the more diplomatic, asked.

Billy leant back, turning his chair to face them fully.

'When she gave me the information on Marek Kováč being a spy,' he explained, 'she also said that an old friend of ours had got back in contact. There aren't many people that I can think of who would fit on a list like that. She suggested that when things were quieter here, you might consider visiting Edinburgh for a couple of days.'

'Aye, laddie, go on.'

Billy glanced at the screen, pausing for a moment, as if unsure what to say next.

'You look like there's more to this,' Declan added.

'There is.' Billy turned back to his screen, pressed a button, and an image appeared. It was a photo taken on a zoom lens somewhere in the Grassmarket in Edinburgh, one of two women standing talking. The first, a younger woman with long blonde hair pulled back into a ponytail was familiar to both Monroe and Declan as Trix Preston, but the other, with a short asymmetrical black bob, was even more familiar.

'When was this taken?' Declan hissed.

'Today,' Billy replied. 'An hour or so ago. Tom Marlowe sent it across. He's in Edinburgh with Trix.'

Declan stared at the image, noting the confrontational body language between the two women.

Between Trix Preston and Francine Pearce.

The long-believed dead Francine Pearce.

'Laddie, book us tickets to Edinburgh,' Monroe hissed. 'We're going to go speak to a ghost.'

Want to know what happens in Edinburgh? Then check out BURNING LEDGERS, the eleventh Tom Marlowe novel, out in March!

Want the next Declan Walsh Novel? CLICK HERE on digital, or turn the page...

Or consider joining the VIP Readers Club, and gain behind-the-scenes access and updates on new releases!

DCI Walsh and the team of the *Last Chance Saloon* will return in their next thriller

DIGGING YOUR GRAVE

ABOUT THE AUTHOR

Jack Gatland is the pen name of *#1 New York Times Bestselling Author* Tony Lee, who has been writing in all media for thirty-five years, including comics, graphic novels, middle grade books, audio drama, TV and film for *DC Comics, Marvel, BBC, ITV, Random House, Penguin USA, Hachette* and a ton of other publishers and broadcasters.

These have included licences such as ***Doctor Who, Spider Man, X-Men, Star Trek, Battlestar Galactica, MacGyver,*** BBC's ***Doctors, Wallace and Gromit*** and ***Shrek***, as well as work created with musicians such as ***Ozzy Osbourne, Joe Satriani, Beartooth, Pantera, Megadeth, Iron Maiden*** and ***Bruce Dickinson.***

As Tony, he's toured the world talking to reluctant readers with his 'Change The Channel' school tours, and lectures on screenwriting, story craft and comic scripting for festivals and conferences such as *Raindance* in London and *Author Nation, The Global Publishing Summit* and *20Books* globally.

An introvert West Londoner by heart, he lives with his wife Tracy and his dog Darcy, just outside London.

Feel free to follow Jack / Tony on all his social media by clicking on the links below, to engage, discuss Declan and put the world to rights.

www.jackgatland.com
www.hoodemanmedia.com

Visit Jack and Tony's Reader's Group Page
(Mainly for fans to discuss his books):
https://www.facebook.com/groups/jackgatland

Subscribe to Jack's Readers List:
http://geni.us/hmVIP

www.facebook.com/jackgatlandbooks
www.twitter.com/jackgatlandbook
ww.instagram.com/jackgatland

Want more books by Jack Gatland? Turn the page...

Printed in Dunstable, United Kingdom

81083907R00231